THE

CHASE

THE

CHASE

A NOVEL

BRENDA JOYCE

ST. MARTIN'S PRESS ⚹ NEW YORK

SEP 3 0 2002

www.stmartins.com

Design by Lorelle Graffeo

Library of Congress Cataloging-in-Publication Data

Joyce, Brenda.
    The chase / Brenda Joyce.—1st ed.
        p. cm.
    ISBN 0-312-28449-7
      1. Widows—Fiction. 2. Serial murders—Fiction. 3. World War, 1939-1945—Fiction.
I. Title.
PS3560.O864 C48 2002
813'.54—dc21

2001048648

First Edition: July 2002

10 9 8 7 6 5 4 3 2 1

In memory of my aunt Edna

PART
ONE

CLAIRE'S FOLLY

CHAPTER 1

There was trouble in paradise and there had been for some time.

Claire turned onto Leavenworth, her grip tightening on the steering wheel. She had been married for ten years; she had known David for almost fifteen. When had they begun to drift apart? How had it happened, when once they had been so happy?

Did it even matter?

David had told her just that morning that she was going to far too much trouble for his fortieth birthday. He had made it clear he was in no mood for a big bash with a hundred guests. And he had refused to even look at her, focusing instead on the task of knotting his Hermès tie.

Claire knew she had been blocking out just how badly damaged her marriage was. She had thrown herself into her work at the Humane Society, where she was a director, and into all of her charities, especially the two for which she was chairwoman. She had always been an overachiever, and it was easy to put in sixty, seventy, even eighty hours a week on all of her projects. In fact, she was frequently solicited by new organizations begging her to join them. These days she had to turn everyone down, as she was stretched so thin. The best she could do was to offer up her valuable mailing lists.

David was a lawyer and had switched firms recently. He, too, worked like a dog. Perhaps this was one of their problems; somehow, they had become immersed in their separate career paths, losing the connection they once had.

Last night they had attended the same fund-raiser, a black-tie dinner and dance. Claire doubted they had exchanged more than a dozen words all evening. He had his social circle, and she had hers. He had also drunk too much.

Maybe this was her fault. Last night she had actually been working—she was desperate to raise another million dollars for the Summer Rescue Kids program. Maybe she was a failure as a wife.

Claire had to let go of that thought. She must not be sad, not now, not when her guests would arrive in two hours. It was a stunning spring day. The skies could not be clearer, and the waters of the San Francisco Bay could not sparkle more. Her dog, Jilly, a chocolate standard poodle, sat in the backseat of the Land Rover with her elegant face thrust out of the car, enjoying the air and the sun. It would be okay, Claire told herself. Tonight their guests would dance outside on the terrace beneath a full moon and a thousand stars. David would be happy. And that would make her happy. She was a pro when it came to making events succeed, to taking care of other people; it was what she did.

Claire turned the Land Rover into her driveway, where the caterer's vans and trucks were parked, causing total congestion. She slid out and opened the door for Jilly, who raced madly for the front door of the house. The stray dogs she housed were also barking. Claire thought she heard childish shouts. She imagined a scene of pandemonium inside, and she smiled, relieved to divert her thoughts from her marriage.

Her house was a big, modern white stucco affair with high slate roofs. From the outside it appeared bulky, but then, four thousand square feet had been crammed into three quarters of an oddly shaped acre. Inside, however, one was greeted with double ceilings and surprising spaciousness—the architect had been a genius. It was their dream house—they had both worked hard for it, had both earned it. Claire slowly entered and paused inside the huge living area, which had smooth wood floors, white walls, and an eclectic combination of modern and antique furnishings. Everything was just perfect. Or was it?

The opposite wall was nothing but double windows. Beyond those windows were the stone terrace and the gardens. From where she stood, Claire could see the sparkling blue waters of the bay, numerous sails, and the red spires of the Golden Gate Bridge. The view was magnificent. She reminded herself not to be sad and smiled.

And it was just in time. "Mrs. Hayden! Mrs. Hayden!" Timmy Kowolski, a neighboring eight-year-old, was shrieking. The chubby boy ran into the room with Jilly chasing him merrily. He was followed by another boy and his sister, as well as three other dogs. The children all lived around the block. Claire adored them. None of them had any pets, and as Claire's house was always filled with strays, it was a second home for the trio. The kids were screaming, the dogs were barking madly, and it was chaos. She loved it.

Claire basked in the warmth of the children and the dogs as they surrounded her and she smiled, genuinely now, tousling Timmy's short, spiky hair. Maybe it was time to get pregnant. She was thirty-two. She had always wanted children of her own. Five or six would do—but David had always said it would be one or two.

Claire knew that getting pregnant would not solve anything.

"Can Jilly come stay with me during the party tonight?" Timmy asked eagerly.

"Only if your mom doesn't mind," Claire said.

"She won't mind!" Timmy cried, beaming.

"You'd better go ask her before taking Jilly over there," Claire said with a fond smile, rubbing her knuckles over his smooth brow.

"I'll call her now," Timmy said, then raced for the phone, Jilly following him.

"Hi, Ben. Hi, Lucy," Claire said to the other children. She was surrounded now by the three other dogs, who had descended enthusiastically upon her en masse, three tails wagging fiercely. Two were mongrels, one a dachshund.

"Hi, Mrs. Hayden," the kids cried in unison. Lucy's blue eyes were wide and earnest. She was a tall, skinny girl with freckles. Her brother was skinny, too, but short, with horn-rimmed glasses. "Did that rottweiller make it?" Lucy asked very seriously.

Claire was petting the ecstatic dogs. Now she straightened and smiled at her neighbor's oldest child, who was twelve going on twenty. Claire patted Lucy's shoulder reassuringly. "The rottweiller will be fine. But still no word on his owner. Don't worry, Luce. We'll get him back to his home." The real truth was, she had hoped by now that someone would have come forward to claim the older dog who had been hit by a car last night. The Humane Society had rescued the stray and, of course, taken him to a clinic. She would not let Lucy worry, though.

Sometimes I think you care more about the cats and dogs you save than me.

Claire stiffened, recalling her argument with David that morning.

That had been a low blow and completely unfair—one he had been resorting to more and more often recently.

If you really cared about me, you would not be throwing this god-damned birthday party. I am overloaded, Claire. And who gives a shit about turning forty?

They had argued fiercely and hurtfully. Or rather, David had argued, because Claire couldn't bring herself to hurl ugly words or insults at anyone, much less her own husband. She wished she hadn't remembered the nasty exchange now.

She had remained calm. *Of course I don't care more about cats and dogs than you, David. That was an unfair thing to say.*

Oh, so now I'm unfair?

That's not what I said. I just thought that turning forty is special—

Yeah, right. Let's announce to the world just how old I am.

Why are you doing this? Do you want to hurt me?

I'm not doing anything, Claire! For crissakes, I am just trying to make a goddamned living! Did it ever occur to you that I want to stay home for my birthday?

"A dog like that, someone has to be looking for him," Lucy was saying, breaking into Claire's thoughts. There was an ache behind the memory, but Claire couldn't entertain it, not now.

Claire forced a smile. "I think so, too," she said lightly. She put her hands in the pockets of her black leather blazer, which she wore over a white cotton T-shirt and slim black pants. Her dark blond hair was pulled into a ponytail, and she wore no makeup other than lip gloss and mascara. The only jewelry she wore was her watch, a gold Rolex with a diamond bezel that David had given her for their last anniversary, the tenth.

"Mrs. Hayden? Are you all right?" Lucy asked.

Claire started. "Of course."

"You just seem . . . sad."

Claire blinked. It was not a good sign if a child could see past her smile and her words. "I'm just tired. It's been a really long day." And that was mostly the truth, Claire reminded herself. She *was* tired. It *had* been a long day.

"It will be okay, Mrs. Hayden. Tonight you can dance to a deejay. How cool!" Lucy's eyes were worshipful.

Claire had to smile, well aware that Lucy thought her glamorous and idolized her. But then she thought about David and the night to come, and her smile vanished. Unfortunately, she felt certain that it was going to be a very long night.

If only they could recapture the past.

In her heart Claire knew that it was impossible.

Claire had just stepped out of the wall-to-wall beige marble shower when she heard the bedroom door open and close. "David?"

"Yeah, it's me," he said from the master bedroom.

Claire tensed even more. There had been nothing warm in his tone, just exhaustion and maybe a hint of irritation.

Refusing to get alarmed, Claire wrapped herself in a big towel and stepped into the room. It boasted high ceilings and views of the bay and bridge. The entire bedroom was done in shades of white, the fabrics each a different texture; even the sofa in the sitting area was a white-on-white wool blend. The mantel over the fireplace was white marble streaked with gold, and one of Claire's favorite paintings in the world hung over the bed—a Gustave Courbet titled *Le Réveil,* featuring the nude Venus reclining while Psychée stood over her, parakeet in hand.

A week ago the painting had arrived at their doorstep, stunning her. Instantly Claire had called her father, once a professor of art and now a world-renowned art dealer, to find out why on earth he had sent them the masterpiece. Jean-Léon had told her that it was a present and he wanted her to enjoy the painting.

His explanation made little sense. The Courbet was worth tens of millions and Jean-Léon was passionate to an extreme about art, especially his own collection, which he had begun in earnest with Claire's mother early in their marriage. Claire's mother, Cynthia Asch, had inherited a sizable fortune, enabling her husband to start a gallery and collection. The Asch family had made their fortune in real estate in the booming years of the sixties.

The gesture of the gift had to mean something, Claire had thought, but her father was a hard man to understand. She still did not understand why he had sent the painting, although David had suggested it had to do with his age, and he was merely getting his estate in order.

Claire watched David now, her heart skipping—for there was a garment bag on the bed. David was placing suits, shirts, and other clothing in it. Claire stared. "Where are you going?" she asked quietly.

He did not even glance at her. "I have to be at a meeting in New York tomorrow. I have an eight A.M. out of here."

Tomorrow was Friday. Not only was he leaving for the weekend—which was unusual though not unheard of—but it would be impossible for him to really enjoy the party, since he would have to get up at the crack of dawn. "Sounds like an emergency," Claire said, hoping to sound calm. The last thing she wanted him to see was her anger, but inside, she was suddenly furious.

Didn't he care about all the effort she was making on his behalf? Didn't he care about them? And what was happening to her? Of all days for her to become unglued, today was the worst possible day. Claire did not have a temper. It served no one, much less herself.

"It's not. Been planned for a few weeks, actually. I guess I forgot to mention it."

He had forgotten to mention that he was spending the weekend of his birthday in New York City. Claire remained very still, trying hard not to be angry, and wondering, not for the first time, if he had a girlfriend. Was it only a few years ago that he would have asked her to come with him? How many times had they booked a five-star hotel like the Plaza or the Carlisle, made love all night, and taken in a show, all jammed between David's meetings?

But she would not have wanted to join him in New York even if he had invited her. She had too much to do that weekend herself. In fact, she did not even enjoy his company anymore. The realization was stunning.

David finished packing and folded the garment bag in half, zipping it closed. "I think I'm going to close my eyes for a half hour before I get dressed," he said, walking past her while stripping off his tie.

It crossed Claire's mind that he hadn't looked at her, not even once. She thought about their argument. It had been eating at her all day. Something he had said was bothering her, but she could not pinpoint what it was.

He was in the dressing room. Claire walked in after him, managing a bright smile. As she stood behind him while he slid off his blue and white button-down, she glimpsed herself in the mirror over the the vanity. She looked half her age—like a teenager, not like the glamorous and professional wife of a brilliant corporate lawyer.

The smiling woman in the mirror seemed so calm and composed. She did not look frightened.

But she was frightened.

Claire turned away. "David? Let's talk." She could hear how tense her own voice was. That would not do, and she coughed to clear her throat.

"Now?" Incredulous, David faced her in nothing but his briefs.

Claire glanced at him. He was a very attractive man, with hazel eyes and thick, dark hair, and he worked out and ate well, so his body was lean. Other women looked at him whenever they went out. David had briefly modeled for extra money while in college. He could still model. If he wanted to play around, he would have no trouble doing so. "I'm sorry we fought this morning, and I'm even sorrier I didn't ask you first whether you wanted a big birthday party," Claire tried with a small smile. A part of her was appalled that she was the one to be the peacemaker when she hadn't done anything wrong. He should be apologizing to her for his boorish behavior.

"I don't want to get into this right now. It's going to be a long night."

Claire stiffened even more, but when she spoke, she made herself sound unruffled. "Wait a minute. Will you accept my apology? I am genuinely sorry we fought. Aren't you sorry, too?"

He stared at her. "Of course I don't want to fight with you. Claire, I have had a fucking rotten day," he said, moving to the sink. He ran water and splashed his face.

Claire was faced with the sight of his black cotton briefs stretching over his hard buttocks. She felt no stab of physical desire. It occurred to her that they needed to make love. When was the last time that they had done so, anyway? "It seems like every day has been rotten these past few weeks," she heard herself say.

He straightened abruptly, regarding her in the mirror, which covered the entire wall. "What's that supposed to mean?"

She bit her lip. "Things have changed, haven't they? I don't think we've made love in months. Do you remember when we made love four or five times a week?"

He turned to face her. "That was eight or nine years ago!"

Had it been that long ago? "We don't talk anymore, David," she said softly, sadly.

"No, we don't." His words were flat.

They stared at each other, the realization unspoken but hanging between them. They didn't make love anymore, they didn't talk anymore, they didn't care anymore.

Claire felt another stab, this one of panic. Was this it, then?

She inhaled and walked away, fighting to recover her composure. It was so hard—her mind seemed to be spinning uselessly now. And Claire suddenly realized what it was that was bothering her about their argument that morning. He had made some crack about earning a living. Claire seized upon the odd statement the way a terrier might a bone.

David had a six-figure income. Claire's income was much lower, obviously—she made nothing working for her charities, and the Humane Society paid little. Still, they were in the highest tax bracket. They had savings and investments, much of which had come from a small trust fund she had come into at the age of twenty-five. Now Claire caught his gaze again. "Are we having money problems, David?" This was a much easier subject, she thought with relief.

His expression was impossible to read. "Things could be better."

She felt her eyes widen. "What does that mean? We have savings, investments, our incomes—"

"I've made some bad investments. We've taken a fucking hit. And I do not want to discuss our finances now," he said flatly.

Claire was stunned, but she knew that monetary problems could be fixed. Clearly, though, this was not the time to raise the subject, an hour before their first guests would arrive. She mustered a smile. "I'm sorry." She touched his cheek. "I want you to have a good time tonight, David. It's your birthday. I want you to be happy and worry-free."

He didn't hesitate. "I am happy. I'm just very pressured right now."

Claire was the one to hesitate. "Are—you sure?"

He paused before saying, "Yeah, I'm sure," and avoided her gaze.

She knew he was lying to her. "Are you sure you don't want to tell me what's bothering you?" she asked with sympathy.

He turned away. "It's just the usual business crap."

She didn't believe him. She said to his back, "David, no matter what is happening with us, we do have a history and I am your wife. I am here for you. You know that." She meant every word. At the very least, she owed him her loyalty.

He slowly turned back. "Actually, Claire, I have screwed up. Royally." There was fear in his eyes.

Claire felt an answering fear. She had never seen him this way. She remained outwardly calm. "What happened?"

He hesitated. "I can't tell you. But I may be in trouble," he said, as he turned away again. "Big trouble."

Claire stared after him. What in God's name did "big trouble" mean?

The first guests were just arriving, and everything was as it should be. The decorations were fabulous—a combination of peach-hued rose petals strewn everywhere, even on the furniture, and hundreds of natural-colored candles in various shapes and sizes and clusters on every conceivable surface, all burning softly and giving the entire house a warm, ethereal glow. The bar had been set up in the closest corner of the living area to the entryway, with the flower petals strewn artfully over the table, amid the bottles and glasses, and over the floor. A tuxedoed waiter stood at the door with a tray of champagne flutes; another waiter stood beside him to take wraps. The deejay had set up in the back of the living room, and soulful jazz softly filtered through the house.

Claire began greeting guests. Her home quickly filled with some of San Francisco's most renowned and wealthy residents; there was also a scattering of Los Angeles media moguls and New York businessmen, mostly high-finance types. Claire knew almost everybody, through either David's business or her charities. Her real friends she could count on one hand, but she socialized frequently, and she genuinely liked many of the people she dealt with.

Claire saw her father enter the house. A mental image of the Courbet hanging on her bedroom wall flashed through her mind.

Jean-Léon Ducasse was a tall Frenchman with a thick head of gray-white hair. He had fought in the Resistance during World War II, and although he had immigrated to the States in 1948, he still did not consider himself an American. Everything about him was very Old World. He smiled as he came to Claire and kissed her cheek. "You look wonderful," he said. He had no accent. His nose was large and hooked, and his hair was iron gray, but he remained a handsome man. No one would guess that he was in his late seventies; he looked sixty, if a day. It never ceased to amaze Claire how many women found him attractive. His current girlfriend was an attractive, wealthy widow in her late fifties, but tonight he was alone.

Claire hoped that her worries were not reflected in her eyes. She smiled brightly. "You look great, too, Dad. Where is Elaine?"

"She's in Paris. Shopping, I believe. I was invited to join her, but I did not want to miss David's birthday party." He smiled at her.

Claire thought he was being sardonic. She was almost certain he would not care if he had missed David's birthday. But it was always hard to tell exactly what her father was thinking, or what he meant. Jean-Léon had raised Claire alone; Claire's mother had died, a victim of breast cancer, when Claire was ten. He had been preoccupied with teaching and later, after retirement, with his gallery. And even when he was not teaching at Berkeley College, he was either traveling around the world in pursuit of another masterpiece or new talent, or lecturing at foreign institutions. Claire had been raised by a succession of nannies. She and her father could have been close after her mother's death, but Claire had never sat on his lap as a child or been told stories at bedtime. "Well, I'm glad you could be here, Dad," she said, still distracted. What kind of trouble could David be in? Surely it wasn't serious.

She prayed it wasn't something illegal.

Jean-Léon was glancing around, taking in every guest and decoration. "You have done a very nice job, Claire. As always."

"Thanks, Dad," Claire said softly.

An elderly couple came up to Claire, smiling widely. The woman, Elizabeth Duke, was tall and thin and quite regal in appearance, clad in a red Armani jersey dress, while her husband, who was in his early eighties and about her height, was somewhat stooped. William Duke embraced Claire first, followed by his wife. "Claire, the house looks amazing," Elizabeth cried, smiling. "And that dress suits you to a *T*, dear." She wore a large Cartier necklace set with diamonds. Somehow she carried the ostentatious piece well.

The Dukes were an English couple, with homes in Montecito, Sun Valley, New York, and East Hampton, as well as San Francisco. Claire had known them her entire life, or so it seemed. They were avid art collectors and close friends of her father's. Elizabeth had adored Claire's mother.

"Where is that handsome husband of yours?" William Duke asked jovially. He was retired, but the company he and Elizabeth had built from scratch in the fifties and sixties was a private one, with financial holdings and properties all over the world. He was fond of David and at one time had hoped to have him join his firm. The deal had never worked out. Claire had never known why.

"He'll be down in a minute," Claire said, hiding her concern. Where was he? What was taking so long? She already had a headache. She fervently hoped that David's mood would have changed by the time he came downstairs—and that he would not drink too much. *I'm in trouble, Claire.* "He's running a bit late." She flashed what felt like a brittle smile.

Elizabeth Duke stared at her. "Is anything wrong, Claire?"

Claire tensed, aware of her father and William regarding her. "It's been a long day," she said, giving what was quickly becoming the party line, but she took Elizabeth's hand and they slipped away.

"I do know that," Elizabeth said kindly. "But don't worry, you know how to plan an event, Claire, as everyone who is anyone knows. I can already see that this evening will be a huge success." She smiled and leaned close to whisper, "William and I thought long and hard about what to give David for his birthday. We decided that the two of you have been working far too hard. So we are offering you the house in East Hampton for a month over the summer, Claire."

It was a magnificent, fully staffed home on Georgica Pond with a swimming pool and tennis court. Claire grasped Elizabeth's hands, about to thank her. But she never got the two simple words out. Somehow, she knew that she and David were not going to spend a month together in the Dukes' Hampton home. Neither one of them would want to. It would be a month of bickering and arguments.

Their marriage was over. It was suddenly clear to her that neither one of them had any interest in salvaging it. It had been over for years.

Oh, God was her next single thought. She smiled at Elizabeth but did not even see her.

"Claire? I know you and David are struggling right now," Elizabeth said kindly. "This might be good for you both."

Claire was an expert at reining in her emotions. She worked hard to keep a sunny facade in place. Perhaps she had learned to do so when her mother had died so suddenly, leaving her, for all intents and purposes, alone. She had certainly felt alone when Cynthia passed away, because her father seemed like such a stranger. But maybe her father had taught her by example how to remain calm and composed no matter what; how to shove any feelings of a personal or emotional nature far, far away. Now Claire felt a sudden lump of grief rising up, hard and fast, impossibly potent. It was accompanied by a real and terrible fear.

"I'm sure it will," Claire said automatically, not even aware what she was saying.

"Everything will work out," Elizabeth said softly. "I am sure of it."

Claire knew she was wrong. "Yes, it will." She had to hold it together, to keep it all in. *Divorce*. The word loomed now in her mind. It was engraved there.

Elizabeth squeezed her hand. Claire watched her rejoin William, then found herself facing her father. She felt uncomfortable and hoped he hadn't overheard them. He said, "I understand you are short a few VIPs for Summer Rescue Kids."

This was a welcome subject. "I am."

"I think I can help. I have a client who's new in town. I'll feel him out for you."

"Thank you, Dad," Claire said far too fervently.

He seemed to be looking right through her. No, he was looking past her. "And here's your errant husband," Jean-Léon added softly.

Claire's gaze whipped to David, who was approaching, and then back to her father. What did that comment mean? But Jean-Léon only smiled at her, and Claire turned her attention back to David.

He was more than handsome and self-assured in his dark gray suit, and the pale blue shirt and yellow tie did amazing things for his leading-man good looks. More than a few women were craning their necks to see him more fully. As David paused to shake hands and accept congratulations, Claire stared. He was beaming as he accepted hearty backslaps from his male friends and soft kisses from their wives and girlfriends. Finally, he seemed to be genuinely enjoying himself.

David reached her father. His smile never faltered, but Claire knew it was a pretense. She watched them shake hands. "Happy birthday, David," Jean-Léon said smoothly.

"Thank you."

"Have you been enjoying my Courbet?"

David extracted his hand. "What can I say? That was so generous of you to give it to Claire."

"She deserves it. So you do like it?" Jean-Léon's tone never changed, but he seemed to be pressing, and Claire tensed.

"It's a masterpiece. Who wouldn't like it?" David returned, his smile frozen.

Claire stepped to his side, glancing anxiously from one to the other. Did they have to be hostile to one another now?

"Then I am very pleased. Where did you hang it?"

"In the bedroom," David said.

"Hmm" was Jean-Léon's response. "A shame. A painting like that should be on public display." He turned his gaze on Claire. "You should hang it in the living room, Claire."

She had the feeling that if she agreed with her father, she would be disagreeing with David, and that was the last thing she wished to do just then. "How about a drink, Dad?"

"Fine." Jean-Léon ambled away into the crowd, greeting those he knew. David stared after him. So did Claire.

"Sometimes he really bugs me," David said.

Claire jerked. "What is going on? How could you argue with him now?"

David just looked at her. "He can be a pompous ass."

"That's not fair," she began.

"Oh, cut it out, Claire. You know that because he's brilliant in the world of art, he thinks he's smarter than everyone else—including you and me. But you know what? If it weren't for your mother, he wouldn't be where he is today. Her money bought him his success. It made him what he is today."

"David!" Claire was aghast. "He's my father! How can you say such things?"

He gave her a look. "Let's do what we have to do. Smile, Claire. This party was *your* idea." He walked away.

She stared after him, his last nasty comment leaving her as angry as she had been earlier in their bedroom. She did not deserve such barbs. And he had no right to talk about her father that way. His accusations hurt, even though they were partially true. It was no secret that Jean-Léon had started both his gallery and his art collection with her mother's generous support. But wasn't that what spouses did for each other?

Claire watched David greeting the Dukes. He seemed a bit curt with them, she thought, before turning away. The night had only just begun, but she needed a moment to herself. She had a massive headache, and she was beginning to feel ill in the pit of her stomach. She hurried down the hall and into the sanctuary of the den.

The doors were open. It was a big room with the same smooth, pale oak floors as the rest of the house but most of this room was done entirely in soft, natural earth tones. Claire plopped down on a rust-colored leather ottoman, cradling her face in her hands. Her marriage was a charade. There was just no point to it anymore.

And David wouldn't care if she raised the subject of a divorce, Claire was certain. But she refused to abandon him if he was in the kind of trouble he claimed to be. They could always separate until the crisis—whatever it was—passed.

Claire began to tremble. She stared down at her shaking knees and realized she was finally losing it.

"I'm sorry. I didn't realize anyone was in here," a man's voice said.

Claire leaped to her feet in surprise. A man had walked into the middle of the room and was regarding her curiously.

Claire smiled immediately, wishing he would turn around and leave. She vaguely recalled greeting him a few minutes ago at the front door but did not have a clue who he was. Somehow she managed to walk over as if nothing were wrong, hand outstretched. To her horror, her hand was shaking. She slid it into his anyway, praying he would not notice. "I'm certain we met. I'm your hostess, Claire Hayden."

He shook her hand, the contact briefly and vaguely surprising. "Yes, we did, Mrs. Hayden," he said, no longer smiling. He was grave. "Ian Marshall. I'm a friend of your husband's."

Claire pulled her hand free, aware of flushing. It was too warm in the den. "Call me Claire." She smiled automatically.

"I hope I'm not interrupting, Claire?" His gaze was searching.

Claire had the unwelcome notion that he knew she was crumbling bit by bit beneath her immaculate exterior. "I was going to make a phone call. I'm with the Humane Society, and I wanted to check on a stray we picked up that was hit by a car," Claire said lightly, hoping that he would take the hint and go.

He did not.

In fact, he just stood there, regarding her. He was a tall man, six feet or so, with dark hair that was neither too short nor too long. He was clad in an impeccable suit, as were most of the male guests. His shoulders were very broad, and Claire knew the suit had to be custom-made. She realized she was staring, but then so was he. She also realized that the room was too quiet. "Can I help you?" she tried.

"I have a feeling that you don't like parties, Claire," he said.

Claire felt her eyes widen as their gazes locked. His kind tone was like a hair trigger, and she turned away, even more shaken. "Of course I like parties." But he was right. Parties were a part of her work. Rarely were they social events and a time to eat, drink, or be merry. Parties were an opportunity to raise badly needed funds for important causes, to pay back or laud those who had helped her in the past. Claire would never let anyone hold a party for her. Her last official birthday party had been when she was sixteen.

"Just not this one?" he prodded.

She turned away. "It's my husband's birthday," she stressed. "It's a wonderful evening for us both." To her horror, her voice cracked on the last syllable.

"It's okay. I know how tough these things can be." His tone was kind, his gaze unwavering.

But their marriage was over. She had seen it in David's eyes, and she felt it, too.

She had been alone her entire life. When she had married, she had thought that she would never be alone again.

But she was different now. She was a strong and successful woman, not a frightened, bereaved child.

"Here."

Claire saw a tissue being dangled over her right shoulder. She accepted it gratefully, and while she was dabbing at her eyes, she heard him wander past her. He was giving her some space to compose herself, but he was not leaving her. Claire peeked at him out of the corner of her eye and saw him studying the seascape above the mantel. Her heart seemed to kick her in the chest.

It was the most shocking sensation.

Claire stared at him, stunned.

He faced her with a smile. "That's better. Beautiful women crying make me all nervous and jittery. I have a whole bunch of sisters, and every single one of them loves to cry."

She had to smile. "How many sisters do you have?"

"Four. All younger than me." He grinned. His dimples were charming—they made him look as if he smiled all the time.

"Growing up must have been chaotic."

"It was hell. Pure and simple. Hell." He smiled again and winked. Then, seriously, he said, "I've got big shoulders. Feel free to lean on them any time."

She felt herself beginning to blush again. Worse, he seemed sincere. "I'm fine now, Mr. Marshall. Truly, I am. I don't know what happened. I never get so emotional." She could not look away from his eyes. They were green.

"Ian, please. And all women are emotional. Trust me. I know."

She smiled. "I'm not emotional." She was firm.

"I doubt that." He wasn't smiling now. "Any woman who dedicates her life to bettering the worlds of kids and dogs has a huge and bleeding heart."

She stared. "How do you know what I do?"

"I'm a friend of David's," he said. "Remember?"

Something had changed, and Claire didn't know how or when it had happened. The room was still. Everything felt silent and unreal. Claire was so aware of the man standing just a few feet away from her; his presence seemed to charge the air.

"Is there anything I can do?" he asked. "Can I somehow make this a better evening?"

She was amazed. He really meant it. "No." Her smile became wide and genuine. "Not unless you can make the clock strike midnight."

He smiled in return. "Well, I could sneak around the house and change all the clocks."

"But all the men are wearing wristwatches."

"We could tell the bartender to pour triples."

Her eyes widened. "Souse them all!" she cried.

"And no cake," he added, dimples deepening.

"No cake. To hell with the birthday," Claire agreed fervently.

"There's always that yacht my friend has moored in the marina—we can probably see the *Lady Anne* from your terrace." His gaze was penetrating.

Claire's smile froze. Her heart lurched with an awareness she should not feel. An image of her and this stranger jumping into a car, driving down the hill, and sneaking aboard his friend's yacht, hand in hand and barefoot, filled her mind.

"I'm sorry." His gaze was searching. "I was only joking."

Had it been a joke? She hesitated. "I hate to say it, but the idea is tempting."

He waited.

Claire realized that if she said "Let's go," he would take her hand and they would go. *It was so tempting.* Claire was actually considering leaving her own party to enjoy herself, and that was unthinkable.

He looked past her, toward the door.

Claire didn't have to look to know who was there, and reality hit like cold water splashing in her face. She turned.

David stood on the threshold of the room. "Claire!"

Claire's shoulders stiffened as if someone had placed a heavy yoke on them. "Yes?" She was going to ask for a divorce. Soon—not that night, because it was his birthday, but tomorrow or the next day.

"Everyone's asking for you," David returned, glancing from her to Ian and back again. The look seemed hostile, if not suspicious.

Claire hesitated, surprised. She looked from David to Ian again. Her husband hadn't spoken to Ian but was regarding him coolly, and Claire knew jealousy had nothing to do with his coldness. David had never been jealous of other men. He knew she would never betray him that way.

Ian smiled. "Hello, David," he said. "Happy birthday. Thank you for inviting me. It's a great party."

David's nod was curt, his words clipped and tight. "Marshall. Thank you. Let's go, Claire."

Claire was bewildered. Clearly David did not like Ian Marshall. Had a deal gone bad? It wasn't like him to be so rude. She walked over to her husband but smiled at Ian Marshall. "Shall we join the others?" But what she really wanted to say was *thank you*.

"Of course," Ian said with an answering smile. But his eyes were on David, and they were filled with wariness.

Claire didn't like it at all. The tension between the two men was unmistakable, and the only question was why.

Guests were finally leaving, most of them smiling and pleasantly inebriated. Claire judged the party a huge success. After the buffet dinner, many of them even danced to seventies rock and roll on the terrace beneath the glowing full moon. Most important, no one except Elizabeth Duke and Ian Marshall seemed to notice her dismal mood or the fact that she and David hardly spoke to each other.

About thirty people remained. It had gotten cold outside, which was usually the case in the Bay Area, and everyone had clustered in the living room on the various couches, chairs, and ottomans, after-dinner drinks in hand. David was playing a jazz tune on the grand piano. He was a gifted pianist, but he had never pursued his talent. Even having had more than his fair share of wine and vodka, he was playing splendidly.

Claire wished he hadn't gotten drunk. Recently—or not so recently?—he had started to slur when he was drinking, and to stagger just a bit. Claire studied him as he switched to an Elton John tune and began to sing. Two women were standing beside him, the blonde clearly mesmerized. They started to sing, too.

Claire turned and saw Jean-Léon watching her. He glanced at David and then back at her, shaking his head in disgust. Claire tensed but gave her father a reassuring smile and turned away. She left the party, and at the stairs, she slid off her gold sandals. Her feet were hurting her.

The night seemed to have become endless; she was exhausted yet eager for a new day. With the eagerness was anxiety and fear. She was really going to ask for a divorce. She was going to leave David and somehow be alone.

It was frightening; it was thrilling.

Slowly, she went upstairs, sandals dangling from one hand. At least she could stop smiling now.

On the upstairs landing Claire came face-to-face with Ian Marshall. "Good God!" she cried, her hand on her palpitating heart.

"I'm sorry," he said quickly, clearly as stunned as she was. "I didn't mean to scare you—you surprised me, too."

Claire's pulse slowed, returning to normal. He smiled at her. "Tough night, huh?" He glanced at the sandals with their precarious heels and tiny straps, then his gaze sharpened, moving quickly back to her face.

But Claire could only stare at him, recovering some of her surprise. What was he doing upstairs? She smiled a little. "It's insanity, isn't it? What a woman does for glamour."

"Not really. That dress is a knockout."

Claire's heart leaped at his words.

"But I'd bet anything you look great in a pair of jeans and a T-shirt," he went on. Then his smile faded. "What's wrong, Claire?"

She did not move. "What are you doing up here, Ian?"

His gaze moved over her features slowly. His smile faded a bit as he understood. "I'm not snooping, Claire. Someone was in the powder room downstairs, and the staff directed me to the guest bathroom up here."

Claire shook her head. "There's another bathroom in the den."

"It was also occupied."

She met his gaze. "I see." She was relieved—but of course, what had she been thinking? He was too nice to have been snooping around her home. "What do you do, Ian?" she asked curiously, leaning against the wall.

"I'm a consultant. Generally for firms who do business in Europe or the Middle East. In fact, I just got back from Tel Aviv a few days ago."

Claire nodded; that hardly gave her a clue as to what his profession was.

He touched her bare arm briefly. "You seem tired. Are you calling it a night?"

Claire shivered and looked up at him. The urge to ask him to drive down to his friend's yacht suddenly overcame her. The evening had been a hard one. She hadn't had a single chance to relax. It would be relaxing, even fun, to sit with this man and sip champagne in a place of peace and quiet. Of course, it was an impossible and forbidden notion. "I wish I could. There's still a good two dozen guests downstairs."

"They're pretty happy down there. I don't think anyone would know if you slipped off to bed."

Claire knew he hadn't been making an innuendo, but the word "bed" made her flush, and she thought—but wasn't sure—he was thinking the same thing. Claire was aware of being a pretty woman. She knew Ian found her attractive. With her marriage in its death throes, she felt vulnerable and even afraid of herself.

But she would never cross any inappropriate lines until she was divorced.

She swallowed. "Did you have a good time tonight?"

"Yes, I did. And thank you for asking."

"I'm glad you enjoyed yourself," she said fiercely, meaning it.

This time he didn't speak. He just smiled at her, as if he did not want to end the moment.

Claire felt herself blush again. It was time to go, and there were no ifs, ands, or buts about it.

His gaze wandered over her, lingering on her dangling sandals. "David is a very lucky man."

"Are you flirting with me?" She smiled because he was, and she needed it.

"Is it a crime? You're blushing, Claire. It's nice."

"It's nice to have a nice man flirting with me," she said honestly.

His eyes widened. "It must happen all the time!" he exclaimed.

"Not really," she said.

He shook his head. "Go figure."

Claire laughed. It was her first real laugh of the evening.

He smiled. "You even have a nice laugh." His smile vanished. "I had better go." He gave her a long look.

Claire tensed, certain she knew what the look meant. He was being swept away by their flirtation, too. And he did not trust himself, just as she did not trust herself.

As they stood there, sounds drifted up from outside, coming around from the front of the house. Good-byes. Car doors slamming. Engines revving.

"Good night," he said quickly, then he turned and was gone.

"Good night," Claire murmured as he disappeared down the hall. She leaned against the wall, feeling as if she had been run over by a truck. Would their paths cross again? She hoped very much that they would.

It was a long moment before she moved. Instead, she replayed their two encounters over and over again in her mind, as if she were a teenage girl with a very severe crush. When she realized what she was doing, she laughed at herself, because she was thirty-two, not twelve. Claire went into her bedroom for another pair of shoes.

A moment later, she stood on the threshold of the living room. A dozen guests remained, but all were in the process of leaving.

She sighed. Jean-Léon was chatting with the Dukes in the foyer. The turquoise-clad blonde who had been hanging all over David for most of the night was slipping on a wrap. Claire suddenly realized that David was nowhere to be seen. Puzzled, she walked to the foyer and said good night to the blonde.

Her name was Sherry. "I had a wonderful time," she gushed.

"I'm glad," Claire said, wondering if she was sleeping with David. It would not surprise her.

Sherry thanked her, glancing past Claire as if looking for David. A moment later she left.

"It was a marvelous party," Elizabeth said to her. "But it's so late! We have to go. Claire, we will talk tomorrow."

Claire nodded as William hugged her. "Dear, once again, you have outdone yourself. The food, the wines, everything was superb. More importantly, you are superb." He smiled at her. "Have brunch with us on Sunday?"

"I'll try." Too late, Claire realized she had said "I" instead of "we." The Dukes stepped out to their waiting car and driver.

Claire said another series of good-byes, then turned to her father. "Have you seen David?" One more couple was putting on their coats, and the bartender was finishing breaking down the bar.

"No, I haven't. He's drunk, Claire," Jean-Léon said with disapproval.

Claire sighed. "I know. Maybe he went up the back stairs to bed."

Her father kissed her cheek. "I hope David knows how fortunate he is to have you as his wife. The party went well, Claire. No thanks to him."

Claire smiled, refusing to buy into the subject, and said good-bye. Finally, all of her guests were gone.

Promptly Claire kicked off her lower-heeled sandals as the remaining two waiters left the house, carrying the last of their equipment. The caterer came up to her. "Everything's done," she said. "The leftovers are put away, dishes and glasses ready for party rentals to pick up first thing tomorrow, and the kitchen as clean as a whistle."

Claire thanked the slim, middle-aged woman, whom she used often

for various events. "Thank you so much, Mrs. Lewis. Once again, everything was just perfect."

Mrs. Lewis beamed. Then she said, "Do try to relax a bit, Mrs. Hayden.
I could see you weren't yourself these past few days."

Claire stared after her. Could everyone tell that her marriage was over?
Could she no longer hide her true feelings? Disturbed, Claire went to the
front door and locked it.

She sighed. Everyone had enjoyed himself, even David; the night had
been a success.

She thought about Ian Marshall and smiled a little.

Don't go there, she told herself sternly. It was only a harmless flirtation.

But somehow, she knew it was more.

Claire turned off the downstairs lights except for one in the hall. The
house was so quiet and still, when just moments ago it had been filled
with conversation and music and so many people. She walked upstairs
quietly, not wanting to wake David but certain he wouldn't wake up even
if she did make noise. The quiet engulfed her. It should have been peaceful. Instead, unease prickled at her.

She flicked on the light in the bedroom.

The king-size bed was empty.

It wasn't even rumpled.

Claire stared at it for a moment, unable to comprehend that David
wasn't there, asleep. *Where was he?*

Her neck seemed to prickle again. Claire went back into the hallway,
turning on the lights, relieved to chase the last of the upstairs shadows
away. Now she was acutely aware of the house being too silent around
her. The dogs were kenneled in the yard out back. She was alone in the
house—but no, that wasn't true. David was also in the house. Except—
the house somehow felt empty.

But that was impossible. David had passed out somewhere, she
decided with a flash of anger, and it was inappropriate. Gripping the railing, she hurried downstairs.

It was so dark.

There were shadows everywhere.

But that was only because everything had been so bright and festive a
few minutes ago. "David?" Claire called, turning on lights one by one as

she entered the living room. She did not expect him to be there, and he was not.

She turned on the last hall light, walking down to the den. She pushed open the door, which was slightly ajar, and hit the wall switch, flooding the room with light. "David?" She saw instantly that he wasn't there, either.

On impulse, she checked that bathroom—it was empty. Her heart began to thud in her chest. Where could he be?

He's only passed out somewhere, she told herself again, trying not to become frightened.

Claire hesitated before the home office they shared. What if he had fallen and hurt himself?

Then she pushed open the door, quickly fumbling for the light, praying that he would be asleep on the couch inside. It came on and she looked around, but the office was deserted.

She felt unbearably alone.

Worse than ever before.

Claire hugged herself.

Somehow, she knew that she really was alone in the house. It was a sickening feeling. Panic assailed her, making her dizzy.

She needed to go get the dogs. But to get to the kennels, she had to cross the backyard, and she was suddenly afraid to step out of the house and into the looming night.

Claire thought she felt a movement behind her. She whirled. The threshold was vacant. It had been her imagination, nothing more.

Where was David? Where could he be?

Was she really alone in the house?

Claire now ran through the entire house, to the kitchen and dining room on the other side. As the caterer had said, her kitchen was as clean as a whistle—no one would ever know that she'd had a party that night. And it, too, was empty.

Panicked, Claire stepped into the dining room. This time she didn't bother to turn on the light—the illumination from the kitchen showed that no one was there. *What was happening?*

She rushed to the phone and called her father, but there was no answer. He lived in Tiburon—he should be home at any minute. She decided not to worry him and did not leave a message. But she would kill David when she found him.

Claire hesitated, then unlocked the kitchen door, telling herself that there was nothing to be afraid of. She turned on the outside lights. The backyard brightened, and across it, she could see the wire kennels. The dogs had awakened and began to bark.

Claire left the kitchen door wide open and ran across the yard to the kennels. She let out the dogs, hugging them all. She was shaking. "Where's David? Jill, help me find David," she cried.

The dogs seemed very happy, oblivious to her worries, and raced ahead of her into the kitchen, all except for her beautiful purebred poodle.

Jilly paused, sniffing the air, and she began to growl.

Claire didn't know what to think. Jilly was very intelligent and a great watchdog. "What is it?" she asked hoarsely.

Jilly growled again—and she took off. Not into the kitchen, but behind the house, disappearing where the terrace was.

The terrace where, just an hour ago, her guests had been dancing beneath the moon and the stars.

Frantic, territorial barking sounded from the terrace.

Claire needed a flashlight. She didn't have one and couldn't think where one was. Filled with fear, Claire headed after her dog. She reminded herself as she turned the corner of the house that her neighborhood was absolutely safe. But she knew something had happened, otherwise her dog would not be so upset. It crossed her mind to call the police, but what would she say? She reached the terrace, and fortunately, the lights she had turned on inside the living room shone directly upon it. Relief filled her.

David was passed out in a chair at the terrace's farthest end.

Damn him! Claire thought furiously, not knowing whether to cry or shout.

Jilly had halted a dozen feet from him, and she continued to bark wildly. Now the other dogs came barreling over to her, and they began to bark as well, causing pandemonium. *They were barking at David.*

Claire stiffened. Why were the dogs so upset? "David?" She hesitated as the barking escalated in urgency. David did not move, and granted, he'd had a lot to drink, but shouldn't the noise wake him now? She broke into a run.

Claire reached David and had a flashing premonition, but she grabbed him anyway and his head fell back—and that was when she saw the blood.

His throat was sliced open. *Bloody and sliced open.*

Blood covered his neck, his shirt, his chest.

He was lifeless.

She screamed.

CHAPTER 2

Claire sat in a chair at the table in her kitchen, clasping a now ice-cold mug of coffee in her hands. She was in shock. Sunlight was streaming into the room through the many wide windows; it was six or seven in the morning. Voices were everywhere, surrounding her, washing over her. Hushed tones. Tones of reverence for the dead and the grieving. Mostly they came from the other room, where detectives and policemen were in various huddles, while other officers where gathering up God knew what kind of evidence in tiny plastic bags. Someone had been taking pictures. Someone had drawn that stupid white line on her terrace where David had died. Someone had even cordoned off the living room and terrace with crime-scene tape. And someone had removed the body, hours and hours ago, loading the covered corpse onto a gurney. David was now a *corpse*.

Was this really happening?

Other voices drifted into her numb mind, too. Claire knew that Elizabeth wanted her to go home with the Dukes. Jean-Léon hadn't countered, and William kept murmuring "Shocking, simply shocking," over and over again.

Claire stared at her milky coffee. David had told her that he was in trouble. Big trouble. Why hadn't she insisted he tell her just what kind of trouble? Maybe, somehow, his murder could have been prevented if she had known the facts. But what kind of trouble could he have been in?

The kind that resulted in murder, clearly.

To make matters even worse, she had been on the verge of asking him for a divorce.

Claire choked on the guilt. It was suffocating. She could not bear it.

Jilly came over and sat down, lifting one slim brown paw. She was an incredibly intelligent animal, and she knew Claire was distressed. Claire looked into her wide brown eyes and felt tears gathering in her own eyes. She smiled at the poodle and accepted the paw. "Good girl, Jill," she managed brokenly. The short tail with the puff of fur at the end wagged enthusiastically.

"Mrs. Hayden?"

Claire heard a man's voice that was unfamiliar. She twisted to look up, stroking the big poodle.

It was the tall, heavyset Irish-American detective in charge of the investigation. Muldoon, or something like that. He had already asked her hundreds of stupid, meaningless, irrelevant questions.

"It would be great if you could find that guest list for us now," he said, his eyes kind.

Claire heard him but couldn't focus on the words. Had David been murdered while she was upstairs flirting with Ian Marshall? Claire felt sick enough to retch.

She looked at him as he waited for her answer, and then she leaped up and ran to the kitchen bathroom, where she was violently ill.

She was never going to forget the sight of David sitting there in their iron lawn chair with his throat slashed open. She clung to the toilet bowl, now heaving dryly, for a very long time.

"Claire, you poor dear." It was Elizabeth. Claire felt her hand on her back, between her shoulder blades. "Come, let me help you up."

Somehow Claire stood. Elizabeth still wore her red jersey gown, and Claire was in her gold lace slip dress. She wore one of David's terry bathrobes over it. "He told me he was in big trouble," Claire whispered. "Why didn't I make him tell me all the details?"

"Because you are human," Elizabeth said gently. "Because you didn't know what was going to happen just a few hours later." Her eyes were filled with concern.

"Maybe I could have seen this coming—and this never would have happened if he had told me what was going on!" Claire cried.

The two women hugged, hard. "This is not your fault," Elizabeth said fiercely, tears shimmering in her eyes. "Do not blame yourself, Claire!"

Claire knew it was her fault. Maybe if she had been a better wife, they would have had a better marriage, and David wouldn't have gone outside alone.

What had he been involved in?

Claire had no idea. It had been years since she had been his confidante.

Claire let Elizabeth lead her out of the bathroom. She could not think, much less make even the most mundane of decisions. The detective was patiently waiting for her. Claire could not recall a single word that she had said to him earlier. "My husband was in trouble," she began. "He told me earlier this evening, for the first time—and he was frightened. I saw it in his eyes."

"You told me all of that, Mrs. Hayden," the big man said gently. "I need the guest list. It's urgent." He smiled encouragingly at her.

Claire blinked. "The guest list. You mean for the party?"

He nodded at her.

Claire blinked. "You don't think . . . that one of the guests . . . could do such a thing?" She had assumed the murderer to be an intruder, catching David unaware when he had wandered outside.

"Just get me the guest list," the detective said.

"He's asked you three times, Claire," Jean-Léon said, coming over to her. "I'll help you look for it. It must be in the office, right?"

Claire stared at her father. He had been the first one she called after finding David dead, and he had been the first to arrive after the initial squad car. "Dad, I want to go home with you," she said impulsively. She had no intention of staying in her own home. In fact, she would never stay there again.

"You know that your old room is always waiting for you," he said. "Come, Claire. Let's look for the party list."

Claire didn't move. Why couldn't he reach out and touch her? It would mean so much just now. It would mean everything.

When she was a little girl, she fantasized about his hugs. She imagined falling off her tricycle, skinning elbows and knees, and then rushing into his study. He would look up from his papers and work, and upon seeing her, he would leap to his feet, concerned. He would rush over to her, lifting her into his arms—holding her tightly, like a real father would.

Claire reminded herself that she was a grown woman. "Sure, Dad."

She headed into the hall. Claire could hardly look into the living area or across it, at the terrace, as she passed. Her home looked more like a Hollywood movie set than a home. The policemen, the detectives in their jeans, the tape forbidding entry, the white line gruesomely depicting

David's body where it had been found . . . Claire hurried past, refusing to see any of it, refusing to see anyone. Words filtered to her—"Helluva party . . . yeah, real good time . . . and no one saw . . . copycat . . . a hundred suspects . . . a hundred and one"—followed by coarse laughter.

There had been exactly 101 guests, including her.

How could this be happening?

"Claire?" Her father stood by the office door, waiting for her to precede him in.

Claire stepped into the sunny corner room and shivered violently. "I wanted a divorce, Dad."

His eyes widened. "You? You asked him for a divorce?"

Claire shook her head, going over to the large desk centered before one window. One corner was stacked neatly with all of her mail, much of it bills, which she had yet to open. Somewhere in the looming pile was the guest list, she thought. When David worked at home, he usually worked on the PC, which was on a smaller, catty-corner table. By mutual agreement, they had divided the larger desk almost in half. His papers and work remained on the left side.

Her space was impossibly neat; his was cluttered and wildly disorganized. Claire had never been able to figure out how he could find anything when he sat down to work.

She refused to believe that one of her guests had murdered David. But automatically, she slipped the rubber band off the stack of mail, and sure enough, at the bottom was a neatly typed guest list, with addresses, phone numbers, and even company names and job titles included. Detective Muldoon would be pleased.

"Is that it?" Jean-Léon asked, coming over.

Claire nodded, suddenly aware of the very first lump of grief rising up within her. It came up from nowhere, hard and fast. In spite of their troubles, in spite of how far apart they had become, she had loved David. He had been a close friend for fifteen years. She would never see him again.

"Could you take this over to Muldoon?" she asked harshly.

"His name is Murphy, Claire. Sure." Jean-Léon took the guest list and left the room.

Claire stared at David's desk.

She had wanted out of her marriage—but not this way. And the biggest question remained. Why?

He had been in big trouble. Apparently he had felt it was his fault. Claire realized she had moved to stand in front of his half of the desk. She stared down at the various legal agreements and notes on the desk. Should she pore over everything? In her state of mind, it would probably be a waste of time. Claire was well aware that her utter daze was a state of shock, and she did not have a clue what she was looking for.

The police would find the killer. It was their job. But she sat down in David's chair. There were half a dozen legal pads, scrawled over with David's frantic handwriting, in front of her. She scanned one—but it was a business deal, and he had made notes involving some kind of merger. Lots of sums had been involved. She glanced at several more, and again, everything seemed to be about work brought home from the office. Claire felt certain that his job hadn't killed him. David had been a damn good lawyer.

"Claire, dear?" Elizabeth was standing in the doorway. There was a hint of anxiety on her tone.

Claire turned. "I was wondering if I might find a clue to David's death somewhere in this mess of his. Did he ever say anything to you, Elizabeth?"

Elizabeth wandered over. "Dear, David wouldn't have confided in me about that. He might have gone to William. You might want to ask him."

"I will." Claire sighed. It felt as if it was well past midnight; it felt as if she hadn't slept in days. And the truth was, she hadn't slept in a full day and more. The extent of her fatigue was beginning to sink in now.

"Elizabeth?" Claire heard William calling.

"Come home with us," Elizabeth said gently.

"I appreciate the offer, but I am going to stay with Jean-Léon," Claire said.

Elizabeth smiled. "Very well. At least let me make you some breakfast."

Claire was hardly hungry, but she understood. "Thanks."

"Scrambled eggs and toast? I think some protein might be a good idea."

Claire nodded, and Elizabeth left the room.

Claire turned back to the desk and saw a large black-and-white photo sticking out from under David's briefs, papers, and legal pads. Slightly curious, she pulled it free, and then she started.

The photo was clearly decades old, taken before the advent of color photography. If she did not miss her guess, she was staring at a photo taken during World War II. Two army officers were standing side by side, smiling at the camera. It wasn't a clear shot, so Claire squinted and finally realized the uniforms were British, that one of the officers was of a higher rank than the other, and that both men were very young—no more than their early twenties. They were standing in front of a granite or stone building, so close to it that the building could not be identified. Claire turned the photo over and saw two names scribbled on the back: George Suttill and Lionel Elgin. Also written there were the words "probably the spring of 1944."

Claire was thoroughly perplexed. She was looking at a photograph of two British army officers taken during World War II. This couldn't possibly have anything to do with whatever David had gotten himself involved in, could it? Claire did not think so. But it was still so odd. David was not a World War II buff. In fact, he wasn't a history buff at all.

Claire was about to dismiss the photo when she realized that another sheet of paper was stuck to its underside. She separated the photograph and the second sheet. For the second time in a minute or so, she blinked in real surprise.

It was a fax from an investigative agency in London.

Enclosed photo of Suttill and Elgin. Possible dead end. Please advise—WC.

Claire stared at the fax. What was going on? Who was Suttill? Who was Elgin? Then she looked at the date—it had been sent just two days ago. What the hell was this about? Why had David hired the Thompson Cantwell Investigative Agency, a firm based in London?

Bewildered, she put the fax and photo back on David's desk. Maybe she was so dazed that her mind was failing her; perhaps there was an obvious explanation for David's sudden interest in two army officers from World War II. Claire realized she was too tired to dwell on the subject. But of course, she must mention to Murphy what she had found.

Claire took both items in hand and went to find the detective.

David's lawyer came to her the following day.

Claire sat stiffly and unfeelingly in the wide-open living area of her father's vast Tiburon home, which overlooked the bay from the top of a hill in a very exclusive neighborhood of multimillion-dollar redwood homes. Jack Thorne, a tall, lanky, bald lawyer, sat on a chair beside the glass coffee table, where the housekeeper had placed two cups of coffee, a sugar bowl, and creamer. Neither one of them drank the coffee. He opened his briefcase and removed documents. He had come to read the will.

Jack Thorne coughed. "Claire?"

Claire wore a straight skirt and short-sleeved turtleneck with stockings and midheeled pumps; everything black. She was devoid of makeup, her hair pulled severely back in a twist. Claire knew she looked like a grieving widow, and it gave her a sense of satisfaction.

She felt like burning everything colorful in her closet. Soon she probably would. She also felt like throwing out all of her makeup—every single lipstick, blusher, and eye shadow.

She felt like rampaging through their home, turning over chairs and knocking over the furniture.

But nothing would bring David back or absolve her of the guilt for her role in his death. Nothing would take away the ball of fear she was trying to keep buried deep inside.

"Claire? I'd like to read the will."

Claire looked at him—he was actually a family friend. She kept her hands clasped in her lap. "Is it really necessary? I assume I've inherited any assets David held singly."

Thorne nodded. "There weren't many, the estate is held jointly. There's the car, the sailboat, a few minor stocks, and it's all yours." He smiled a little at her.

Claire shrugged. She did not give a damn about David's Mercedes, Sunfish, or some small stock portfolio. "You didn't have to come all the way out here just to tell me that."

"Of course I did, Claire. He also specifies that he wishes to be cremated, his ashes scattered over the bay."

Claire nodded. "I know. He mentioned it once or twice." She inhaled to fight sudden tears. "I just always thought I'd be scattering his ashes in fifty years or something." Her voice broke.

"I know. This is terrible. Are there any leads?"

Claire shrugged and quickly recovered her composure. "I haven't heard from the police since I left the house yesterday morning."

Thorne nodded.

She looked more closely at him. Something was wrong. There was something in his eyes that she did not like. "Jack? What's wrong? Is there something you have to tell me—that you don't want to tell me?"

"Yes, there is, Claire. But maybe we should wait a week or so to go over some details that eventually you will have to deal with."

Claire was as rigid as a board. She stared at his heavily lined face. "What kind of details?"

He hesitated.

"Jack?" Her tone was as sharp as any whiplash, and she heard it. But she was alarmed now. "If there is something serious that I should know about, then I must know, and so be it."

He sighed. "Claire, David has been in trouble financially for some time."

Claire looked at him, not quite understanding. "What?"

He repeated himself.

She fought to make sense of what he had said. "David told me we'd taken a hit recently. All of our money is held jointly. When I was twenty-five and came into my trust from my mother's family, he took charge of that money. I hope you're not talking about our mutual investments?"

"I am."

Claire just stared.

"There's not much left, Claire," Jack Thorne said grimly.

"What?"

"In the past several years, he moved most of your portfolio into technology stocks. You surely know what happened. There's not much left."

Claire was stunned. "What do you mean? My mother's family left me a quarter of a million dollars, which David invested for us when I was twenty-five. That was over seven years ago. I believe he added a percentage of his earnings every year. By now, we should have close to a million tucked away."

He pursed his lips. "Actually, the net sum in that portfolio is forty-two thousand dollars."

Claire stared. Surely she had misheard.

"Claire?" he asked softly.

The comprehension crashed over her all at once. She stood. "Oh, God." Their investments had been reduced to almost a bit more than her annual income—but less than one fifth of what David made. *He had literally lost everything.*

"Are you okay?" Thorne was also standing.

She was going to have to move. Soon. She could afford to live in their house for maybe two or three more months. Not that she wanted to live there now, but she had never dreamed she would have to sell out of necessity and under duress. The sooner she moved, the better, she realized with another stab of fear. So she would not deplete all the savings that she had left.

Claire smiled brightly. "I'm fine, Jack," she said with conviction, but it was an utter lie. "I'm a little surprised, but that's all." Her lifestyle would have to change as well. Immediately. But she could manage that. She had no intention of leaving the Humane Society to look for a better-paying job, even though she had a master's in business administration; she would never give up the work that meant so much to her.

"When you want to talk about it, you should give me a call," Jack Thorne said. "I'd be more than happy to advise you, Claire, with no charge."

"I appreciate the sentiment," Claire said. "But you must bill me for your time." She held herself proudly. "I might just give our accountant a call." She would have to plan a budget instantly.

"You should do that," Jack said. "As soon as possible." He began packing up his briefcase. "I'm leaving a copy of the will and some other reports, including financial statements, here for you. They're yours to keep."

"Great," Claire said, the smile plastered on her face. She must not unravel now. After all, this was a low blow, but it was nothing compared to finding David on her terrace with his throat slashed about thirty-six hours ago.

"I can find my way out," Jack said.

"I'll walk you to the door." Claire smiled firmly and marched him to the front door of the big house. Paintings of various sizes and value, representing hundreds of different schools, covered every inch of space in every room. Claire shook his hand and let him out. Suddenly she was aware of the art that surrounded her. She had never really paid attention to its value; now, she wondered if Jean-Léon had really meant for her to own the Courdet.

Then she turned and walked back into the living room. She could never sell it. She refused to cry. Crying would not solve anything. But she

couldn't help wondering if her financial straits were, somehow, her just
desserts for failing David in his time of need.

It was cold and windy at the beach where the mourners had gathered to
scatter David's ashes. Claire stood between her father and the Dukes,
foremost among the crowd. A cleric was speaking. Claire did not hear a
word he said.

Claire had worked hard to gather up her last reserves of strength. In
the past few days, she had hired a broker, and as soon as word of David's
murder died down, the broker would put the house up for sale. Her entire
life had changed, or at least it felt that way. It was as if she had stepped
unknowingly across a huge divide—and there was no way back. David
was gone. She would sell the house and move. Although she would continue to devote herself to her work at the Humane Society, Claire somehow felt as if she had changed fundamentally inside. She did not feel like
the same person. She wondered if she would walk through the rest of her
life carrying the huge burden of her guilt while hiding the little, intrusive
knot of fear.

And David's killer still had to be brought to justice.

If the police had any suspects, they were not revealing anything.

A hundred somberly clad people—everyone bundled up in coats due
to the weather—were listening to the cleric drone on about David's
exemplary life and God's will. Most of the mourners had been at David's
birthday party, and the detective, Murphy, had also come to the service.
David's family had appeared—they lived in Atlanta—but his parents
remained dry-eyed and aloof on the other side of the crowd. Occasionally
one of his sisters dabbed her eyes with a tissue. Claire wondered if the
murderer was actually present now.

It was a horrible thought. Claire tried to tune in to the cleric, but
again, it was so hard to understand what he was saying. He kept saying
how wonderful David had been. A wonderful husband, a wonderful son,
a wonderful partner to his associates.

Claire closed her eyes. Clearly the cleric had not known David at all.
He had been a decent husband, but he hadn't had anything to do with his
own family. Or maybe he hadn't even been a decent husband—he had
somehow lost almost all their savings, most of which had been inherited
from Claire's mother.

She realized she had stiffened and her fists were clenched. The anger was trying to take her over again. She must not blame David. He hadn't intended to lose their money. But she could be angry with the killer for what he had done.

Claire tuned out the droning voice of the cleric. Elizabeth took her hand and whispered, "Just a few more minutes, dear." Claire managed to smile at her.

Elizabeth smiled back, but concern was reflected in her reddened eyes. She had also been crying. She had loved David, too.

In spite of the wind, the day was blindingly bright. Claire wore sunglasses because she did not want anyone to see into her eyes and past her facade. That facade felt so incredibly fragile now, yet Claire was determined to cling to it with all of her power. She was determined to accept condolences, but she didn't want people to tell her how sorry they were. She just wanted to go home—and find David's killer.

Except she had no home, not with her house currently under a police quarantine, and soon to have a FOR SALE sign in front of it.

She was vaguely aware of William leaning between her and Elizabeth and whispering to her. "It's almost over. Just a few more minutes, Claire."

Claire nodded at him, a small smile adhering to her face as if it had been sutured into place. Her mouth was beginning to ache.

Claire suddenly noticed what the cleric was doing. He was approaching her. Panic filled her; he was holding the urn.

He gave her a kind smile.

I can't do it, Claire thought wildly. David was in that urn, and she was supposed to scatter him across the bay? It was ridiculous, absurd—grotesque. As grotesque as finding him dead just minutes after she had been contemplating when and how to ask him for a divorce.

The cleric handed her the urn.

And a face in the crowd suddenly came into focus just to the left and behind the cleric's black-garbed shoulder. Ian Marshall was staring at her. He was wearing aviator-style sunglasses with reflective lenses; still, his expression seemed grim, and there was no mistaking who he was.

Claire realized she was holding the urn. She didn't quite know how that had happened, but now her smile failed her. She stared at Ian, and her heart began a heavy beat inside her breast.

Jean-Léon had her arm. Claire did not move.

She had been flirting with Marshall upstairs while a killer had been cutting David's throat. Claire had no doubt. David had been playing the piano when she had gone upstairs; when she had come back down, he had been gone.

What had Marshall been doing upstairs in the first place?

Suspicion and hostility consumed her.

Claire stared at him. Her father was speaking into her ear, but she did not hear him. *He had said he'd gone upstairs to use the toilet, because the one downstairs had been occupied. But there were two other bathrooms downstairs, as well as the powder room off the foyer. How could they all have been occupied?*

What had he been doing upstairs?

It was wrong. Something was wrong with his explanation.

Of course, he was not be the killer. The killer had been downstairs murdering David while Ian was upstairs, right?

No, that was not necessarily true. When she had gone downstairs, Ian was gone, and David had also been missing.

"Claire?" Jean-Léon tugged on her arm. "Everyone's waiting. Or should I do it?"

Claire looked from Ian Marshall, whose stare was unremitting, to her father. She had only vaguely heard him, but she knew he wanted her to scatter David's ashes. She nodded, allowing him to lead her across the sandy, pebbled stretch of headlands, and somehow they were walking over to the edge of the cliff.

David had been cold and hostile to Marshall. They were not friends—that had been obvious. So Ian had lied to her when he had said, oh so calmly, that they were.

Claire faced the swirling waters a hundred feet below. Now she was supposed to turn the urn upside down and scatter David's ashes. Tears blinded her. The one last wave of grief and loss took her by surprise, washing over her richly, sickeningly. David was gone. The bay sparkled and glittered. Jesus. David was gone, reduced to a handful of gray ashes, and maybe, just maybe, Ian Marshall was somehow involved.

She had to tell Murphy. Immediately.

There were rocks on the beachhead below.

Claire stared down at the water; she stared down at the rocks on the small strip of beach. She saw neither the sand nor the shore nor the rocks.

Instead, she saw David sitting in the iron lawn chair with his body covered in blood. Then she saw Ian in her den, intruding when she had escaped there to be alone.

Why had he wandered off and into the den, alone, when the party was confined to the living area and the terrace? None of the other guests had ventured around her house.

Claire turned and looked over her shoulder, directly at his silver reflective lenses.

"Should I scatter his ashes?" Jean-Léon asked. "Claire? Everyone's waiting."

Claire focused. She wasn't holding merely a pot of ashes; she was holding David. There had been a will, she had read it, and this was what he had wanted. Claire clutched the urn to her chest. She looked down. The water was so bright. The rocks, so big and jagged. And she thought, *Good-bye. Good-bye, David.*

This is really good-bye.

Claire stepped abruptly forward to the very edge of the cliff and turned the urn upside down. As she did so, it slipped and fell; David's ashes lifted on the wind. Claire watched the urn crashing down onto the rocks below, finally shattering.

She shivered as she watched a few last ashes drifting on currents of air.

There was a pressure on her arm. Jean-Léon was guiding her back toward the crowd. People were approaching them. Claire sought the smile she had somehow lost minutes ago, managed to find it and drag it back into place. Instantly, her mouth hurt, aching from being held so long in one impossible position. Claire began accepting condolences, shaking hands.

"So sorry . . ."

"Claire, how terrible . . ."

"In time . . ."

The murmurs and gazes were being directed at her. Claire was surrounded now by strangers—she knew everyone but couldn't recognize anyone. Voices and more voices, pity and more pity. She had become separated from her father, whom she saw on the other side of the crowd. Control. Now was not the time to unravel and lose control. Her smile became firmer. Yet there was a pressure in her chest that was uncomfortable and sickening, even frightening, and it would not go away. Almost desperate, she looked around for the Dukes and finally saw Elizabeth, who, being so tall, stood out. But she, too, was far away, with dozens of dark-suited men and women between them.

"Terribly, terribly sorry . . ."

"If there is anything we can do . . ."

"We truly must tell you how sorry we are. . . ."

Claire looked for Elizabeth. Across the crowd, their eyes met, and Elizabeth understood and began to weave through the mourners to come to her. It was then that Claire saw Marshall again.

He had left the crowd of mourners and was waiting for cars to pass so he could cross the road and find his own vehicle. Anger sizzled inside of her. Why had he lied about being David's friend? And just who the hell was he?

Claire shoved into the crowd. Someone gasped her name; Claire ignored it. She thought she heard Elizabeth calling her, and then her father. Claire did not stop. Resolution filled her. It was a good feeling to have. It chased away the panic.

Somehow she made it through the crowd and to the road, where the cars were double-parked up and down the far side, against the steeply sloping ridge of the headlands. Just as Claire reached the blacktop, she saw Ian Marshall, pausing before the door of a black sedan. Claire ran across the road—almost in front of an oncoming car.

It swerved to avoid her, the driver honking angrily at her.

"Claire!" Ian ran to her and grabbed her arm. He seemed pale, but surely not because of her close encounter.

Claire shook him off abruptly. "We have to talk," she said.

"You have to be careful," he began. "That car almost hit you!"

"Hardly." She looked at his black Mercedes. "I need a lift." She started toward his car, feeling just how squared her shoulders were. Her short strides felt hard.

He fell into step beside her. "Claire, are you all right? Maybe you should stay with your father. I'm sorry about David." They paused beside the driver's door of the sedan and faced each other. He slid off his sunglasses.

"Are you?" She did not remove hers.

He seemed startled. "Excuse me?"

Claire felt herself flush. "I'm sorry. What I mean is, I need to ask you some questions, Ian."

His eyes had seemed soft with concern. Now they filled with a wariness she had seen once before—when David had stepped into the den and caught them there together. "What about?"

"You said you were David's friend. We've never met."

"I guess David and I were more business associates. What's this about, Claire?"

"You said very distinctly that you were his friend."

He stiffened. "It was just a way of speaking. Like, hey, how are you, nice to meet you—I'm a friend of David's."

So she had been right, they weren't friends. "What kind of business are you in? Are you a lawyer?"

He hesitated. "No, I'm not."

Claire began to feel like he didn't want to answer her questions. "What kind of business could you have had with David? And what do you do?"

"He was advising me—in a kind of offhand and *friendly* way. As a favor to a mutual friend. And I told you what I do. I consult for firms doing business mostly in Europe and the Middle East."

Claire didn't get it. "Consult how? On what?"

"Look, Claire, I can see that you are feeling a bit upset right now—"

"I'm not upset, I'm pissed," she said, shocking herself.

"Maybe we should give this conversation a rest for a few days. I could call you next week."

Claire didn't really hear him. She was stunned. Had she just said that she was "pissed"? She didn't even use that kind of language. Her heart was racing now. "What?"

"You're upset." His tone was gentle. "As you should be. What happened to David was terrible. I can call you next week, when some of the shock has subsided."

She looked him in the eye—through the black lenses of her sunglasses. "You don't want to answer my questions, do you?"

He stared. "No. Not today. Not here. Not now."

Oddly, his answer made her feel savagely satisfied. *He was hiding something.*

"Shall I give you a ride to your father's?" he asked.

As if she wanted to get into the car with him, when he refused to answer her questions, when he might somehow be involved in what had happened to David. "I'd like one of your cards. I'll call *you*," she said.

His eyes widened. "Okay," he said, drawing out the single word. He reached into his breast pocket, then said, "I don't seem to have my wallet, or my cards."

He was full of shit. He was lying. What was going on?

"I see," Claire said, feeling her cheeks burning. She was going to speak with Murphy the minute she got back across the street.

"Claire, what is this about? I can understand why you might be angry—but surely you're not angry at me?"

She smiled her socialite's perfect smile. "Why would I be angry with you, Ian?"

"I don't know. We just met. In fact, I thought we hit it off rather well." His gaze was searching.

She felt triumphant for not having removed her sunglasses. "I am a married woman, Mr. Marshall," she warned. Too late, she could have kicked herself, as she was a widow and the warning was certainly a give-away that she knew he was not being straight with her. Besides, today he hadn't made a pass. Today there was no chemistry.

"What?"

She corrected, "I mean, I'm a grieving widow."

"I am aware of that. Have I done or said something inappropriate? Because if I have, I am terribly sorry."

She wet her lips. She wanted to ask him if he had left the party the moment he had left her upstairs in the hall, or if he had lingered. But she did not. Murphy could ask him that.

But did she really think him capable of murder?

Claire wasn't sure. She knew only that he was being highly evasive—he didn't want to answer her questions, he had no business cards, he wanted to call her next week. She would not hold her breath. And she still didn't know what he did for a living.

But she could find out. David's secretary, Geraldine, knew everything in David's life, right down to the size of his shoes and suits.

Ian suddenly touched her shoulder. Claire stood very still. "Things will get better, Claire. I mean, as far as David goes."

She stared, not responding.

"Can I call you next week? To see how you are doing? As a friend," he added quickly.

They weren't friends. They were strangers who had been attracted to each other briefly during a party. But that was before David had been murdered. "Of course." She put on her smile again.

"I wish you wouldn't do that. It hurts me when you try so hard to pretend that you're okay and nothing is wrong," he said quietly.

Her chin came up. Her shoulders squared. "I will deal with life my way, Mr. Marshall, and you may deal with *your* life *your* way." She nodded abruptly and turned to cross the road.

"You're a strong woman, Claire. It's obvious. You'll get through this. It will just take some time," he said to her back.

This time, Claire waited for the traffic to subside before crossing. She did not answer him.

The moment she settled in the car beside her father, she reached for the phone. Murphy had not been present when she had rejoined the mourners, clearly having taken off with his partner.

"I think that went well," Jean-Léon said, pulling back onto the road carefully, easing into the slow-moving traffic.

Claire didn't answer. Instead, she dumped the contents of her purse into the center of her lap.

"What are you doing?" her father asked with surprise.

Claire was usually neat and organized. "I'm looking for that card Murphy gave me. You know. The detective in charge of the murder investigation." She sorted through tissues and a mirrored compact, several bobby pins, her wallet, her house keys.

Jean-Léon took the phone from her lap and hung it up. "What's this about, Claire?"

She finally took off her sunglasses. "I want to know if he's questioned Ian Marshall about David's murder."

"Marshall? The guy from New York? The one you were just talking to on the road?"

"Yes. He's from New York?"

"That's what he said," Jean-Léon said as they drove alongside the bay but hundreds of feet above it. "I met him at the party. We only spoke briefly. I didn't like him."

That made Claire stop searching among the items and debris in her lap. "Why not, Dad?"

"I don't know. An instinct, I guess. I think you should stay away from him. Why did you chase him over to his car?"

"Because he claimed to be a friend of David's, and that's not the case. I want to know who he is and what he does," Claire said. "Do you know?"

Jean-Léon stared at her searchingly for a moment. "He said something about consulting for firms that are start-ups in foreign countries. I didn't push. A few people commented about how you two were together after that night. I told everyone he was an old family friend to explain your behavior. I think everyone accepted it."

Claire met his eyes. "I'm sorry. You didn't have to lie on my account." God, even her father, who was so astute, could not figure Ian Marshall out. He was becoming a full-blown mystery. Or was she the one who was paranoid and hysterical, in her state of loss?

He stared at her directly again. "Claire, I am worried about you. You know you can stay with me as long as you need to, as long as it takes for you to get settled again."

Claire started. Her father was not the kind of man to worry. He was too preoccupied with acquiring new talent or old masters to think about much else. She was touched. Her heart melted instantly. "Thanks, Dad."

"I don't want anyone taking advantage of you right now," Jean-Léon said, surprising her anew.

Claire stared. "What?"

"We don't know this Ian Marshall, and I don't think you should be involved with him. We don't know what he wants, Claire."

Claire trembled. He was right. But why the warning? "Dad? Do you know something about him that I don't?"

"I told you everything that I do know. Again, it's just my intuition, but I have very good intuition, and I think the man might be trouble. I'll call Murphy for you as soon as we get to the house. I want an update on the investigation, anyway."

Claire nodded, relieved that her father would help, and suddenly exhaustion overcame her. She stuffed her things haphazardly back in her purse and closed it. She would take a nap the moment she got back to the house, she decided, and then she would call Geraldine and find out just who Ian Marshall really was, and what it was he was after.

She was determined to reach the truth.

The following morning, Claire called David's secretary from her car.

They exchanged greetings, and once again, Geraldine told Claire how sorry she was. Her voice broke as she did so.

"Thank you, Gerry. But I'll be okay," Claire said, thinking it was oddly true. She was still scared, but somehow, she had banished that lump of fear to a very distant place where she was able to ignore it. It was much easier to be angry and burning with determination to uncover the truth. "Maybe you should take a week or so off?" Claire asked her.

"I just can't, Claire. The partners are transferring me to a new lawyer, either that or I'll have to leave the firm. You know I've been David's secretary for ten years!"

"I know. I'm so sorry you have to go through this, too."

"Of course I do. David could yell and curse with the best of them, but he was a good guy and a great boss." She sounded weepy.

Claire smiled grimly—she did not want to reminisce now. "Gerry, were you aware that David was in some kind of trouble before he died?"

Geraldine hesitated. "Sort of."

"What does that mean?" Claire turned onto the two-lane highway leading to the freeway that would take her south and across the Golden Gate Bridge, reaching out a hand to calm Jilly.

"He never said a word. But the past week, maybe two, he was very short-tempered and distracted. I've known him so long. I can tell when he's upset. He was pretty upset, Claire."

Claire felt the guilt surging through her again. She had been his wife, but she hadn't noticed that something was wrong, other than with their marriage. "Are you sure he didn't say anything? Anything at all?"

"Yes, I am. And Claire? Detective Murphy already asked me these questions."

Claire absorbed that and said, "Geraldine, have you ever heard of a man named Ian Marshall? I met him the night of David's birthday, and he said he was David's friend but later amended that to his being advised by David in some offhand way."

"That name sounds familiar, Mrs. Hayden," Geraldine said. "But off the top of my head, I'm afraid I can't help you."

Claire felt slightly excited. She was crossing the bridge now. Traffic had slowed but was moving at a steady pace. Claire took a sip from her coffee. "Would you want to check for me? Would you check his things, maybe his calendar, his address book?" David had been meticulous with his Palm Pilot, and Geraldine had backed up his agenda, calendar, and address book routinely.

Geraldine said she would do that immediately and get back to Claire as soon as she had something for her. Claire thanked her profusely. A moment later she was descending the bridge and entering the city.

Something was nagging at her. Then comprehension struck her. Ian Marshall was from New York City. *And David had been on his way to New York City.*

Claire turned onto Lombard Street, where rush-hour traffic was heavy. It wasn't unheard of for David to go to New York on business; surely there was no connection. After all, Marshall had been in San Francisco the night of David's party. They could have met earlier in the day, right there in the city. Claire's excitement died. David's trip to New York probably had nothing to do with Ian Marshall.

Claire turned into the driveway of her home a few minutes later, instantly uneasy. She got out of the car, carrying her coffee, letting Jilly jump out as well. She unlocked the front door and let herself into the silent, almost brooding house.

Claire was almost sorry she had come back. But the answer she wanted might very well be in her own home. Claire started down the hall, going straight to the office. She refused to glance, even once, into the living room or beyond it, at the terrace.

But from the corner of her eye, she saw that it looked exactly as it had the morning she had stumbled out of the house, with the Dukes and Jean-Léon. Police tape remained, as did the white dust the technicians seemed to have used everywhere.

She felt relieved to be in the office, which seemed normal and untainted by the madness and evil. Jilly seemed happier, too, going over to the couch and leaping onto it, where she promptly lay down.

Claire walked over to the desk and stared down at it. The World War II photograph was on top of David's papers now; the detective hadn't been interested in it. "Everyone acquires new hobbies, Mrs. Hayden" was all that he had said. He barely glanced at the fax from the investigative agency in London.

Claire began sorting slowly through David's papers. It was a laborious process, especially because she did not know what she was looking for, and she was afraid that even if she found it, she would not know it was significant. Eventually she began going through the first of the desk's three drawers. She went to take another sip of coffee and found her cup empty.

A page torn out of a newspaper was on top of the pads, pens, and notes in that first drawer. Only slightly curious, as David was not the type to cut something out of a newspaper, she took it out and unfolded it.

It was a middle page from the *San Francisco Examiner*. The first thing Claire saw was a small headline: TOURIST BRUTALLY MURDERED IN FINANCIAL DISTRICT.

Her heart stopped. The lead-in read, "Throat slashed with no motive."

Claire's hands began to shake. The words on the page in front of her began to blur. *Copycat.* Jesus. Hadn't she heard someone, somewhere, mention something about a copycat? Claire blinked hard to reestablish her vision. Her hands were shaking now, so that the page she held wavered before her eyes, making it harder for her to read.

The tourist had been an elderly man named George Suttill, on vacation from Great Britain with his lady friend. Claire could not read any further.

She sank down in a chair, stunned.

Then she grabbed the old photograph and turned it over and dear God, there was no mistake, the back read, "George Suttill and Lionel Elgin, probably the spring of 1944."

Claire looked at the fax from the investigative agency in London. *Enclosed photo of Suttill and Elgin. Possible dead end. Please advise—WC.*

Obviously something was going on—obviously there was a connection between this Englishman's murder and her husband's.

Claire grabbed her purse and upended it. The items inside scattered all over her office floor. Amid Kleenex, a lipstick, house keys, and breath mints, Claire found Murphy's soiled white business card. She dove for it.

She dialed frantically, trying to calm herself, but it was impossible.

"Murphy," he said.

"Detective!" Claire cried. "Do you remember the photograph I showed you of the two army officers during the war? I just found a news clipping in David's desk! George Suttill had his throat slit just the way David did!"

"Mrs. Hayden? Is that you?"

Claire nodded, aware that tears had slipped down her face. She was shaking uncontrollably.

"Please calm down," Murphy said, sounding as relaxed as if he were discussing the weather. "We are very aware of the similarities between the two murders, and we are working on the connection. Actually, I'm glad you called. I'd like to ask you a few questions, if I may."

Claire had been standing; now she sat back down, nodding breathlessly. "So you know about George Suttill?"

"Of course we know. Suttill was murdered two days before your husband."

"But you didn't say anything." Claire was bewildered. She did not want her mind to fail her now.

"No, we did not. It's department policy not to discuss the details of an investigation with anyone outside of the investigative unit, Mrs. Hayden."

"Bullshit," Claire cried, and then she blinked, amazed with herself for being so rude.

He did not seem offended. "Mrs. Hayden, do you have any idea why David would deposit cash into his private savings account, five days in a row—just before he died?"

Claire blinked another time. "What?"

He repeated the question.

Claire stood up. "I'm not sure I understand. David had a private savings account?"

"Yes, he did, at First National."

Claire could hardly breathe. "I didn't know. We do our banking at Citibank."

"I know that."

"How much cash did he deposit?"

"Nine thousand nine hundred and fifty dollars—five days in a row."

"You mean he put almost fifty thousand dollars' cash into a secret bank account—one I did not know about?" Claire asked, aware of her voice becoming impossibly strained.

"Yes, he did."

"But . . . why?"

"Any sum below ten grand isn't reported. Clearly he was into something dirty."

"Something dirty," Claire repeated. But of course the detective was right. Honest citizens did not deposit fifty thousand dollars in cash, in increments that the authorities would not learn about. Honest citizens did not get their throats slit. Claire felt fear welling within her—and it had nothing to do with her being alone in the world.

"We found another interesting fact," the Irishman said. It sounded like he was smoking a cigarette as they spoke.

Claire whispered, "What?"

"David had lunch at the Garden Court on April second, ten days before he was murdered. The reservation was for one P.M. but his agenda doesn't say who his guest or guests were. Although the restaurant keeps records, and says it was a party of two."

"And?" Claire asked, managing to swallow. She needed a glass of water.

"Suttill's girlfriend, Frances Cookson—a New Yorker, by the way—told us that they'd had lunch there that day, around the same time. They were walk-ins, so they're not on the books. But we believe her. We have no reason not to."

Claire tried to understand. "What does it mean that David and Suttill were both dining there, separately, on the same day—at the same time—in the week or so before they both died?"

"I don't know. But if it means something, I will find out."

Claire was certain that he was smiling. He was smiling, and suddenly she was scared. She wet her lips. She spoke hoarsely. "Detective? Is there a serial killer on the loose?"

"Mrs. Hayden, do not be alarmed. We have no reason to think that you are in danger."

That thought had never crossed Claire's mind. Now it gave her pause. "But was it the same killer?" she asked.

He hesitated and sighed. "Yes. Same killer, same MO. Same weapon, in fact." He paused.

Of course, this wasn't a surprise, not after finding that article, but Claire felt ill.

"In fact, the killer used what is called a 'thumb knife.' It's a three-inch blade, one side completely sharpened. Only an inch of the other side is usable. It's a very odd weapon."

Claire hardly cared. She was reeling.

"I'd never even heard of a thumb knife, and I've been on the force for twenty years. My partner has learned it was sometimes used by German operatives during World War II."

Claire tuned in those last three words: *World War II.* "I beg your pardon?"

"German spies used thumb knives, Mrs. Hayden. Now you tell me what that means," he said.

Claire was sitting in her car with Jilly, her forehead on her hands on the steering wheel, when her cell phone rang. She was mindless. She just couldn't seem to think now.

She was going to skip the call, but instead, she straightened and picked it up.

"Claire!" Geraldine cried. "I've got it! I found a number for Ian Marshall in New York City. Are you ready?"

Claire had stiffened and was completely alert now. "What did you find out?" she asked warily. She knew an ax was about to fall. She could feel it as if her own head were right there on the chopping block.

"Ian Marshall is a director of an unusual organization, Claire. It's called the Bergman Holocaust Research Center. Mostly it's an educational group, privately endowed. He has a good reputation, and an M.A. in European history and a Ph.D. in Holocaust studies, the former from Oxford, the latter from the Hebrew University of Jerusalem."

"I don't get it," Claire said uneasily. But she kept thinking about the thumb knife that had killed both David and someone named George Suttill. A weapon used in World War II. Marshall seemed very involved in World War II. "What does this guy do? And how could he have been involved with David?"

"I have no idea why he and David were involved. His exact title is director of special investigations, Claire," Geraldine said with excitement. "No one at the BHRC will discuss current and ongoing investigations, so they won't really discuss him."

"Special investigations?" Claire echoed. Her pulse was drumming. "Special investigations of what?"

"War crimes," she replied.

Claire stared through the windshield at her house without really seeing it. It took her a moment to comprehend Geraldine. "He's a Nazi hunter?" she asked incredulously.

"It seems that way."

Claire stared, but all she saw now was David sitting in the lawn chair on the terrace, his throat slit, his torso covered with blood—and all she could think was that the killer had used a thumb knife, a weapon used by Nazi agents over fifty years ago.

Claire somehow said good-bye and hung up. It took her only a second to lift the receiver again and dial the number she had scrawled on a pad. She did not know what she was going to say, and as she had seen him only yesterday at David's funeral, she did not even know if he was back in New York yet.

Her message sounded breathless to her own ears. "Ian, this is Claire Hayden. I'm sorry about our abrupt conversation the other day. I must speak with you again. It's urgent. Thanks." Claire left her numbers and hung up.

She was shaking. She was insane. He was a Nazi hunter, which made him an expert on Nazis, and maybe, just maybe, a killer from those days was on the loose. A killer . . . or a copycat. And that would explain why he had so suddenly appeared in their lives, if he was somehow involved in what was going on. But involved how? If he knew something that she did not, he was going to cough it up. But why hadn't he been honest with her from the start? If he was investigating this killer, then why hadn't he said so?

She could not know that thousands of miles away in a sunlit corner room in a brand-new building on the east side of Manhattan, Ian Marshall sat at his desk, listening to her message, his hands bridged in front of his face.

And when he moved them, it wasn't to reach for the phone, it was to turn a photograph on his desk more fully toward him.

It was a color photo of a young man with dark hair who looked remarkably like Marshall. The man was wearing a beaten-up bomber jacket, jeans, and scuffed Frye boots, and he was smiling at the camera, squinting against the sun. He was standing in front of a World War II fighter plane with the Royal Air Force insignia, but the man's long side-burns and shoulder-length hair earmarked the picture as dating to the early seventies and not the war. Marshall stared at the photograph for another moment, and then he turned it away.

He did not return Claire's call.

CHAPTER 3

One week later, Claire began the process of moving. She had signed a year lease for a small two-bedroom apartment in Mill Valley, which was just over the Golden Gate Bridge. Actually, she was leasing half of a home that had been divided into two apartments. The house was charming, set back in a rustic wooded area, and it had a yard for the dogs. Her neighbors were a young professional couple who owned the house. Claire had liked them both instantly.

She would be moving her things next week; she had a ton of packing to do. In the past, the few times she had moved, she had hired movers to do everything. Now she would pack up what she wanted, to cut back on the expense of the move. She was intending to sell her San Francisco home mostly furnished.

Claire was glad to be so busy now. She planned to go back to work full-time—to throw herself into it completely. She was sleeping about four hours a night; she had also lost eight pounds.

And Ian Marshall had not returned her calls.

He was avoiding her. Her every instinct told her that.

She had reported to Murphy; he told her Marshall was being helpful, and politely, he told her not to worry about the investigation.

Now Claire double-parked her Land Rover in front of her father's art gallery on Maiden Lane, just a few blocks from Union Square. She was about to begin packing, but she dreaded the time it would entail. Claire was hoping to drag Jean-Léon to lunch. She would also offer to return the valuable painting. Even if he would not take it back, she could never sell it. In her heart, she felt that the painting belonged to her father.

Clad in a black jersey shirtdress and a black leather belt with a silver buckle, Claire slipped down from the big four-wheel-drive vehicle. She wore dark sunglasses, her hair was pinned back in a twist, and she had a print scarf knotted around her throat. A chic outfit, but Claire knew damn well that she looked haggard and hard. She had been slender to begin with. She could barely afford to lose more weight.

The receptionist smiled at her as she walked inside the spacious front room, filled with paintings and sculptures. Claire smiled back and asked Beth how she was. Voices drifted to her from her father's office, which was just behind the showroom. She could see from where she stood that the door was ever so slightly ajar. "I guess Jean-Léon is with a client?" she asked, realizing that she should have called.

"Yes, he is, but there was no appointment," the receptionist said, glancing down at her pad. "So I can't begin to tell you how long he will be."

There was no reason to become alert. But Claire walked over to her desk. A walk-in potential buyer was not unusual. Still . . . Claire glanced down at the receptionist's pad. Even though she was reading it upside down, she saw his name as clearly as if it were right side up. *Ian Marshall.*

Claire gasped. "Ian Marshall is with Dad?"

"Yes, he is," Beth said.

But Claire was staring at the door to Jean-Léon's office, the vast expanse of the gallery between her and the doorway. Her pulse had accelerated.

Claire's feet carried her rapidly across the room. When she was inches from the slightly open door, she slowed. She was agitated and breathless.

Claire looked back at Beth, who was on the telephone and not even looking at her. Claire inhaled, then stepped closer—as close as she dared.

"So you do not recognize this man?" Ian Marshall was saying.

"I've told you twice, I do not," Jean-Léon returned very calmly.

"And the name George Suttill does not ring a bell?"

"What's this about?" her father asked, with no loss of composure whatsoever. "I have a busy day, Mr. Marshall. I do not have time to spare. Besides, the police already asked me these questions."

Claire almost fell against the door. Why was Marshall asking her father about George Suttill? Why had the police spoken with her father?

"George Suttill was murdered on April tenth. His throat was slashed. It was not a mugging—there was no apparent motive."

Claire peered around the door, her heart palpitating wildly. Marshall stood before her father's huge antique desk; her father stood on the other side, facing him. And although both Marshall and Jean-Léon were speaking in quiet and conversational tones, their body language was that of two adversaries braced for blows.

Jean-Léon walked around his desk. "My son-in-law seemed to be murdered the same way. But you're not a police officer. You're with the Bergman Holocaust Research Center. Why are *you* asking me these questions? I don't have to speak with you."

"I thought perhaps you might have some answers for me."

"What kind of answers?" Jean-Léon was incredulous. "Unless I have had business with this Suttill, I do not know him. Of course, Beth can check our files if that would help. And as far as David goes, I have no idea what happened."

Marshall stared. "The same killer murdered Suttill and Hayden, Ducasse. That's off the record, but it's a fact, and the police have confirmed it." Suddenly he glanced over his shoulder, toward the doorway where Claire was standing.

Claire jerked back flat against the fabric-clad wall.

"What does any of this have to do with me? Other than the fact that David was my son-in-law and I could not stand him?"

Claire's heart raced. Of course she had known that David and her father did not care for each other. But it hurt a little now to hear Jean-Léon speaking so bluntly and so fervently.

"You gave David a painting for his birthday," Marshall said. Claire had to muffle her own gasp of surprise. How had he known that? "How did you acquire the Courbet?"

"Actually I gave Claire the painting. And how did I acquire it?" Jean-Leon sounded surprised. "I bought it. I bought it just after the war, I believe in forty-eight. I bought it in Paris."

"From whom?" Marshall asked.

"I don't recall," Jean-Léon said, sounding amused. "Good God, Marshall, that was almost sixty years ago."

"Fifty-three, if you want to be exact," Marshall said flatly.

A silence fell.

Claire tried to recover her composure; she tried to deepen her shallow breathing. What the hell was going on? Why was Marshall asking her father about George Suttill and David? And why the questions about the Courbet, which she had been about to pack up and return to her father?

At least Marshall was acting like an investigator—and not a copycat psycho killer.

Claire was not really relieved. She stole back to the opening between the door and the wall, to sneak a peek inside the room.

The men stood a few feet from each other, in front of Jean-Léon's massive desk. They were staring at each other. Marshall spoke.

"I'd like to see the bill of sale."

"Really?" Two bushy white eyebrows raised.

"Really."

"You know, Marshall, you have truly been wasting my time. And you are arrogant. What gives you the right to come in here and demand to see an ancient bill of sale?"

"The pursuit of justice," Ian Marshall said. "The pursuit of a killer."

Jean-Léon made an abrupt sound.

"You do want to see your son-in-law's killer brought to justice, do you not?" Marshall said, staring coldly.

"Of course I do. Claire shouldn't have to be going through this."

"Then humor me."

"Perhaps I will. It might take some time to find a record like that," Jean-Léon responded. He returned to his chair behind the desk but did not sit down.

Marshall walked right over to the edge of the desk and leaned on it with both hands. The desk was placed in the center of two corner windows, and it faced the doorway where Claire stood, and the expanse of the room to Claire's right. When Jean-Léon sat at his desk with the office door open, he could see into a wide, angled portion of the gallery. Now Claire stared at both men from a side view. Ian Marshall said, "Maybe you don't have a bill of sale."

The action of leaning on the desktop had pushed aside Ian's black sports jacket, and Claire saw very clearly that he was wearing a gun in a shoulder holster.

She gasped and ducked away from the door, sweating. *Why was he wearing a gun?*

Because a killer was on the loose.

"What does that mean? I bought the painting, Marshall. It was just a long time ago."

"That's my card. Fax me a copy when you can. I'd appreciate it—and I'm sure your son-in-law would, too."

He was leaving. Claire didn't think twice. She ran across the gallery and ducked into the bathroom, locking the door behind her. Then she began to breathe.

What was going on? Clearly Marshall was after David's killer, but why ask her father if he knew Suttill? Why ask him for some stupid bill of sale that dated back fifty-three years? Somehow, the Courbet must be significant to Marshall, or linked to the killer, but Claire could not make heads or tails of it.

But by damn, she would find out.

Claire came out of hiding as rapidly as she had gone into it, unlocking the door and leaving the bathroom. Ian Marshall was nodding to Beth on his way out.

Claire hurried across the gallery. Marshall was outside on the sidewalk, and he had paused, but briefly. Then he lifted an arm.

He was flagging down a car and driver.

"Mrs. Hayden?" Beth asked, stunned.

Claire ran out of the gallery. Ian Marshall was climbing into the backseat of a dark Mercedes. He was about to shut the door. Claire got her hands on it.

He looked up, startled. "Claire?"

Claire leaped inside, mostly onto his lap. "We have to talk!" she said, pushing herself onto the seat on the other side of him.

He looked at her, and he wasn't smiling. "Christ."

Ian had directed the driver to take him back to his hotel, the Mandarin Oriental.

Claire stared at him, thinking that the backseat of the Mercedes had somehow shrunk in size. It wasn't big enough for the two of them.

He faced her, and he was clearly annoyed. "Hello, Claire. How are you?"

She crossed her arms. "My, so formal. You haven't returned my calls. Let me guess. Answering machine broken?"

His jaw flexed. "Do you always leap into cars with men you don't know?"

That gave her pause. He had a gun. Someone had murdered David and George Suttill. This wasn't a silly game or make-believe. And until she understood why he had been so evasive, and why he had lied to her, she would consider him with suspicion. "Do you have a license for that gun?" she asked uncomfortably.

"Yes, I do," he said evenly.

"Why? You're not a cop."

"You know why. Murphy told me you made the connection between Suttill and David. By the way, I'd like to borrow that photograph and fax."

The gun was for protection. And he wanted the World War II photograph and the fax from the London investigators. "What is going on, Ian? Why was David killed?"

But Ian was telling the driver to turn around, giving Claire's home address.

"Are you going to answer any of my questions?" she asked uneasily.

"Yes, but not here, in the car. We'll talk at your house while we get the photo and the fax."

Claire stared at him; he was staring directly ahead, as if past the driver. Did she want to get out of the sedan and walk into her home with him? They would be alone.

She felt chilled. They would be alone, and David had been ruthlessly murdered in her house only a week or so ago.

But Ian Marshall was one of the good guys. Wasn't he?

For the first time, Claire directly faced her worst suspicion—one she wished she never had. He was an expert on war criminals, on the Holocaust, and surely, on the subject of World War II. But he *was* one of the good guys. Wasn't he?

David had been hostile to him. Ian had been wary in return. The tension between the two had been unmistakable.

And Claire knew that Ian Marshall had not been on the guest list. Murphy had made her go over it at length, discussing everyone present. Claire hadn't been able to point the finger at anyone.

He had crashed the party, and he had been far too charming, and he had been snooping around her house. Today, he'd been asking her father all kinds of questions, and he wasn't even a cop. He had misled her about his real occupation, he had lied about his relationship with David. Why?

Claire stole a sidelong glance at him. His profile was hard and chiseled; now she found little attractive about it. Beneath the beautifully cut sports jacket was a gun.

Claire tried to remain calm. Normal people did not carry firearms. At least not in her world. She made a snap decision.

"You know what?" Claire said quickly. "I left my car double-parked in front of Jean-Léon's gallery. Why don't you take me back there and I'll follow you up to the house?" She smiled at him. "I'm going to get a ticket. Or worse, towed."

"You won't get a ticket, and I'll make sure that if you are towed, you'll have the car delivered back to your front door."

Claire stared. He turned his head toward her, and their gazes locked. "Can you do that?"

"Yes."

Okay, so he had connections. That was a plus. "How does one acquire a thumb knife?" she heard herself ask.

He twisted to face her. "Well, you could steal it from a museum. Or you could have one made. Murphy's got a big mouth. He should lay off the whiskey."

"Why are you trying to keep me in the dark?" Claire whispered, unable to look away from him. "Why won't you tell me the truth?"

Their gazes held. "I don't want to see an innocent bystander hurt."

Her house looked vacant and lifelessly dull now, Claire thought, as they stepped out of the car. Ian told the driver to go get a cup of coffee.

Claire tensed as the sedan began backing out of her driveway. "Why did you do that?" she cried, turning to face him, aghast.

"Why are you acting as if you're afraid of me?"

Claire swallowed. "Why do you refuse to answer any of my questions?"

"Are you afraid of me?"

"Yes!"

He stared, his eyes widening fractionally. "Well, that is just great." He seemed very irritated now. "I sent the driver to get coffee because I am beat and I need some caffeine."

"Bull."

He smiled for the first time since she had seen him that day. "You're cute when you curse." He started up the walk to the house.

Was she crazy enough to follow him? Claire decided that she was not.

She stood where she was, by the drive, like a statue. "That was not a curse, by the way."

He tested the front door, which was locked. "Coming from you, it most certainly was."

Claire moved. Acutely interested now, she turned to see what he was doing.

He didn't look back at her. "I need the keys."

"I don't have them," she lied.

He dipped his hand into an interior pocket and produced something long, like a pick. Claire felt her eyes bulge as he inserted the object into the lock. Was he an accomplished burglar, too, as well as a Nazi hunter? Oh, this was just too much. "Are you picking my lock?"

"Yes, I am." He sounded infinitely patient. Claire could not help herself, and she walked over to him.

He slid the object from the lock and opened the door. "After you," he said with a slight gesture.

Claire did not precede him in. "After you," she said firmly. She had changed her mind. This was just too rich to avoid. However, she would remain on alert, and she would keep her distance, for now.

He stared down at her. "Are you thinking that somehow I'm involved in the murders of David and Suttill?"

"No. What I'm actually thinking is that you killed both men, imitating some ancient espionage-ish form of murder."

He smiled, then he started to laugh.

"That's funny?" She was annoyed now.

"Yes, it is. It's hysterical, actually. Claire, FYI: I've never killed anybody. Let's go inside."

He had never killed anybody. Claire hoped that was the case. But what would he do if the opposite was true, stand there and confess? "After you," she said.

He sighed in exasperation and walked inside, going directly down the hall on their left to the office. Claire followed, leaving the front door wide open. Hopefully a cruiser would go by and come to see what was going on.

"So, why did you really send the driver away?" she asked nervously. She hated the house. It felt like death. It even smelled like death. Claire knew her imagination was overactive, but the shadow of evil seemed to be present everywhere. What was actually present were tons of cardboard boxes.

"Privacy," he said, entering the office.

She was a schmuck, Claire decided. He hadn't wanted to talk in front of the driver, that was all. He did not have a dire or foul intent toward her.

Still, Claire remained at the door while he went to the desk, keeping the width of the room between them. She watched him pick up the photo and fax. He studied the photo for a long time.

"Are we going to talk now?" she asked finally.

He turned, and she saw his face. It was grim, and there was no mistaking his anger.

Claire stiffened.

"We can talk now," he said. "But I'd like to see the Courbet."

She stared. An idea struck her. "Is that why you were wandering around my house the night of the party? Are you also a collector, like my father?"

"Yes and no," he said, coming toward her. Claire forgot to move away. "The Courbet belongs to the Elgin family," he said. "It was the centerpiece of their collection, and it disappeared sometime during the latter years of the war. Lady Elgin reported it missing or stolen after the war."

"It's in the master bedroom," Claire whispered. Had her father bought a stolen painting? "Is Elgin dead also?"

"No. He is very much alive," Ian said, moving past her without looking at her. "In fact, he's our killer."

Claire ran after Ian. To go upstairs, she had to cross the living area. She refused to glance at it or the terrace. She found Ian in the master bedroom, standing in front of the Courbet, staring grimly at it. Claire suddenly realized that the painting should be moved, perhaps back to her father's. "I demand an explanation," she cried.

"That's a problem," he said, not looking at her. He was studying the painting, and suddenly, he shivered.

"What is it?" Claire asked quickly.

He shrugged, still studying the masterpiece. "I don't know," he said softly. "I just had the weirdest feeling. . . ." He stopped himself. Still, he did not glance at her. "I'd hoped to have a chance to see this someday. I don't think this painting was stolen. I think that when Elgin disappeared, he must have taken this painting with him."

"You were interviewing my father. Did my father buy this painting from Elgin? And who is Elgin? And will you look at me, damn it!" She grabbed his arm. "Is my father in danger, too?"

He looked at her. "You are a double-edged sword, Claire. I do not want you involved. You don't need to know any of this. You already know too much for your own good."

She reeled as if struck. "You're kidding, right? You are kidding?"

"I am dead serious," he said grimly.

"My husband was murdered right outside and just below where we are now standing. He was in some kind of trouble. I think you know what kind. Now maybe my father knows the killer, too. And you expect me to just walk away, pretending that everything's hunky-dory, while this killer runs around scot-free?"

"Yeah, I do. Hunky-dory?" He smiled.

She felt her fists ball up. If he laughed at her again, she would flatten his nose, and to hell with the gun he carried. "I seem to be regressing to some adolescent stage of behavior and language usage," she snapped. "But you cannot keep me in the dark."

"Actually, I can. This is an official homicide investigation. You are not a cop."

"Neither are you!" she shouted.

"I am not a policeman, and no, I don't work for any government agency. The center is privately funded. But I do work closely with the police and other government agencies, including foreign ones, whenever the need arises," he said. "Like now."

Claire was very angry. "I want my photo back. And the fax."

He made a sound. "That's juvenile."

"As I said, I seem to be regressing." She held out her hand.

"Claire."

"No."

"I mean it, Marshall. I know you want that photo. I bet you don't have a photo of Elgin, even if he's only twenty in it. I bet you want to dash over to a computer and do some imaging and aging. That's my property in your hand, and I want some goddamned answers. Do we have a deal or not?"

He said, his mouth curling a bit, "Talk that way at your fund-raiser next month, and you won't raise a dime, much less that million you're fishing for."

"How the hell do you know so much about me?" she asked with fear.

He handed her the photo and the fax. "No, Claire, we do not have a deal." And he walked out of the room.

Claire was still, but only for an instant. Then she ran after him. "Ian, please. *Please,*" she cried. She heard the desperation in her tone and knew she was begging, but she did not care.

He halted in his tracks. "Shit," he said.

Claire allowed the tears to fall. It was the oldest trick in the book, but her tears were real—David was dead, and she was alone and terrified.

"Claire, cut it out," he said, turning helplessly.

She shook her head. "I can't," she lied. Actually, the brief need to cry had ended. Her tears were drying up as fast as they had flowed.

Ian sighed. "You don't want to hear any of this," he said. "Trust me, Claire."

Alarms went off, right there inside of her head. "David told me he was in big trouble," she said. "What kind of trouble could it have been?"

"The killing kind," he said.

"Ian?" The tears shimmered in her vision again. "Please. He was my husband. We were together for almost fifteen years."

His jaw tightened visibly. "He may have been blackmailing Elgin, Claire. And to make matters even worse, he witnessed George Suttill's murder."

Had David been out of his mind? No wonder he was dead.

Claire was stunned.

"Claire? Driver's back. I'll drop you at the gallery so you can pick up your car."

Claire hardly heard Ian, who stood in the driveway sipping from a Styrofoam container of coffee. She was reeling. If only David hadn't done something so stupid—and illegal. She remained on the steps in front of her house. What should she do now?

Find Elgin. Bring him to justice.

"Claire? C'mon. I have a flight to catch."

That got her attention. She came down the steps. "What do you mean?"

"I mean that I have a flight to catch," he said. He looked closely at her. "Are you all right?"

"Am I all right?" she echoed in some disbelief. "You drop that bomb-shell on me and ask me if I am okay? No, I'm not okay. Is my father in danger?"

Ian hesitated, then said, "No."

Claire was incredulous. "You're lying to me!"

"Why won't you leave this alone," he exploded. "God damn it, if only I had gone to the gallery a bit earlier, we wouldn't even be standing here hashing this out."

She was alarmed now, and filled with caution. She couldn't trust this man because he was a stranger—a stranger with a temper who carried a gun and was so damned evasive. "How do you know that Elgin is the killer? And not someone else?"

He turned a hard gaze full-force upon her. "Get in the car, Claire. I have a plane to catch. I am not about to miss it because of you."

Claire didn't like his tone. It was threatening. She got into the car.

This time Ian jumped into the front seat, beside the driver. Clearly, he wished to avoid close contact with her. That was fine with Claire as well. He handed her a container of coffee. Claire took it but made no move to drink it as they headed down the hill, merging into the traffic on Leaven-worth Street.

Shit, she thought. He was refusing to tell her anything, and he had lied—her father might be in danger. Why was he flying out of town so fast? Did that mean that Elgin—if he was the killer—was no longer in town? Claire hoped that was the case. "Where are you going?" she asked.

"I'm making a brief stop to speak with Murphy, and then it's back to the hotel to pack and check out."

"No, I mean where are you flying to?"

He didn't turn to look at her. "You are awfully nosy. I liked the dolled-up, glam-queen version of Claire Hayden better."

"She's gone."

Now he twisted to look at her. "Take off those sunglasses," he said.

"Like hell I will," she said, having just put them back on.

He reached out and removed them.

Claire bit back a protest—and this one might have been a real curse.

His face softened. "Look, Claire, right now everything's okay, and you don't have to worry."

She saw that he was concerned. "But I am worried. This is not a case of ignorance being bliss."

"Can't you see that I'm an old-fashioned kinda guy, and I am trying, in my own way, foolish as it may be, to protect you?"

Claire stared into his eyes, which happened to be green. "That's a nice way to be," she heard herself say. "That is, if you are telling me the truth."

"I also happen to be a basically honest guy, too. Which is why I hunt down people like Elgin."

Claire smiled a little, and it was genuine. "Is that a Brooklyn accent?"

"Queens," he said with a small, answering smile. "Friends?"

She hesitated. She did not dare trust him yet. "Friends."

He stuck out his hand. She took it. The shake was brief but firm. Claire realized his touch flustered her. Unfortunately, she still found him highly attractive.

Then, "Can I borrow the photograph and fax, please?"

Her mind sped. If he was tight with the police, she could be forced to hand over the items anyway. "Sure. What are friends for?" She smiled her perfect socialite smile at him.

"I hate it when you do that," he said.

She ignored the remark and handed him the photograph and fax.

"Thank you, Claire," he said. Then he hesitated. "Look," he said. "I want you to lay low for a while."

Her eyes widened. "Why?"

He avoided her gaze. "Because there's a slight chance, a very slight chance, that you may be in danger, too."

Claire wished Ian a good trip, then waved after him as the sedan crept away. Then she leaped into her Land Rover, which, miraculously, had a ticket but had not yet been towed, and she sped out of Maiden Lane in the opposite direction. By the time she reached the Mandarin Oriental Hotel, four and a half minutes had elapsed. She had run three red lights, and she doubted he would appear for a half an hour, if not more.

Her heart felt as if it had become permanently lodged in her throat. She was in danger? Could this be happening?

Claire had the valet park her car and watched to make sure it was whisked away into the underground garage, because if it remained in front of the hotel, she had not a doubt Ian would notice it. She was going to con her way into his room so she could find the answers he refused to give her. Determination fueled her now. She ran into the lobby. Having connections paid off. She had used the Mandarin Oriental Hotel for a fall gala for San Fran Save a few months ago, and had attended many events there over the years. Claire knew several of the concierges, as well as the events manager and the general manager. One of the concierges was only too happy to help her out, and she learned that Ian's room was 514.

Good God, she thought, going over to the marble bank of elevators. Had she just bribed the concierge? It was unbelievable.

She could not be pleased. What kind of danger could she possibly be in? And more important, why?

On the fifth floor, Claire found his room and went through the process of pretending to discover that she did not have a key. A hotel maid with a housekeeping cart approached. "I will call security," she said in a heavily accented voice.

"I am going to divorce the bastard," Claire cried, beginning to weep. "He left me stranded—stranded—at the Embarcadero, and I have no money, no change, he has the bank card, he is such a shit! And he has the keys! I am divorcing him, I have had it, screw men!" She wept. It was amazing what fear could do. She had never been a good actress before.

Someone banged on a wall or door and shouted, "Be quiet!"

"I divorced my husband, and I am very happy, you will be happy, too," the maid said, shaking her head. "Here, honey, go in." She unlocked the door for Claire and smiled. "Just don't tell anybody, I break the rules."

"You are so kind," Claire said, giving her ten dollars.

The maid stuffed it in her apron, and Claire decided she had better ease up on the bribes or payoffs or whatever they were. She was on a budget now.

And then she was inside Ian Marshall's room, and she double-locked the door. Now he would not be able to get in, not even with his electronic key.

Claire collapsed against the door. And then she smiled, at once incredulous and disbelieving. God, she had done it. She had broken and entered into a hotel room. It was as if she had become someone else.

She looked around.

The room was state-of-the-art and modern. There was a king-size bed, two stark white stone bed tables, interesting iron wall sconces, and a desk. There was also an entertainment center, which probably housed a minibar. A laptop was on the desk.

Claire sat down at the desk. As she booted up, she looked down at Ian's briefcase.

Claire didn't hesitate. She bent and opened it. Inside were various folders and pads. She took everything out and began skimming over his notes. The problem was, they were illegible to her eye.

She flipped pages, then frowned, because the one name that did leap out at her was Robert Ducasse.

Robert Ducasse was her uncle, who had died in 1944, just before D day. He had been a hero of the French Resistance.

Claire did not like finding his name on Ian's legal pad. She stared at it. Why was there a question mark next to his name?

Windows ME came up. Relieved, Claire put down the pads by her feet. She hesitated, deciding to check his agenda first. She opened up his Task Scheduler and, with a click, found the second week of April, the week of David's death.

"Hayden" was entered for April 12, as was the note "Party, 7 P.M." Her home address was there, and her home telephone number. Inhaling, Claire scrolled back to April 10, the day George Suttill had been murdered. His name was listed under the date.

Claire didn't know exactly what she was looking for, but she opened up his address book, and sure enough, David was listed under Hayden—all of his numbers, and his work address as well as that of their home. There was a notation that read "Wife—Claire."

Claire stared at the page. Why was she so uneasy?

She turned to D. Instantly, she found her father's name, address, and numbers, as well as those of the Dukes. What were the Dukes doing in Ian's address book?

Claire's fear increased.

Claire closed the scheduler and opened up the Documents folder. She saw a file named Elgin and clicked on it, her pulse racing with excitement. She quickly read that Lionel Elgin had been born in 1922 at Elgin Hall, his family home just outside of London. Claire stopped, stunned. *They were after an Englishman?*

She exhaled loudly and continued to read. He had come from an old and wealthy family. His father, Randolph Elgin, had been a baron; his mother had died when he was a young boy. He had attended Eton and was in his first year at Oxford when the war began. He inherited his father's title and estates when his father disappeared in August 1940. By then, Lionel was a lieutenant in the air force.

Something sounded behind Claire, but she did not quite hear it. Elgin was an Englishman, not a German, and if he had been born in 1922, he was only seventeen when the war began in 1939.

Elgin was an Englishman—and William Duke was in Ian Marshall's address book.

Claire's heart felt as if it had dropped from her body and right through the floor. Like a damned World War II rocket.

How old was William Duke? Good God, he was in his eighties. He was older than Elgin, who was in his late seventies.

Something jiggled behind her. Claire froze. *Ian had opened the door, and now he was trying to open it fully, but the safety latch wouldn't allow him to open it more than an inch or two.*

Claire was afraid to breathe, to move.

A silence fell. He had stopped trying to pull open the door.

Shit and damn and double damn, Claire thought, panicked.

Slowly, she turned and looked at the door, now slightly ajar. She saw nothing, and too late, she recalled that he had a gun.

And then it struck her that he might think someone else was in his room—someone like Elgin.

"Ian, it's only me!" she cried, jumping to her feet.

His eye appeared in the crack between the door and the wall, and with it, the nose of his black gun. "God damn it," he said, very low and succinctly. "Open the door, Claire. Now."

Claire wet her lips. Of course she had to let him in.

"Open the door, Claire. Before I shoot the latch off."

"You wouldn't."

"I would. I have a silencer. Open the door."

Claire opened the door.

Ian came in. She looked at his gun as he closed the door, her heart exploding in her chest with fear and dire predictions. The gun did not have a silencer attached to it. He had lied—again.

Not a good sign, she thought.

He shut and double-locked the door behind her. "What the hell are you doing?"

Claire shrugged helplessly. She was trying to figure out how many seconds it would take her to unlock the door and flee.

He scanned the room and cursed. "You just don't give up, do you, Claire?"

Tears of fright almost came. She shook her head. "No. I can't."

"Under other circumstances, I would admire your gumption. But right now, I'm pissed."

"Sorry," she whispered meekly.

He put his gun down on the desk by the laptop. He studied the screen, then glanced at the notes at his feet. He looked up—at her. "So now you know."

She swallowed, but she was short of saliva. "I know Elgin is English. I know that you have William Duke's name in your address book." *And he's English, too,* she wanted to add, but wisely, she did not.

He sighed.

Then she heard herself say, "William is one of the nicest and kindest men I know. I've known him my entire life. He is not a killer. He is not Elgin."

Ian stared.

"You think it's him!" she cried, horrified. It was impossible. Wasn't it?

"Go home, Claire," Ian Marshall said, sounding tired. He walked over to the closet and took out a garment bag, throwing it on the bed. Then he turned, removing his jacket, which he tossed on the chair. He unbuckled and slid off his holster. "I wasn't kidding when I said you might be in danger."

"But why?" Claire managed.

He was unbuttoning his pale blue shirt. "The killer may be someone you know, and that's all I can say right now."

Claire stared. Oh, God. *It could not be William Duke!*

He stripped off the shirt, tossing it aside, and shrugged on a red polo shirt.

Claire flushed. The man was all muscle—either he had a great metabolism or he worked out. She suspected both. "I can't go home," she said.

He put two suits into the garment bag, and a pair of shoes. "How come I thought you'd say that?"

Claire hadn't moved since he had come into the room. Now she wrung her hands. "Why is my uncle's name on that pad?" she asked fearfully.

He zipped up the garment bag, and folded it over. He straightened and turned. Their eyes met. He was silent.

"My uncle died over half a century ago," she cried. But she was feeling ill.

His face darkened with anger. "Fine. I give up. You know what, you're a ballsy lady for a society dame, and being as you are hounding me out of all patience, I concede the day, Claire. You win."

He was shouting. Claire pressed her spine into the door.

"I'm not sure your uncle is dead," Ian Marshall said. "I'm not sure he's dead, and I'm not sure that *he* isn't Lionel Elgin."

CHAPTER 4

If a bomb had exploded right in front of her, she would not have been more stunned. "Are you nuts?" she demanded, but she began to shake.

He crossed his arms and stared. "No. I'm not crazy, Claire." He hesitated. "And I'm sorry to be the bearer of bad tidings."

"*The bearer of bad tidings?*" She felt shell-shocked. "Excuse me. My uncle died in May of 1944. So if he was Elgin, Elgin is dead—and someone is a copycat killer!"

"Elgin is alive," Ian said.

"And my uncle was a Frenchman," Claire cried. "What are you suggesting, that he was born in England, that he was born an Elgin—which would make my father what, Ian?" Fury overcame her. "A liar, that's what it would make him."

"I'm sorry," Ian repeated grimly. "I am more sorry than you can know."

Claire didn't like that. She stiffened in alarm. But this would explain why Ian had been so reluctant to be honest with her. "My father was born in a small village in France, about a hundred kilometers south of Paris. So was Robert. End of story. And Robert is *dead.*"

"So it's been claimed," Ian said.

Claire stared at him, her breathing fast and shallow. So much fear consumed her that she could hardly think straight or see clearly. "Maybe you're Elgin," she said, jabbing her hand in his direction.

"I'm thirty-nine, Claire," Ian said quietly. "Maybe you'd better sit down. You are as white as a sheet." Kindness had crept into his tone. He seemed reluctant to allow it in.

"I'm not sitting anywhere," Claire shouted. "You know what I meant. Maybe you're copycatting Elgin!"

"You're hysterical. I'm hunting Elgin, Claire. I'm *hunting* the man who killed your husband, George Suttill, and a number of others as well."

Her uncle was dead. And he was a Frenchman—her father was a Frenchman. Robert Ducasse was not alive, and he was not an alias for Lionel Elgin. It was impossible.

"But you suspect William, too." She met his gaze. She had been hoping to calm herself, but accusing William Duke, who was more of an uncle to her than Robert had ever been—obviously, since Robert had died twenty-odd years before she was born—did not help her to recover her composure.

"There's three years missing from William Duke's life in the mid-forties—it's highly suspicious and too damn coincidental for me."

Claire turned away. She felt ravaged, more so than she had ever thought it possible to be. But her father could not have deceived her all of these years, claiming to be a Frenchman, claiming that his brother was dead. "My father is fluent in French," she said.

Ian was studying her very closely.

Claire shivered.

"What is it, Claire? What is it that you really want to ask me?" Ian asked softly.

Claire continued to tremble. She went to the bed and sat down, gripping the edge of the mattress. She hadn't really heard him. "I need to understand now, Ian. I need to understand everything. Tell me about David . . . and Elgin."

He seemed somewhat surprised by her response. "You don't need to know."

Claire launched herself at him. She grabbed his arms, on the verge of tears. "You can't do this to me!" she cried. "You can't appear in my life, and then the next thing I know, David is dead! You can't come into my life this way and accuse someone I love of being a horrible, horrible liar." She knew she referred to her father now, when it had been William she wanted to discuss. "If you have any ethics—and any kindness—you will explain everything to me." Tears swam in her eyes. His face, so close to hers, was blurring. Claire released him abruptly. There was too much compassion in his eyes—and too much pity.

Claire turned her back to him. *There was something else there, but she must not consider it.* "Besides," she said harshly, "I'm your partner now."

He grabbed her arm with incomprehensible speed and whipped her around. "Like hell."

"I'm your partner now, and if you don't like it, that's tough!"

"I need a rich, blue-blooded socialite in my work like I need a hole in the head," he said, his voice raised.

"I happen to be broke, flat broke—David lost almost everything. And," she snapped angrily, "my blood is red, not blue. You've just told me that William, a dear friend, whose wife has been a mother to me ever since my own mother died, could be Elgin. Then you say that maybe my uncle is alive—and that my father has been lying to me my entire life! Not to mention that my husband has been murdered—and you said I may be in danger, too! Well guess what? You're stuck with me."

He stared. "Like hell," he said.

She faced him unblinkingly, and amazingly, she did not feel any fear. Not from him. She was too afraid of the truth to be afraid of Ian Marshall now. "Which flight are you on?"

He turned away, cursing and pacing and raking one hand through his dark, curly hair.

"I can find out," Claire said to his rigid back. It was a threat, said sweetly. "Any of the concierges will tell me which airline your driver is taking you to and at what time. If you're going back to New York, the last flights are after six. You'd be leaving here by four-fifteen at the latest, just in case there's traffic. I won't have to be a genius to figure out which flight you're on."

"So now you're a detective," he said with disgust.

"No, now I am your partner. Spill the beans, Marshall." Her hands were on her hips.

He turned. "What will you do if I call security and have you hauled out on your ass?"

"I'll go to William, who I believe is innocent anyway. And I'll warn him."

Ian's eyes went wide with unfeigned shock. "That is low and dirty, Claire. That isn't you. You cannot breathe a word of this to anybody, not William, not your father, and not even that big mouth, Murphy."

She had him, Claire thought, astonished. He was afraid of her now. "I don't know who I am anymore. How do you like that? I only know that William is dear to me and he is not Elgin, and that my father was born in

St. Michele, and his last name is Ducasse." She stared coldly. But it was true. Was this really her? The Claire Hayden she knew would never be so bold, so brave, or so aggressive. Not in a million years.

Perhaps the old Claire had died along with David.

"What if William is the killer? What if he really murdered George Suttill—and David?" Ian asked, his gaze as hard as hers. But Claire also saw real worry flickering there.

"I just don't believe it."

"Appearances are always deceiving."

"Tell me about it."

"Nothing is ever what you expect it to be."

"I agree."

"What do you want to know?"

Claire smiled, triumphant. She had done it. She had Victory Number One. "Start with David and Elgin."

Ian glanced at his watch. Then he walked over to the chair behind the desk and pulled it out, turning it around. He straddled it. "I'm leaving at four," he said, making it clear that their time was limited.

"American or United?" They both had six-fifteen or six-thirty departures for La Guardia.

He ignored her. "I believe that David stumbled onto the truth about Elgin. I also think that Elgin was blackmailing him for his silence, which would explain the cash he'd deposited before his death. These are the facts: David was having lunch with someone we have not been able to identify. I think it was Elgin, in his alias. George Suttill was having lunch at the same restaurant with his girlfriend, Frances Cookson. Apparently Suttill spoke to David's companion, and I can only assume he recognized Elgin. You see, Suttill was Elgin's aide during the war."

"The photograph of them both in uniform," Claire remarked, interested in spite of herself.

"Believe it or not, Elgin was assigned to the ministry of information. He was army intelligence." Ian shook his head.

"Oh my God," Claire whispered. "They had a spy right in their midst."

Ian's face hardened. "Yes, they did. Anyway, David saw Suttill murdered. I'm guessing that he went to Suttill's hotel, hoping to learn more about Elgin. That was when he called the center—not the police—and we had a very brief phone conversation. I wanted David to identify the killer. He said he would think about it. He was afraid."

"He didn't go to the police because of the scandal that would have come out for his part in a blackmail scheme," Claire said grimly. "I know David. He'd be smart enough to make a deal to avoid prosecution, but he would want to avoid scandal at all costs."

"Maybe. Unfortunately, David and I never had a chance to speak again at length. When we met at his birthday party, it was face-to-face for the first time, and I could see he had changed his mind. He was very hostile. It was pretty obvious he was regretting ever having contacted me. We did speak privately once. He told me he would handle this alone, his own way. We were interrupted before I could talk him out of it."

"So he wasn't flying to New York the following day to meet you?"

"No."

"How do you know for sure, Ian, that the murders were committed by Elgin, who must be in his late seventies or eighties by now, and not someone else?" She thought about what she had read on his laptop. "The Elgin file says he was born in 1922. William Duke is older than that." Claire was wondering now if Robert was born in 1922. It seemed like a possibility—her own father was born in 1925 and Robert was a few years older.

As if reading her mind, Ian said, "Birth dates can be fudged, Claire. We have to look for a ballpark age on this guy. And how do I know it's Elgin? Suttill and David were not his first victims. There was an RAF pilot whose throat was slit and his body dumped in a pond not far from Elgin Hall. Two other intelligence officers also bought it the same way. And there were two other murders, an SOE agent and a German agent who had rowed himself to shore but was caught in Dymchurch by the Home Guard. The last two murders were different, but Elgin always leaves a thumbprint of some kind. The SOE agent was killed with a German-made explosive. Of course, being SOE, he might have had the explosive on him and it was used against him. But the German agent had a sketch in his pocket. A sketch of a swan."

Claire's mind was spinning now. There was so much to absorb. "A swan?"

"The one thing we do know was that Elgin's code name was Swan.

And that was just before Elgin vanished, in late 'forty-four, when it was clear that Germany was losing the war."

"How in God's name does someone simply disappear?"

"I believe he fled first to either Belgium or France before emigrating to the United States—under a new identity, possibly the very same identity he uses today. Some of the coded material was found in an empty flat adjacent to his, with instructions on how to slip out of the country with a newly forged identity. It wasn't hard to do back then. Also, Elgin was fluent in French."

Claire was beginning to piece it all together. "So he vanished and hasn't been seen—or heard from—since."

"Yeah. The file on Elgin has been open but forgotten—until I got that call from your husband."

"Until Suttill ran into Elgin at that restaurant. And since he could have identified Elgin, he's dead. David could have made the ID as well. So now they're both dead." Claire shivered. "But there's something I don't understand. Why would Elgin reappear this way? By using that thumb knife, he's sending us a red flag that he's here. Why not shoot his victims?"

Ian was grim. "I know he's arrogant, Claire. But actually, it's simpler than that. Guns make noise. Guns can be traced."

Claire stared. "I'm surprised Elgin doesn't want to go after you."

Ian shrugged. "I can't ID him without a reasonable doubt. And Frances Cookson, a potential witness, seems to have been in the rest room during the exchange. She told the police that when she came out, Suttill had paid their check, and they left without finishing their meal."

"A dead end."

"Maybe. Maybe not. She's with family in Florida right now, grieving, but she'll be back in a few days, and I have an appointment to speak with her."

Claire felt a ripple of excitement. "When?"

He gave her a dirty look. "You're not coming." He stood. "So that's the story. Elgin is as clever as they come, and very arrogant. After all these years, he's back in the game—he's taunting us, Claire. Because he thinks he can outwit everyone again."

Claire also stood.

"The only problem is, as much as I'd like to see Elgin put away for treason, I'll take murder one. Because the authorities only have circumstantial evidence as far as his activities during the war go. So far," Ian said, his eyes glittering, "Scotland Yard believes the same perp got the RAF pilot, the intelligence officers, Suttill, and David. They're working with the feds and the San Francisco police department now that Elgin is back in the game. If we can identify Elgin, and the other agencies do their job we should put him away for the rest of his life."

Claire felt a flicker of answering excitement; Ian's was contagious. Then she became grim. He was hunting William and, worse, Robert Ducasse.

Ian looked at her closely. "Are you okay?"

She smiled at him. "I'm fine."

He gave her a look. "Can the socialite act, Claire. I don't like it."

She was hurt. Inexplicably so. The artificial congeniality that had served her for so long, so well, did not work with Ian. It helped her raise millions of dollars for her charities. It helped her win, define, and prolong important relationships. She had thought her persona pleasant and charming. And when she had first met Ian, he seemed to think so, too.

But now she knew why he had been at David's party, and why he had been flirting with her. It had been a ruse. A simple ruse. Now the knowledge was a very bitter pill.

She did find him attractive, mostly when they were not arguing, but clearly, he found her too blue-blooded, rich, and phony for his taste. Claire was half Polish and half French. Her mother had been Jewish, and Claire had been bat mitzvahed at thirteen. Her father was a French Baptist, although he never went to church.

Her blood was hardly blue. It was damned red and certainly ethnic, as far as she could see.

She looked up at Ian. "Excuse me for not being born in Queens." She walked to the door.

"You're leaving?" He sounded surprised and eager.

"You have a flight to catch," she said, turning so she could give him her best and most perfect society smile.

"Yeah, I do." He scowled.

"Bon voyage," Claire said nicely.

Suspicion crossed his face.

Claire left. She had a flight to catch and, if possible, some minor packing to do. And she had to speak with her father first, before it was too late.

* * *

Claire drove at a frantic pace back to her father's art gallery. As she did so, she called her travel agent and instructed her to book any seat on Ian's flight, which was the six-fifteen on United. One of the concierges had been more than willing to tell her which airline Ian was being driven to.

Miraculously, there was a parking space not far from the gallery, and when Claire ran inside, Beth told her that Jean-Léon was in his office alone, and on the phone. Claire thanked Beth and dashed across the showroom.

Jean-Léon smiled at her as she came inside, gesturing for her to close the door behind her. Claire was more than happy to oblige.

Ian's stern admonition that she not tell a soul any of what she had learned thus far came to mind, but she felt no guilt. Claire felt certain that Robert Ducasse was dead. If he was alive, and that was a very big "if," then her father had been lying all these years to protect the brother he so loved. But would that make him an accomplice? And would that mean he knew that his brother had been a traitor and a killer for so long?

Claire did not want to let her thoughts race so far ahead. There was no point, because she just did not believe that Robert was alive. But she had a feeling of dread hanging over her now, like a dark and frightening shadow.

Jean-Léon hung up the phone, smiling. "And to what do I owe this surprise?"

"Hi, Dad." Claire realized she was nervous. "I dropped by to tell you that I'm going out of town for a few days." Actually, she had no idea how long she would be gone.

His smile faded. "Where are you going, Claire? And when did this happen?"

She hesitated. "I'm off to the Big Apple." Another pause. "With Ian Marshall."

Surprise filled her father's eyes. He stood up. "What?"

Claire repeated herself.

"I don't understand. What is going on? We spoke about Marshall the day of David's funeral. We agreed he is a suspicious character. We agreed that you should stay away from him."

Claire felt like a child being chastised for a childhood crime. "Ian

Marshall is a Nazi hunter, Dad. And he's chasing David's killer. I intend to help."

"You what?" Jean-Léon seemed genuinely shocked and out of his depth for the first time that Claire could ever recall.

"Dad, I'm an adult now. A pretty successful one. If something was wrong, you'd share it with me, wouldn't you?" Her unease escalated suddenly.

Her father's eyes changed. They became very watchful. "What are you trying to say, Claire?" His tone wasn't fatherly now.

Claire had become impossibly tense. "Is there any chance that Robert is alive?"

He blinked. His eyes reminded her of an owl's. The watchful hunter, waiting for the innocent prey to become unaware, just for an instant. "Who?"

"Robert. My uncle. Your brother."

Her father seemed absolutely shocked—and bewildered—by her question. "What? Claire, my brother died in 1944! In France! He was on a mission for the Resistance! What the hell is going on?"

Claire felt utter relief. There was no doubt in her mind that Robert Ducasse was dead. "Nothing," she whispered, sitting down in one of the bergères in front of Jean-Léon's desk.

Jean-Léon strode around it. "I don't like this. Why are you going to New York with Marshall? Did you know that he was here today, asking me all kinds of questions?"

Claire nodded. "Yeah, I know."

"You do?" He seemed briefly surprised.

"Yeah. Look, Dad. It seems like David was blackmailing someone who once spied for the Germans during the war. And he got himself killed for his efforts. There's a killer on the loose, and I am going to help Marshall catch him."

"Are you insane?" Her father shouted at her.

Claire was stunned. Her father never raised his voice—and now he was yelling. "I hope not."

"Claire, I do not want you involved with this man."

She felt disturbed all over again. "Why not?"

"Why not? It's dangerous, that's why not. You're not a policewoman.

You're my daughter. And something's wrong with Marshall. I don't like him. I don't trust him. I do not want you involved, not with him—not with any of this far-fetched Nazi nonsense."

Claire got to her feet. "I'm a grown woman, Dad. You can't order me around." She kept her tone gentle, amazed with herself. She was arguing with her father. She never argued with him. For most of her life, she had wanted to please him.

His eyes popped. "I am not ordering you around. When have I ever ordered you around? But you are not thinking clearly. Use your head, Claire. Ian Marshall is a stranger, and this is a dangerous situation. David is dead, Claire. Dear God, I don't want you to get hurt."

The guilt almost overcame her. "I have to do this, Dad. I have to find David's killer. I just have to. Please try to understand."

"Why?" he asked.

Claire stared. "I don't know why." But she thought about the fact that Ian was after William Duke—and Robert Ducasse.

Who was dead, of course.

Then her mind wanted to go forward, and she stared at her father and refused to allow it to make the next obvious step, leap to the next obvious conclusion. *She just could not.*

What is it that you really want to ask me, Claire? Ian had asked.

"What is it, Claire?" Jean-Léon asked so softly that had a pin dropped, they both would have heard it.

"I have to go." She turned almost blindly.

"No, Claire," he said firmly, sternly. It was the voice of authority, and it halted Claire in her tracks, halfway to the door. "You are not going to New York."

She squared her shoulders but did not turn. "I'm sorry, Dad. I have to go."

Claire arrived at the United gate with a carry-on and her purse. She had run home, thrown some clothes haphazardly into a small garment bag, and grabbed a few toiletries. At the last minute, because Elgin hailed from the U.K., she took her passport as well. She'd given her father's housekeeper instructions for Jilly's care while in her car and racing to the airport.

They had just begun the boarding process. Claire saw Ian from behind, walking up to the attendant at the gate to the jetway, clad in tan trousers and his black single-breasted jacket. Clearly he had a first-class ticket, and so did she. She could not afford it, but the flight had been sold out in coach and there hadn't been any choice.

Claire grew nervous in spite of herself. Maybe Jean-Léon was right. Maybe she was crazy. Ian did not want her help, and she could go home, reorganize her life, move to Mill Valley, and pretend that she had never spoken with Ian Marshall. She could forget all about Lionel Elgin and let the police, the FBI, Scotland Yard, and Ian Marshall do their jobs. And she could hope for the best.

But Claire was afraid. It would be like ignoring a bad leak in the kitchen and hoping it would one day go away. When instead, the probability was, it might soon produce a flood, sweeping away the floor, the house, and her life.

What if Jean-Léon was protecting his brother? Or worse?

Claire bit her lip. "Ian!"

He had been showing his boarding pass to the attendant. Slowly, he turned to face her.

Claire smiled at him. Perfectly. It was no easy task, because she knew he hated the particular expression, and because she was so worried. She could no longer believe her father implicitly. But she could not understand why.

Ian's eyes widened, and then he began to flush, and Claire knew it was a sign of anger.

Claire stiffened as he strode over to her, forgetting about boarding their flight. "What is this?" he demanded.

Claire put down her carry-on and dug her boarding pass out of her purse. "Gee. We're on the same flight. Same class, too. Oh my God! Are we sitting together?"

"This is not funny," he ground out.

Claire lost the smile. "No, it's not." She felt a huge groundswell of fear rising up, engulfing her, choking her. "I told you," she said quietly, "I'm your partner, Ian. And I don't care if you don't like me, I only care about doing what must be done."

"You can't help," he said tightly. "You can only slow me down!"

Claire shook her head. "What if Robert Ducasse is alive?" she whispered, and to her horror, she heard how broken her tone sounded. Broken and fragile and pitiful.

Ian didn't comment, but then what could he have said?

Claire bit her lip again. Her heart was drumming so fast and furiously in her chest that she felt faint.

She mustn't do this. Mustn't go there. She must not. But she had to give voice to her worst unspoken suspicion. "You suspect Jean-Léon," she said flatly. And slowly, she looked up.

The answer was in his eyes. "Yes, I do," he said.

She felt dizzy and faint. She had known this from the beginning of their discussion about possible suspects, but somehow, she had blocked out the inkling. She could bear David's murder and the guilt for their failed marriage and whatever part in his death she was responsible for. But she could not bear this new, incomprehensible, unthinkable burden. She just wasn't strong enough.

He put down his garment bag and took her by both upper arms. "Claire."

Claire stared, meeting the depths of his green eyes. His hands were very large and very strong, and she felt their warmth through the rolled-up sleeves of her jersey shirtdress. Claire shivered, but his grip was not unpleasant, and she knew what it meant.

"Claire, this is the real reason you should not be involved. Clearly you know that. You can't help. In case Elgin is Jean-Léon."

She shook her head. It suddenly struck her that she had told her father what Ian was doing; that she had told him too much. But no, it would be too much only if he were a traitor and a killer. That was impossible, wasn't it? "Don't be angry," she whispered, not looking away. "Please don't be angry now. I can't bear it."

"Don't." His hands tightened. "I'm a sucker for a helpless female, don't."

She swallowed. Thank God he had four younger sisters. "I told him."

His hands tightened again. *"What?"*

"I had to know if Robert was alive or not!"

Ian released her, appearing disbelieving. "I trusted you!"

"I'm sorry," she said and meant it.

He whirled away, then turned back. "And? What happened?"

"At the time"—she swallowed hard—"I believed him. He seemed stunned that anyone would think Robert was still alive. I am so sorry, Ian. I'm not a woman who betrays any confidence."

"Did you mention me?" Ian asked abruptly.

Claire nodded. "I told him I was going to New York with you."

"What! Jesus! Claire, how could you? Don't you get it? A killer is at large. A ruthless killer—a sociopath—someone who will do whatever he has to. Elgin intends to win what is, to him, a game. You've put yourself in real danger, Claire," he added tersely. "Frankly, that is untenable, as far as I am concerned."

"First of all, if, and it's almost an impossibility, *if* Jean-Léon is Elgin, I don't believe for a second that he killed my husband or anyone else. My father would never hurt me!"

"Go home, Claire," Ian said tightly. "You've done enough. Go home, pack your stuff, move into your new place, and go back to raising money for kids and dogs. You do it well. It's what you should be doing. They need you. Go back to your life and let me and the authorities take care of Elgin."

He was right. She had betrayed him, but she was in this now. "I can't," she said plaintively. "I cannot."

"Oh, yes you can." He was firm.

The new Claire rose up quickly, taking over once more and chasing the frightened and vulnerable Claire far away—at least for now. "No, Ian." Her tone was every bit as resolute as his. "From now on, I am sticking to you like glue. Not rubber glue, not nail glue, not the kiddie roll-on kind. From now on, until this is over, I am Krazy Glue. Do you got that?"

He looked at her, and a long moment passed in which Claire felt her cheeks heat. Had she really said that? Then he rolled his eyes, perhaps toward God in prayer, and he walked away, past the attendant and onto the ramp leading to the Boeing 747 destined for New York City.

Claire picked up her bags and she followed. She was, oddly enough, exhilarated. Until she remembered what was at stake.

CHAPTER 5

"Nice digs," Claire said. It was two in the morning, New York time.

Ian did not answer, turning on more lights. They had actually been in the same row on the transcontinental flight, but on opposite sides of the aircraft. Ian had slept the entire flight. Claire had spent most of her time pretending to watch movies while watching him.

He had not been talkative in the taxi on the way into Manhattan, either. The ride was only forty minutes, and Claire had actually fallen asleep.

Now she looked around. His building, on Eightieth and Third, seemed very new. The doorman had been ingratiating, the lobby high-ceilinged and magnificent. Ian's apartment was on the twenty-fourth floor with catty-corner views of the city south and west. It could have been a model apartment for the aspiring big-city *Cosmo* bachelor-of-the-month. The furnishings were very Ralph Lauren—a combination of leather, tweed, and fabric, all rustic and new, in contrasting solids and prints. She wondered if he had a maid. It was as neat as a whistle.

"Spend a lot of time at home?" Claire asked sweetly, for the first time wondering if he had a girlfriend. Maybe she did the cleaning—and the laundry.

He ignored the comment, walking across the living area and throwing open a door. He hit a wall switch. "Guest room. Good night."

Claire folded her arms across her chest. "Aren't you hungry?"

He did not look at her. "Kitchen's right there." She could see it; it had no door. "Help yourself."

She wondered if he would punish her for days, weeks, forever. Claire walked over to a cast-iron bookcase. There were lots of books—all, she saw, on World War II, European history, and the Holocaust. There were also several photographs of pretty women who looked like Ian, two of whom had handsome husbands and cute kids. There was a photograph of a middle-aged woman with gray hair and dimples. Claire picked it up. "Is this your mother?"

"Yes."

There was no picture of his father, she realized as she put it down and turned. "Did you sleep well on the flight?"

He stared at her. "What do you want, Claire? You're like a kid desperate for attention. Do you really want my attention in the middle of the night in the middle of my apartment with the two of us alone?"

She straightened. She was breathless. "What does that mean?"

"It means you're a pretty woman, and I'm a normal guy, and we're here alone." He smiled. It was tight and humorless.

"Are you trying to frighten me? Or distract me?"

"I'm trying to get you to go to bed, and maybe, in the light of tomorrow, you'll go home."

He turned and walked into another room, hitting the lights as he did so.

Claire followed. This was the master bedroom, she saw. The carpet was a rich dark blue, the walls eggshell white. The bed was covered with black and blue blankets, striped and patterned, the shades of blue competing. There were blue and white sheets and too many pillows. He had either a girlfriend or a decorator.

"I want to talk," she said.

He turned abruptly. "Are you always this way?"

Claire met his gaze frankly. "No. I seem to have changed."

"I think so. Maybe you have multiple personality disorder."

"Why are you being so rude?"

"All right!" He threw both hands in the air. "I apologize. It's been a while since I had a woman barge her way right into the middle of my life."

Absurdly, his comment pleased Claire to no end. "But Ian, I'm not in the middle of your life, just your investigation."

He looked at her and sighed. "I stand corrected."

"Do you?" She was more than curious. "I think this is somehow very personal for you."

He said, "Please go to bed, Claire. We'll talk in the morning."

In spite of the hour, Claire was wired, not tired. "Can't we discuss the case?" she asked.

Ian sighed again and dropped down in a faded black leather chair. He kicked off his lug-soled loafers. "Fine."

Claire smiled and sat down on the edge of his king-size bed. She tried not to glance around at it. She knew she should not be speculating about what kind of lover Ian Marshall was.

On the other hand, she had spent most of the flight trying to recall when she and David had last made love. She had assumed it to be about six months ago, but finally she had decided it might have been last summer, in July, when they had gone to Hawaii for a week.

"Ian, what led you to my father, his brother, and the Dukes in the first place?" she asked.

"David," Ian said, standing suddenly and shrugging off his jacket. "Want a beer?"

"I hate beer," Claire said.

"Be right back." In his socks, he padded out of the room.

Claire took that moment to really glance around. She could see into a large master bathroom, and it was wall-to-wall red-veined marble. From the two bedroom windows, the millions of city lights winked back at her. There was a huge blond chest against one wall, covered with more books. The chest looked Chinese or Japanese and antique. There were several tasteful framed reproductions on the walls. The art was modern; she recognized Miró, Pollock, and a new artist, Dworman.

Then Claire saw something by the edge of the chest, next to the other side of the bed. *Airline tickets.*

She slid off the bed—it was so high she had to jump down a few inches—and ran around to the monster chest. She inspected the tickets. He had flights to London and Cardiff, Wales, tomorrow!

Ian returned. "What are you doing now?" He sounded resigned.

She held up the tickets. "You're holding out on me! These are for tomorrow night."

"That's right."

"What's in Wales?"

"Claire—"

"If this has anything to do with Elgin, I'm on board. Glue, remember?"

"Krazy Glue," he said. "How could I forget?" He lifted the beer bottle, a Budweiser, and drank.

But she had seen the smile he'd tried so hard to contain.

"Maybe you can help," he said finally. "I am going to visit Lady Elgin in the north of Wales."

She went on alert. "Lady Elgin?"

"Elgin's stepmother."

Claire stared. "She's still alive?"

"She's only a few years older than Elgin. His father remarried a very young girl."

Excitement sizzled inside her. "I wonder if they've been in touch."

"I doubt it."

"But you wonder, too!"

He smiled a little and drank down half the beer. "Yeah."

"Do you think she could recognize him today?" Her excitement vanished, replaced by an equally intense fear. *Her father was not Elgin.* It was absurd. And how could it be William? He was the one who had always picked her up when she had fallen down as a child.

Suddenly she couldn't help recalling the first Christmas after her mother was buried. Her family had celebrated both Hanukkah and Christmas. Only a few weeks had passed since the funeral, and Claire and her father had been invited to spend Christmas Eve with the Dukes. That morning, Claire had not wanted to get up. She hadn't cared about all of the presents underneath the huge Christmas tree. But Santa had come knocking on her door, towing a bag of the presents behind him. And in spite of the Santa costume and disguise, there had been no mistaking who it was. William had made her laugh for the first time since she had buried her mother.

"I have no idea. But we will find out," Ian was saying.

Claire stared, jerked back into the present painfully. "You have photos, don't you? Of Jean-Léon, of William." Elgin had to be someone else, someone other than her father, William, or the uncle she believed to be dead.

"I do."

Claire grew uneasy.

"What is it?"

Claire shook her head. She was not going to tell him something that was just now striking her as strange. There were no family albums at home that predated her father's marriage to her mother. Or were there? Perhaps they were in an attic somewhere. For surely her father had photographs of himself—and Robert—as children, as boys, as young men.

Claire smiled her best smile. "Whatever happened to Elgin's father? I read in the file that his father disappeared in 1940."

Ian reached out and pressed his thumb to the side of her cheek. "Don't play brave."

Claire froze at his touch.

He dropped his hand, turning away and slugging down the rest of the beer. "He disappeared in August 1940, and no one ever learned what really happened to him." Ian sat and tore off his socks as if he had not just touched her face. Claire told herself that the gesture had not been intimate. It hadn't meant a thing. He began lifting the polo shirt, revealing his navel, his hard abs.

Claire was about to protest, then decided to enjoy the show. "That was a bit convenient," she said, staring as he pulled the polo shirt over his head. He dropped it on the floor, and she looked away.

"Very," he said, walking over to a built-in closet. He opened it and grabbed a torn T-shirt from a shelf, as well as very faded jeans. Claire glimpsed rows of beautiful suits, dress shirts, casual slacks, and trousers. There was a rack of ties. On the floor, she glimpsed half a dozen pairs of black loafers and one pair of tan oxfords. She glimpsed shelves of sweaters, mostly in shades of beige, brown, and blue, and they looked to be cashmere. She saw ragged tees and beat-up jeans. She saw running shoes, biking shoes, a cycling helmet. She saw a tennis racket and a gym bag.

She had never before realized what a closet could tell you about a man. He was impeccably dressed and very athletic. His girlfriend did not live in.

"At the time, the elder Elgin left letters behind suggesting that *he* was the fascist, and that he'd fled to Germany. It was a joke, Claire. So much incriminating evidence was left behind at Elgin Hall—I doubt any self-respecting spy would be so lackadaisical." He faced her. His eyes glittered again. "Lionel inherited his title and his estates, his respectability and his connections, *everything*, upon Randolph Elgin's death."

"What are you saying?" Claire whispered, enthralled. "Surely you don't think Lionel killed his own father?'

"I don't know what to think—except that it was convenient as all hell." He smiled grimly at her, jeans in hand, poised to enter the master bath. "Sandwich?"

"Sure." She waited while he disappeared behind that closed door, and when he came out, barefoot, in the soft jeans and torn tee, she followed him out of the master bedroom and into the kitchen. "Ian? I need to book those flights."

"At this hour, you'll have to call the airline directly," he said.

She could hardly believe it. "Really? You finally accept the fact that I'm your partner?"

"Did I say that?" He took a loaf of bread and a jar of low-fat mayo from the refrigerator. "Lady Ellen is in her eighties. Remember, I grew up surrounded by women. I *know* women. At least, I know women when I'm not romantically involved." His grin was crooked. "She'll do better with another woman than with me."

"So now we're officially partners," Claire said, feeling a rush of adrenaline.

He sniffed a package of deli-sliced ham, made a face, and tossed it in the garbage. "Peanut butter okay?"

"Only if you have bananas," Claire said. "Or even better, bacon."

He looked at her. "You're joking, right?"

Claire smiled. "I'm in the market for a heart attack. PB's okay. You do have jelly?"

He smiled, and it reached his eyes. "I have a maid, Hayden. She does all the shopping."

Claire watched him replace the mayo in the fridge and take out no-sugar-added jam. "Is your girlfriend on a diet?"

He popped bread in the toaster, not even looking at her. "Broke up almost a year ago. She wasn't what I wanted."

Claire felt relieved. She scolded herself for feeling so. "Why not?"

"She wasn't too bright," he said.

Claire liked that. "Beautiful?"

"Yeah."

She didn't like that. She watched him make the sandwiches, realizing she was envisioning his ex-girlfriend as a Cindy Crawford or Gisèle Bündchen. It made her spirits sink to a new low.

She had to stay focused. This was not a lark or an adventure. A real killer was out there. And what if he was William? Claire couldn't even begin to imagine how it would hurt Elizabeth.

But she would prove that Jean-Léon was not even remotely connected to Elgin. That was why she was standing in Ian Marshall's kitchen at three A.M. There was no other reason.

He handed her a plate and a glass of skim milk and they went over to the very small kitchen table by the single window in the room. Claire realized she was famished even though she had eaten every single crumb of her two airline meals.

"You're too thin," Ian commented. "Want another sandwich?"

"Could I?"

He laughed and got up.

"I'll call the airlines while you do that," Claire said. She tried to remain focused as she went to the telephone. Ian's ticket was business class. Claire knew she had to travel coach, but she really wanted to sit with him. That way she could make sure he remained annoyed and did not forget that she was his official partner. She smiled a little as she called the airline, calculating how many months it would take her to recoup the amount of money spent on such a fare. If she stayed under her new budget by two hundred dollars a month, for a year and a half, she could afford the fare. She booked her seats and returned to the kitchen, this time barefoot. "Done."

His eyes slid over her and they seemed warm. "Done." He handed her the gooey sandwich.

Claire ate more slowly this time, somewhat self-conscious, aware of Ian's regard. When she finished, she realized she was finally tired. "You never told me how you came to suspect William and my father and even Robert Ducasse," she said, sitting back in her chair.

"Through David. There's been no trace of Elgin for years, Claire. And then David calls me. Frightened and able to identify him. I have a team working for me, a small team, but they did a full bio on David in less than twenty-four hours. The two significant men in his life who are in Elgin's age range and who are both European are William and your father. And then there's the Courbet." He had been studying his hands as he spoke, as if his mind was racing ahead with other thoughts he did not wish to share with her.

"My father bought it in Paris," Claire said sharply. "Clearly it had been stolen."

"Maybe," Ian said. "It's fortunate he loaned the painting with several others to the Met a few years ago. One of my guys made the connection; he'd seen the Courbet there, and when he read lady Elgin's report in the Elgin file, a quick call revealed the painting's provenance."

Claire was silent. "And there's the missing years from William's life."

"Yes." He nodded. "And both men emigrated to the United States in 'forty-eight, within two months of each other. Interesting."

She realized she was exhausted. "But that doesn't mean anything."

"Maybe, maybe not." He stood. "You look beat. Why don't you hit the sack?"

She looked up at him, thinking suddenly about his very large bed. It was large enough for two.

A deliciously warm feeling unfurled inside of her, and she knew what it was—desire.

Her body was charged with an animal attraction for Ian Marshall. It had been so long since she had felt this way. Not since the early years with David.

Ian might have sensed her thoughts, because he flushed and walked abruptly out of the kitchen. Claire stood slowly. Feeling this way just wasn't right. Not only was it too soon, it was disloyal and far too complicated.

She took their plates and glasses to the sink and washed them, trying to rein in her wayward sexuality. When she finished, she realized he had been standing for some time in the doorway, watching her. Claire turned as she removed the rubber gloves and their eyes met.

"You didn't have to do that," he said.

She shrugged. Her breathing wasn't as even as it could be. "Habit."

"I got you a spare quilt. I like to keep the AC high at night."

She nodded. Would it be so terribly wrong if, after all that she'd been through—all that she was going through—she found solace in his arms? Claire had never slept around. She'd had one boyfriend before David. She'd had only that boy and David as lovers. For her, sex was anything but casual.

But this was the new millennium. Claire knew that many women took lovers as casually as experienced playboys. Many women faced the fact that they had the same physical needs as men. Today such behavior was not just heard of, it was sometimes even applauded. No one would condemn her if she went to bed with Ian Marshall in a casual way.

But Claire knew herself. She would condemn herself the morning after. Either that or she'd be head over heels in love.

"Thanks." Claire gave him a stiff smile and hurried past him to her room. As she closed the door, she dared a glimpse of his face.

His expression seemed odd, strained, but she might have been imagining it.

Then she realized she had no pajamas. It was the devil, of course, prompting her to misbehave. Claire slipped out of her room.

Ian's door was open and he was moving around. He sensed her and turned.

She kept her eyes wide and innocent. "May I borrow a T-shirt?"

Ian wasn't home when Claire woke up at noon, clad only in Ian's soft pale blue T-shirt. It was only nine in California, so there was no guilt. And amazingly, for the first time since David had died, she felt refreshed and well rested. For one moment, Claire lingered in the queen-size bed, wiggling her toes and enjoying the soft, worn cotton on her bare skin. The T-shirt had come out of the laundry, but she loved wearing it and thought she could detect a masculine scent upon it.

Claire got up and walked over to her bedroom window, which looked out over a part of the terrace that adjoined the living area and his bedroom. It was a beautiful spring day, and tonight they were on their way to Wales.

The bathroom was in the hall. Claire did not hesitate. Still in her makeshift pajamas—the T-shirt covered about four inches of thigh—she stepped out of the bedroom with her toothbrush in hand. The moment she did, she knew Ian wasn't home. The apartment was silent, and worse, it felt empty. She sighed.

As Claire brushed her teeth, she regarded her gray-eyed reflection in the mirror. She had her father's eyes, and they were sparkling. She did not look haggard this morning; in fact, she looked okay. Maybe she'd go on a diet of peanut butter for a while, peanut butter and Ian's company.

Claire wandered into the kitchen after finger-combing her hair. Ian had left her a brief but nice note, telling her he'd gone into the office for a few hours and to make herself at home. He also wrote that a car would pick them up at four; their flight departed at seven P.M. Claire found herself smiling as she read the note and scooped coffee, which he'd left out on the counter, into the coffee machine. He was an awfully good host for a bachelor.

As Claire sipped, she debated calling her father and pressuring him to produce the bill of sale for the Courbet. That would do a lot to redirect Ian's suspicions. And while Claire wasn't a policewoman, now she was wondering if her father should volunteer to hand over a sample of DNA. If the killer had left anything behind, Claire was convinced it would not match her father's bodily evidence.

Claire found eggs in the fridge and was scrambling them up and toasting bread when the telephone rang. She assumed it was Ian and did not hesitate. She lifted the receiver before it could ring twice.

"Hello?"

"Claire, is that you?"

Claire blinked, stunned, at the sound of Elizabeth Duke's voice. "Elizabeth?" Guilt filled her. She had left town without calling Elizabeth or saying good-bye. Worse, she hadn't said anything about William, and should she? William could not be Elgin, but what if she was wrong?

"Claire!" Elizabeth's voice filled with relief. "I'm so glad I found you. Your father was so distraught, and he called me a few moments ago. Oh, Claire. Are you all right?"

Claire turned off the burner and sat down at the tiny kitchen table. "I'm okay. Much better than I've been, actually." But her mind was racing. What had Jean-Léon said, exactly?

"You sound better, and for that, I'm relieved. But Claire, I am worried about you."

"Please don't worry. I'm in good hands," Claire said, envisioning just that—herself in Ian Marshall's large hands.

"Don't worry? Your father says you've teamed up with Marshall to find David's killer. He's afraid you might be in danger, and I am, too. Claire, this isn't like you."

"No, it's not." Claire wondered what else Jean-Léon had told Elizabeth. "How did you get this number? And how did you know I was here?"

"Your father had the number, Marshall gave it to him yesterday morning. I didn't expect to find you there, but I was hoping Marshall would tell me where you were staying."

"It was easier to stay at his place. We got in very late last night." Claire felt herself flush. Of course, never in a million years would Elizabeth suspect that Claire was having fantasies about jumping into bed with her host. She would never in an eternity suspect a real affair, either.

There was a pause. Then, "Claire, will you consider coming home? The police will find David's killer. That's their job."

Claire hesitated. "I can't, Elizabeth. I just have to do this."

"But why? You were about to move into that charming house in Mill Valley. You're in the middle of planning a fund-raiser. Why? What if, God forbid, you get hurt?"

Claire actually considered the question. "Elizabeth? I know this sounds strange, but for the first time in years—and I do mean years—I feel young and alive."

There was absolute silence on the other end of the phone.

Now Claire blushed. She felt her cheeks burn.

"My God, Claire, you're in a state of grief. Has Marshall taken advantage of you?"

"Have you and Jean-Léon been comparing notes?"

"We have. He doesn't like him, Claire, and I trust your father's judgment completely."

"Well, I sort of do like him," Claire said, surprised because she was actually bristling.

"Very well. You know, your mother was a very determined woman, and I have always thought you were so much like her. Now more than ever." Elizabeth's tone was soft but resigned.

"Wish me luck?"

"I'll do more than that. Is there anything at all I can do to help—or see you through this safely?"

Claire thought about it. "Yes. Would you please make sure that Jean-Léon finds a bill of sale for the Courbet he gave us for David's birthday?"

Elizabeth seemed surprised. "That's an odd request."

"Just please make sure he does it." Claire felt relieved. Apparently her father had not mentioned everything she and Ian were up to. Just in case

William was, somehow, a ruthless and sociopathic killer, it was best that Elizabeth did not know about their hunt for Elgin.

"Very well. Which hotel will you be in?"

Claire started. She realized that Elizabeth assumed she was staying in New York, and that she would be more comfortable in a hotel. "Actually, I'm off to Wales. But I'll call from the U.K. so you don't worry."

"Wales? Claire—" Elizabeth began in a worried and motherly protest.

"Trust me, Elizabeth. I'm a grown woman and I can handle this."

Elizabeth sighed. "I know you can. But how can I not worry? It's almost as if you've run off with an absolute stranger, and it's just not like you."

"Maybe I had a lobotomy in my sleep," Claire said.

"What?"

"Bad joke. How's William?"

"I haven't told him yet what's going on. He loves you so, and I hate worrying him." She hesitated. "He hasn't been feeling well recently, Claire, and I didn't want to say anything. He's going in tomorrow for tests. He's been complaining of dizziness."

Claire froze. "Oh, no. Please tell me he's all right."

"I'm sure he is," Elizabeth said, too firmly—as if trying to convince herself. But they both knew that William was in his early eighties, and at that age, any number of medical conditions could occur.

"I'll call you tomorrow night," Claire said decisively, worried now about the man who had showered her with so much affection for most of her life.

"You do that, dear. And Claire? If you need anything, call."

Claire promised that she would, and they exchanged good-byes. Then Claire stared at the phone, concerned about William. This was not the first time in her life she had faced the fact that life was so unpredictable and so fragile. She had learned that horrific lesson at the too tender age of ten.

Claire finished her breakfast. It was almost two, and she decided to shower and dress. But on her way to the shower, she found herself making a detour. The one room in Ian's condo that she hadn't even glimpsed was his office.

Claire walked past the bathroom and to the end of the hall. His office door was closed; she pushed it open. A room with wood floors and three walls of bookcases, all crammed with books and notes, faced her. Also facing her was a wall of windows, and his desk and PC.

This was a very serious office indeed, Claire thought, wondering if it was off-limits. But they were partners now, so he should not have anything to hide.

Claire walked in, glancing at one shelf of books. Medieval history tomes faced her. She smiled. Clearly he was a Renaissance man.

She walked over to his desk, and the first and only thing she saw was the photograph. Her smile vanished.

It was black-and-white. Clearly the young man was an officer, for he wore a belted uniform and beret. In fact, as Claire picked it up, she saw wings over the man's left breast pocket, as well as half a dozen medals. And the officer resembled Ian.

Almost exactly. Like twins, or like a father and son. He was smiling at the camera, a reckless gleam in his eyes. And those were Ian's eyes, Ian's nose and chin, and one but not two of Ian's dimples.

Chills crept over Claire. This explained why it was so personal for Ian Marshall. The officer had to be his father.

And clearly, this was a dated photograph. Claire squinted at it, but there was no way she could tell if the uniform was American or not. She wasn't certain why it mattered, but a gut feeling told her that it did.

"I was wondering how long it would take you to ferret out Eddy," a voice said from behind her.

Claire whirled. Ian stood in the doorway, leaning against the wall. His eyes were on her intently.

Claire held up the photo, then the question she was about to ask died. Ian was taking a long look at her legs.

She flushed, even though this had been her silly plan all along.

"You could lift that photo a bit higher," Ian said a touch roughly.

Claire realized what he meant, and she felt her color heighten. She dropped her hand to her side, and the T-shirt fell an inch or so. "You could have knocked."

"My office. My T-shirt. You could have changed."

"I was just about to jump in the shower."

"This does look like the bathroom," Ian agreed.

Claire walked over to him, not quite steadily. "I was snooping. Guilty as charged. But not with malicious intent. Is there a reduced penalty for good intent? I *am* sorry," she added.

"Are you?"

Claire bit her lower lip, because how could she be sorry? She had just found Ian's personal connection with World War II. "You win. I'll go to jail," she said.

"Not funny. I happen to know you don't have a malicious bone in your body, Claire," he said. "I also know you're dying to ask who that man is. *That* is Eddy Marshall."

He took the photo from her hand and put it back on his desk. Then he walked over to a bookcase and handed her another photo, also in a frame.

Claire blinked and her heart jumped. She took everything in almost at once. She was looking at the same handsome young man, only now he was with two other men, everyone wearing beaten-up bomber jackets and standing arm in arm, grinning, in front of some kind of old, open-air, single-seat plane with a big propeller and a round nose. Clearly they were pilots, and now she could see the RAF insignia on the plane.

And there was a RAF pilot whose body was found in a pond not far from Elgin Hall, his throat slit. Ian had told her so.

"Who is Eddy Marshall? Your father? He was in the RAF?"

He went to her and took the photo from her hands. He stared down at it grimly. "No. Eddy Marshall was my uncle—my father's oldest brother."

"And?" She held her breath.

"And he was Elgin's first victim," Ian said. "His first victim, but clearly not his last."

CHAPTER 6

He was the pilot Elgin had murdered. This helped to explain so much. "When was this taken?" Claire whispered finally.

"The summer of 1940." Ian put the framed photo back on the bookshelf. "Eddy quit his job and took off for France to join L'Armée de L'Air so he could fight the Germans in April or May of 1939. He went over with two or three other American boys."

Claire stared back at him. Her mind was racing. "How did it happen?" she asked.

"He never got a chance to fight in France; the country fell before he could complete his training," Ian continued. "He somehow got to Britain, claimed he was a Canadian, and joined a Canadian squadron of the RAF. By July of 1940 he was fighting Germans, all right. He was the first American to down a Gerry—an ME-110. Before he died, he had ten kills on his record, and he was wing commander of an Eagle squadron. He was a hero, Claire." Ian was harsh and grim. "An all-American hero."

"And?"

"Elgin murdered him. Eddy was on to the bastard, and Elgin murdered him in late December 1940. In fact, it was Christmas Eve."

Claire stared, her heart skipping a dozen beats. "This is why you are burning to get Elgin."

"I am determined—not burning—to get Elgin because I believe in justice, and thus far, Elgin has eluded all justice. I am determined to get Elgin because his is the most heinous of the cases I have on my desk."

Claire only half believed him. Her mind made rapid calculations, and all the while, she tried to remain skeptical and logical. "How did Eddy uncover Elgin? I mean, no one else did."

Ian sighed. "Eddy's job before he took off for France was with the FBI."

Claire's eyes widened.

Ian shrugged. "My baby sister is a fed right now. It sort of runs in the family."

Claire stared. "Are you an agent?" She didn't know anything about the FBI, but it might explain the gun he carried. Claire felt certain that the average Nazi hunter was no Indiana Jones.

He did smile. "Are you kidding? You know what I do and where I work. Besides, federal agents make squat. If that was my income, I couldn't live like this."

Claire knew he was telling the truth. "So what are you saying? Eddy had some training and he stumbled onto Elgin by sheer chance?"

"Yes and no. Eddy was in love with Elgin's cousin, Rachel Greene." He gazed at Claire. "That was how he met Lionel Elgin. So my guess is that he stumbled onto Elgin's activities by chance, but after meeting him through Rachel."

"How did they meet?" Claire asked after a moment. "Eddy and Rachel, I mean."

"I know what you meant. I don't know how Eddy and Rachel met. The family myth is he crash-landed right at her feet." Ian smiled then. "Which makes a cute story, but I doubt it's true. However, they were newlyweds when he was murdered."

Claire had to shiver again. "Poor Rachel," she heard herself whisper. "Poor Eddy."

"Yeah," Ian said flatly. Claire took one last look at the handsome, care-free young fighter pilot in the photos on the bookshelf. An idea occurred to her. "Is there any way to know if the same person killed all three—Eddy and George Suttill and David?"

"Special Branch believes to this day that the same killer did in Eddy, the intelligence officers, Suttill, and David. It's the assumption they, the SFPD, and the FBI are working on. The bad news is that the killer is a pro. He didn't leave any evidence behind with either Suttill or David, just the deed itself."

"Well," Claire said, "the plot thickens."

"You need to pack. And change." He started for the door. "Unless you intend to get arrested for indecent exposure."

Claire followed him out, smiling and satisfied. "Do you think this is indecent? I kinda thought it was sexy."

He ignored her, heading into his own bathroom. Claire stared after him, glad he'd returned—until an image of the reckless and handsome Eddy Marshall came to mind. His resemblance with Ian was eerie. So, being in the FBI ran in the family? There was something about that statement, or the way Ian had made it, that gave her pause. She could smell a rat. He was holding out on her again, she felt certain of it.

And she was still wondering why he didn't have any photographs of his father anywhere, when the rest of his home was like a family museum.

Claire went to get dressed.

They arrived in London just before seven, managed Immigration, and killed two hours over breakfast, bleary-eyed, waiting for their short flight to Cardiff. There they rented a car, a small hatchback Fiat. The map proved deceptive. Wales was a region filled with hills, mountains, rivers, and lakes, and the route north had not been direct, although the scenery had become more and more breathtaking the farther they went. By the time they reached the small town of Ruthin, outside of which Lady Elgin now lived, it was early evening.

The town was set on a ridge in the southern end of the Vale of Clwyd, surrounded by lush, wooded hills. They had alternated the driving, with Ian doing his manly best to do most of it, and now he parked on St. Peter's Square, just a stone's throw from the old church of the very same name. Two-story buildings, mostly of stone, with timbered fronts, lined the square. Claire felt as if she had walked back in time; having been to England before, she knew that, in many ways, she had.

Claire and Ian stepped out of the Fiat. She looked around with rising excitement. St. Peter's Church was on her right, surrounded by many old buildings, including a cloister. The town hall, clearly marked, was just across the square. She was standing in front the big brick Castle Hotel. Another inn was next to it, the Myddleton Arms, where she and Ian were staying. Numerous shops lined the square, and to her far left was a fairly new and sprawling castle—Claire guessed it had been built in the last hundred years—which was also a hotel. The outer walls were obviously older and a part of the original ruins.

Claire smiled at Ian. "What a sweet village."

"It's cute." He didn't smile, hefting both her carry-on and his.

"I can carry my own bag," Claire said, coming around the car to his side.

"Forget it, Scarlet," he said.

She was briefly insulted. "I have nothing in common with Scarlett O'Hara," she said.

He started walking toward the Myddleton Arms. "Who's talking *Gone with the Wind*? I was referring to your nails."

Claire glanced down at her fingernails, which were a brilliant crimson, matching her toenails. She usually wore red nail polish to the evening functions she attended so often, and it had become a habit. She couldn't even recall her last manicure, but obviously, she'd had one. "Are you one of those guys who hates red nail polish?"

He shrugged. "It's sort of sexy."

Claire smiled at his back.

There was hardly any traffic, and far more tourists than Claire had expected. Many of the tourists were visibly American, lumbering about in shorts and sneakers even at this hour. As they navigated their way across the square, her gaze took in the hills surrounding the town again. "Ever see *The Sound of Music*?"

"Fifty years ago," he said, snorting.

"Party pooper," she returned.

He gave her a look. "Are we having a good time yet?"

"You're a great companion," she said frankly. "What is it, Pavlov's training? I mean, the minute you sit down in a plane, you fall asleep. Don't eat, don't drink, don't snore, don't use the john, just sleep. It's really fun traveling with you."

"That's what you're supposed to do on night flights to Europe, Claire," he said, pushing open the front door to the inn with his shoulder. "And I read on the flight to Cardiff."

"The conversation was scintillating," she said.

"You remind my of my second baby sister. She had an identity crisis when she was twelve, and it's still going on."

She made a face at him, and he caught her in the act. He raised one eyebrow. She grinned. "I'd rather fly with Sleeping Beauty than Garrulous George, anyway," she said.

"Garrulous George?" He looked up for God. "Heaven help anyone involved with you."

It felt like a compliment and Claire felt somewhat pleased as they checked in.

However, there was a problem.

"What do you mean, you have only one room? We called last night from JFK and explained that we needed two rooms, and a gentleman assured me that he had the extra room." Ian was trying to keep his tone contained but not doing a good job. Claire could see that he was pissed.

"I'm so sorry, sir. I don't know how there could be such a mix-up. But the town is full. We're full. I could ring up a few inns, though, and see what we've got." She smiled helpfully at him.

Ian did not soften. "I'd like to see the manager," he said flatly. His eyes were cold.

Claire broke in. "Ian, if they don't have another room, they don't have it. It's okay. It's only one night. I promise not to be witty. And I won't wear your T-shirt to bed," she added slyly.

He turned to look at her. "We are not sharing a room."

Claire's smile faded. His eyes were black with resolve. "What, do I have cooties or something?" She should not be disappointed but she was.

"You know that is not why." He ground his jaw.

"BO?"

"Claire, cut it out. This is serious."

"Warts?" she asked, wide-eyed.

He started to sigh and laughed instead, and the girl behind the desk giggled. She said, "Sir, we do have a cot. I can give you a cot. Will that be any help at all?"

Ian turned away.

"Bring on the cot," Claire said with gusto. But she was nervous, all the same. Not that anything was going to happen, which of course it was not.

After they had settled in, there was a knock and a bellboy appeared, holding a silver ice bucket. In it was a bottle of champagne. There was no cot in sight. "Compliments of management, sir, miss," he said with a freckled grin.

Claire watched as Ian let him deposit the tray on the small table by the window. Ian thanked him and the boy left.

"Now we have a perfect excuse to eat in," Claire said.

He glanced at her, then lifted the bottle. "Amazing. Veuve Clicquot in this place. Good stuff."

"Open it," Claire said. "And it's not good, it's excellent, my dear."

He faced her, his hands on his hips. "Let's talk, Claire."

She became still. "About Elgin?"

"No. I do believe that, for the moment, we have exhausted that subject."

Claire wished she could think of something silly or witty to say. She couldn't. So she waited, with no small amount of dread.

"For some odd reason, we're partners now. And believe me, it is odd, and I can't seem to recall just how this happened."

Claire nodded a bit guiltily. "I pressured you. Because of my dad and William."

"That's hardly a rational explanation."

"Maybe you should open the champagne."

"Are you listening?"

"I am all ears."

"I want to talk about this goddamned chemistry that's between us."

Claire blinked. The word "chemistry" seemed to hang in the air. "Okay," she said, and her voice sounded like a squeak.

"Why are you acting so surprised? It's obvious you are attracted to me, and it's a natural thing. I mean, David just died—"

"Hold on!" Claire was on her feet. "Who said I'm attracted to you, buster? And what does David have to do with anything?" The pulse in her temples was hurting her now.

"You didn't let me finish," he said softly. "And why are you getting that hurt look in your eyes?"

She folded her arms tightly across her chest. "Well, rejection isn't the most pleasant of life experiences."

He stared. "Claire, we have to be sensible now."

"Of course." She was an idiot, she told herself, to even think about him. Damn it! Why couldn't she have kept her eyes in her head just a few times?

"Look, I think you're rebounding after David's death, and—"

"You are not a shrink, and don't go analyzing me."

That shut him up.

"Please open the champagne," she said. She picked up her carry-on and purse and stalked into the bathroom. It was immature, but she slammed the door, then locked it. She had the urge to cry.

Now she hoped they would bring up the cot. She said through the door, "You are so arrogant, Marshall! I'll bet you think that reception girl was in love with you, too!"

"Actually, no, I don't, and you didn't even let me finish" was his calm reply from the other side of the door.

"Well, I know you hate having me for a partner, but get this: you're stuck with me now!" Claire turned on the shower while stripping off her black pants and white knit top. A thong and triangle bra, both white and lacy, followed.

"Believe me, Claire, I know you are sticking to me like glue. Krazy Glue, remember?"

"No, now it's worse. Like a tick to a dog. Like a blood-sucking tick! I hope you're opening that champagne, because I am in desperate need of a drink."

"I am."

She stepped into the shower, and the pain of his rejection brought a sick feeling to her chest. She heard the cork popping as she scrubbed herself and then quickly washed her hair. But truly, what did she expect? A torrid love affair while they were chasing Elgin? That wasn't even her style, and maybe he was right. Maybe she was on the rebound after David's death.

Claire stepped out of the shower, shivering, as it was very cool in Wales at night. "By the way, I am not rebounding because of David," she said through the door, toweling off and jumping into a pair of jeans. "I was going to ask him for a divorce." She pulled on a T-shirt; unfortunately, it was his. "Our relationship died years ago. I can't even remember the last time we had sex." She opened the door, wrapping a towel around her head.

He stared. "That's nice to know," he said, and he was flushing. He held out a flute of champagne.

Claire snatched it and downed half in one gulp. "Like that?"

"Impressive. Is this a contest?"

"Maybe. Let's see who gets drunk first." She would win, hands down.

His mouth quirked. "Claire, you never let me finish. Okay, so maybe this isn't about rebounding for you. I'm not rebounding from anyone, remember?"

Claire went still. "What are you saying?"

"What am I saying?" He was incredulous. "What I'm saying is that I am dedicated to bringing Elgin in to the authorities, preferably with a case that will hold up in a court of law. I am determined, Claire."

"I know," she said softly. "I'm determined, too. For David, and to prove William and Jean-Léon innocent."

"Will you stop interrupting?" He smiled and shook his head. "I'd really like to finish."

"Okay." She managed a smile, still afraid of what it was he wanted to stay, but not as afraid as before.

"Quit looking so wounded, Red," he said softly. "Stop putting words in my mouth and feelings in my heart before you even know me."

Claire nodded uncertainly.

"I'm not on the rebound. You're a gorgeous woman. I thought so the first time we met. I was a bit deluded, because you seemed so perfect, the reigning society queen. But I saw some of the real Claire Hayden that night. You were upset. Vulnerable. You got me then, Red. Beauty and brains and fear, all tied up in one very pretty, superglam package."

She began to tremble. "Got you? How?"

"I'm a guy, remember?"

She snorted, then was mortified. "Like anyone could forget."

He grinned. "I really wanted to sneak you down to my friend's yacht and spend the night talking and drinking and fooling around."

"You did?" She began to imagine just what they would do if they really did fool around.

"Yeah. I really wanted to." He paused, grim. "Nothing's changed, Claire."

She gaped.

He stared back.

"That's the problem, and I want it out in the open," he said.

Claire watched him walk away. He'd removed his jacket and was wearing a chambray button-down shirt, tucked into beige trousers. Nothing was fitted, but she knew what his body was like—it was the superbly conditioned body of an athletic man in his prime.

Claire unsteadily put down her flute. She'd finished it in under five minutes—had to be a first. She went up to him and laid her palm on his incredibly hard and wonderful back. "Why is it a problem?" she asked softly. "It's only a problem if you let it be."

He didn't turn. "One does not mix business with pleasure."

"Why not?"

He turned. Their gazes locked. "I know you're not really the wacky lady you pretend to be. Sometimes I see this frightened little girl in your eyes. It disturbs me, Claire."

She trembled. "How can you possibly see her? She's gone, Ian. I'm a grown woman now."

"I see her. And I don't know if I'm man enough to protect her from what she's afraid of."

Claire inhaled hard.

So did he.

A clock began ticking in the room—either that or it had been ticking all along and only now was resonant and audible. "I'm a big girl. I won't break."

"Damn right," he said. "I won't hurt you, Claire. Not now, and not tomorrow."

He was rejecting her. In a goddamned heroic way.

"Don't look at me that way," he exclaimed softly. His palm cupped her face. "You pretend to be tough and strong, but right now you're crying inside, and I can see the tears as clearly as if they were falling down your face."

She pressed her face more fully into his hand, and her lips opened on the soft flesh in the middle of his palm. "Okay. There's a place inside that hurts. I didn't mean to find you so attractive. The plan was to protect my father. And William. I swear. But it happened, Ian, it happened, and I like you, and I'm stuck."

"I like you, too," he said. He looked down and she looked up.

Claire had never wanted a kiss more. Just a single lousy kiss. Except it wouldn't be lousy. Claire knew that if he kissed her, her world would never be the same.

This was the moment.

He put both hands on her shoulders, as if to keep her—or him—at bay. "You're growing on me, Red. Wisecracks and all. Let's make a deal."

"What kind of deal?" she asked, at once elated and dismayed by his words.

"We're partners, real partners, from now until we bring Elgin in." He smiled a little at her, but there was uncertainty in his eyes.

"Go on," she whispered, hope flaring.

"No funny business."

"No hanky-panky. And?"

"When this is over, we go out on a real date. I'll even bring you flowers when I pick you up." He smiled a little at her.

Claire bit her lip. "Red roses or white?"

"Whichever you prefer."

"White."

"White," he agreed.

"And Godiva."

He sighed. "And Godiva."

"Where will this date be?" she asked.

His eyes finally widened. "What a little negotiator! Your choice."

She grinned then. "Hmm. Sydney, Australia."

"You're kidding, right?"

"Well, I was, but now that I think about it, I have never been Down Under."

"Claire . . ."

"Okay. Beijing."

He laughed. "Beijing. You do realize we might not get visas?"

"You have clout."

"I forgot."

She became serious. "Is this a promise?"

"Only if you do not keep trying to seduce me," he said.

"Trying to seduce you?" She pulled away, incredulous. "I have not tried, not even once, to seduce you."

"Like hell," he retorted. "You've been parading around with those red toes and those gray eyes and those tiny clothes of yours, not to mention the body, and what about my T-shirt? Like now?" His eyes flashed.

"Like now? Last night I understand; I was naked underneath." What was he talking about?

He groaned.

She was pleased. "But I have jeans on, Ian, so don't go telling me your T-shirt is an attempt at seduction!" She had to laugh.

He crossed his muscular arms over his chest. "Okay. I won't. So put on a bra."

"Excuse me?" she said in disbelief, no longer laughing.

"Don't tell me you are not strutting around braless on purpose."

"I came out of the shower, and who the hell wears a bra when they're going to sleep?"

"It's six o'clock at night!"

"But we're staying in! I didn't sleep on the plane! I'm going to bed! Besides, I'm no Pamela Anderson!" She could hardly believe he was distracted by such a simple issue.

"You're about one million times better than any Pamela Anderson. Christ! I'm going for a walk. I'll bring back something to eat. Try to get decent, will you? Or you'll make me a very crotchety old man before my time."

Claire stared as he marched out of their room, slamming the door. Then she ran to it and cracked it. "You don't have to be crotchety, you know. We can always renegotiate."

He ignored her, walking downstairs.

And breathless, Claire closed the door, leaning on it, filled with giddy delight. He thought her a seductress.

It was a first.

"I have a hangover," she said in a thick, unhappy tone.

"That's what you get for drinking an entire bottle of champagne while I was out looking for food."

"That's what men do. Bring home the bacon. Gather berries. Hunt mammoths. And I did not drink the entire bottle." God, her head hurt. The sun was way too bright. Claire closed her eyes tightly.

"I had one glass."

"Well, you upset me."

He turned off the motorway onto a two-lane country road. "That was not my intention, Claire, and you know it." He glanced at her. "And I don't think you were upset. You loved our little deal."

"I cannot trade quips with you today," she said, almost meaning it.

"Thank God," he said, and clearly he meant it.

Claire groaned to herself.

"Should I pull over?" He sounded amused and not at all concerned. He was enjoying her hangover.

"I am not going to barf."

"Well, that's a relief."

"I need food."

"But you passed on breakfast."

"I'm a vegan."

"Since when? Two seconds ago?"

"Since last night." Claire opened her eyes and found a PowerBar in her purse. She hadn't even eaten last night, because jet lag combined with the champagne had caused her to fall asleep by the time he had returned. Or had she passed out? In any case, the effect was the same. She hadn't heard him come in, and the next thing she had known, the alarm clock was going off and a grinning Ian was not so gently rousing her.

Claire dug into the peanut-butter-flavored PowerBar. She had not been able to face the smorgasbord of eggs and sausage an hour ago. She hadn't even been able to take a sip of coffee. Now coffee sounded great. "Can we find a cup of java?"

Ian patted her back. "Feeling a bit better, are we?"

"Don't gloat."

He laughed. "I'm not gloating. I'm commiserating. This is our turnoff. If you're lucky, Lady Elgin will have coffee in the house."

Claire saw a white sign with Welsh words that she could not sound out, much less read. "Why does she live way out here when Elgin Hall is outside of London?"

"The National Trust owns Elgin Hall, and it's open to the public a few days a week. Most of these old aristocratic families are broke, and they can't afford to keep up their ancestral homes. Her family seems to go back to the earliest Marcher lords. Why she lives out here, I don't know. Maybe because it's more affordable."

They entered a long, winding private drive. The grounds were unkempt and overgrown, with clusters of towering elms and oaks, and here and there what once might have been gardens and were now patches of bushes and weeds. Claire imagined the grounds as they might have been a half a century ago. Undoubtedly the area had been a vast and magnificent sweep of lawns and gardens. They passed a gleaming pond. Claire blinked in surprise when she saw a pair of swans gliding upon it.

A charming stone manor with a timbered roof and two corner towers came into view. A car was parked in front, but other than that, there was no sign of activity or life. Ian whistled as he parked their Fiat next to it. "An antique Rolls. That baby's worth a small fortune."

"She needs a new paint job," Claire remarked as they got out of their rental car.

"And probably a complete overhaul under the hood," Ian said, studying the car. "I can't help wondering how old she is."

Claire looked at him. She knew he was hoping that the car dated back to the war—and that Lionel Elgin had ridden in it. "You're a romantic guy, aren't you?" she said.

"Not really," he responded as they went up to the front door.

"You don't have to believe in true love or knights in shining armor to be romantic."

"Let's not debate the definition of the word," Ian said. The door opened.

Claire hadn't known what she expected. What she had not expected was this gray-haired little old lady with the surprising bright brown eyes, who had to be the mistress of the house.

As surprised, Ian said, "Lady Elgin?"

She was smaller than Claire. She smiled, revealing perfect dentures. "Mr. Marshall? Do come in. I have been waiting all morning for you."

Lady Elgin led them into a large living room, offering them a choice of tea or coffee and telling them that she had been so looking forward to their visit. The room was falling apart and badly needed new flooring and fresh paint, but Claire took one look at the antiques, then another look at the frescoed ceiling, and a third at the original art on the wall. There were even two crystal and brass chandeliers. The rugs would probably go for tens of thousands of dollars. She felt as if they had truly stepped through the window of time into another era and another way of life.

Then Claire saw the sterling silver tray of baked pastries that had been placed on one of three coffee tables in the room. Her stomach growled at the sight of so many scones and muffins. Clearly she was on the mend. "Please, Mr. Marshall, Mrs. Hayden, do sit down," Lady Elgin said happily.

Claire sat down on a pale green chair with claws for feet, tufts of stuffing coming through the faded silk upholstery. A servant who was old enough to be Claire's mother poured coffee as Ian sat down on a cream-colored damask settee. The servant used a cane. Lady Elgin took a chair similar to Claire's and smiled. "Please, do have a bite to eat. It's so pleasant to have visitors from the United States."

"Thank you," Claire said. "I cannot be shy." She picked up and bit into a raisin scone that was as close to heaven as she could get on that particular morning.

"Your friend is hungry," Lady Elgin remarked to Ian, appearing pleased.

"My friend drank too much champagne last night," Ian said pleasantly, but he did send Claire a grin.

"Oh, I do so love champagne," Lady Elgin said with a sigh of nostalgia. "I remember when we were first married and Randolph spoiled me with La Grand Dame."

Claire made a mental note to send her a bottle along with a thank-you card. "You have a beautiful home," Claire said when her mouth was no longer full. "I've never actually been in a home like this—it's almost like there are ghosts in the room with us, there's so much history permeating everything."

Ian gave her an incredulous look.

"I've always loved this place," Lady Elgin said. "It's so peaceful here. If there are ghosts, they are happy ones. My memories are of my childhood and those first few years of my marriage, before Randolph disappeared." She sobered.

Claire raised both brows and glanced at Ian—they had a very willing subject.

Ian said, "Childhood memories are often the best memories. Lady Elgin, can we ask you a few questions? I'd also like to show you a few photographs."

"Of course. That's why you came. To ask me about that traitor, Lionel." She was eager and unblinking and amazingly calm.

"I am sorry for the grief his treason must have caused you and your family," Ian said. He took out a small state-of-the-art tape recorder. "May I record our conversation?"

"Of course." She beamed at him and then at Claire.

Ian turned it on while Claire reached for another scone. "You'll get fat," he remarked.

She smiled, because she knew he was teasing her. "Then we can cancel Beijing."

"I don't think so."

She was very pleased.

"The two of you are traveling to China?" Lady Elgin said with apparent delight. "How wonderful. I have always wished to visit the East."

"Actually, we'll probably substitute SoHo for Beijing," Claire said.

Lady Elgin blinked in confusion, and Ian said, "Lady Ellen Elgin, stepmother of Lionel Elgin, April twenty-sixth, 2001, nine-thirty A.M." He smiled at her, but before he could speak, she said, "You know, there was so little family grief when the rumors began. I do thank God that Randolph was not alive to hear those rumors. I myself did not care. In fact, Lionel's treachery hardly surprised me."

"Randolph, your husband," Ian said.

"Yes."

"You speak as if you know that he died. I thought he disappeared, and his disappearance was never resolved?" Ian asked.

"I know something terrible happened to him," Lady Elgin declared stoutly. "It was absolute hollyhock that he ran off to join the Germans. My husband was a patriot, Mr. Marshall, from the day the war began. I told that to everyone, I might add."

Claire saw Lady Elgin was indignant, even after all these decades, and touched her hand lightly. "They never solved his disappearance?" she asked softly.

"No, they never did," she said, calming down. "Before the war, he was somewhat admiring of Hitler. But so many of us were! You see, it was the communists who were the real threat in the thirties. Once we went to war, Randolph was Hitler's most avid opponent." She nodded decisively. "He was a fan, a friend, and a supporter of Churchill. The prime minister even dined with us once at Elgin Hall."

"I believe you," Claire said. She glanced at Ian, and he gave her a look that she understood: he wanted her to take over the interview. Claire smiled at Ellen Elgin. "Lady Elgin, do you have any ideas of what happened to your husband that summer? It was 1940, I believe?"

"Yes, it was 1940. I last saw him on a Friday night in early August. He went out rather early in the day, as he usually did. I assumed he was off to the club and the Lords. But he never came home," she said, eyes wide. "It was just horrible. Briefly, the police seemed to think he had been murdered, but they never found his body. To this day, I wish they had discovered what really happened to him."

Claire patted her hand again. "I am so sorry that you had to live with such an unresolved tragedy your entire life," she said, meaning it.

Lady Elgin sighed. "One survives," she said simply.

"Yes, one does. I lost my husband recently. It was very unexpected. One does go on."

"I am sorry," Lady Elgin said, meeting her gaze. "But you were no longer in love with him, were you?"

Claire started. Then she glanced at Ian, growing uneasy. "No, I was not."

Lady Elgin smiled at Ian before looking back at her. "I do believe that there is a reason for everything, my dear." This time, she patted Claire's hand.

Claire could not believe that this little old lady had put two and two together so easily. She could feel herself flushing. Were her feelings so obvious? "Tell us about Lionel."

"There's not much to tell. He was a peculiar boy and an even more peculiar young man."

"Peculiar how?"

Lady Elgin shrugged. "He was very cool, very remote. I doubt red blood ran in his veins."

"You didn't like him," Claire said, a bit surprised. After all, they were family.

"No, I did not. Few, if anyone, did."

Claire nodded. "Were you at all close? He was your stepson."

"We were not close," she said stiffly. "He was too odd. Let me see. He was nine, I believe, and I was eighteen when I married Randolph. I do recall trying to befriend him initially, but he laughed at me for my kindness. Not overtly, but the laughter and the scorn were in his eyes. I do hope he is dead," she said as if commenting on the color of the flowers on the side table.

Claire's radar went up. "Why?"

"Well, do they not claim he was a spy for the Germans during the war?"

"Yes, they do," Claire said. But she sensed that Lady Elgin's antipathy went deeper than that.

Ian suddenly said, "Did you ever meet my uncle, Lady Elgin? He was an American in the RAF, and he was in love with—and eventually married to—Lionel's cousin, Rachel Greene."

She blinked and smiled. "Eddy Marshall? Of course I met Eddy, but only once. They spent Christmas Eve here, and that was the first time I'd seen Rachel in years. Oh, they were such a lovely couple, and they were so in love! She was so pretty and so kind, and she was in the women's auxiliary air force, you know, and he was so dashing and so handsome. It was just wonderful seeing them together." She hesitated. "Lionel did not like him. I feel certain it was because he had feelings for Rachel."

Claire looked at Ian, who stared back at her. Then Claire faced her hostess. "What do you mean?"

"Lionel clearly did not like Eddy. That evening was so tense. I could see he wasn't pleased to learn that Rachel had married him secretly. I think, in his own odd way, Lionel loved her himself."

Claire was still. So was Ian. Then Ian said, "I hadn't realized their marriage was secret."

Lady Elgin nodded. "I am sure it had to do with her being Jewish. I only met her father once, but he was a difficult man. Very set in his ways."

Claire almost fell off her chair. Ian seemed equally stunned. "Rachel Greene was Jewish? But . . . how was that?"

"My husband's sister ran off with Rachel's father, and was disowned."

"Wow," Claire said, her mind spinning. She could barely begin to imagine the Romeo and Juliet story of Rachel's parents, and then Rachel must have gone through the very same thing.

"It was a terrible scandal for the Elgin family," Lady Elgin continued. "That was well before I ever married Randolph, but I was present when he tried to reconcile with the Greenes. There was no reconciliation to be had. It was far too bitter and far too late."

Ian seemed to be dying to speak. He was leaning forward in his chair, his eyes glittering. After a pause, he said, "You were one of the last people to see Eddy alive."

"Yes. He disappeared that night, and I believe his body was found somewhere not far from Elgin Hall a few weeks later. It was so terrible, especially for poor Rachel."

Claire could imagine Rachel's frenzy, hysteria, and later, grief. For if Eddy had been at all like Ian, the loss would have been too terrible to bear.

She stiffened, stunned by her own train of thought.

Ian said, "Do you have any idea what could have happened?"

"No, I do not," Lady Elgin whispered. "But it was such a tragedy. He was a fine young man. And he was a famous pilot, a real RAF hero. And then to have Rachel die the way that she did, a year later . . ." She trailed off. "Perhaps it was for the best, as they were so in love. Maybe she did not want to live without him." Lady Elgin shrugged.

"Rachel Greene died a year later?" Claire gasped, sharing a look with Ian, who was also stunned.

"Yes, she did. In fact, I do believe the last time I saw Lionel was at her funeral, which was over the holidays in the winter of 'forty-one." Lady Elgin frowned. "He did not shed a tear, but I could tell that he was very upset."

"Over the holidays," Ian echoed. "You mean, like Eddy, she died around Christmas?"

"I believe so."

"How did she die?" Claire asked, shivering. She had a very unpleasant feeling now.

"She was hit by a car," Lady Elgin said.

"Where do you want to have breakfast?" Claire asked when they were ensconced in their tiny rental car after she had won their brief argument about whose turn it was to drive.

"Very funny. You ate three scones."

"I'm starved," Claire said, lying. She had no appetite. She was so sad. And on top of everything, Lady Elgin hadn't been able to identify anyone in the photos Ian had shown her. "I need beef."

"Beef? It's eleven in the morning. What happened to the veggie thing?"

"That was yesterday," Claire said.

"You mean this morning," Ian corrected.

"Look at the map," Claire ordered instead. "Let's have our date somewhere on the sea." She drove down the driveway, thoroughly shaken. Had Rachel's death really been an accident?

He stared at her and shook his head. "You're not serious. Not about the date. About beef."

"You're right—I ate three scones, and there's mad cow disease." Her smile fell apart in spite of her best intentions. "I'm trying to distract you," she said.

"I know," he said quietly, "and you don't have to be so upbeat when I can see the sadness in your eyes."

"I'm wearing black sunglasses!"

"Claire."

"All right." She glanced at him. "I smell a rat. And his name is Elgin."

Ian was silent for a moment. Then he said, "Look, Claire, we'll probably never know if Rachel was an innocent accident victim or not. However, I can't even begin to tell you how many innocent civilians were injured or killed by motorists because of the blackout during the war."

"Really? Or are you just saying that?"

"Really."

She glanced at him as they cruised down the country road, heading for the motorway. "It is a big coincidence, first Eddy, then Rachel."

"Maybe. Maybe not."

"You're holding out on me, Marshall. I can sense it. There's something you're not telling me." Claire exited onto the A525, going north, paying attention to the traffic cruising ahead.

As she did, Ian glanced behind them.

She glanced once in the rearview mirror but then focused on merging into the traffic. "So what shakes, Dick?"

"Nothing. Who the hell is Dick?"

"Dick Tracy."

Claire caught him glancing over his shoulder again. "Claire, move back into the right lane," he said quietly.

Claire didn't like his soft, calm tone. She glanced into her mirror and saw that a BMW which had gotten onto the motorway with her had moved into the left lane behind her. She signaled with her blinker. "Ian, we're not being followed. That only happens on TV."

"Just move into the right lane and let's find out. Speed up while you're at it."

He was for real. He thought that someone was following them. Her heart sank as she obeyed, slipping into the center lane while increasing her speed. She looked into her rearview mirror, and for a moment, nothing happened. Claire pressed down on the accelerator, eating up the distance between her and the next car—leaving the BMW behind.

She was relieved. She turned to smile at Ian. "Nuts. I really thought this was my big break. Did I ever tell you my secret dream is to be an actress? An action heroine?"

"Shit," Ian said.

At the same time, Claire saw the big black car out of the corner of her eye. The BMW swerved abruptly, weaving in and then out of the left lane, slowly but surely catching up to them. "We're being followed," she whispered, stunned.

"Yes, we are. Stay calm," Ian said.

"Easier said than done," she muttered, because her hands had become wet on the steering wheel. "What should I do?" The BMW was keeping one car length behind them, even though Claire had changed lanes again.

"We'll get off at the next exit," Ian said calmly. He sounded almost bored.

They had just passed the exit for Rhuddlan Castle. Claire nodded and looked in the mirror again. The driver was so close she could see that he wore aviator-style sunglasses.

The driver blared his horn at them. Ian was twisting to look. "Do you know him?" Claire asked hoarsely.

"No," Ian said as the BMW came abreast of them.

Dread washed over her in sickening waves. Claire turned her head, too—and was met with the direct and reflective stare of the driver of the BMW. She realized that he was gesturing to them. He wanted her to pull over to the shoulder of the road.

Claire's fear skyrocketed.

"Don't pull over," Ian said. "Keep up your speed. Ignore him now. And when I tell you to go, pop onto the shoulder and hit the brakes. Jam into reverse and back up to the Rhuddlan exit."

Sweat trickled into her eyes. "Okay," Claire whispered, clenching the steering wheel. Could she do as Ian asked? What if she destroyed the gears? She was a good driver, but could she reverse at high speed without causing an accident?

"You can do it, Claire," Ian said matter-of-factly.

Claire nodded, not sure if she believed him or not.

"Go," Ian said.

Claire didn't think. She wrenched the wheel hard and swerved onto the shoulder of the road, slamming on the brakes. They screamed. Tires burned. The BMW sped past.

Claire jammed into reverse, hit the gas, and began driving backward along the shoulder. Horns blared at her from the passing cars on her side of the road.

Claire didn't have to look forward to realize that the BMW had gotten off the road, was also on the shoulder, and pursuing her in reverse.

Still in reverse and on the shoulder of the road, Claire passed the exit. More rubber squealed and burned as she slammed on the brakes and shifted into first. Facing them was the BMW, reversing at an impossible speed, seemingly intent on ramming them from the front.

"Go, Claire," Ian shouted. "Go, damn it, go."

She shot forward, wrenching the wheel and turning onto the exit ramp, missing impact with the other car by centimeters. Tires squealed again. Claire knew the other driver was doing exactly what she had done.

Sweat was pouring into her eyes. Claire floored the gas pedal. A stop sign was ahead. "Don't stop, he's right behind us," Ian shouted at her.

"Shit" was Claire's reply, because the intersection was not empty.

Two cars had just entered it as Claire shot through. Both vehicles veered away from her to avoid a collision and almost collided into each other instead.

Claire swerved around the pair, straightened out, and stomped down on the gas.

"Good driving, Claire," Ian said, relief in his tone.

"Fuck," Claire said in reply. The Fiat flew over the now bumpy road. She looked back. The BMW was going around the two stopped cars, and he was farther behind her now. "What does he want?" she cried.

"He wants me."

Claire had to look at him.

"Watch the road!" Ian shouted, grabbing the steering wheel and straightening them out. "We need to get to the next village. We'll be safe there. We need to ditch the car, call the police, and stay in public."

Claire faced forward grimly. They were on a country road, just one lane in either direction, with no clear demarcation in the center. "Is there a village on this road—" she started to ask, when Ian cursed and the Fiat jerked abruptly forward, hit from behind.

Claire screamed, looking in her mirror—the BMW was back.

This time the driver was going to ram them until they spun out or crashed.

Ian cursed, moving to hold the wheel with her. He looked back. "Watch out—here he comes!"

Claire held the wheel as hard as she could and felt another huge impact from behind.

This time it was so brutal that the wheel was wrenched out of both of their hands, and the Fiat, going fifty or sixty miles an hour, went screaming into a 360-degree spin.

Claire felt her head and neck snap from whiplash as the little car spun around and around, rubber burning, trees and bushes whirling in her vision, and then it veered off the other side of the road, hitting a huge bump. Claire realized what was happening—the road paralleled a ravine of some sort. She screamed again when the Fiat shot into the air as if launched by a catapult.

It landed with a thud, bouncing again, spraying water, landing a final time, and coming to a quivering standstill.

Claire sat there, paralyzed.

Ian spoke first. "Are you okay?"

Claire didn't know. The car sat in a small creek or river. She wiggled her shoulders. Christ. She seemed to be intact. "I think so."

The water was just lapping the hood of the car.

Ian was already unrolling the window, then reaching for and unsnapping her seat belt. "C'mon. Through the window. Now."

Suddenly Claire heard the sound of a car door closing—above and behind them.

Breathless, Claire watched Ian shove his considerable frame through the window. The seconds seemed to be ticking by. She craned her neck around but could not see onto the bank above them. "Hurry, Ian," she whispered.

He made it. Claire followed quickly, easily. The frigid waters of the Clwyd stunned her, taking her breath away. Ian gripped her hand as they found their footing and started slugging through the waist-high water to the opposite bank.

The water began popping around them.

"Hold your breath, Claire!" Ian shouted, as Claire realized they were being shot at by a gun with a silencer. She inhaled as Ian pulled her under water with him.

It was pitch black beneath the surface. The water was rippling around them; Ian continued to hold her hand. And then the ripples stilled. Claire's eyes began to adjust to the darkness, and she could finally see Ian's hands, his face. She made out his eyes. Ian tugged on her hand and she nodded and they crawled along the bottom on all fours, continuing in the direction they had been going before.

Her lungs began to beg for air. They hurt. Claire tugged on Ian's foot. He understood, and together they lurched upward and through the surface of the water, gasping for air.

The Clwyd wasn't wide, and they were only two feet from the opposite bank and knee-deep in water. They staggered through the last bit and up onto the muddy embankment, still panting.

Claire glanced over her shoulder as Ian pulled her forward and into a run. On top of the ravine on the other side of the Clwyd stood the driver of the Mercedes, a huge and frightening silhouette in dark clothing. Claire watched him raise the gun. "Ian!"

They dove into a line of several trees, and the dirt began popping up all around them. Grass and dirt were flying.

The pings stopped. So did the bursting of the earth. Ian and Claire crouched behind a tree that was just too narrow to provide any comfort or protection. Ian wrapped one arm around her. "Listen to me."

She met his gaze, nodding, unable to speak.

"We're going to have to make a run for the ruins. We can hide there—try to trap him. When we get there, we split up. Don't worry. Just find a spot to hide. I'll try and come up on him from behind."

"That's the plan?" she managed. "You don't have that gun with you, do you?"

"I can't carry it out of the States," he said, holding her gaze. "Claire." He touched her face. "It will be okay. I promise."

Time slammed to a standstill. Claire looked into his eyes and knew he meant his words and felt herself fall hopelessly for him.

"Let's go," Ian ordered, as if he were a marine.

Claire looked back and saw the gunman scrambling down the ravine, about to wade or swim through the river.

Claire looked ahead. A wide-open expanse of green faced her—and beyond that, the ruins of the castle.

They ran.

They ran across the meadow, Claire praying that there would be tourists at the ruins. The car park was on the other side of the fortifications, so she couldn't see if any cars were parked there or not. She hated Ian's plan—she didn't want to split up—but she knew it was the only way to save their lives.

Claire glanced over her shoulder, stumbling on the uneven ground as Ian pulled her at an impossible speed—he was stronger and faster than she was. The gunman was emerging from the river, and now he was running up the bank. In a moment he would hit the stand of trees they had just left.

Claire gasped raggedly and drove her aching legs even harder. They reached one of the first sections of broken wall and darted behind it. Ian grabbed her by both shoulders, and their gazes locked. "Go left. Hide behind anything you can. Just stay there."

Claire nodded fearfully. Before she could tell him to be careful, he disappeared around another section of wall.

Fear overcame her. Claire did as he had told her, turning left around another corner, and another, until she could see into the heart of the ruins and past that into the car park. It was deserted. She wanted to collapse and cry.

Claire backed between two jutting sections of stone, crouching down. She was so afraid. Ian was unarmed. And even though he had said the gunman was after him, Claire wasn't so sure. They were in this together, after all—she knew so much. And then she heard the footsteps.

She knew they weren't Ian's.

Claire picked up a rock and tried her best to melt into the stone wall at her back, praying the gunman would walk right past without ever seeing her. She raised the rock in case he did not. Waiting for him to step around the corner on her right.

Silence.

It yawned about her.

Vast. Frightening.

Claire's own heartbeat was now interfering with her ability to hear.

Worse, her labored breathing was loud and resonant—giving away her position.

Claire knew he was close. She could feel him. Every hair stood up on her body. She held her breath.

He stepped out from an adjacent wall on her left.

Claire looked into the muzzle of the gun. It was pointing directly at her.

Then she looked at the gloved hand holding the gun—and she saw the finger on the trigger. Then she looked up, into the man's face, into his eyes.

She didn't know him, but their eyes met and held, and she knew she was looking into the eyes of death.

He fired.

PART
TWO

SARAH'S CHOICE

CHAPTER 7

North Wales, summer 1935

They had changed trains at Oswestry, and the closer they got to their final destination—they were being met at the rail station in Ruthin—the quieter and quieter Papa became. Rachel kept glancing anxiously at him. He no longer pretended to read the *Daily Mail,* which he had brought from Aldgate Station in London. The newspaper had fallen to the floor hours ago and had gotten tromped upon by his recently polished shoes. Papa's reading glasses hung upon his chest, and he stared out of their window at the countryside.

Rachel didn't know what to do. Sarah, who was sixteen, was making paper dolls with Hannah, who was turning six in another two days. Both sisters were smiling and it was nice to see. In fact, Sarah was starting to look like herself again. The weight she had lost when Mama died was finally returning. Her cheeks were filling out again, her hips had a womanly curve, and the sparkle Rachel was so accustomed to seemed to have reappeared in her hazel eyes. Hannah, however, had been the most inconsolable when Mama died—after Papa, that is. She had refused to speak for several weeks and had to be forced to eat. Now she was actually giggling as she made her paper doll dance and pirouette. Rachel was relieved to see her older and younger sisters so cheerful.

She didn't know if she would ever be cheerful again.

Rachel shot another worried glance at Benjamin Greene. He was a handsome man in his late thirties with dark hair that was showing threads of silver at the temples and in his beard. He was a good man, Rachel knew, honest, godly, and hardworking. He owned a shoe store and a leather-goods factory. Growing up, he had been a cobbler like his father. Hard work, long hours, and frugality had paid off. Rachel had never known a time when she did not have a clean dress, new shoes, piano lessons, and plenty of food. There were even cinema tickets once a month for the entire family. For as long as she could remember, they had lived in a small, pleasantly furnished house with a little backyard on Fournier Street in East London. Fournier Street was a few blocks north of Brick Lane, the road made famous a half century before by Jack the Ripper. Papa owned the house and rented half of it to their neighbors, the Schwartz family. The Greenes had a parlor, one bathroom, two bedrooms, and a kitchen. They had an old stove, but Mama had insisted on a new refrigerator. Like the house, their backyard was evenly divided, but the whitewashed fence was low, and in good weather, both families often sat outside after dinner, reading the day's papers and weeklies or playing a game of checkers or horseshoes.

Papa was an observant Jew. He observed the Sabbath as his father had before him and his father before that—on that holy day they did not cook, read, work, or even use electricity, and anyone who decided to go anywhere did so by walking on their own two feet. Even an emergency caused no exceptions. The Sabbath was God's day. Privately, Rachel thought it quite bothersome, but she kept her irreligious thoughts to herself. Sarah had recently defied Papa on the Sabbath— she had used her bicycle to meet some friends. Papa had almost hit her, but Rachel had begged him not to, and in the end, he had realized some of Sarah's stubbornness might be an offshoot of Mama's illness and death.

Papa treated others fairly and often gave to those less fortunate than himself. He believed his success and bounty in life were due to living in an honest and morally upright way.

Rachel had thought so, too. Until recently. For now there was a huge problem. Why had God let Mama die?

Mama had been the kindest, nicest person Rachel knew, and she had not deserved to die at the age of thirty-five. Papa did not deserve such a loss, either. It made no sense. Rachel no longer understood God.

Papa suddenly realized she was staring at him, because he glanced at her, and their eyes met. Rachel was so distraught now, her musings adding to her worries, that she could not smile at him. Papa looked at his other two daughters. He seemed to soften when he saw that Sarah and Hannah were enjoying themselves. Then he turned and took Rachel's hand, squeezing it. "Don't be thinking so hard, Rachel-lay. You'll be having frown lines before you be twenty."

Rachel finally smiled, wanting so badly to make him smile, and the pain of it hurt her the way a knife might. "I'll try not to think so hard, Papa," she whispered. "But it's not easy, you know."

Their eyes held. "Mama's happy today," Benjamin said roughly. "You know that, don't you?"

Rachel felt a lump of grief rising up in her and couldn't speak, so she nodded instead. She wished Papa would not talk about Mama as if she were still alive.

Benjamin smiled once at her—a bit grimly— and said, "A few more minutes and we'll be at Ruthin." He turned away to gaze out at the sheep on the hills again, but he continued to hold her hand.

Tears flooded Rachel's eyes. It was so unfair. Her whole life, Mama had wanted nothing more than to have peace between her and her brother, Randolph Elgin. But there had only been bitterness and anger, and Rachel knew very well why. Because Mama had married Papa, a Jew, and the rich and fancy Lord Elgin was a terribly mean and prejudiced man.

Rachel wondered if he was one of those Blackshirts. A few months ago, she and Sarah had been on their way home from school, which was held in the synagogue on Whitechapel High Street. They had turned a corner and come face-to-face with a parade of men in black uniforms, holding banners that vilified the communists, the Jews, Labour, and even Neville Chamberlain. Bobbies lined the street, with their hands on their nightsticks, but Rachel had been frightened anyway. The parade of men seemed ominous, as if foretelling some terrible disaster. Even Sarah, who was always audacious and never afraid, had been pale and speechless. Ultimately the girls had hurried home another way. Neither one had ever spoken of what they had seen.

Rachel knew that she had been to the Elgin home once when she was very little and just beginning to walk. She could not remember the visit, although Sarah claimed that she could recall white marble floors and a beautiful woman playing the piano. That would have been Elgin's first wife. But they had never been invited back, not ever, and from time to time over the years, Rachel would hear Mama and Papa arguing. Their argument was always the same: Mama wanted to invite her brother and his family to dinner, and Papa would not hear of it. "They hate you now, Deborah, and when will you realize it?" Papa would finally shout. "His lordship's ashamed of you because you are now a Jew!"

The argument always ended the same way, with Mama crying first, and then Papa. It was horrible.

Rachel knew Mama was somewhere watching over them all, because she loved them too much not to, even in death. And yes, Papa was right, Mama had to be happy now, even thrilled, because her brother, Randolph Elgin, had invited Papa and the girls to the country for a weekend. Finally, the two families would reconcile. But for Rachel, it was too late and horribly unfair.

How she missed Mama.

The train was slowing. Rachel blinked back tears just as Sarah nudged her with the toe of her patent-leather shoe. Rachel looked up and saw that Sarah's eyes were sparkling with excitement and her cheeks were flushed like berries. "We're almost there," Sarah said in her unusually husky voice.

"I think it's a ways to the manor house from the station," Rachel said, clasping her hands in her lap. She wished they weren't going, then was ashamed of herself for her cowardice and for betraying Mama's hopes and dreams.

"We are being met by a chauffeur, Rachel, and a motorcar. Can you believe it? I have to pinch myself to remind myself that this is real." Sarah was smiling. She was a beautiful young woman with dark blond hair, exquisite eyes, high cheekbones, and a full, rosy mouth. Rachel had noticed a few years ago how the boys looked at her; recently, men looked at her the very same way. Rachel found this open admiration for her sister fascinating. And Sarah, as a result, had become rather coy. She knew men adored her, and she seemed to enjoy it.

The train's whistle was blowing. Hannah had jumped onto Papa's lap. Rachel looked out of the window and saw that they were indeed entering the village. Her heart sank. In a few minutes, they would disembark, and after that, they would drive up to the country manor where Lord Elgin and his family were waiting.

Rachel was sick with apprehension.

And Papa knew. He patted her hand, Hannah still on his lap. "Don't think so hard," he whispered.

Rachel tried to smile and failed. "What if they still don't like us?"

His smile faded. "Just be yourself, Rachel-lay. And his lordship will love you almost as much as I do."

Rachel wanted to believe him, but she only had to recall all the times Mama had wept over her brother, and she could not.

The chauffeur wore a suit that was as fine as Papa's, and a peaked cap as well. He carried their bags for them, refusing to allow Papa to help. Rachel knew this was the way the rich lived, and it felt odd for them to be treated this way now. The chauffeur opened their doors for them. Sarah jumped in first, so eagerly that her skirts went flying about her thighs. Papa murmured an admonition that nobody heard, as Hannah was following Sarah into the backseat, squealing with excitement. Rachel glanced at Papa. He was so grim.

He doesn't want to be here, she thought with a pang. *He's only doing this for Mama.*

"Your turn, Rachel-lay," Papa was saying.

Rachel sent him a smile and slid onto the smooth, gleaming leather seat beside her sisters. Papa closed the door before the chauffeur could and went around to the front of the car to sit beside the driver.

"Look, a cow," Hannah cried.

None of the girls had ever been to the country before, but Rachel knew the difference between a cow and a pig. "Honey, that's a sow."

"It is?" Hannah seemed surprised. She was glancing all around the street. "Where is the chip shop?" she asked.

The chauffeur pulled out of the parking space in the lot behind the rail station. "No chip shop in Ruthin, little lady," he said.

"No chips?" Sarah asked, bemused. She glanced at Rachel. "Just how big is this town?"

"We've got about two thousand people," the chauffeur said proudly.

"Is there a cinema?" Sarah asked, holding back a snicker.

"Afraid not."

Sarah looked at Rachel again. *Aren't you glad you don't live here?* her eyes clearly said.

Rachel poked her, warning her not to be rude.

"How far is the manor?" Papa asked.

"About half an hour, if we don't get held up by farmers and their sheep. They like to cross a few kilometers out of town."

Now Sarah jabbed Rachel. "Are there any boys in this town?" she asked.

"Sarah." Papa turned to cast a stern glance at her.

Sarah pretended to be chagrined. "Just asking, Papa."

The driver knew better than to answer. He said, "This is only the second time his lordship and her ladyship have used the house here. We're all so pleased that they've come out to Wales. We're hoping they will like the house enough to come more often. It's awfully quiet without Lord and Lady Elgin."

Papa stared out of his window.

"So why do they keep the house if they never use it?" Sarah asked, leaning forward.

Papa turned. "Randolph Elgin inherited the house from his new wife, who is Welsh." His glance strayed briefly over Sarah. "I do believe Lady Ellen is not much older than you."

Sarah's eyes widened with a look of delight. "Really, Papa?"

"Do not get any ideas." He turned back around.

Sarah smiled. "Now why would I get ideas from my uncle marrying a girl a few years older than me?"

Rachel looked at her and turned to gaze out of her own window; they were leaving the small, quaint village behind. Sarah had always been a handful, but recently, she was becoming even more than that. She had started dating a young man who had emigrated from Germany and then joined the army. Every time Rachel saw Sarah and her handsome beau, she couldn't help thinking that, at twenty, he was too old and worldly for her. In truth, Rachel was afraid Sarah would do something terrible, like elope.

Papa turned to face the backseat again. "Listen closely, girls," he said. "I expect everyone to mind their manners. Be on your Sabbath best." His face was stern.

"Yes, Papa," they chorused in unison.

"No mischief." He looked at Sarah. "Randolph's got two boys about your age. I expect everyone to get along."

"We will, Papa," Rachel promised. In spite of herself, she was curious to meet her two cousins, Lionel, who was a year younger than she was, and Harry, who was a bit older than Sarah. Mama had shown them photos once. They were handsome boys with blond hair. Rachel had thought they looked like Mama.

"Make Mama proud," Papa said.

They were lined up in the entry to meet them. Lord Randolph Elgin was tall, thin, blond, and impeccably attired in his hunting clothes and knee-high boots. He looked as rich as any prince and as used to giving orders and being obeyed. He seemed a little older than Papa. In contrast, his wife seemed no more than twenty. Lady Ellen was black-haired, sloe-eyed, and very pretty, although not as pretty as Sarah. She was wearing more diamonds than Rachel had ever seen in her entire life, and more than she had thought any one woman could wear all at once. She wore a triple-tiered diamond necklace, dangling diamond ear bobs, a chunky diamond bracelet, and a diamond ring with a stone the size of Rachel's thumb. She glittered just like a diamond, Rachel thought, in her pale cream sateen dress. Rachel looked down at the woman's shoes. It was the middle of the day and she was wearing ivory shoes of sateen that matched her dress exactly. They had high heels. How did she walk?

A maid in a black uniform and a white apron stood behind her. She held Lady Ellen's two-year-old son in her arms. The little blond boy seemed to resemble his father; he was sucking his thumb and squirming to get down.

The older boys stood beside their father. They looked like miniature Lord Elgins, dressed similarly, both blond and blue-eyed and quite handsome.

Rachel took in her family in one blink of an eye and then, as Papa and Elgin shook hands stiffly, she gaped at the hall she found herself in.

It was hardly a manor, she thought, eyeing the huge paintings on the walls and the high, high ceilings. It seemed more like a castle. Indeed, there were swords and banners hung on one wall. She turned to look at Sarah. But Sarah was smiling at Harry Elgin. Harry was smiling back.

Rachel felt a pang. It wasn't jealousy, it was more like . . . longing.

Introductions were made all around, and the maid left to take little John off for a nap.

And then the two families stood facing each other, with several feet in between as if an invisible barrier lay there on the stone floor. No one spoke.

Rachel was aware of being uncomfortable, but on the other hand, she was trying to see past the Elgins and into a huge salon with gilded furniture and crystal chandeliers. Did real people live like this? Maybe the Elgins weren't real!

She smiled to herself. Maybe they were a figment of her imagination, and maybe being there, in the north of Wales, at this fancy house, was only a dream.

Her smile faded. Maybe she would wake up at home and Mama would still be alive.

A man coughed. It was their host. "I trust your trip was without event?"

Papa looked at him as if he spoke a foreign language or sported two heads. "It was without event," he said.

Rachel bit her lip. Elgin could not know that, in his own angry way, Papa mocked him. But Sarah knew, because she glanced at Rachel with worry. Rachel realized that Harry also suspected Papa of being sarcastic, as he was studying both men too closely. Her heart lurched. If only Papa were less angry! She was afraid of the conflict simmering inside him.

Elgin was speaking. "Lady Ellen will show you up to your rooms. We'll take tea as soon as you get settled; supper is at nine."

Rachel blinked. Supper was so late! They would all die of hunger well before nine. As if reading her thoughts, Harry glanced at her and gave her a reassuring smile. Startled, Rachel realized at once that he was a nice young man. She found herself smiling back at him.

"I've given you a wonderful room overlooking the gardens out back. From it, you can see the Clwyd and the ruins of Rhuddlan Castle," Lady Ellen told Papa eagerly.

Papa made a gruff sound, which meant thank you.

Sarah stepped forward. "Actually, I think I will take a stroll around the house. The gardens are so beautiful," she said. "And it's such a beautiful day, I can't bear to be inside."

Elgin seemed startled. For the first time, he really looked at Sarah. "Surely you have some things to unpack?"

"I'll unpack later," Sarah said with a quick smile.

Elgin just looked at her.

Rachel grew uneasy. She did not like his stare.

"That is, if you do not mind, Uncle Elgin?" Sarah asked, gazing back at him directly.

He seemed startled to be called "uncle."

Papa said, "Sarah, why don't you go upstairs and unpack first, as our host wishes?"

Elgin added, "If you unpack your evening gown now, it will be pressed and made ready for you. And anything else that you need for supper tonight."

"I can iron my dress in a tick," Sarah said, but more slowly. Rachel was wide-eyed herself. They would have maids to wait upon them?

Harry stepped forward. "I'll show her the grounds, Father," he said, his gaze on Sarah, not Elgin. Then he glanced at Rachel. "I'll show you both, if you like."

The last thing Rachel wanted to do was to go upstairs and unpack— she was curious to see an old ruined castle. It would be her first; there were no old castles where she lived. Exploring the grounds sounded wonderful. Rachel glanced at Papa with yearning.

He understood and faced Elgin. "The girls have been cooped up in the train all day. I think they'd like some fresh air and a bit of a stroll. Rachel and Sarah can press their own dresses. We don't believe in others doing our work for us."

Elgin nodded rigidly. He turned. "Ellen, see to it that their bags are brought up to their rooms." And then, as if he had not heard Papa, "Make certain someone can press my nieces' gowns."

"Of course," Lady Ellen said. "Bessie will be more than happy to do it." But there was a funny expression on her face. She hesitated.

Elgin turned. "Lionel? Why don't you join Harry as he escorts your cousins about the grounds." It was not a question.

"Yes, sir," Lionel said with no inflection at all. Briefly, his eyes strayed to Rachel, and their gazes met. It was awkward, as they were strangers, and Rachel quickly looked away. She wondered if he liked her family, disliked them, or had no feelings at all. She could not tell.

Rachel took Hannah's hand. "We're ready," she said brightly. Then a thought struck her. What was poor Papa going to do while they were out?

"Let's go, while the sun is high," Harry said, waiting for Sarah to pre-cede him. Sarah smiled at him as she walked past, and Rachel was well aware of the flirtation.

She did not move. "Papa? Sarah can take Hannah and I can help you unpack."

His eyes softened for the first time since entering the old manor. "Go and have a good time," he said. "No one deserves it more."

"Are you certain?" Rachel whispered, not wanting the Elgins to hear. Of course they did. They were standing so close, and no one else was speaking.

Papa nodded.

Rachel smiled at their host and hostess, and with Hannah in tow, she followed Sarah to the door, Harry and Lionel trailing after them.

Behind her, she heard Lady Ellen say, "My lord?" She was breathless. "Maybe I should go with them?"

Rachel glanced over her shoulder and saw the plea on Ellen's face.

"Ellen, I prefer it if you make certain everything is in readiness for our guests," her husband said.

Rachel turned away, but not before she saw Ellen's face fall.

They trooped past a small lake where several swans were gliding by. No one spoke, but it wasn't as awkward as it had been a few minutes ago, inside the house with the adults. Rachel's steps slowed. How lovely the shady lake with the beautiful white swans was.

"Those are pretty ducks," Hannah said softly, clinging to Rachel's hand. She was beaming.

"They're swans, dear," Rachel said as softly. She had never seen a live swan before, but she'd seen them rendered in art and books, and she knew exactly what they were looking at.

"Well, they're pretty. I wish we could take one home," Hannah said.

Rachel was about to smile and chide her for such a thought when she felt eyes on her back. She shivered as she turned. Lionel was studying the sisters.

Rachel didn't know what to say, so she said, "Your swans are so beau-tiful."

"Thank you," Lionel replied. "They actually belong to my stepmother. Lady Ellen had them shipped here from the south of Wales. She likes swans." His eyes moved over her slowly.

Rachel didn't like his gaze. It was so intent and so opaque. She almost felt as if she were under a microscope, and that he was studying her, dissecting her, trying to understand how she worked, as if she were a machine.

"Hey." Harry and Sarah were ahead of them, turning onto a small meandering path that led through a grove of silvery birch trees. "Are you all right back there?" Harry called with a wave.

"We're fine," Rachel said gratefully, tugging on Hannah. "Let's go."

"I want to stay with the swans," Hannah said with a stubborn set to her chin.

Rachel realized the little girl was going to be pigheaded, and her heart sank. She glanced at Lionel. He smiled, but it was a strange smile, neither warm and inviting nor cold and forced.

"We can watch the swans," he said. "We can feed them if you like."

"What do they eat?" Hannah cried excitedly.

"Bugs," Lionel said, looking at Hannah. "And things on the bottom of the pond."

"I want to feed the swans."

Rachel was dismayed. She realized she didn't really like Lionel, or at least she didn't enjoy his company and would prefer to remain in one group. Then she heard Sarah's laughter. It was light and free. Rachel glanced ahead and saw Sarah with her hand on Harry's arm, her smile as bright and sunny as the day. Harry was also grinning. Apparently they were sharing some kind of joke.

Rachel was a bit alarmed. She told herself not to worry, as Sarah might be a bit reckless, but there was nothing she could do just then to get herself into trouble.

"She likes him. All the girls do. But then, he is Father's heir."

Rachel jerked and met Lionel's pale gray stare. "Surely any inheritance will be divided between you. You're both his sons," she said, meaning to be kind.

He looked at her as if she were a madwoman. "This is Great Britain. Inheritances are not shared. The oldest son gets everything. Oh, I forgot. You're not English, you wouldn't know."

Rachel stiffened. "I was born in London."

Lionel shrugged. "But you're a Jew."

Rachel hesitated. "I'm also English."

"Can you be both?" Lionel asked, brows raised.

"I think so. I mean, I know so," Rachel said, flustered.

Sarah was laughing again. Rachel glanced toward the path and saw her sister and Harry strolling down it, almost out of view. They were walking so closely that Sarah's skirts repeatedly brushed his thighs.

"I told you. All the girls like him. He will be baron next. He will have the entire Elgin estate."

Rachel studied Lionel but saw no jealousy in his eyes. "Is that how your laws work?"

He nodded.

"That is so unfair," Rachel exclaimed.

Lionel smiled then, clearly amused. "If estates were divided up, a family as old as ours would have nothing but the tiniest parcel of land."

Rachel absorbed that.

Hannah said, "I want to feed the swans."

Rachel glanced anxiously at the path, but Sarah and Harry were gone. "We had better go join them," she said. She heard how worried her own tone sounded.

"Why? Will your sister seduce my brother?"

Rachel whirled. "That is a horrid thing to say!"

He put his hands in the pockets of his tweed riding coat. "But Harry is highly moral. He will never seduce her. He will be a virgin on his wedding night, I assure you of that."

Rachel felt herself turning crimson. "Let's go, Hannah," she said.

But Hannah whined in protest.

"Why are you offended? I'm merely being truthful. Harry will be a lord one day, and he will take a wife. There are many fortune hunters thinking to ensnare him."

She almost strangled on her shock. "My sister is not one of them. She is . . . a romantic!"

Lionel smiled at her. "How absurd." He shrugged. "In any case, she has no chance with Harry."

Rachel felt herself flushing again. But now she was so angry. "Because she is a Jew?"

Lionel nodded, watching her closely.

"Your aunt married my father," Rachel pointed out.

"Only by running away and eloping. She lost her name, her title, and her fortune. Her parents disowned her. My father disowned her."

"I know what happened to my mother," Rachel said, tears coming to her eyes. But she hadn't known the extent of it, and she was shocked and angered by his words.

"Let's feed the swans," Lionel said lightly, glancing at Hannah. "Wait here." He turned and ran back toward the house.

"Is he a mean boy?" Hannah asked Rachel with curiosity.

Rachel wiped her eyes. "I don't think so. But sometimes the truth is mean, dear."

"But he was saying mean things about Mama."

Rachel stooped to hug her. "No, he was not."

"Then why are you crying?"

Rachel froze. She met her sister's dark eyes. Unlike Sarah and Rachel, Hannah had their father's swarthy complexion and dark, nearly black, hair. "I'm crying," Rachel said, feeling the bubble of grief rising, "because I still miss Mama and it hurts sometimes when we talk about her."

Hannah nodded solemnly. "I miss her too. But I want to feed the swans."

Rachel smiled and stroked the girl's curly hair. "We will. I expect Lionel went to get us some swan food." She hoped he did not intend to hand them bugs. And why had Sarah taken off with Harry like that? She had seen the look in her sister's eyes. She was more than flirting with him, she was taken by him.

Rachel made a mental note to tell Sarah that she would never stand a chance with Harry Elgin; not that Papa would ever let her marry a gentile, anyway.

"Here we go."

Rachel looked up at the sound of Lionel's voice, which was rather cheerful. In fact, the sound of it alarmed her. If she had learned one thing since arriving at the manor, it was that he did not have a particularly pleasant disposition.

He was carrying a small pail. He smiled at them and led them to the grassy, pebbled bank of the little lake. The swans began drifting toward them, their dark eyes bright with expectation.

Lionel dug into the pail.

"What are you feeding them?" Rachel asked warily.

Lionel opened his fist. In it lay a beautiful goldfish. It was alive.

"Can I? Can I?" Hannah asked excitedly.

Warning bells went off in Rachel's mind. "That fish is alive. And it's a goldfish. Surely you don't feed these swans goldfish!" she cried.

The fish began to flop in Lionel's palm, gasping for air. "Here," he said, ignoring her, handing it to Hannah. "This swan will eat anything, even your fingers, so throw it toward him carefully. He's very fast. He won't miss the fish."

Hannah was giggling, and before Rachel could react, she threw the tiny red and gold fish at the swan, which dove into the water for it. A moment later the big bird came up, the fish between its beak. It snapped the fish in two, then dove back into the water for the latter half of the fish.

Rachel looked at Lionel in shock. His eyes seemed to be laughing at her and Hannah both. She felt ill. Somehow she broke free of his gaze, and she grabbed the pail. Inside it was an assortment of beautiful, exotic, dying fish. "You took these out of an aquarium," she cried.

He shrugged. "So? Lady Ellen will buy more."

"They're your mother's fish?" Rachel gasped.

Lionel took the pail from her, reaching in. Rachel watched him take out a beautiful pale blue fish with yellow and orange fins. He tossed it to the waiting swan. "She's not my mother," he said calmly. "She's my step-mother."

Rachel jerked the pail from his hands and scooped it into the lake, filling it with water and trying not to lose any of the fish. She was relieved when she saw the colorful fish start to swim about in the pail. Slowly, she looked up.

Hannah had realized what was happening, and she was now grave. Lionel had his hands in his pockets, and he was watching her carefully.

"Here." Rachel extended the pail toward him. "You can put these back where they belong."

Lionel stared. "You do it," he said. And he turned and walked away.

CHAPTER 8

"Look at this dress! How can I wear it?" Sarah wailed dramatically.

Rachel was in Sarah's room. Like Papa's, it had views of the river and the old castle poised on the opposite bank. The view was stunning: a sweep of green hills and the river winding through. But Rachel didn't know where to look first, since Sarah's room was one of the most beautiful she had ever seen. The walls were painted a dark yellow, and all of the furniture was upholstered in yellows, blues, and greens. The four-poster bed was canopied, and there was a huge fireplace on one wall. The curtains were a dark green brocade that pooled on the floor. It was a room fit for a princess, not Sarah Greene.

Rachel's room was next door. It, too, was beautiful, all pale pink and mint green. The fact that the three sisters would all have separate rooms was also amazing.

Rachel turned away from the window to study her sister, who looked ready to cry. She was holding up a pale blue dress that was practically new. "That is a very nice dress," Rachel remarked calmly.

"It is not an evening gown, and I hate it," Sarah snapped. "How could Papa bring us here if we do not have the proper clothing?"

Rachel folded her arms. "That's quite enough, Sarah Greene. Don't you dare berate Papa now. You know how sad he is and how much he still misses Mama."

Sarah gave her a look and threw her dress onto the four-poster bed. The underside of the canopy was pleated in gold silk, while the rest of it was pale blue. "They will think we're farmers," Sarah said.

"No, they will think we're honest, hardworking, middle-class folk," Rachel returned. But now she was thinking about her conversation with Lionel. What they would really think is that they were Jews.

"Well, I suppose I have no choice if I wish to have supper with everyone," Sarah sighed. "At least the maid pressed the dress."

Rachel walked over to her as Sarah fingered the blue silk dress. "You will be beautiful in that dress, with Mama's pearls."

Sarah looked up. "Do you think so?"

"Yes, I do." Rachel smiled. Then, with worry, "Why did you and Harry go so far ahead of us? What were the two of you doing?"

Sarah began to smile. It was a somewhat smug and secretive smile. "We were just walking. And talking. He was telling me about his life. He is so interesting!"

Rachel folded her arms. "And handsome?"

"Did you notice?" Sarah gushed, her eyes shining.

"Sarah, he is not for you!" Rachel was now very alarmed. Her sister had stars in her eyes.

"Why not? Because we're poor and they're rich? Mama married Papa."

"And look at what it cost her. It cost her all of her family, Sarah. She had to give up her parents and her brother in order to marry Papa. And you know it!"

"But she loved Papa, and she was happy. You know that."

Rachel did know that Mama had loved Papa. But their arguments over the Elgins echoed in her mind—there had been too many of those arguments, just as there had been too many tears. And what about all the times that Mama, Rachel, and Sarah had been doing the dishes after dinner? Or cleaning the house? And what about Sunday, which was wash day? So often Mama had been so tired, and maybe so sad.

But she had never complained. Now, seeing how her mother had once lived, Rachel couldn't imagine how she couldn't have had some nostalgia for the life she had left behind. But if there had been regret, Rachel had never noticed it. "Yes, she loved Papa very much," Rachel said quietly.

"Harry thinks I am beautiful. I can tell by the way he keeps staring at me when he thinks I am not looking." Sarah gave her back to Rachel, who began to unbutton her dress.

"And what about Saul?" Rachel asked, referring to Sarah's new beau.

Sarah stepped out of her dress. "Truthfully, I have not given him a single thought since we arrived in that little village today."

"But you're in love with him," Rachel said, hoping it was true. Now

Saul didn't seem like such a bad choice, and in any case, he was safer, because he was Jewish and at least he and Sarah came from the same world.

"Not anymore," Sarah said after a pause. She sat down and undid her garters while rolling down her hose. "Aren't you going to get dressed?"

"Sarah." Rachel ignored the question, kneeling before her. "Harry will one day be a baron. He is an aristocrat and a gentile. He will never be serious about you. No good can come of this flirtation."

Sarah flushed. "Mama married Papa."

Rachel stood, incredulous. "Is that what you are thinking? To marry Harry? So he can be disowned? So you can both be disowned? Papa will disown you, too!"

"I hadn't even thought about it," Sarah said fervently. "But maybe we will fall in love, and if that is the case, then so be it!"

"No," Rachel said, shaking her head. "Sarah, there are hundreds of boys to choose from. Please don't choose this one."

"It's too late." Sarah looked her in the eye. "He kissed me, Rachel. And it was my first real kiss. Not a silly little peck on the lips. It was deep and dark and wild." Her eyes changed. The light in them was one Rachel had never seen before.

She stared in horror at her sister, whom she no longer recognized. Before her very eyes, Sarah had changed. Finally, she had become a fully grown woman. The girl on the verge of womanhood was gone forever.

"He didn't kiss you," Rachel said, thinking of what Lionel had said. "You kissed him."

Sarah smiled at her and shrugged.

Rachel followed Sarah and Hannah down the winding spiral staircase. Papa was waiting for them in the hall below, and he was so handsome in his black suit that Rachel smiled. His eyes brightened as he gazed at his daughters, his pride evident. "How lovely you all are," he said in a hushed and reverent tone.

Rachel glanced at Sarah, who was breathtaking and so very much like Mama, and at Hannah, who was so pretty that she looked angelic. Her heart swelled, and she wished Mama was there.

Elgin strode into the hall in a white dinner jacket. His trousers had satin seams. He wore a blood-red signet ring on one hand, and he looked every inch the wealthy and blue-blooded aristocrat. His wife trailed behind him, wearing even more jewels than she had earlier in the day. Her dress was an amazing combination of gold lace and gold silk. It was also scandalously low-cut and full-length. Her hair was upswept, and her lipstick was red, but she still looked impossibly young. Rachel was beginning to wonder if she was even twenty. Sarah now appeared the elder and more sophisticated of the two.

Rachel realized her anxiety was soaring. Her family was shabbily dressed in comparison to the Elgins. She could not even imagine what Lady Ellen's dress had cost.

"And how was your afternoon?" Ellen asked, smiling brightly.

"We fed the swans," Hannah chirped before Rachel could reply.

Rachel felt her smile vanish and her heart lurch. Images she wished to forget assailed her. She took Hannah's hand and squeezed it warningly. Then she smiled at her hostess. "Your swans are lovely. Your home is lovely. And the gardens! It was a wonderful afternoon." She refused to think about the mocking look in Lionel's eyes that afternoon.

Ellen smiled happily. "My family used to summer here. I am so glad to be back."

At that moment, Harry walked into the hall. He took one look at Sarah and he flushed. Sarah sent him an enticing smile.

Their soaring interest and attraction to each other were only too plain. And Rachel was not the only one to notice; Papa saw, and his expression turned incredulous. Ellen noticed as well, and her eyebrows shot up. But mostly, Elgin saw. Their host stared wide-eyed, and then the dark flush of anger crept over his refined features.

Sarah must have sensed his dismay, because she smiled brightly at him. "I do so love your home, my lord," she said softly to her uncle. "I cannot thank you enough for having us. Coming to the country is no small thing for my family. Truly, the air is so much fresher here!"

Elgin started. Then, gruffly, "It was what Helen wanted."

Sarah appeared bewildered. "Helen?"

Rachel coughed and whispered, "That was Mama's name before she converted."

Sarah blinked at Rachel. "I never knew."

"You look just like her," Elgin said abruptly.

Everyone had always compared Mama and Sarah. They had the same hazel eyes, the same oval face, and even close to the same hair, with Sarah's being just a shade or two darker blond, with more curls. "I beg your pardon?" Sarah said.

"I cannot get over it," he said grimly. "You are Helen's exact image. The dark blond hair, the eyes, even your features are the same. Helen spoke the way you do, too. She was always happy and far too forthright. It is like being thrust back in time, or like looking at a ghost."

For one moment, no one spoke. Lady Ellen seemed genuinely surprised by her husband's remarks. Even Harry looked a bit taken aback. Perhaps, Rachel thought, Elgin rarely expressed his feelings.

Ellen smiled then, her expression remaining bewildered, and she tucked her arm in her husband's. "I do wish I had known my sister-in-law," she said gamely. "I have heard so many wonderful things about her."

At this moment Lionel entered the hall, also clad in a white dinner jacket. He was actually more handsome than Harry, but Harry's sunny nature far outweighed his younger brother's good looks. "Really?" Lionel murmured, his lashes sweeping down over his gray eyes. "And to think I thought we never dared to utter her name, much less speak about her."

Rachel gaped, appalled, but then realized she had been the only one to hear his aside, as he had come to stand directly beside her. He shot her an odd smile, and all she could think was how he had fed the swan those two beautiful fish.

But Elgin had heard and he turned red. "It is too late now for regrets," he said flatly. "Shall we?" And he gestured toward the dining room.

Both oversize mahogany doors were wide open, and through them, one could see a vast table set with crystal, silver, and china, and a huge chandelier above. "Are we really going to eat in there?" Hannah asked in breathless wonder.

"Yes, we are," Papa said gently but grimly.

Rachel moved closer to him. She sensed he needed her loyalty now. He was still, clearly, unhappy and hardly impressed with the wealth of Mama's family.

Elgin spoke. "Lionel, you may escort your cousin Rachel in. Harry, you may do the same for Hannah. Sarah?" He held out his arm.

Rachel was not quite sure what to do, and she saw that Sarah was also uncertain. But then she saw Papa take Lady Ellen's arm, tucking it against his side as if he were a real gentleman and leading the way to the dining room. Relieved, Rachel watched Sarah smile at their uncle and tuck her arm in his. She made a comment, and although Rachel couldn't quite hear, Elgin did smile. Then she realized that Lionel was offering her his arm.

Rachel shivered, thinking about the poor fish. Reluctantly, she looped her elbow in his.

"I don't bite," he said calmly, walking with her across the hall. "Only mad dogs—and swans—do that."

Rachel shot him a glance. "I prefer not to think about the swans just now, thank you."

Lionel smiled. "Perhaps you should take a lesson or two from your sister Sarah. I doubt feeding the swans with Lady Ellen's fish would so bother her."

He was right, but Rachel was prepared to deny it. "Of course she would be bothered by an act that is wrong."

"And what was so wrong with feeding the swans?" There was laughter in his eyes, but it was too sardonic to be pleasant.

Rachel pulled her arm free. "You stole the fish," she said in a very low voice so no one might overhear. "They did not belong to you."

He smiled with real mirth. "They will not be missed," he said with an indifferent shrug.

Rachel paused by the long table, no longer paying attention to her cousin. She noticed that a small, fancy name card was in front of each place setting. Lionel was pulling out a chair. Clearly it was for her. She checked the name on the card, which was scripted in gold, and took her seat. Her host was on her left and Lionel was on her right. Sarah and Harry were seated together, across from them, with Papa next to Harry and Hannah on the other side of Lionel. Lady Ellen graced the foot of the long table.

Rachel looked around. There were meters and meters between every diner. The table could probably seat twenty or more. Did the Elgins always dine in here? And if they did, what was it like when they did not have guests? Rachel thought it would be awkward, cold and even lonely.

Two servants entered the dining room and began pouring wine and water. Rachel started, turning to look at Papa. They never began a meal without lighting candles and saying a simple blessing. Papa just smiled at her. His eyes were even sadder than they had been earlier.

Rachel glanced across the table at Sarah, but Sarah was eyeing Harry out of the corner of her eye, and Harry was flushing all over again. Sarah smiled as if pleased. Rachel suddenly realized that she was doing something under the table to her cousin. Were they somehow holding hands? What could Sarah possibly be thinking?

"I don't drink wine," Hannah suddenly announced. "Except for a sip during the seder."

The servant moved on.

"And what is a seder?" Lady Ellen asked with a bright smile.

"We celebrate being free people," Hannah said proudly. "We used to be the pharaoh's slaves."

Lady Ellen blinked, not understanding a word Hannah had said.

"It is a Jewish ritual," Elgin said, taking a sip of his wine.

"It is one of the holiest days of the year," Papa corrected, seated on Lady Ellen's other side. "It is a high holy day and a celebration. But Hannah is right. Once we were slaves. Moses led our people to freedom. In fact, the Red Sea parted to allow us to escape the tyranny of bondage in Egypt."

"Oh," Lady Ellen said, sipping her white wine, wide-eyed.

Papa seemed irritated. Elgin made a sound.

Food was served.

Rachel could not believe her eyes—there were several different kinds of chicken, as well as a platter each of lamb and beef. There were green vegetables she did not recognize, and a salad of fresh greens. There were roasted potatoes and yellow rice. There was so much food! It was a meal fit for a king and queen. Did they always dine like this?

Her stomach growled. Of course, her family kept a kosher table, so they would not be able to eat everything.

Harry turned to his father. "Father, what do you make of this new post for Anthony Eden?"

Rachel realized they were going to talk about politics. Anthony Eden was some government official, but that was all she knew.

Elgin made a scoffing sound. "Absolutely absurd," he said. "We hardly need a post like 'minister without portfolio for League of Nations affairs.'"

"Yes, I do agree," Harry said. "Enough of the League, war will never be out of fashion as the Leaguists hope—unfortunately."

Sarah was gazing at Harry with wide, worshipful eyes. He turned to grin at her.

"I disagree," Papa said, sitting up straighter. Rachel took one look at his face, and her heart fell. He had an expression she recognized well: he disagreed and was going to set everyone straight—come hell or high water.

"If more men were Leaguists, war would most definitely become out of fashion, as you put it. Collective security is the answer to the troubles of our times," he stated firmly.

"So you support the League," Elgin said with a cool tone. "It is useful enough, I suppose. Pacifists like yourself have a legitimate venue. I am sure the Japanese admire the League as well, after all, the Leaguists let them walk off with Manchuria."

"The Japanese exited the League in response to the Lytton report," Papa said, his eyes darkening. "Our government betrayed the League of Nations. There is no doubt about that."

"Our government hardly betrayed the League by concurring with the report of an independent commission. For God's sakes, man, for all intents and purposes this country runs the League—so why would our government betray it?"

"To support our interests in Shanghai," Papa shot back fiercely.

Rachel looked from one man to the other. They were both so angry. How could they be stopped? She knew it would be terribly rude for her to make a comment to Sarah or anyone else just then. And everyone else at the table seemed mesmerized by the debate.

"Rearmament is what we really need," Elgin said firmly. "Not collective security or pacifism, and certainly not a bunch of conciliatory and cowardly men sitting around a table in Geneva discussing world affairs! Rearmament—and sanctions. We should have used a blockade in the Far East."

Papa made a scoffing sound. "As if we would ignore the Americans! They would never allow a blockade in a place where their interests are so vast."

"If we had men of moral fiber leading this country—men who do not ignore the recommendations of our chiefs of staff—Great Britain would reign supreme on land, on sea, and in the air," Elgin said, slapping his fist on the table.

Rachel jerked at the sound. She glanced around and saw that Sarah was eyeing Harry out of the corner of her eye, while his gaze darted back and forth between Elgin and Papa. At the foot of the table, Ellen seemed frozen with a fork poised over her salad. Lionel was staring at Papa, fascinated.

"Should we choose to back up the League in a real crisis, we will find ourselves in an unnecessary war," Papa said, flushed now, his voice every bit as raised as Elgin's.

This was going too far, Rachel thought desperately. She tried to catch Papa's attention, but he had eyes only for their host.

"Well, lucky for you, we cannot support the League in a real crisis, as we do not have the armaments to do so without a plan of rearmament!" Elgin said.

Papa's face was so dark that Rachel was afraid he would pound on the table as well—either that or have a heart attack. "I suppose you would support Germany's domination of Europe as well as Japan's domination of the Far East?" Papa asked harshly.

Oh, no, Rachel thought. They were not going to debate the subject of Germany now! "Papa?" she whispered.

He did not hear her.

Elgin was speaking. "Germany has many legitimate grievances due to the Treaty of Versailles, which is one reason Hitler rose so quickly to power."

"Oh, so now you support Hitler? He is a threat to Britain's security and that of all of Europe!" Papa cried. "Can you not see? Capitalism is in its last throes. Here, finally, is the proof. Hitler has been secretly supported by the city of London these past few years. Otherwise there would not be a fascist state."

"My God!" Elgin was on his feet. He had paled. "You are a communist!"

Papa stood also. "And if I am?"

"Sarah?" Rachel whispered, scandalized.

The embittered men had Sarah's full attention finally. She glanced at

Rachel, her eyes wide with alarm. Rachel could read her thoughts exactly. She, too, wanted to stop them before they came to blows. And never mind that Sarah's motives were completely different from Rachel's.

Elgin was red-faced. He shouted, "National socialism is a far better alternative than communism, my friend. Hitler has saved his country from communists like yourself!"

"That is profascist propaganda, my friend," Papa said coldly. "Disseminated by both Labour and Conservatives alike, solely with the purpose of denigrating the Communist party. Perhaps you should don a black shirt and join Mosley's British union of fascists?"

"Papa!" Rachel cried. "We are guests here!"

"I am hardly a fascist," Elgin gritted. "I am a Conservative, Greene."

"Point made," Papa said coolly.

Elgin and Papa stared at each other like two bulls in the same pen. Would they come to blows?

Rachel was perspiring. How had this evening come to such an end? Then, thankfully, Harry stood and went to his father, touching his sleeve. "Father? It doesn't matter what he thinks. It will not change anything. And this is a free country. One is allowed to express one's political opinions—for the most part." He smiled winningly at Elgin.

Rachel wanted to hug him. He was a wonderful young man! "Papa? Mama would hate this." Rachel whispered, and as she spoke, tears filled her eyes. "Is this how we treat her memory?"

Papa started. So did Elgin. The two men glanced at her and then at each other. In unison, they sat down, leaving Harry standing. He returned to his seat.

Lady Ellen spoke, her voice high and strained. "How is the guinea hen? You must try that plum sauce!"

Everyone attacked the food. Except for Lionel. He said, "The Blackshirts are marching next Saturday in Cheapside. Anyone care to attend? We can throw tomatoes if you like."

Rachel felt like kicking him. No one bothered to respond.

Rachel thought that she was the very first one to arise the following morning. How could she sleep? The sun was barely casting its glow over the river running through the hills when she went to her bedroom window. The sight was glorious, and it made Rachel smile.

She quickly washed and dressed, then went into Hannah's room. Her sister was still in bed and barely awake, clutching a rag doll to her chest. "Let's take a walk before breakfast, sleepyhead," Rachel said. "We shouldn't waste one single minute of this weekend holiday!"

Hannah yawned. "I'm too tired to get up," she said.

"Then I will take a walk. I'll be back in an hour," Rachel promised.

Hannah did not reply. She had fallen back asleep.

Rachel knew better than to stop by Sarah's room. Given the choice, Sarah would always sleep in, and last night she had sat out on the terrace with Harry for an hour or so after supper. Lady Ellen had been their chaperone.

Rachel did not want to disturb Papa, either. He was always up at dawn, except on Shabbat, when he rose an hour or so later. It would be good for him to oversleep, she thought, so she went downstairs by herself, pulling a cardigan on over her skirt and shirt, to ward off the early-morning Welsh chill.

No one was about. The house was absolutely silent. Rachel found herself smiling. Briefly, she wondered what it must be like to be the mistress of such a home.

She slipped outside without seeing even a servant. She would never be the mistress of such a home, and she knew it. One day she would marry someone like Papa, a handsome Jewish boy who made an honest and respectable living. She would marry for love, not money or position. She would have a life very much like the one she now had.

Rachel wandered through the first garden, which was filled with roses of every imaginable color. The sun was higher now, shining and full, an orange ball. Fingers of apricot drenched the hills and the horizon. The lake was ahead, surrounded by elm trees, cloaked in mist. From a distance it was hard to see, but Rachel thought she could see one of the swans drifting upon the water. She refused to think about the previous day's episode. Her steps quickened. She would sit out at the lake for a while. She was sorry she hadn't brought a book to read.

The mist clinging to the lake was beginning to lift. As she approached, one of the swans glided toward her, emerging from the silvery wisps of vapor. As he came closer, his black eyes became visible. They were intent. Rachel wondered if he expected food. She had nothing to give him.

Another swan appeared, approaching. The mist was disappearing.

The sun had become yellow and bright. They were such beautiful creatures, Rachel thought. She did not blame Lady Ellen for bringing them here to the north of Wales.

Birds were chirping madly now. As if on cue, the entire lake became drenched in dazzling sunlight. The two swans waited expectantly by the edge of the lake, regarding Rachel.

"Where's your friend?" she asked, her hands in the pockets of her lilac cardigan. And her gaze lifted.

Her smile vanished. The third swan was at the opposite edge of the lake. Like its two brethren, it was not moving, but Rachel's heart lurched—something seemed very wrong.

A feeling of dread overcame her. Rachel hurried around the lake, closing the distance between her and the third swan. She realized that the other two swans had lost interest in her and were swimming to the opposite bank.

The third swan wasn't just still, Rachel realized, it was floating on its side.

She halted abruptly, in disbelief.

It was floating on its side, as though dead.

But that couldn't be. Rachel broke into a run. As she approached, she realized its face was in the water—it was most definitely dead.

She stopped breathlessly and saw as clearly as if she were a veterinarian that its neck had been ruthlessly twisted and broken.

Rachel sat alone in a small but elegant parlor. She did not move. In fact, she felt afraid to move, as if by doing so she would cause something horrible to happen. Her hands were clasped in her lap. There was a huge, gilded clock in one corner of the room, and it was ticking loudly. Tick-tock. Tick-tock. The room—and the house—were so silent, it was as if everyone were in mourning. But then, someone—no, something—had died.

It was only a quarter to eight.

Rachel wondered if Lady Ellen had awakened yet, and if she knew the fate of her beautiful swan. Rachel wondered if she would grieve in her room or come downstairs. She wondered who could have committed such a gruesome deed.

Rachel heard voices and the front door of the house slamming closed. She leaped to her feet, wringing her hands—she was quite certain she had heard Papa speaking, but his words were low and hushed and indecipherable. Papa and Elgin walked into the room, trailed by Harry and Lionel. Papa was grim. Elgin seemed taken aback. Harry was wide-eyed.

Rachel finally looked at Lionel. His expression was the picture of surprise and innocence.

Papa's gaze met Rachel's. "You were right. The swan's neck was broken. Someone deliberately twisted the bird's neck to kill it."

"I'm so sorry," Rachel whispered.

"No, I am the one who is sorry," Elgin said. "I am sorry you had to wake up and find such an unpleasant sight."

"Who would do such a thing?" Lionel asked.

"That is a very good question," Elgin said, shaking his head. "It must be a prank."

"Or worse," Papa returned evenly. "There is so much dissatisfaction now, with entire villages out of work. Perhaps an unemployed worker decided to take out his ire on you, Elgin. The wealthy are an obvious target for the disaffected."

"I had already thought of that," Elgin said. "But the north of Wales has not been as hard hit as the south, where unemployment is almost one hundred percent. Still, I think that in this case you may be right."

"Perhaps a local villager is disaffected not because of lack of employment, but because of some feud with the Llewyllens," Lionel offered. "This is only the second time you have come to the manor, Father." Ellen's maiden name was Llewyllen.

"I have been to Ruthin twice," Harry said. "My reception was nothing but warm and eager."

"Well, for the moment, we can only speculate. Do not say a word to your mother. I will speak with Lady Ellen when she arises." Elgin glanced at his watch. "That will not be for another few hours."

Everyone nodded.

"I am going in for breakfast," Elgin announced. "Greene?"

Papa nodded, glancing at Rachel, who had no appetite. "Rachel?"

"I'm not hungry, Papa. I think I'll see if Sarah and Hannah are up."

When the men were gone, Harry came over to her. "Are you all right? I must say, you are holding up bloody well. You are a brave girl, Rachel Greene." He smiled at her.

Rachel flushed with pleasure. "I am fine, and thank you," she said.

"We'll get to the bottom of this eventually," Harry assured her.

"I doubt it," Lionel said easily. "Unless there is a rash of incidents like this one, we will never know who murdered the swan."

Rachel stared at him. *Murder.* That's what this was. Was he amused by the whole sordid affair?

Harry was speaking. "You are ever the cynic, Lionel." He shrugged. Then, to Rachel, "We are going hunting. Perhaps you and Sarah would like to join us?"

Rachel blinked. "I don't hunt."

"We will teach you how to shoot."

"I could not kill any animal."

"We eat the pheasants, rabbit, and deer that we shoot," Harry said. "We don't hunt for the joy of killing some innocent creature."

"I'd prefer not to go hunting," Rachel said, meaning it.

"I'd like to go," Sarah said brightly.

Everyone turned. Sarah was dressed and glowing and standing on the threshold of the small salon. She was also smiling—at Harry.

He grinned and strolled over to her. "Do you know how to shoot a gun?" he asked.

"No, but I would like nothing more than for you to teach me," she said.

CHAPTER 9

Rachel wished Sarah had refused Harry's offer. Instead, the foursome had gathered up two rifles and ammunition and were now entering the woods, leaving the grounds of the house behind. Rachel felt horribly uneasy. She did not know why. It was almost as if she had a premonition of disaster.

Sarah and Harry walked ahead. Sarah was talking up a storm, entertaining Harry with funny stories about life in the city of London. Harry was grinning and laughing. He had a big rifle slung over his shoulder, as did Lionel. Rachel had never realized before that she hated guns.

It was cooler out in the woods, where the growth was dense and few rays of sunlight could penetrate. Birds sang overhead. Squirrels and chipmunks raced along the leafy branches of trees. They passed a small glade where a doe and her fawn were grazing; both animals took flight at once.

"I hope we are not going to kill one of those beautiful deer," Rachel whispered nervously.

Lionel glanced at her. "Surely you've had venison? The meat is delicious."

"No, I have not, and I do not intend to," Rachel said more tersely than she intended.

"We will shoot hare," Harry said, smiling over his shoulder at her. "But first I will give Sarah a lesson in marksmanship." He had paused. "This meadow looks like a good place to practice." He pointed at a wide, stunted tree. "We can use that oak as a target."

"This is exciting," Sarah said eagerly.

Harry gave her a fond glance, loading his rifle.

"I wonder how excited you will be when Papa finds out what we have been doing this morning," Rachel said. Papa would be furious. He was a pacifist in all things. He would abhor the idea of his daughters even touching a gun.

"You would never tattle on me," Sarah said, and she was right.

Lionel hadn't moved. He carried his rifle casually, with the stock pointed at the ground. Harry finished loading, the rifle making an ominous click, and he glanced at his brother. "Why aren't you loading your gun?"

"It's already loaded," Lionel said.

Harry stared. "You know that's against the rules. We are to load the guns only when we are ready to use them."

Lionel shrugged. "Father will never know."

Dismay crossed Harry's face. "Sometimes I wonder about you," he said.

Lionel smiled. "Don't we all wonder about others?"

Harry shook his head and turned away.

Rachel looked at Lionel. The exchange just increased her apprehension. "Sarah? We should let the boys hunt by themselves. I think we should leave."

"I hope that's a joke," Sarah said as Harry came to stand beside her. She wasn't even looking at Rachel.

Rachel's heart sank.

"They'll be fine," Lionel said softly in her ear.

She jumped and moved away from him. "I'm worried," she admitted nervously.

"You think too much," Lionel said. He smiled. "But that's what I find so charming about you."

Rachel blinked and felt herself flush. To hide her loss of composure, she turned back to Harry and Sarah. She was hardly trying to impress Lionel. She had decided that he was far more than enigmatic, he was peculiar.

Harry was explaining to Sarah how one placed the rifle in one's hands, how to support its weight against the shoulder, how to sight carefully, and then how to gently squeeze the trigger. Sarah was wide-eyed with fascination. Rachel knew Harry was going to fire the gun, but nothing could have prepared her for the sound. It was deafening. She leaped, crying out.

Lionel chuckled and patted her shoulder. The gesture was patronizing.

"Sorry," Harry said with an apologetic glance. "I forgot to mention how loud the shots are."

Sarah was running toward the tree, holding her skirts high. "You hit the tree!" She cried breathlessly, inspecting the thick old oak.

Rachel crossed her arms as Sarah laughed and hurried back to Harry. If she wanted to be the center of attention, she was succeeding; both boys had been gaping at her legs.

"Your turn," Harry said, a flush high up on his cheeks.

"This is not a good idea," Rachel managed, hugging herself.

"Oh, posh," Sarah said as she accepted the huge rifle from Harry. "This is so heavy!"

"Here." Harry helped her position it and then hold it correctly. Rachel noticed that for him to do so, he had to stand with his body behind Sarah's, so that his weight supported hers. She felt herself blushing. The two of them were almost glued together—an embrace could not have been more intimate.

"Is that better?" Harry asked, his tone oddly husky.

Sarah turned her head to look back at him. "Perfect," she whispered.

Harry coughed. "Look through the sight, Sarah. Look very carefully down the length of the rifle."

Sarah obeyed. "All right."

"Now the point is to try not to jerk the gun when you fire it. Remember, there is a kickback. When you fire, the power of the shot will jerk the gun in your hands. So hold tightly, that's right, and now, slowly, squeeze the trigger."

Rachel put her hands over her ears.

Sarah fired. The gun jumped visibly in her hands, but Harry had never let it go, and he steadied it. "Did I hit the tree?" Sarah cried breathlessly.

Harry smiled at her. "No, sweetheart, you did not."

The endearment seemed to have just slipped out. Sarah ceased smiling. So did Harry. They remained standing together, staring at each other. The gun was lowered, and suddenly they were kissing.

Rachel did not know what to do. She turned to look at Lionel in shock. He shrugged, laughter in his eyes. Clearly he did not give a whit about propriety, or about what was happening before their very eyes.

"Sarah Greene!" Rachel shouted, marching over to the pair. "Enough! How shameless can you be?"

Harry and Sarah slowly broke the kiss. It was as if they hadn't even heard Rachel, for they stared at each other like two lovesick idiots.

"We should go," Rachel continued fervently. "This has been a terrible idea from the very start."

Sarah faced her, hands on her hips. "You can't tell me what to do, Rachel," she said.

Rachel was at a loss. "Please think about what you are doing!" she finally said.

"What am I doing, Rachel? You are making a big to-do about nothing at all. I am learning how to fire a gun, that is all."

Harry stepped forward. He seemed rueful. "This is all my fault. Rachel is right. We have not behaved the way that we should. I apologize." He looked directly at Rachel. "It won't happen again."

Rachel wasn't relieved. The problem was hardly a single kiss. Harry was a wonderful young man, sincere, intelligent, and ethical. He would be so perfect for Sarah—if the gulf of religion and class did not separate them. But that gulf did exist, and it was very real. Rachel was afraid that it was too late, that they had already fallen in love. The outcome could only be tragic.

She knew Papa could not live through another marriage like his and Mama's. She wasn't sure that she could, either.

"She can't tell us what to do, or how we should feel," Sarah said to Harry, appearing mulish and cross. "She is afraid we will fall in love like Mama and Papa did."

Harry was grim, absorbing that.

"That would definitely be the end of the world," Lionel remarked.

Harry looked at him angrily. "Of course it would not be the end of the world."

"Look at how poor Helen lived," Lionel said calmly. "Penniless and cut off from everything she loved."

Rachel stiffened. "We are not penniless, Lionel. And Mama was not cut off from everything she loved—she loved Papa and she loved us."

"Did you know that until her death, Helen wrote Father frequently, begging him to accept her again? Her heart was broken when my grandparents and Father disowned her. She said so. She begged for their acceptance."

"That's enough!" Harry snapped, pushing Lionel.

Rachel was rigid with dismay. "She loved us and she was not heartbroken." But she kept recalling Mama's tears.

Lionel had lost his balance, but he hadn't fallen. "I think she wanted to come home. I think she wanted her life as Lady Helen Elgin back."

Rachel gasped.

"What has gotten into you?" Harry shouted. "Why are you trying to upset everybody again? Aunt Helen was happily married to Benjamin Greene, and you know it."

"I know nothing of the sort," Lionel said with a defiant tilt to his chin.

"Mama was happy," Sarah said, ashen. "But she would have been happier if your family hadn't been so rotten as to disown her for marrying the man she loved."

"She wasn't disowned because she eloped with your father," Lionel said.

"Lionel," Harry warned.

"She was disowned because she became a Jew," Lionel finished, and there was a note of triumph in his tone.

Tears came to Rachel's eyes. Sarah started forward, but Rachel restrained her. "Let's go back to the house," she said.

"No. He's a horrible boy. A horrible little boy."

"I'm like Father. I'm a fascist," Lionel said.

Rachel thought he was teasing, but she could no longer be sure.

Harry stepped between the girls and his brother. "What you are is mean," he said. "You killed that swan, didn't you?"

Lionel looked at him. "That's absurd."

Rachel was stunned, and she saw that Harry meant it. She looked from brother to brother and thought that Lionel was telling the truth. This had gone too far. "Sarah, we must go."

"I saw the pamphlet in your valise," Harry continued, flushed with anger. "The one about the Blackshirts. What are you doing, reading that kind of bloody trash?"

Lionel shrugged. "Capitalism is collapsing." He smiled at Rachel. "You see? I agree with your father on that point."

Harry gaped. "Don't tell me that you think fascism is the answer?"

"You said it, I didn't."

"Do you know what they're doing to the Jews over there?" Harry said, pale. "Jews can't run for political office or even serve in the government, they can't teach in the universities, they can't become lawyers or doctors! Even those who are lawyers and doctors can no longer serve their professions. Jews can't even marry non-Jews if they're German. They're starting to take their homes and possessions away from them. It's insanity!"

"Who cares," Lionel said.

Silence fell over the group.

Rachel realized she had taken Sarah's hand and was clinging to it. She hadn't known that the Nazis were doing those things. This was the very first she had heard of such atrocities. She glanced at Sarah and saw that her sister was as upset as she was. "Let's go, please, Sarah," Rachel whispered.

Sarah nodded. "I haven't had breakfast." She smiled sadly at Harry. "We're going back to the house."

Harry was alarmed. "Sarah! Please, don't go—"

"I'll see you at the house."

"Don't go like this!" Harry cried. "Lionel is always doing this. He's always ruining everything for everyone!" Harry grabbed Sarah's hand. "Please, Sarah, do not be upset!"

She let him hold her hand for one moment before gently disengaging it. "Thank you for the shooting lesson," she said softly. A tear slipped down her face.

Rachel and Sarah turned to leave, Rachel fighting the urge to cry for Sarah and Harry and stunned that her sister had come to her senses. As they headed toward the path that would take them back to the house, they heard Harry say angrily, "Now look at what you've done!"

Rachel cast one last glance over her shoulder. Harry faced Lionel, his face etched with anger.

"I am going to hunt a deer," Lionel said. He slung his rifle over his shoulder and disappeared into the woods.

The doe was grazing quietly by a small pond in the glade they had passed earlier. Lionel froze, becoming as still as a statue, standing behind a thick tree. The doe continued to graze, unaware of his presence. He was upwind, he knew.

The doe reminded him of Rachel. As he stared at it, he saw his cousin instead, with her wide, honest eyes—eyes that looked at him and could not hide their confusion and mistrust. Lionel smiled to himself and slowly lifted the rifle.

How innocent and good she was. How pure and kind. She was also so beautiful, far more so than her older sister, who was nothing but a whore. Lionel had stayed up most of last night thinking about Rachel. He found her purity fascinating; he could sense when purity was genuine and sincere. What made a human being so holy? So worthy? What life experiences had she had to be so kind and caring, so compassionate? What was her motivation? Was it God? Or did she seek to please her father? It was very curious, very interesting.

Rachel would hate it if he killed the doe. He had been somewhat amazed by her reaction to the death of Ellen's swan.

Thinking about his stepmother brought disgust. Lionel sighted down the scope of the rifle. Now he saw Ellen there instead of the doe. His blood thrummed in his veins. He would not grieve if his stepmother met with an accident. It would be a case of good riddance. Of course, she wasn't the doe now trapped in his sights. And that was too bad—the doe would have to do.

He began to squeeze the trigger. And then Rachel said, as if she stood beside him, *You're not going to hunt deer, are you?*

The doe lifted its head, listening intently, as if suddenly aware of an intruder.

Lionel did not move.

But someone was crashing through the woods. And just before Lionel pulled the trigger, the doe leaped away to safety. It disappeared in the woods on the other side of the glade.

Lionel lowered the gun, staring in the direction the doe had gone. He knew who was in the woods. Harry had interfered with his kill.

Harry, who was always so good, so perfect, the perfect student, the adored son, the heir apparent—the Prince Charming. Harry, his brother, whom he truly despised.

Lionel closed his eyes, overcome by intense and debilitating hatred.

When he had gained control of himself, he slung his rifle over his shoulder and headed back into the woods. For how much longer should he put up with his perfect brother?

Lionel began to track the doe. He had never been able to understand what Harry's allure was. Clearly, Sarah was smitten with him. He had seen his stepmother eye him as well. Even Rachel seemed fond of Harry already. And Harry had dozens of male friends, all of whom adored him.

And somehow, Harry had known he was the one who had wrung the swan's neck. Lionel considered the notion. It wasn't the first time that Harry had overstepped his bounds. Harry knew too much about him, and Harry was in his way.

The woods were dark now, and damp, the scent of rot and decay potent. He found the odors in the heart of the woods as attractive as they were repugnant. But then, life seemed divided into polarities: good and evil, light and dark, truth and lies. Extremes of nature faced him at every turn, it seemed.

Like Rachel and Sarah. Like him and his brother.

Lionel smiled a little. Except his nature was hardly evil. Or did planning the murder of one's brother constitute "evil"? Perhaps it did—by society's definition of the word. But society was a bunch of fools. And it had never mattered to him what others thought. Except, of course, for Father.

Something moved in the woods ahead of him. Lionel paused, fighting a surge of anger. He had learned years ago that he was more effective without any emotions at all.

Today was the day, he decided. He had waited patiently for the perfect opportunity, and now he had it. He would forget about the doe. And then he imagined Rachel's reaction when she learned of Harry's fate.

Soundlessly, Lionel moved through a pair of trees, raising the rifle to his shoulder. It was a shame that he would never be able to tell her the truth.

The doe did not stand on the deer trail ahead of him. His brother did.

This was the moment he had waited years for. Lionel froze, and images tumbled through his mind swiftly, a kaleidoscope of the past. Harry and their father in earnest debate, as they had been about to engage in last evening at supper; returning from the hunt, muddy and happy and arm in arm; or discussing affairs of estate in the study, privately—fervently. Harry and Sarah, entwined and kissing shamelessly. Ellen, hungrily gazing after Harry. Rachel, looking at his brother with obvious admiration in her eyes.

Lionel realized he was sighting through the scope of the rifle. Excitement surged through his veins. *This was it, then.* He was a perfect marksman, but now he was trembling ever so slightly. Father would be destroyed by Harry's death. Elation surged in his chest even though he tried to breathe deeply and calm himself—he must not think of Father or Rachel or anyone now. He must think only of the kill.

He squeezed the trigger slowly—the way Harry had instructed Sarah just a few minutes ago.

The rifle boomed. It jerked in his hands, an event that had not happened in years. And because he was shaking, the shot hit Harry in the back, just off center, instead of in the back of his head, where death would have been instantaneous.

Still, Harry crashed to the ground, face first, where he lay unmoving.

Lionel stepped back behind the pair of trees, stunned. *Good God.* He had just executed his deepest, darkest fantasy—he had shot his brother.

The elation began. Lionel fought it.

Harry moaned. The sound was weak and pitiful.

He was alive.

It wasn't too late, Lionel could go to him, claim it was an accident, and help him to survive.

Lionel moved around the tree and stared. Harry was clawing the earth. A red blossom was spreading rapidly from the hole in his back, staining his tweed coat almost black. Lionel realized his heart was thundering in his breast. He had only minutes in which to decide whether to grant life or dispense death.

The power of it was fantastic.

Harry began crawling forward. His moan sounded again. And this time, Lionel thought he heard the whispered word "Help."

"Help me. Please."

He had done it. The disbelief was fading; reality and comprehension were setting in. And euphoria. For he had decided. *Harry would die.*

He had planned a hunting accident like this for years, and he had a plausible story. He had hit the doe, but she had run off, and he assumed he had grazed her. When they found Harry, they would quickly realize

Lionel had shot his brother instead of the deer, thinking him to be the doe. Lionel almost smiled, except he was too giddy to do so.

He had the perfect story.

All of his problems were over.

Except for Father, that is.

Harry continued to crawl on his belly through the woods. Lionel wondered what he thought to do. He would never make it back to the house. Besides, the river was ahead—he was going in the wrong direction. How stupid the effort was. Why not just die in peace?

Harry paused, a soblike moan escaping him. He was covered in blood. He could not have much longer to live.

Curious, Lionel couldn't help peering more closely at him, wondering what he would do next.

Harry turned his head. Their gazes met.

"Lionel," he cried in a hoarse whisper. "Lionel."

Lionel did not move.

The comprehension came then, and Harry's eyes filled with shock. "Lionel! Help me!" Blood spewed from his mouth.

Lionel turned and melted into the woods.

Sarah was walking so quickly that she was outpacing Rachel. Rachel broke into a run and caught up with her. "Sarah, I am sorry," she said, and she meant it.

"No, you're not." Sarah had tears in her eyes. "You're jealous, aren't you? That's what this is about!"

"I'm not jealous!" Rachel gasped. "I just don't want you to get hurt! Or even Harry."

Sarah ducked her head, continuing to walk rapidly through the woods. A gunshot sounded somewhere behind them, not that far away. Both girls flinched. "What difference does it make if we're Jews? Who cares? Harry doesn't care!" Sarah said.

"But his father cares, and you know it. And our father cares very much about our religion. Poor Papa. He has been through so much. I hate to see him go through more tragedy. Sarah, it's best for everyone—you, Harry, Papa, Elgin—if you forget all about Harry."

"I don't want to talk about it," Sarah said, and she broke into a run.

Rachel paused and watched her sister disappear as the trail curved away. She rubbed her temples. Life could be so unfair. "Why, God?" she whispered. "They are perfect for each other in almost every way. Why do this to them?" She wiped a touch of moisture from her own eyes. "Why take Mama?" she had to add. Rachel sighed. She really didn't expect an answer, not even one from herself.

She had no desire to go back to the house. It was only midday, and dinner would not be for another few hours. Besides, Papa would want to know why Sarah was crying. Rachel would never lie, not to him or anyone, and she did not want to tell him what was really happening between Sarah and Harry.

The woods were thinner where she stood. Through the trees, she saw the river flowing, and on the opposite bank there was a wide-open sweep of hilly ground and the ruins of the castle. Rachel wondered if she could somehow cross the river. Maybe she would wander alongside it and find a bridge. Exploring Rhuddlan Castle would be the perfect antidote for her somber mood.

Rachel threaded her way through the waving birch trees, which were dappled with bright sunlight. The river ahead was slow and sluggish, but the landscape beyond was breathtaking, especially with the castle perched on the hill just above it. Rachel decided she would ask her uncle about its history. It would surely be fascinating.

Rachel left the edge of trees behind her, beginning to step down the embankment. But it was damp and slick, and she had to pause or lose her balance. She reached down and steadied herself.

And when she looked up, she saw the body floating past her.

Rachel cried out, realizing that Harry was floating down the river. It took her a moment to react. "Harry!" she shouted.

Rachel scrambled down the bank, using both hands, trying to understand why he was drifting in the current facedown and not swimming to shore. *As if he was hurt.* She reached the soft mud by the water's edge and righted herself. Harry floated past her, and his motionless form filled her with terror.

No.

Rachel ran along the river, screaming his name. And now she realized that a bloody wake was trailing behind him.

And he was motionless.

No.

Rachel screamed, rushing into the water. It was frigidly cold, shocking her, as she plunged in to her waist, her shoulders. Her chin. But then the water leveled off, and using her arms to help her move, as if she were swimming, she managed to catch Harry's foot.

"Harry!" She was sobbing. "Harry!" She reeled him in.

As her arms went around him, she rolled him over onto his back, and she saw that he was dead.

PART
THREE

THE CHASE

CHAPTER 10

Huge weights were pressing down on her. Her limbs and torso, every inch of her, felt heavy, paralyzed, useless. And there was so much blackness. It enveloped her; it was everywhere.

A man spoke to her.

She struggled to rise up through the heavy layers of darkness. It seemed an impossible feat.

"Claire?"

Claire blinked and was blinded by a light that seemed to be shining right into her eyes. She realized that someone was holding her hand. The cobwebs shifted. An image of a big black steel barrel filled her mind. Claire was awake and fully cognizant. Her head was hurting her. "Ian!"

He pushed a wisp of her hair from her face. "You're fine. It's just a graze on the side of your head. Can you understand me?"

Images of that terrifying car chase, and worse, the chase on foot through the river and the ruins at Rhuddlan, assailed her. Claire met Ian's gaze. *"Someone tried to kill me."*

"I know. I was there. Or don't you remember?"

Claire's heart was going wild. She tried to sit up. In that instant, all she could remember was facing the gunman as he pulled the trigger. "What's happening?" she asked fearfully. She realized she was in a hospital room, and that she was woozy from whatever painkillers she was on.

"Take it easy, Claire," Ian said as she tried to sit up. He helped her, propping more pillows behind her. Her bed was curtained off from whoever else was present in the room. She could not tell what time of day it was; the light inside the curtained-off cubicle was a sickly shade of yellow, although far too bright. "There's a policeman outside. But he won't come back."

Suddenly exhausted, she sank back against the pillows. "This can't be happening. What *is* happening, Ian?" She stopped. Their gazes locked. *"Elgin."*

He was grim, but he smiled a little at her. "Yeah."

Claire stared at him. But it was not Ian she saw. Instead, she saw the gunman with his impossibly cold eyes, regarding her as he aimed his gun. She would never forget the moment he had pulled the trigger. Her heart had literally stopped.

And that had been the exact moment that he had been knocked down, tackled from behind by Ian.

"What happened?" she asked. "The last thing I remember is seeing you hit him from behind and being shot. I must have blacked out."

"We struggled over the gun. Fortunately, I was stronger, and I had just gotten it when some teenage boys appeared. I think they had entered the ruins to smoke some dope, but it was perfect timing. I had the gun, and our gunman decided it was time to make a hasty exit." He touched her. "It's okay, Claire."

Claire was finding it hard to breathe. "No, it's not okay. That gunman was working for Elgin, wasn't he?"

"Yes."

Claire stared, and their gazes met. Elgin . . . who might be William Duke, who might be Robert Ducasse. But he could not be Jean-Léon, obviously. Her father would never try to kill her!

"Was it a mistake?" she asked tersely.

"Look, Claire," Ian began, reaching for her hand.

"No!" Claire had raised her voice, which was a huge mistake. Pain lanced through her temples. "Surely you are not still suspicious of my father." Her tone was shrill.

"Elgin is a killer," Ian said flatly. "Whomever he is masquerading as, he is a *killer*. I believe that gunman was after me, not you. I feel certain his shooting you was his own idea. These thugs aren't renowned for their high IQs."

"You did not answer my question."

"You're not up for this discussion now."

She wasn't, not physically, but having someone try to kill you negated that. "What about your theory that my uncle is alive? Or that William is Elgin?"

Ian sighed. "You're on painkillers, Claire. You have a very slight con-cussion. From falling on stones, though, not from the bullet. You should rest."

"Like you care!" She was so angry, and suddenly so afraid. It was all sinking in. This was no lark. Someone wanted Ian dead—and maybe her as well.

"I care."

She had to focus on him. It was no easy task with the panic creeping over her. "I have known William Duke since I was a little girl. He would *never* make an attempt on my life."

Ian hesitated. "If Duke is Elgin, then he might, and he most definitely would if you were a threat. If Duke is Elgin, then he is not what he appears to be, and you don't know him at all."

"So far, nothing in my life is what I thought it was!" she cried, thinking of Ian's suspicions and recalling David's brutal murder. "There has to be someone else out there, Ian. There just has to be."

Ian settled his hip beside her and brushed her bangs out of her eyes. Her head was bandaged, she realized. "Maybe there is, Claire, and if that is so, I will find him sooner or later." He smiled at her.

Claire could not smile back; but she was exhausted now. "So now what happens? We were hunting Elgin, and now he's hunting us." Renewed fear filled her.

"What happens next is that you go home," Ian said softly. "Enough is enough, Claire. You don't need to be in this kind of danger."

Their eyes connected and held again. Go home. Of course she should go home. She was truly afraid now—she was a real coward.

He seemed to take her silence for acquiescence, because he said, "I had to tell the police everything, and they're a bunch of village cops more used to dealing with parking violations and drunkards than anything else. They're not going to be much help, Claire. But they need a statement from you. Just tell them the truth."

"I can't speak to them," she said quickly. "I'm tired and woozy. I can't think straight."

"I'm afraid they won't take no for an answer. You're conscious—they'll insist on speaking with you sooner rather than later. This is a big deal out here, Claire. We're in the boonies, and someone has shot you."

Claire stared into his eyes. They were more green than ever, not a hazel green, not a golden green, but a real Irish-clover green. "He'll try again, won't he? That gunman."

"That hired thug is in France by now. And I'd be surprised if Elgin dared set foot in the U.K. right now, with the authorities closing in on him."

"He'll try again," Claire repeated stubbornly.

"If he does, you won't be in the picture, Claire."

But she didn't really hear him—she was thinking about the fact that the Dukes often traveled to London. Still, William would never hurt her. She just knew it.

And Jean-Léon was innocent. She would prove it—she had to.

Ian was speaking. "Look, I'll book you a flight for tomorrow night. They're talking about releasing you in the morning, and that will give you enough time to get to London. You'll feel like a new person when you get home and put all of this behind you."

Claire took a sip of water from a paper cup beside her bed. How could she prove Jean-Léon innocent if she went home? And as far as putting this behind her, it would take years: David was dead, and that was not how she had intended to end her marriage. Even if she did go home, Elgin had tried to kill them.

Claire put the paper cup down. "I can't go home. I can't and I won't." Oddly, having made the decision somehow calmed her. She had never felt more resolute.

He stood up abruptly. "Why the hell not?"

"We're partners, remember? Concussion and all."

"Whatever agreement we had, it's over. Negated by the fact that you were shot, Claire. Elgin wanted me—and he got you. That is unacceptable as far as I am concerned. Absolutely unacceptable."

Claire smiled a little. "I'm growing on you, I can tell."

"You're growing on me like a gray hair. Unwanted—and with real bad timing!"

"You're comparing me to gray hair?" Claire tried to be insulted.

"That's not what I said and you know it. Damn it, don't look at me with those big eyes. You don't have an innocent bone in your body—not when you're after something."

"If only you knew," she murmured, her mind veering in the most absurd and forbidden direction.

"What?" he shot back.

"I don't want to spend the night in the hospital," Claire announced. "In fact"—she threw the covers aside—"I want to go now."

"What are you doing?" he cried as she tried to stand up.

There were two problems. One, she was wearing a typically ridiculous and ugly hospital gown that exposed her backside. Two, she was dizzy the moment she stood up. So reaching to close the gown, instead of holding on to the bed, was a bad call.

Claire fell into Ian's arms, then decided it was a good call after all. "I like that little inn we stayed at last night. Our stuff is still there. We never checked out," she said against his chest. It was broad and hard and he smelled great.

"You're not leaving the hospital," he said firmly, anchoring her with one arm around her back. "What gets into you at times like these?"

Claire looked up. "Man, I am light-headed," she said.

He pushed her back onto the bed. "Mule-headed is more like it. I'm going to see if the police will wait to speak with you tomorrow. And I am booking you a return to the States."

"And I'm not going. You're stuck with me, big guy. Like it or not."

He stared at her, clearly angry, and she stared back, hoping her smile was seductive and alluring. Trading jests with him was hard work, given her weakened condition.

"Cut it out," he finally said. "The sweet stuff won't work. And if you think you're sexy, forget it. Your head is bandaged and your hospital gown is hardly by Valentino."

"Shucks. I'd hoped Val made it just for me."

He sighed, shaking his head. "All right. Truce. We'll finish this when I come back tomorrow."

"But won't you miss my company tonight?"

"No!" He smiled then. "I'd have to lock up the minibar with you around."

"There is no minibar in the B&B."

"Do you always have to make the last quip?"

"Only since you came into my life." Claire smiled happily at him. Her temples no longer throbbed. The painkillers were definitely working.

"Has anyone ever told you that you are really stubborn?"

She smiled slightly. "No. Not ever. Stubbornness has never been one of my major character traits."

"Great. I clearly bring out the worst in you."

"Or the best," she said, still smiling.

He gave her a dark look. "I'm going to see the doctor, tell him what a lousy patient you are, speak with the cops, and then I'll be back to say good night."

"Fine," Claire said meekly.

Ian strode from the room.

Her smile faded as she realized that, filled up with painkillers, concussed, and having just escaped an attempt on her life, she was making jokes and oddly happy. This time there was no denying it. There was also no denying that this was not the time to fall for Ian Marshall.

Unfortunately, Claire had the feeling that the deed was already done.

"Claire?" Ian popped his head back in the room, startling her. "It looks like you're off the hook. The cop in charge has gone home for the night. They'll take a report from you in the morning."

Relief washed over Claire. "Great. That was quick."

"Doc's gone, but I spoke with one of the nurses. She's going to keep a close eye on you, so stay in bed."

Claire saluted him, thinking with real nostalgia about Veuve Clicquot and their small guest room at the Myddleton Arms. "Aye-aye, *mon capitaine.*"

He laughed a little, shaking his head. "I'll be back first thing tomorrow. Good night."

"Good night. Don't let the bedbugs bite."

"I won't," Ian promised.

"Or the Reception Girl," Claire had to add.

He rolled his eyes at her and left. Claire wiggled her toes and smiled, until the memories of the horrible and frightening afternoon began to assail her in vivid Technicolor. In spite of her injury, it was a long time before she slept, and when she did, her dreams were filled with the men she loved the most, William, Jean-Léon, and Ian Marshall. Everyone was chasing everyone, and everyone carried guns. Even Robert Ducasse was present.

Except the dream changed, and one gun became a thumb knife. It was dripping blood.

And in her dream Claire saw Elgin's face and realized who he was—who he had been for all of these years—and it was so obvious, it made so much sense, that she just didn't understand why they hadn't figured it out sooner.

Hospital rules required that she use a wheelchair to leave the premises. The next day, Claire sat in the wheelchair, a nurse behind her, on the sidewalk by the hospital's entrance. Ian was retrieving his car from the parking lot, which faced them.

Claire was brooding. She was recalling the vague, shadowy images of her dreams, which had left her very disturbed. What was worse, in her dream she had uncovered Elgin's real identity, but in the light of day, she could not recall it. She had been racking her brain ever since awakening, but to no avail.

Ian stopped the sedan at the curb and jumped out. Claire thanked the nurse and got out of the wheelchair. The huge bandage on her head had been reduced to a large Band-Aid. She felt fine, for the most part. She attributed any lingering shakiness to stress, not the mild concussion. There was a killer out there and there was no forgetting it now.

"Okay?" Ian smiled at her, opening the car door.

"Okay," Claire said with a return smile, slipping into the passenger side of the front seat.

Ian said something to the nurse, and a moment later he was seated beside her and they were leaving the hospital grounds.

"Are you really okay?" he asked, steering onto a busy two-way thoroughfare. "How did it go with the cops?"

Claire rolled down her window so she could inhale the sweet, salty sea air. "You were right. They're not big-league guys. But the officer in charge said he's going to call the San Fran PD and Scotland Yard to coordinate with *their* investigation." Claire gave Ian a look. "He was really excited by the case. Delusions of grandeur, I believe."

Ian shook his head. "By now, MacIntyre from Scotland Yard has spoken to him and burst his bubble. These village cops will be demoted to foot patrol, if it hasn't already happened."

"Anything new on the case?"

"Only the attempted homicide yesterday," Ian said, glancing at her.

"When we get to London, you need to go through some mug books with MacIntyre and some guys from Interpol."

"Wow," Claire said, meaning it. "First the SFPD, then the FBI, then Scotland Yard—Special Branch no less—and now Interpol. Do we get to call in the cavalry, too? The CIA kind?"

"No."

"The Secret Service?"

He ignored her.

"IRS?"

"Claire."

"What about you?"

"Me, too, of course. I already gave the best description I could of the assassin," he said.

The assassin. Claire shivered a little. "Maybe when this is done, I'll have found a new calling in life. From glam queen to global PI. Now that's a midlife crisis if I ever heard of one."

"I like what you do," Ian said quietly.

Claire twisted to stare at him. "You do?"

"Yeah. It's really admirable, Claire."

A tiny compliment—and she was ecstatic. "It fits the red toes. If you have red toes, you have to be a fund-raiser."

"Got it," Ian said, smiling.

Claire fell silent, also smiling. Her head still throbbed from time to time, and when it did, her happiness would vanish, replaced by fear and dread. They were driving alongside the promenade. Gulls wheeled overhead. Tourists strolled on the beach while sunbathers stretched out on towels and children splashed in the gentle surf. There was a long pier jutting out into the water with an arcade. Children, families, and teenagers milled about the length of the pier, playing pinball and eating hot dogs. It seemed almost absurd that yesterday she and Ian had been chased and shot at by an assassin.

Claire refused to think about the events of the day before. Instead, she wondered what it would be like to be driving through this town with Ian under normal circumstances. Say, as bona fide tourists, or as lovers.

She looked out of her window again. She had an injury, Ian suspected two of the men she loved most in the world of being Lionel Elgin, yet she was more smitten with him than ever. Damn and double damn. What was to be done?

"Are you okay?" he asked again, a different inflection to his tone.

"As okay as I'll ever be," she said.

"You're a helluva trooper, Claire." He smiled then. "I've begun to see why you're so good at raising money."

"Why's that?"

"Other than the red toes, you have the determination of ten men."

She twisted to meet his gaze and did not smile. "It's an illusion. Nothing more. The truth is, I'm scared."

He glanced at her. "Which is why you're going home."

"I thought we settled that. You Lone Ranger, me Tonto, remember?"

He sighed. "I suppose you have the memory of an elephant, too?"

Claire had to smile. "Not until recently."

He sighed again, but then he met her gaze and smiled back. "You're booked. Tonight."

Claire smiled more widely. "Like hell I am."

He didn't answer, and she looked out of her window, her mood unquestionably lighter now that that was settled. They had left the promenade and beach behind. The fresh sea air was wonderful, and the town was a tourist trap but very picturesque. A silence ensued. It was easy and comfortable, as if they really were lovers. Claire finally said, "Can I ask you some questions?"

"Can I stop you?"

"They're not personal." But as she spoke, she wondered if he'd seen Reception Girl last night or that morning.

"What a relief."

"Changed my mind. How was last night?"

He blinked. "I went to bed. Alone—as if it's any of your business."

"Just checking. There's a lot of disease out there."

"What is really on your mind?"

"The case. Eddy Marshall." She looked at him and thought she saw him stiffen.

"I thought we went over that."

"We did. But you couldn't have known your uncle if he died in December of 1940." This point had been bothering her a bit. "And you are so into Eddy Marshall. He was only a relative from another generation. You're after Elgin for murdering a relative who died probably twenty years before you were ever born."

"If you're fishing for my age, I was born in 'sixty-two," Ian said.

Claire smiled.

"He was a hero, remember? And in truth, because of Eddy, I fell into my fascination with World War II, the Holocaust, and ultimately, my job."

Claire would have used the word "obsession," but she kept silent. She waited for Ian to open up the subject of his murdered uncle, but he did not. She said with a smile, "He looked just the way Hollywood might have portrayed an RAF pilot in one of those fifties films. Handsome and dashing, stereotypically so. Sort of like a tougher, rougher version of Errol Flynn." Actually, Eddy Marshall had looked almost exactly like Ian.

Ian was silent for a moment as he drove, changing lanes. "He was the oldest of the five Marshall boys; my father, Bill, was the youngest. When Eddy was murdered in 1940, he was only twenty-three. My father was twelve."

"Your father must have worshiped his oldest brother," Claire said, twisting in the seat to face him fully.

"He did. Eddy sent letters home to everyone, including my father. Dad kept not only his letters, but everyone else's."

"Those letters must be a treasure trove," she said.

"The ones to my father are light," Ian said. "He was writing to a kid. He kept it light with my grandparents, too, obviously not wanting to alarm them. But my uncle Joe, who is seventy-nine now, received some heavy-duty stuff."

Claire had to tug his sleeve. "Such as?"

Ian glanced at her. "He had some hairy dogfights. He wrote once about a dogfight he lost to an ME-109. He was flying against the sun. He was blinded. He was badly hit—he lost his tail. He ditched out over the English Channel. Rescue workers picked him up in a dorry."

"Wow," Claire said, visualizing Eddy in a parachute over the rough waters of the channel. "Did he ever mention Elgin?"

Ian gripped the wheel. "My uncle Joe has Alzheimer's, Claire. But twenty years ago he was okay. Before he became ill, he told my father that Eddy told him Elgin was a spy." He looked at her, his eyes dark. "Eddy was on to him, that's obvious, and that is why he was murdered at Elgin Hall with a thumb knife and dumped in a nearby pond."

"At least your dad remembers the conversation with Joe." She hesitated. "When did Joe tell your dad all of this?"

"In 1972," he said shortly.

Warning bells went off for Claire. She stared at Ian, who seemed grim and even upset. How in God's name would he remember that date? And the original conversation between Joe and Eddy had taken place sometime before Christmas of 1940. Thirty-two years was a huge gulf between the original conversation and Joe discussing it with his youngest brother, Bill.

"You know, Ian, I hate to rain on your parade, but there's a bit of hearsay going on, don't you think?"

He looked right into her eyes. "Is there?"

"How would Joe recall that conversation thirty-two years later?"

"He did. My father recorded the conversation. I've heard it. I still have the tape, in fact. His memory seemed fine to me."

Claire was taken aback. "Your father *recorded* their conversation?" she asked, amazed.

Ian nodded, his gaze on the road.

"Okay," she said, more bewildered than before. "Why did your father record a conversation with his own brother?"

"How would I know?" He was curt.

Claire winced. Why the sudden black mood? "Is anything wrong?" she asked cautiously.

"No."

Claire realized they were passing signs for the exit for Rhuddlan Castle. She tensed involuntarily and found herself holding her breath. The exit disappeared behind them, and Claire forced herself to relax.

"Do you feel confident that if we bring Elgin in, he will be convicted for all the murders he committed? You mentioned there isn't a solid case against him for treason."

"There isn't. Scotland Yard dropped the investigation in the late forties—I think I mentioned to you that the Elgin file was forgotten for all these years. However, things have changed. The odds will be in our favor now. If Scotland Yard and the FBI can't hang the guy in today's modern world, who can?"

"Not to mention the SFPD and the Llandudno police force," Claire had to add. Llandudno was the tourist town they had just left.

"Don't be snide, Glam Girl," Ian chastised mockingly. "It doesn't match the smile."

"Okay. 'Reform' is my middle name."

"There's something I haven't mentioned before," Ian said slowly.

"What's that?"

"Eddy's wife went to the authorities after his death with a claim." He glanced at her.

"What kind of claim?" Claire asked curiously.

"Rachel Greene claimed that Eddy had taken some very incriminating photographs of Elgin just before he died. The only problem is, she not only did not know their content, she also did not know what he did with them."

The hairs stood up on Claire's neck. "I believe her. She was his wife. She would have been his confidante. We have to find those photographs, Ian." Excitement filled her.

"It's a bit hard to look for something when you don't even know what they contain," Ian said. "Besides, maybe Elgin got there way ahead of us and everyone—say about sixty years ago—and destroyed them."

Claire studied his chiseled profile. "I wonder what those photographs contained?"

He shrugged. "It could be anything. It could be as simple as photographing Elgin using his German-made wireless radio."

"I'm no lawyer, but that might not be the nail in his Hamburg-made coffin."

"No, I don't think that would be strong enough."

"It would be very cool to find those photos," Claire said, this time more to herself than to him.

He only smiled as if he thought her amusing, and then his eyes went back to the road. The smile vanished. "Claire? There is one more thing," Ian said, exiting at the road that would take them south and to Cardiff.

This time she did not like his tone; instantly, she was wary. "What's that?"

He glanced at her.

"What?" She sat up straighter.

"Elizabeth Duke called."

Claire stared.

"Several times. She's been calling my office in New York City. Apparently she's in London and she insists upon meeting with you," Ian said. "Immediately."

CHAPTER 11

It was almost ten that evening when they finally closed the door of their London hotel room. Claire had slept quite a bit during the long drive to Cardiff, but on the short flight back to London, she had started to worry about the Dukes. Why had Elizabeth followed her to London? Claire could hardly believe the trip was coincidence; she would have known if the Dukes were taking a holiday in Britain. She hadn't heard a word about any such travel plans. *What could Elizabeth want?*

Claire walked over to one of the twin beds and flopped down on it. They had decided to share a room, but not because of the expense. Claire had looked at Ian with wide eyes and told him in a quivering tone that Elgin was out there, hunting them. It had been hard not to blow it, and even though she had kept her agenda hidden, Claire felt certain that Ian understood her scam. But he hadn't seemed angry; he had seemed resigned.

Of course, Elgin really was out there, and yesterday she'd been shot. Maybe they'd have shared a room anyway, but Claire hadn't wanted to leave anything to chance.

Claire knew what Elizabeth wanted. She wanted to protect her husband. Why else come all this way to meet with her? Claire felt sick. There was no joy in the knowledge that if William were Elgin, Jean-Léon was off the hook. In some ways, William had been more fatherly to her than her own father had ever been. Claire did not want to go down memory lane now.

But she was meeting Elizabeth first thing in the morning. It was hard not to.

"I'm exhausted. I need a hot shower and some food," Claire announced.

"Do whatever it is that you have to do," Ian said, not paying her any attention. He was already taking his laptop out of its carrying case and setting it up on the room's single desk. Clearly he intended to work.

Claire watched him sticking a floppy into the laptop's drive. He didn't seem to care that they were sharing a room, which told her that he wasn't as interested in her as she was in him. Which was a good thing, of course. That way she could stay out of trouble.

Except she had been thinking about it, and she didn't want to stay away. Not anymore, not after yesterday. She had a yearning for this man that made no sense. And it got to her ego that he could be so immune to her charms.

Claire studied him. He was so intense. He had probably forgotten that she was present, and didn't even know that she was watching him and thinking very unholy thoughts.

Claire folded her arms. "Hmm. I'm in the mood for birdbrains. What do you think?"

Ian's response was "Mmm." He began typing away on the keyboard.

Claire lifted the phone, becoming quite annoyed. "White or red with that?"

"Whatever," he said.

She narrowed her eyes. Maybe that was the key. She could get him drunk and then take total advantage.

His head whipped around. "What the hell are you doing?"

She flushed. "Ordering room service."

"You're boring holes in my back."

"I was not," she said with mock indignation. "I beg your pardon!"

"I'm going to work for a few hours. Then I'm going out to meet MacIntyre for a drink."

Claire hung up the phone. "Without me?"

"It's a guy thing—and don't start with the big eyes, Claire," he warned. He turned abruptly back to his laptop.

She couldn't believe it. They would dine—and then he would abandon her to her own devices. Not that she needed to be entertained. Claire knew she had better things to worry about, like meeting Elizabeth the next morning at her hotel, the Berkeley, on Wilton Place. That was only a few blocks from the Hilton Tower. Claire knew she should prepare herself for what might come.

Claire picked up the phone, her spirits sinking. God, how could this be happening? If Elizabeth was here to protect William, then she knew everything, then she was an accomplice of sorts, and Claire loved her so. Maybe she had so suddenly come abroad because she was worried about Claire tracking David's killer; maybe she knew nothing about their hunt for Elgin. Claire couldn't help praying that was the case.

Ian's typing stopped. He turned to look at her. "Now what?"

"I'm worried."

"I can see that. Elizabeth?"

Claire nodded. She suddenly felt so sad, enough to cry.

"Claire, let's not anticipate or predict anything. Let's see what she has to say. Stay in the present. Don't start thinking up worst-case scenarios. You'll only scare yourself."

He was right. "How about a nice filet mignon?" she asked.

"Great." He actually smiled at her, and it was warm. So much that she felt its warmth right down to her curling toes. "Get a good Burgundy or Bordeaux while you're at it."

"Okay." Claire smiled back, and their eyes locked. Ian was the one to turn away first.

She had to face it. She was definitely in love. She no longer considered Ian a stranger. And things would work out—somehow. Claire would settle now for any scenario as long as William and Jean-Léon were innocent. If her father had lied to her all of these years to protect his brother, she would be able to understand. She promised herself that and refused to consider any implications or how shaky it actually felt.

After ordering their meal, Claire got up abruptly and went into the bathroom, closing and locking the door. She tossed her purse on the vanity. She didn't want to look at herself in the mirror, because she felt horrid and filthy. As she stripped, she wished she had a sexy nightie—even better, some sultry makeup. Claire had left her red lipstick and kohl eye pencil at home. She quickly showered, then debated the choice of dressing for dinner in jeans, Ian's soft T-shirt, or a hotel towel. The hotel wasn't ritzy enough to offer bathrobes to its guests, which was a relief. Claire chose the towel, dusted some blush on her cheeks, put gloss on her lips, pasted a smile on her face, and walked back into the room.

She was nervous. Really, really nervous.

He spoke without turning. "I found something."

Claire went to stand behind him, silently ordering him to turn around and look up. But telepathy had never been her thing. "What?"

"A copy of a paragraph from the *Evening News.* Jesus, Claire." Ian turned to look at her. "It's from—" He stopped. "Where are your clothes?"

Claire smiled and hoped it was serene. "I was going to wash out some things, either that or I need to buy new underwear." Total lie. "This hotel is cheap. No plush bathrobes for us to steal."

He was flushing. "What happened to my T-shirt?"

She smiled. "I promised not to wear it, remember?"

"I recall no such thing. Go put it on," he snapped.

"What's wrong, Indiana? A case of the schoolboy jitters?"

His eyes widened. "I know what you're up to. You're as transparent as glass—Miss How-Can-I-Seduce-Ian."

"Honey, I am not trying to seduce you," Claire scoffed. "I mean, please, in this thing? If I were trying to seduce you, I'd be in a thumb-size G-string, a Wonderbra, and stilettos. All black," she added as an after-thought.

"You own a Wonderbra? I don't think so." His hands were on his hips. He was red-faced.

"I own stilettos." She smiled, feeling triumph at hand.

"No, you don't."

"Three inches qualify."

"Fine." He threw up both hands. "Now please, go get dressed."

She blinked. "Just like that?"

"Yeah. I'm working, remember?"

"Am I making you uncomfortable? I thought you were a man of the world." It crossed her mind to go back into the bathroom and come out naked.

He stared at her. "Do you want to jump into that bed with me?"

"I thought you'd never ask," she said, feeling her own cheeks begin to redden.

"Put some clothes on," he said harshly.

"Great," Claire huffed. She walked into the bathroom and slammed the door behind her. "And by the way, deal's off, screw Beijing," she shouted. She pulled on his T-shirt, then instantly regretted her choice. She tore it off. "You should just accept the inevitable," she shouted through the door, fully aware that she was contradicting herself. But was their love affair—or better yet, love—really inevitable? Or was the whole thing wishful thinking on her part? She put on her jeans and a plain white ribbed tank top. When she returned, he said, not looking at her, "Maybe I have."

"What?" she gasped.

He remained engrossed with the computer screen. "Maybe I have accepted the inevitable. Claire, now is not the time for us to lose our heads in a wild affair."

"Yes it is," she said stubbornly.

He sighed and looked at her. "Go figure."

"Because what if we really do lose our heads? Or what if one of us does? I was shot yesterday, Ian, and what if I had died? What if you die?" Her mouth was trembling with a mind of its own. "I know I make a lot of jokes, but maybe I care a lot about you, and maybe I need you, and maybe I'm scared."

Claire was frozen. She hadn't meant to reveal herself this way. Claire Hayden never let out her real feelings. It was like letting the world look at your laundry while it was hanging out to dry. "Forget it," she whispered, turning away.

"No." He quickly came up behind her, turning her around. He did not drop his hands from her shoulders. "I know you're scared. And I wish I could make the fear go away."

"You can," Claire whispered, drowning in his eyes. "For a while, anyway." She could barely believe she was begging him to make love to her.

He was silent.

But Claire had meant every word. "It won't be the end of the world. The end of the world might come—via Elgin, or another assassin—but not over there, in that bed."

His jaw tightened. "You're killing me," he finally said. "And I like you a lot. That's the problem. This is very complicated. William, your father—"

"Ssh," Claire said, putting two fingertips on his mouth. She was almost amazed with herself—she had never been so assertive before. But she was compelled. There was no turning back. "It's only complicated if you make it that way. We're both consenting adults."

His eyes were turning dark. "No. You're consenting, I'm not. This is coercion, plain and simple," he said roughly. And his hands tightened on her shoulders.

Her heart soared. "Ian." His name rolled off her tongue as a sigh.

Their eyes held. Silence filled the room, along with the sounds of traffic on the street below.

"There's nothing I want to do more than make love to you," he ground out. "Damn it, Claire." He didn't look happy. "I've been telling myself for days not to complicate matters."

Claire was elated—he'd been thinking exactly as she had. She felt as if she'd won the lottery. "See—talking to yourself is only a good thing if you're old and lonely."

"Sometimes I feel like I'm talking to myself when I'm talking to you. Why won't you listen?" he cried.

"Because . . ." She gulped hard. "Because I think I'm in love with you."

He went white.

"Oh, God." Her brain went into shock. "Now *I've* complicated matters."

"Yeah, you certainly have," he said. He leaned over her, and Claire found herself pressed against his body and wrapped in his arms. His kiss was long, slow, and deep.

Claire tried to fuse her body with his. Emotion overcame her. Elation, euphoria, triumph, love, fear. The latter was niggling.

There was also truth. This was so right. He was so right. Everything about him was simply perfect.

She had never wanted to be with any man more. She had never wanted anyone the way she wanted him.

"Hurry," she urged, running her hands up and down his back with growing urgency. She pressed her thigh against his erection. It was large and solid and she was pleased.

"No," he said, lifting her into his arms while slipping off her tank top. It fell away, undoubtedly to the floor.

Claire began to argue as he carried her to the bed. "No. I need you now."

"Shut up, Claire," he said with so much affection in his tone that she could not take offense.

Claire did intend to protest his choice of words. She really did. But he was removing her jeans, and she wasn't wearing any underwear. She was also on her back, and he was leaning over her, inspecting her from head to toe while running one large palm from her shoulders down to her toes. She shivered in delight as his fingers grazed her breasts and nipples, her belly, her pubis and inner thighs. Their gazes met on her gasp.

"How long has it been?" he asked frankly, his eyes shining now.

His hand was moving back up the inside of her calf, her thigh. Claire had to shift her legs wide for him. "Nine months, a year," she managed.

"What a fool," he said, bestowing a somewhat chaste kiss on her sex.

She knew he referred to David. Claire bit off another gasp, and he moved over her, their eyes holding. Claire began to tug at his belt.

He grinned, but it was brief, and quickly his expression became strained. His lips found hers, and as he kissed her, Claire fumbled with and opened his belt, his pants. He kicked off his trousers, his briefs.

Claire reached for him. "This is my lucky day," she heard herself whisper.

"I hope," he said, tonguing her ear.

She loved him even more for not being an arrogant jerk. "Hurry."

"Don't think so," he said, sliding his tongue over her jaw and down her throat.

Claire realized his ultimate destination and she lay still, except for her thundering heart. He reached her breast, her nipple. But his attentions there were brief.

Claire moaned as he kissed and tongued his way down her belly. When his tongue slipped between her labia, she managed, "Keep this up and I'll buy you a Wonderbra and a whip."

"Do you ever stop talking?" he asked, shifting slightly to take her hand and wrap it firmly around his penis. Then he went to work.

His tongue did amazing things to her sex, and Claire came, shouting God's name in vain.

Someone banged on an adjoining wall.

He pulled her close and she found herself wrapped in his arms again, but this time he was thrusting his huge hardness inside, and it was heaven-sent. "Come again, Claire," he whispered, moving slow and deep but with real urgency. His words were tight and hard. "This time, shout *my* name, okay?"

She wanted to jab his ribs and call him Dick, buster, whatever. She couldn't speak. She couldn't breathe. This was it, the experience she had been waiting a lifetime for.

He said something, his own rendition of worship and sacrilege. He was moving faster, harder, now.

Claire clung. "Oh, God."

"Ian," he gasped, and it was an instruction.

"Oh, God, I love you," Claire screamed.

And as she was on the wings of another huge orgasm, carried far, far away, she felt his release, too, and she thought but wasn't sure that she heard him breathe her name at last.

Room service came and went. Claire kept her eyes screwed shut, hiding under the sheets, pretending to be asleep.

She had to be the idiot of all idiots. Of all time. Who the hell shouted to the world—literally—that they were in love?

Claire knew it would be even stupider to hope he hadn't heard her. After all, hadn't she said the same thing while totally sane?

Of course, she could write the last instance off to being absolutely mindless while in the throes of an orgasm. That was fairly close to the truth.

Except the real truth was she had meant every word *both stupid times,* and now she could not be more mortified.

"Claire," he called softly, and she felt the bed dip by her feet. "Dinner's on."

Should she continue to play possum?

"I know you're not asleep," he said, and there was amusement in his tone.

She felt him tugging on the sheets.

"Fine," she snapped, sitting bolt upright and clutching the covers to her chest. "I am *starving,*" she said. Her cheeks were already burning, and she could not look him in the eye.

"You are also loud," he said, laughter in his voice.

She stole a glance at him. He had slipped on his briefs. They were chambray blue and very revealing. "I hope the waiter wasn't gay."

"I borrowed your towel." He was smiling, his eyes twinkling. "Here." He handed her the tiny ribbed tank top. Her jeans followed.

Claire gave him a dirty look—as if her loquacious moments were his fault—and tossed aside the covers. She knew he stared at her as she hopped into her jeans and then shrugged on the tank.

"You know, we do have neighbors," he said, holding out a wineglass.

Claire snatched it. "Fine. You know, you could be a gentleman right now."

He grinned. "But what fun would that be?"

She stared. "I could toss this at you."

"Why are you so angry?" He began to laugh.

"This isn't funny."

"It isn't?" He laughed harder, saw her face, stopped. "You seduced *me*."

"Oh, God. I cannot take this!" She set the wine down on the table that had been rolled into their room with their food.

"I'm sorry. Truce. Pax Britannica," he said, still sputtering with laughter he could not repress.

Claire faced him with her hands on her hips. "You men are all the same. Egomaniacs!"

He laughed all over again.

"Why are you so happy?" she cried.

He seized her hand and reeled her in as if she were a trout on his fishing pole. "C'mon, Claire, we both know you aren't dense."

She found herself against his mostly bare and newly aroused body. "Well . . ."

He slid his hands down to her behind and lifted her up. "I'm a happy guy. Got me a gorgeous dame." He kissed the top of her head. "One who shouts and screams. Never had a screamer before," he teased.

She had melted, from the top of her perspiring head to the tips of her painted toes. "I never was such a 'screamer' before, either."

"Hmm. More grist for my ego." He began tugging up her tank top.

Claire pressed her hips against his distended loins. "More grist for your mill."

"Like that." The tank top was tossed to the floor.

"I don't want to be a screamer," Claire complained breathlessly as he cupped her small breasts in his hands.

"I don't want you to change," he said, and he made love to her again.

They brought their plates into bed, the bottle of wine and glasses on the left-side night table. Claire had shrugged on his T-shirt, and Ian put on his briefs. They inhaled oven-warm rolls and their filets in near silence. The wine went down like water. Ian ordered another bottle.

He had forgotten all about MacIntyre. Claire chose not to remind him.

Ian had also ordered something called Chocolate Decadence. It was actually a sampler of five different chocolate desserts. Claire dug into a chocolate pastry, washing it down with wine. "So what did you find, Ian? You started to tell me about something in the *Evening News*." It was a newspaper she had never heard of.

He was eating a huge chocolate cookie with creamy white filling. "God, I forgot to tell you. According to this article, the Elgin heir died in a hunting accident in June of 1935. I didn't know that Lionel had an older brother at one point."

Claire blinked, tempted to lick her fingers, and then decided, *Why not?* "Is that significant?"

"I don't know." He smiled at her.

Claire licked her fingers and took the other half of the cookie. "Thanks, you're a gent after all."

"I'll call my office in a bit and have them do some checking on the older brother."

Claire suddenly got a chill. She put the last bite of cookie back on the plate that sat in the middle of the bed between them. There was chocolate on the white sheets. Not to mention crumbs—and lots of great sex. But she didn't want to reminisce now.

Surely Ian didn't think, because Lionel Elgin had an older brother who was dead, and her father also had an older brother who was dead, that they were one and the same?

"Claire? What's wrong?" Ian asked, pausing in the act of digging his fork into a piece of chocolate-chocolate-chip cake that looked mega-fattening.

"You aren't trying to make a connection between my father and the fact that Elgin had an older brother who's dead, are you?" She could hear how terse she sounded.

"It's an interesting coincidence, but I wouldn't make too much of it," he said way too indifferently.

Claire put her hands behind her head, leaning back against the pillows, and stared almost blindly at the door. He had said that their lovemaking would complicate matters, and she had refused to listen. Claire tried to control her pulse rate, which had accelerated. It seemed impossible to remain calm now.

It really didn't mean anything that both men had deceased older brothers.

But who was she fooling? What if it did?

"Hey, Screamer, pass over that bottle of wine."

Claire turned and looked at him.

"Not even a tiny smile?" Ian asked, but his own smile did not reach his eyes.

"Ian, I just know that my father is not Lionel Elgin."

He was silent.

Claire realized she was biting her lip. Worse, she saw on his face that he seriously considered her father a suspect and that nothing had changed for him. "Why can't you trust me? On this one simple thing?"

After a pause, he said, "That's not fair and you know it. First of all, there is nothing simple about this case. You're too involved, Claire. Against my wishes and better judgment, I might add."

Claire slipped out of the bed, standing and facing him. She said, low, "I loved my mother," and saw the look of surprise flit across his face. "She was everything to me. She was an angel, Ian, a real, live, flesh-and-blood angel. She was so kind, so warm, so loving . . ." Claire had to stop. It was so hard to speak.

Ian looked down at his sheet-clad lap. "It's okay, Claire. I think I understand."

"Do you?" She shook her head, barely able to speak. "No, it's not okay. It will never be okay again. Because one day she got sick. And then every day she was sicker than the day before. I was only eight when she was first diagnosed with breast cancer. She died a few days after my tenth birthday. Do you have any idea what it's like to watch your mother dying like that?"

"No. I don't."

"I still love her. I still miss her. I always will."

He didn't say anything; there wasn't much he could say.

"My father is an aloof man. You've met him. He's reserved and preoccupied with his world—art. But he's my father. He raised me alone. And right now, he's all I have."

"I understand."

"Do you? Jean-Léon has never lied to me. He may have sucked as a dad, but he's honest—through and through. Robert Ducasse was a hero of the French Resistance. He died a few weeks before the invasion of Normandy. Period. End of story." She stared at him through blurry eyes.

Ian remained silent. He quaffed down some more wine.

Claire crossed her arms. "What makes you think that my father has been lying about his real identity all of these years, anyway? What could possibly make you think that Robert Ducasse is still alive?"

Ian hesitated. Claire stared at him unblinkingly and almost felt his mind race. She was certain he was deciding what to say—and what not to say. Why did he feel the need to hold back now?

"Have you ever been to St. Michele, Claire?" Ian finally asked.

She tensed. "Where my father and his brother were born? It's a small village about fifty miles south of Paris. Yes, I've been there."

"Actually, so have I."

Claire didn't like his answer. "When did you go there?"

"Three days after David's death."

Claire looked away. "Okay," she said, fighting more anxiety. Then she met his eyes. "What did you find, Ian?"

"Every parish keeps records," he said. Then he patted the bed. "Come sit down, Claire. We're not adversaries. We're lovers, remember? You owe me a Wonderbra."

She did not move and did not crack even the slightest smile.

He sighed. When he spoke, his tone was very gentle. "There is a Ducasse family. It's a huge family—siblings and cousins, and they're all over the province. During the war, there were five brothers in that town who went off to fight, some in L'Armée Française before Dunkirk, several slipping into Vichy to fight in the Resistance. I believe one brother remained behind after the German occupation, he was a butcher or something. There was a brother named Robert Ducasse. He did not fight the Germans in Vichy France. He was interned in a German POW camp for most of the war, where he died. His brother, Jean-Léon, died fighting the Germans in May of 1940. Neither one of them were ever in the Resistance. He died in northern France on the Belgium border, near Bruly-le-Pêche."

Claire stared at him. "It's a different branch of the family." But she was sick in her gut.

He said softly, "I've done some research into the French Resistance in Vichy to double-check. Ducasse is a common name, but if Robert Ducasse existed in the whereabouts of Lyons, there are no records about him, no accounts, not even any myths."

"The Gestapo imprisoned him for a week in Lyons early on in the war," Claire said breathlessly. "He was released when they couldn't prove any of the charges against him. That should be easy enough to verify."

"There are no records, Claire," Ian repeated softly. "Not in Vichy."

It was simply impossible. "You haven't looked hard enough." She stared at him, light-headed all over again. It was hard to think clearly, rationally. What was he trying to say? *That her father and his brother had stolen identities from these Ducasse brothers?* She did not believe it. It could not be possible.

"Forget about it for now," Ian finally said, throwing aside the sheet and standing. He came around the bed. "You don't need it now. You need it like you need a hole in your head."

"I have a hole in my head," she muttered, the urge to cry overtaking her.

"No, you have a graze, which is a very different matter." He took her hands in his.

She pulled away. "Jean-Léon, Robert, Ducasse—they're all very common names."

"Yes, they are," he said.

"Now you're patronizing me!" she shouted furiously.

"I'm not. All I want to do is . . ." He stopped.

"What? Tell me what it is that you want to do, Ian? Other than nail Jean-Léon or Robert or William and hang one of them like they hung the Nazis at Nuremberg?"

He stared somberly at her. "I want to protect you, and God, I am so sorry you are involved in this."

She crossed her arms across her breasts. "You can't protect me," she said grimly. "No one can."

He stared at her; Claire turned away. Then he said, "Look, it's late and tomorrow is a big day." They were flying home that night—Ian had an appointment with Frances Cookson, George Suttill's girlfriend, who was finally returning from her visit to Florida. "Let's go to sleep, Claire."

Claire looked at him. She thought about the Ducasse family currently living in St. Michele, she thought about her breakfast with Elizabeth in the morning, and she thought about all the lovemaking they had just shared. "I've really complicated matters, haven't I?"

"Yeah, you have." He put his arm around her. "But you were right. It was inevitable. So don't go blaming yourself now, Red."

Claire tried to smile and for the first time in her life, found that she couldn't.

CHAPTER 12

They paused on the wide steps before the entrance to the Berkeley Hotel. It was a cool morning, and Claire felt chilled. She was certain it had more to do with meeting Elizabeth and hearing her out than the weather.

"You'll be fine," Ian said, smiling at her.

She met his eyes, and a rush of warmth swept over her, but it was followed by dread and fear. This morning, after the night they had shared, she was dangerously in love—with the man who might, at any moment, destroy her father or her dearest family friends. Becoming lovers now was fraught with complications. She felt as if she were out on a limb that might be sawed out from under her at any moment.

"We're meeting in the salon right off the lobby. Elizabeth suggested breakfast. That must mean other guests will be present." As Claire spoke, she realized she was extremely anxious. Yet that was absurd. William would not be present, and Elizabeth would never hurt her—she considered her the daughter she had never had. Claire was also determined to believe that Elizabeth was blissfully ignorant of the extent of Elgin's crimes—should Elgin be unmasked as William Duke.

"Do you want me to come with you?" Ian asked.

They had already discussed this. Ian felt Elizabeth would speak more freely if speaking with Claire alone. "No. I'll be fine." Claire smiled at him and turned to go.

"I'll wait out here, and every now and then I'll walk into the lobby and glance into the salon just to make sure you're all right. We met only briefly at David's party, and I'm sure she won't be able to pick me out of a crowd."

Claire nodded, about to leave, feeling as if she were about to face a firing squad, when Ian took her arm, halting her. Confused, she hesitated.

"Break a leg, O'Hara," he whispered, kissing her on the lips.

Claire's heart melted. "Thanks. I guess that means it's show time."

"It does."

Claire walked inside. The lobby was small and brightly lit. Uniformed hotel staff were everywhere, smiling at her and murmuring crisp greetings. To her left was a bar in shades of blue that seemed to be closed. Claire turned to her right and saw the salon, a grandiose and old-fashioned room filled with plush couches, club chairs, and antiques. At the same moment, Claire saw Elizabeth *and* William. She faltered.

What was William doing there? She hadn't expected him to be present. Ian had said Elgin wouldn't dare to set foot in the U.K. right now. Did this mean he was innocent?

But why wouldn't he dare? He had dared everything else—he had killed George Suttill and followed that murder by killing David under everyone's nose during the party. And he had tried to kill them, for God's sake. He had dumped Eddy's body in a pond close to his home, Elgin Hall. He was arrogant and clever. He might very well dare to come back.

Claire was shaken, and worse, she was ill. The sick feeling was induced by a real and raw fear.

Elizabeth had seen her and was standing, smiling and waving. Her expression was clearly anxious, and now that Claire had been seen, she could not turn around and flee, nor could she procrastinate further. Filled with dread, she was unable to smile back at the woman she loved.

Elizabeth hugged her. The embrace was brief, but it seemed warm. As she pulled back, Claire looked into her blue eyes and saw more anxiety.

"Claire? I am so glad we found you!" Elizabeth cried.

Claire finally turned to face William. He was grim, and instead of hugging her as he might have, he pecked her check. She did not mean to pull away from him, but she did. The action was a reflex.

William started. "Claire? You don't look well." His tone was avuncular. How could this kind old man be a killer? "I'm fighting a cold."

"You've been under too much stress," William said. "Whenever I am overloaded, the first thing that happens is I catch a cold. Take lots of vitamin C and echinacea," he said.

"I will," Claire managed.

"I'm so glad to see you. Claire, I have been so worried about you," Elizabeth exclaimed. "Let's sit down. I ordered coffee, I know that's what you drink in the morning, and we can order breakfast." Her smile flashed. "Where is your Mr. Marshall?" Her gaze had strayed beyond Claire to the lobby.

"He's not here," Claire said as they sat down, Claire on the sofa, William and Elizabeth each in a flanking chair. A coffee table was in the center. The moment she sank onto the small, plush couch, Claire realized she had made a mistake and was at a disadvantage. She was a half a foot lower than the Dukes.

"I just spoke with your father," Elizabeth said after signaling a waiter. "He is rather frantic, Claire. You must call him. How can you just disappear in this kind of situation? We've both been afraid that something happened to you when we didn't hear from you."

Claire hesitated, a game plan going through her mind. "I'm sorry," she said. "I didn't realize that silence might make it seem like I'm in trouble. But actually, that has been the case."

"What?" Elizabeth gasped. "What kind of trouble?"

"I spent the night before last in a hospital. Someone tried to shoot me—kill me. And Ian," she added. She regarded them both closely.

If they knew—if William had hired the assassin—Claire never would have been able to guess, not in a thousand years. Elizabeth seemed stunned. So did William.

"What happened?" he asked grimly.

"Someone tried to drive us off the road, up in Wales. He succeeded, actually—we wound up in the river Clwyd."

The Dukes remained pale. "Dear God," Elizabeth said, reaching for Claire's hand and holding it tightly.

Claire looked from their joined hands to Elizabeth's pale face and felt tears gathering in her own eyes. Claire squeezed her friend's palm. "It gets worse," she said softly. "We were chased on foot into some ruins— the driver had a gun. I got a graze just over my ear." She lifted up her hair to show the Band-Aid and the small patch where her hair had been shaved around the wound.

"A terrible, terrible thing," William said soberly. "You shouldn't be involved in this, Claire. You must come right home."

Claire twisted to stare at William. Was there a double meaning to his words?

"You did call the police," Elizabeth said.

Claire met her gaze. "Of course." She almost added, *And Scotland Yard and the FBI and Interpol,* but she refrained. Some things were better left unsaid. "How is Jean-Léon?"

"Frantic," Elizabeth said. "You must call him immediately."

"I will," Claire said, meaning it.

"Dear, surely now you are going home. Surely after such a threat on your life, you will cease with this absurd investigation."

Claire looked right into her blue eyes. "Actually, we are flying home tonight."

"That is wonderful," Elizabeth said in vast relief.

Claire turned to look at William, who was uncharacteristically serious. "How are you feeling, William?"

"Just fine," he said. "Claire? Why are you so nervous?"

Claire stared, feeling how wide her eyes must be. "Nervous? Who said I'm nervous?"

"I have never seen you this jumpy. Of course, that's understandable, considering that someone tried to kill you. But every time I look at you, you fidget and look away. Am I making you nervous?" William asked, his blue gaze direct.

Claire stared, and it seemed as if her ears were ringing. If the Dukes were involved with the attempt on her life, then she was in the midst of a nasty cat-and-mouse game—and she was in no way up to it. "William, how could you make me nervous? When I was a little girl, you read me bedtime stories—while I sat on your knee."

He smiled fondly. "Yes, I did." His smile faded. "I suppose it is that Nazi you are after. Does Marshall think he will strike again? And why, dear God, did he strike at you?"

Claire wet her lips. "He was after Ian. That's what Ian thinks. I don't know why he took a shot at me." She shrugged. "I don't know what to think," she had to add. Then she was afraid she had given all of her suspicions away.

"Well, thank God you have come to your senses and are going home," Elizabeth said, taking her hand briefly again. "Nothing could make me happier, Claire."

"Is that why you flew over to London? To make sure I go home?" Claire asked, too late realizing she had asked the question in such a leading way that the Dukes could seize on the obvious answer, getting themselves off the hook.

"That is one reason. Perhaps you should invite Mr. Marshall to join us now," Elizabeth said. It was not a suggestion.

"That's a good idea," William seconded the notion. "We have information for him."

Claire was startled. She looked from the one to the other, and in that short moment, as she stared at them, she tried to decipher their innermost thoughts and feelings. Was he a killer? Did Elizabeth know? Or were they innocent, her dear and cherished lifelong friends, whom she believed to have hearts of gold?

An answer eluded her. Any intuition she might have had was not forthcoming.

"Claire? Isn't that Mr. Marshall in the lobby?" Elizabeth asked, breaking into her thoughts.

Claire leaped to her feet as William said, "Yes, that's him. Fortunately, I never forget a face."

Claire saw Ian as he paused in the lobby, a map in hand, looking very casual, as if he were a tourist and a guest. Claire waved at him.

He did a double take when he saw William, then slowly he came over to them.

Elizabeth stood. William, who seemed to be relying more heavily on his cane than he had in the past, did not. "Mr. Marshall. I believe we met briefly at David's birthday party, and at his funeral." Elizabeth extended her hand.

"I believe so," Ian said, accepting the handshake. He gave Claire a brief glance, but when their eyes met, it was in silent communication. Claire responded with a slight shrug and knew he understood that she had not learned anything.

"I am a very good friend of Claire's," Elizabeth said, still standing. "I must tell you, I am quite bothered that you have dragged her into something she should not be a part of." Claire gaped. The Dukes were very proper, and to set Ian down was completely out of character. "Like Jean-Léon, I want her to come home." Elizabeth looked at Claire. "I am just speechless that she was shot. And I am thrilled that she is coming home tonight."

"I prefer that she goes home as well," Ian said, making Claire want to kick him.

"Good. We agree on that, at least." Elizabeth smiled. "Please, let's sit down." She signaled the waiter, who came over. "Coffee, Mr. Marshall?"

"Thank you."

"We need another cup. Shall we order breakfast?"

"We've eaten," Claire said, and then she blushed. They'd had a continental breakfast in their room—after making love. But the Dukes wouldn't know that.

Elizabeth ordered toast for her and William, then turned to Ian. "We wish to help your investigation, Mr. Marshall."

Ian glanced at Claire. "Why do you want to help, if you don't mind my asking?"

"Why?" William spoke up. "I'll tell you why. I'm an Englishman, even if I have chosen to live in the States, and if I can do my patriotic duty, then I shall."

Claire and Ian looked at each other again. "What is it that you wish to tell us?" Ian asked.

"William went to school with Harry Elgin," Elizabeth said.

Claire started, then she turned to stare at William in surprise. He nodded, and she turned to look at Ian. Ian also seemed surprised. "The older brother? The one who died in some accident?" she asked.

William nodded. "Harry and I were great friends at Eton," he said. "We played football and sculled on the same teams. We dated together. He was a wonderful chap. Good wit, intelligent, at the top of his class. Good manners, too. His death crushed me. I couldn't get over it."

"He died in a hunting accident, I believe," Ian said.

William looked at him. "Yes, he did. It happened at his family estate in the north of Wales. A terrible, terrible tragedy," he said. "And now this. This whole affair with the younger brother. It makes me think."

"It makes you think what, William?" she asked.

He looked at her. "You are chasing Lionel Elgin, believing him to have spied for the Gerries during the war. I always thought he was an odd duck, indeed. The brothers were not close," he added with some venom. "Of course, that was not unusual, as Harry was the heir. Lionel was most definitely jealous of his brother, especially as one and all adored Harry."

"Could you identify Lionel Elgin?" Ian asked.

William laughed. "I last saw him fifty or sixty years ago. We ran into each other briefly sometime during the beginning of the war. No. I would not be able to recognize him. But what I have been wondering now is if it was really an accident."

"If what was an accident?" Claire asked, perplexed.

William looked at her as if she was rather foolish. "Harry's death."

Claire sat up straighter. "I beg your pardon?"

"You didn't know? Lionel shot his brother. That was how Harry died. The two of them were out hunting in the woods, and Lionel shot Harry, supposedly by mistake."

Claire felt as if the breath had been knocked out of her. Her ears began to ring. She just knew that the man who killed Eddy Marshall, George Suttill, and David had also murdered his own brother. It was the strongest, most sickening gut feeling she had ever had.

"I had no idea," Ian said. "I saw one news clipping, and it was brief. There was no mention of how Harry died."

"There wouldn't be. It was so tragic and, of course, all hushed up," William said.

Claire found her voice. "But wouldn't Lionel have been a boy at the time?"

William nodded. "Harry was only seventeen. Lionel was several years younger. He might have been twelve or thirteen."

"Hunting accidents happen frequently," Ian said.

Claire gaped at him. Was he now defending their quarry?

Elizabeth finally spoke. "I did not meet William until 1940, shortly after the Blitz began. I was only fifteen, and we didn't begin dating for another year and a half. I never met Lionel, not even once, but I do recall the splash that the death of the Elgin heir made in the dailies at the time." She shared a glance with William. "But it only lasted for a few days. I am certain Lord Elgin must have quashed the story. I would have done the very same thing."

Claire tensed when Ian shifted forward slightly in order to speak. "William, when did you immigrate to the States?"

"In 1952," he said without hesitation. "Why do you ask, Marshall?"

Ian smiled benignly. "It's important. If you do not mind?"

William shrugged.

Claire's tension increased. She doubted she could move her shoulders if she tried.

"You lived in Paris for a few years," Ian remarked.

"Yes." William stared at Ian, and if he was surprised that Ian knew a bit about him, he did not reveal it. "I was offered a job with a very prestigious investment banking firm in 'forty-eight, and a part of the job offer was a transfer to their Paris branch. I didn't mind. Elizabeth had just been accepted at the Sorbonne, so it worked out perfectly." He smiled and glanced at Claire. "That's where I met your father. At some small art gallery holding an exhibition for several young, unknown artists."

"So you were in Britain until 'forty-eight?" Ian asked.

William looked right at him. "Yes, I was. Of course, in 'forty-four I was posted to a destroyer in the Mediterranean. I was a colonel in Her Majesty's Navy. But after the war, I returned to London. Elizabeth and I were married in a very small and private ceremony that summer, and we lived quite happily in a small flat in Chelsea until the move to France."

Claire wondered if Ian was itching to take notes. This was the first she had ever heard about William being in the navy during the war, but then, World War II was not their usual topic of conversation. She understood what Ian was doing—he had told her there was a huge gap in the records of William's life in the mid-forties.

A silence fell over the group. Claire was absorbed with her own thoughts, and they were frightening. She looked at Ian. He nodded at her, indicating he was ready to leave, much to her relief, but he spoke to the Dukes. "Thank you for you help."

"It was no bother, really," William said, and smiled. "And I do hope we did help."

Claire was already standing, aware of Elizabeth's close regard. The Dukes walked them into the lobby. Claire managed to smile at Elizabeth, who hugged her. She seemed reluctant to release Claire. "We're leaving tonight, now that we've had a chance to see you. You really are coming home, aren't you?"

Claire met the other woman's eyes, surprised that Elizabeth was in doubt. "Yes, I am."

"But you are not finished with this, are you, Claire?" Elizabeth asked quietly.

Claire hesitated; she did not want to lie. "No. David's killer needs to be caught, Elizabeth."

Elizabeth shook her head as if sad, resigned. "You are so much like your mother now, Claire. She would never quit anything, not once she had started it. Please stay safe," she said softly.

"I promise," Claire whispered back, moved and tearful.

They exchanged another hug, and Claire turned to smile at William. He was regarding them obliquely, and the hairs on her neck seemed to rise when their gazes met. He smiled a little at her, but it seemed sad, and then he moved stiffly away with the use of his cane, not bothering to embrace her or say good-bye.

Claire was more distressed than previously. She watched the Dukes walk around the corner to the elevator, and then they were out of sight.

"Ready?" Ian asked her, touching her elbow lightly.

She nodded, inhaling harshly. A doorman opened the front door, and they stepped out of the hotel.

"Taxi?" another doorman asked.

Ian told him they would walk, as the Hilton Tower was only a few blocks past Hyde Park Corner. He took her arm as they started down the block. "Chin up, Red," he said.

Claire blinked back a tear and met his gaze.

"Jury's not in," he said softly, pausing in the middle of the block. Pedestrians glanced at them curiously but walked around them.

"What do you think?" she asked hoarsely.

"I think they came over here to help, but what did they tell us? That William went to school with Harry Elgin. That maybe Lionel meant to shoot him and Harry's death was no accident. The latter has no bearing on anything, Claire, since we already know how ruthless Elgin is. And the former could well be a smoke screen."

Claire looked at him. "It's worse than that. I never, ever mentioned Elgin's name, not to my father and not to the Dukes."

Because of the time change, they arrived at JFK just an hour or so after they had left the U.K. "Eightieth and Third," Ian directed their taxi driver. He glanced at Claire. "How you doing, kiddo?"

Claire put on her seat belt carefully as the cab left the terminal. She smiled. "Couldn't be better, bud."

But she was tired. More so mentally than anything else. Had she arrived in Wales only four days ago? A lifetime seemed to have passed since then. And now she was back in New York—with Ian Marshall, who was no longer a stranger but a lover. Had anyone even suggested to her a week ago that she would survive a hit attempt and be having an affair with Ian Marshall—while in the midst of a hunt for a Nazi—she would have accused them of being crazy.

But maybe she was the crazy one now. Claire looked out of her window. For hours and hours, she had replayed every word and every nuance of their conversation with the Dukes—while trying to avoid thinking about her conversation with Ian the night before. Had William been Harry Elgin's best friend when they were boys? Or had Harry Elgin been his older brother?

The latter was a sickening prospect.

Ian was on his cell phone. As he wasn't speaking, she guessed that he was picking up messages. She noticed that he had not put on his seat belt. It was a very New York way to tempt fate, as New York cabbies only pretended to know how to drive. Claire had never been able to figure out how they acquired their licenses.

Claire was tense and torn. Looking at him made her heart want to sing a little, and it made her wonder when they would make love next. Being in his arms was the best thing in the world, as far as she could tell. And thinking about making love was a good distraction. But maybe it was a dangerous distraction. Maybe he had been right; maybe this was a complication that neither one of them needed right now—when they did not know for certain just who Elgin really was.

She had yet to call her father, who was, according to Elizabeth, sick with worry about her.

"Good news," Ian said. "Frances Cookson is back, and we're confirmed for first thing tomorrow morning." He smiled at her, but his gaze was searching.

"Great!" Claire exclaimed, knowing she had to be the worst actress in New York.

The taxi was now speeding down the Van Wyck Expressway. "Claire, give it up. You've been tense since we departed Heathrow."

"I am hardly tense. I mean, we get to relax tonight. How's that? Relaxation. That's a word we've both forgotten, I think. My vote is for Patsy's Pizza and a video. Something easy. Like *The Big Easy*."

"Claire." He took her hand. "It's okay to be frightened."

She faced him. "That is easy for you to say." She grimaced, then said, "It's William. I know it. He was acting differently around me."

"Let's not jump the gun."

"Why not? Why not have him picked up and see if you can match his DNA to another Elgin's?"

"There is no other Elgin. Lady Ellen is not an Elgin by birth, and her relatives are all from her side. We could go for a match on Randolph Elgin's body, but he was never found. I don't want to bring in the wrong guy so the real Elgin can disappear again—this time forever." He hesitated, then added, "Besides, I'm not a cop, remember? Technically, I'm supposed to do research and point the authorities in the right direction."

Claire flopped back against the sticky seat of the cab. "I need panties."

"What?"

"I didn't do the best job packing in two minutes flat. I'm short a few things. Do you want a list of unmentionables?"

"Not really."

"Who are you calling now?" He was on his cell phone.

"My office."

Claire tuned out. Guilt tried to get a hold on her. She shoved it away. Yes, she did need a few things, but her shopping could wait. What she really needed was a moment alone—so she could call Jean-Léon.

She promised herself that she would not violate Ian's trust. She would not compromise the investigation. But there was no way she was going to speak with her father with Ian listening to their every word.

Ian hung up. "There's a few shops in my neighborhood. Mostly boutiques, but—"

"Why don't you just drop me off at Bloomingdale's?"

He studied her. "Okay. Claire, I hate seeing you upset like this."

Claire sighed. "Believe me, it's not fun."

"You could change that stubborn mind of yours and go home."

She looked at him. "So now you want to dump me? You guys are all the same, wham, bam, thank you, ma'am."

"Be serious."

"I'd rather not."

"Things might get worse."

Claire flinched. "How much worse?" She stared fearfully into his eyes, but she was seeing Jean-Léon, not Ian.

"I don't know. But maybe you should prepare yourself."

The cab dropped Claire off in front of Bloomingdale's, which she hadn't been to in years. They were in New York City. No one knew where they were. They were safe for a while. She was safe. So why did she feel uneasy splitting up from Ian now? It was absurd.

She waved briefly and walked to the front doors as the cab pulled away. Then she halted, not going inside. Ian had given her his cell phone, just in case she needed to call him.

The crowd was amazingly dense as it moved around her. She stood there in front of the store, hesitating. Ian hadn't told her not to speak with Jean-Léon again, so she did not need to feel so guilty. Still, she knew he would not be happy for her to be in touch with her father, not now. Claire made her decision—she just had to speak with Jean-Léon one more time.

And she did not like the train of her thoughts. Why had her brain formed the words "one more time" as if it might be the last time?

Claire remained sick at heart. She quickly dialed Jean-Léon at the art gallery, but the only reply she got was his answering machine. She dialed his cell and it was answered instantly.

"Claire! Where the hell are you now? And where have you been? *Why didn't you tell me you were shot?*" he demanded.

"How did you know that I was shot?" Claire asked, taken aback. "Dad, it was only a graze."

"How do I know? I spoke with Elizabeth this morning before she left London, just after she met with you," Jean-Léon said flatly. "Why do you think she went over there? I asked her to."

Her heart was pounding erratically now. What was this? A conspiracy of Jean-Léon and Elizabeth? "How long have you known the Dukes, Dad?"

"Why?"

"I need to know."

"We met in the late fifties, around the time I met your mother."

Claire froze. *He was lying.*

Or had the Dukes been lying?

"What? I missed that. What did you say?" she asked, her heart pounding.

"I met them at a party here in San Francisco. I remember very distinctly—I had just begun dating your mother. Claire, what is this about?"

Was he lying? Claire refused to believe it—the Dukes had to be lying. "Dad, this is important. Did you find that bill of sale for the Courbet?"

"What?" he exclaimed. "What are you talking about?"

"I need the bill of sale, Dad. I need you to fax it over to me."

"What are you and Marshall up to? And where are you, Claire?"

Claire wet her lips. "Dad, what would you do if I told you that Marshall thinks your brother is a lie? What would you say if I told you that he thinks your brother was never a Frenchman? That he thinks your brother is Lionel Elgin—David's killer?"

There was only the briefest instant of silence on the other end of the line. Jean-Léon said, mirth in his tone, "The man is certifiable. That would make me a liar, Claire, a liar and an Englishman, and I have *never* lied to you."

She collapsed against the big window of the store, thinking, *Dad, what would you say if I told you that he thinks you are Elgin?* But she did not dare voice her inner thoughts and her very worst fears. "I know you wouldn't lie to me, Dad. I just know it."

"Are you crying?" he asked, surprised.

Claire shook her head, unable to speak. "No," she managed. Then, "I need proof, Dad, proof that Robert's dead and that you and he were born in St. Michele."

"Is this a joke? A bad joke?"

She couldn't speak; she could only shake her head.

"Where are you now? New York? Elizabeth said you were on your way home."

"I'm at Heathrow," Claire lied. She closed her eyes, hating herself.

"You're on your way back to San Francisco?"

Claire made a sound that indicated yes.

"Good. Are you out of this now, Claire? Really, truly out?"

"Yes," Claire said harshly. Then, prodded by some inner devil, she whispered, "No."

"What? Did you just say no? Claire, is the line breaking up?"

"Dad, I need birth certificates for you and Robert. Surely they are stashed away somewhere?"

"I thought you said you were finished with this sordid affair," Jean-Léon shouted.

"I will be—when I get those birth certificates!" Claire cried.

"Now you listen to me, Claire," her father said, and he was angry. "I've checked Marshall out. Are you aware of the fact that he has a terrible reputation, Claire? You can't trust him. He's considered a cowboy—worse, a loose cannon—with his own agenda. I've spoken to the Bergman Holocaust Research Center. They said that, at times, he is good at what he does, but at other times, he's crazy. Reckless. Impulsive. Like now. They *told* me, Claire, that Elgin *died* in 1980 in France. Of natural causes. *He's dead, Claire.* He's been dead for over twenty years! Elgin isn't even on their wanted list! He's not even *alive*, Claire."

Claire was frozen.

"Claire?"

No, she did not believe it, not for a single second.

"Claire! Are you there?"

"You're wrong," she said flatly, finding it hard to breathe now. "Elgin killed George Suttill, and he killed David. Just like he killed Eddy Marshall in 1940," she heard herself say. Her pulse was thundering in her ears now.

"Says who? Marshall?" Jean-Léon was sarcastic.

"Yes," Claire whispered, feeling very much like her father's punching bag.

"Did Marshall tell you why he's so obsessed with Elgin, Claire? Did he tell you the real reason?" her father demanded. *"Did he tell you the truth?"*

Claire swallowed in order to find her voice. "Elgin murdered his uncle. Eddy Marshall was his uncle, Dad."

Jean-Léon made a sound. It was abrupt, both mirthful and mocking. "No, Claire, that's not it. That's not why your boyfriend is obsessed with Elgin. He believes Elgin murdered his *father*, Claire. In the winter of 1972."

CHAPTER 13

Claire stared blindly at the passersby milling around her on Lexington Avenue. "What?" she managed.

"Bill Marshall was hit over the head with a tire jack while fixing a flat on the side of a highway somewhere in upstate New York," Jean-Léon was saying. "Ask the center. They'll tell you. It was an unfortunate, accidental crime; I think he was mugged for a few hundred dollars. Your friend Ian Marshall is convinced that Elgin—who is dead, Claire—murdered him. You are on a wild goose chase."

"I've got to go. Bye, Dad." Claire flipped the cell closed. She realized she could barely breathe and that she was shaking like a leaf.

Then she stood there in front of the huge storefront window, as still as the mannequins behind her. The crowd hurried to and fro past her, a mass of faceless humanity.

Claire took a few deep breaths, trying to steady herself. It was impossible. She tried to think clearly. That, too, seemed impossible.

Why hadn't Ian ever told her about his father's death?

No wonder he recalled that the recorded conversation between his father and his Uncle Joe had taken place in 1972, the year of his death.

Elgin was dead?

Claire inhaled. If Jean-Léon was right, then this entire nightmare was over: the Dukes would be as innocent as anyone, Robert Ducasse would remain dead, a hero of the French Resistance, Jean-Léon was exactly who he said he was, because they were a different branch of the Ducasse family, and she could go home.

But how could Elgin be dead? David had been blackmailing Elgin, and he had died for his efforts. Or so Ian said.

George Suttill had discovered Elgin's current identity, and he was dead. Or so Ian said.

Claire couldn't even begin to imagine why Ian would make up such stories. Elgin had to be alive, because Claire could not imagine any other explanation for David's and George Suttill's deaths, not even at the hands of a copycat.

She just could not believe that Ian was crazy. Still, clearly, he was a man bent on revenge.

Whom should she believe? Was Elgin alive or dead?

Claire shopped mindlessly, picking up twos of everything, no longer certain of what she needed—slacks, knit tops, underwear, hose. By the time she left the store, she wasn't sure what time it was; she didn't know what she had purchased, either, or how much she had spent—and she didn't care. She stepped out onto Third Avenue, took one look at the traffic, and realized the odds of getting a taxi at this hour were nil. *Great,* she thought with a sudden fury. *Just great.*

Claire decided that walking would be faster than taking a bus. She didn't feel up to figuring out the subway system, which she had never used in her previous travels to the city.

She began walking uptown, carrying her two bags. Shopping had been a badly needed distraction from the ramifications of that terrible phone conversation with Jean-Léon. Now, against her will, she began to turn over all the possibilities.

Ian thought that Elgin had murdered his father, Bill Marshall. That much Claire believed. Why hadn't Ian told her the truth about his father? The omission was a terrible lie, especially now, when they were lovers and friends. And it made no sense.

Her father claimed that Elgin was dead—that he had died twenty years ago in France of natural causes. Could her father be mistaken? Claire could not really believe that Elgin was dead. Had they both lied to her in different ways?

She told herself that if Jean-Léon was lying to her, he was doing so only to protect Robert Ducasse, who had to be alive, who had to be Lionel Elgin. This *had* to be the case.

As far as Ian went, they truly had complicated matters, Claire thought with real anguish. She had been incapable of objectivity before. Now her feelings for Ian were further clouding her ability to be rational. Compounding matters was a pervasive sense of doom that was dogging her.

Claire had reached Seventy-second Street. Her sandals were hurting her feet, and her shopping bags seemed to have gained ten pounds each. But neither her feet nor her shoulders hurt the way her heart did. Her world had been turned violently upside down in a handful of minutes. She was so upset and angry—at Jean-Léon, at Ian, at everyone. Just then she wanted to be alone. But being alone wouldn't help her to sort anything out.

If only she hadn't gotten involved in this, or with Ian.

Claire could hardly believe her last thought. But she still loved him. Even frightened and angry, Claire knew that, and it only made matters worse.

Claire realized a bus had stopped on the other side of Third Avenue. The light was green and she ran across the intersection, somehow leaping onto the bus just before it closed its doors. She was too tired—and too distressed—to walk anymore.

The bus was so jammed that Claire saw no way to walk farther back. She scraped together the fare, deposited it, and grabbed onto a pole, all the while aware of receiving numerous stares. Claire realized she must look as frazzled and frantic as she felt. She had to pull herself together before she reached Ian's apartment; otherwise, how would she be able to confront him? The cell phone rang. Claire jammed her shopping bags firmly between her knees so they would not overturn, then fumbled with her purse. She found the phone and looked at the screen. A 212 number that she did not recognize was illuminated on the dial. Ian had to be the caller.

"How does Italian sound?" he asked in a friendly tone, with no preamble, when she answered.

"We need to talk, Ian," she said tersely.

There was a moment of surprised silence. "Okay. What's happened?"

"I'll be there in five or ten minutes," she said, and flipped the lid closed. She was trembling.

Ian was waiting for her. He was standing in the open doorway of his apartment, and he wasn't smiling.

Claire looked him in the eye as she came out of the elevator.

"What happened?" Ian asked quietly as she approached.

She walked past him and into his apartment, and dropped her bags, then whirled. "You did not tell me about your father, Ian."

"What?" He paled, closing the door.

"You had every opportunity to tell me that he was murdered—*murdered*—in the winter of 1972!"

"Who have you been talking to?"

She folded her arms across her chest. "Was he murdered? In the winter of 'seventy-two?"

"Yes, he was," Ian said, and he turned and walked away from her.

So that much was true. Claire fought tears. She was so tired that she had to sit, and sank down on the rust-colored leather sofa. She cradled her face in her hands.

She heard Ian's footsteps and looked up. He handed her a framed photograph.

Claire blinked. A handsome man with longish, curly black hair was standing in front of an old fighter plane that seemed to seat one person. He wore jeans, Frye boots, and a beat-up leather jacket—the kind pilots wore. He wasn't smiling, and he was squinting against the sun. "Is this your father?" she asked with a lump in her throat.

"Yes. He's standing in front of an old Spitfire at the RAF museum in Hendon, which is outside of London. This was taken in the mid-sixties. My dad was a pilot. Not professionally, but he had a Cessna. He just loved to fly."

Ian was also a pilot, Claire had learned during a casual conversation on one of their flights. "Why didn't you tell me that he was murdered?"

Ian shrugged as Claire set the photo down on the glass coffee table. "Who told you?" His eyes were dark, and all of his facial muscles had tightened.

"Jean-Léon."

"I see." If he was surprised, he gave no sign, but Claire knew he wasn't. "What else did he say?" He was so calm—too calm.

"He said that you think Elgin murdered him."

"He did."

"How can you be certain? Maybe it was a mugging," Claire said, strained.

"No, it was not a mugging, Claire."

"You were ten years old when he died," she pointed out.

"That's right. And when I was a sophomore in college, I decided to investigate the 'mugging.' My father was hunting Elgin, Claire, when he died. He had figured out who he was, and he was about to nail the bastard." Ian's eyes flashed. "My mother told me the whole story. She had begged him to let sleeping dogs lie, but he wanted revenge for Eddy. He had adored him, and he never forgot his death. I didn't tell you the truth. My father opened up the Elgin investigation in 1972. And he knew what he was doing. Remember when I said being a fed runs in the family? My father was an agent. He had the bureau's resources at his fingertips. And one night, during a blizzard, Elgin hit him over the back of the head with a goddamned tire iron when he was changing a fucking flat tire, because he was getting too close." Ian stared at her. He was flushed with anger. "It was Christmas Eve, Claire. December twenty-fourth, 1972."

Claire stared back. In spite of herself, she was chilled. Bill Marshall had been murdered on the same day as his brother Eddy. "So this whole thing with Elgin is a personal vendetta. This whole chase is about Elgin having murdered your uncle *and* your father."

"It's more than that and you know it," Ian said. "Thanks for selling me so short."

"What if it was a mugging?" Claire asked, but less forcefully. She just had to ask. "Could Elgin be dead, Ian? Is there any way he could be dead?"

"Is that what he told you? And you believe him?" Ian was incredulous. "Have you forgotten the reason David disappeared? David saw Elgin murder George Suttill, and he was afraid he'd be next! The man is a killer, Claire. A mastermind and a killer."

Claire felt as if she were facing a huge brick wall, one she would never break though. Instead, that wall would come crumbling down on her, burying her alive the way rubble had buried civilians in World War II. "David saw *someone* murder George Suttill. Maybe Elgin is dead and there's a copycat—"

He made an exasperated sound and threw his hands up in the air. "There was a rumor. Briefly, in the early eighties, the rumor reached various agencies, including Special Branches at Scotland Yard, that Elgin was dead. That he died in France. But it was only a rumor, Claire, one I know Elgin started. Unfortunately, my father hadn't shared his investigation or files with anyone. To this day I've never found them—I think Elgin destroyed them."

"So my father made a mistake," Claire said harshly.

"When David called me, I had to practically start this investigation from scratch," Ian stated. "Your father is sticking his nose way deep into affairs he shouldn't have any interest in," Ian said flatly.

And the rest of it remained unspoken, *if he isn't Elgin.* "Don't. Stop right there. My father knows I'm in danger, and he wants me to come home. Period."

"Then go home," Ian said.

Claire just stared. Ian stared back. The apartment became frighteningly silent. The only sound she could hear was the air-conditioning unit. But a new fear rose up inside of her chest. "Is that what you want me to do?" she got out.

"Yeah, that's what I want you to do," Ian said roughly.

Claire couldn't seem to get enough air. "I thought we were friends."

"We are," he said, his face tight and closed.

"But you're kicking me out."

"It's for the best now."

"No, it's what's best for you," she said, choking. She turned almost blindly and made her way across the foyer to the guest bedroom.

His hand appeared on the door in front of her, effectively preventing her from entering the room. "That is so unfair. This is for your own good."

She turned and faced him. Unfortunately, he was only a few inches away. "We're partners."

"I don't need a partner anymore, Claire, and my decision has nothing to do with our personal relationship."

"Do not even try to tell me that you are protecting me," Claire said harshly.

"I am."

"Then find someone other than my father to pin the Elgin rap on." She meant every word.

"I wish I could," he said with regret.

Claire turned abruptly, shoved his hand away, and slipped into the dark bedroom. She closed the door hard behind herself as she did so, and only then did she dare to fight the sobs that were threatening. Damn it. Damn him.

Suddenly she thrust the door back open. "What about your reputation?" she shouted.

He was standing right where she had left him, in front of the door. He appeared stricken. "What?"

"They said you have a terrible reputation. That you're reckless: a cowboy with your own agenda."

"Who the hell is 'they'?" he demanded angrily. "Wait—let me guess. *Your father.*"

"He checked you out," Claire cried.

"I'll bet he did," Ian said in a dangerous tone—one Claire did not like at all—and he turned his back on her and disappeared down the hall.

Claire was the one who felt stunned now. She hadn't meant to attack him, and she didn't really believe he had a horrid reputation—which meant that she did believe that her father was lying through his teeth. And now she had lost Ian, too.

She stumbled over to the bed and sat down hard, trembling. Everything was happening so quickly that she felt dizzy.

The lights in the bedroom came on. Claire blinked.

Ian stood in the doorway, a heavy brochure in hand. He smiled at her mirthlessly. "Would you like to speak to one of the executive directors at the center, Claire?"

She froze.

"Claire?"

The evening had become surreal. Claire was aware of Ian waiting for her response, but she couldn't respond because she didn't want to, because she didn't dare. He seemed angry and hateful now. He was angry with her, that she knew—but surely he did not despise her as well? Claire felt almost as if she were outside of herself, watching the drama unfolding—the frightened, paralyzed woman, the angry man, and a bunch of ghosts surrounding them, patiently waiting for justice.

Ian didn't wait for her answer. He handed her a beautifully published brochure. The cover was dark green, and embossed on it was a circular logo that read BERGMAN HOLOCAUST RESEARCH CENTER with a Star of David in its center.

Claire realized her hands were trembling as she opened it. The inside of the front cover listed the names of the institution's directors and various employees. Claire found Ian's name listed about twelve names down, as executive director of special investigations. Tears came to her eyes, blurring her vision.

She flipped through the brochure. There were different sections, some of which were education, information, research, and investigations. The final page listed hundreds of contributors, huge familiar corporations among them, as well as several philanthropists whose names she recognized. Claire closed the brochure and held it to her chest. Slowly, she looked up at Ian, feeling a lone tear trickle down her cheek.

His face was set. He took the brochure from her hands and opened it to the first page. He pointed to a name. It read "Leonard P. Feinstein, Executive Director." Then he went to a phone, lifted it, and dialed. He handed Claire the phone without saying a word.

Claire heard it ringing. A woman answered. "Feinstein residence," she said.

Claire found it hard to speak. "Mr. Feinstein, please," she said. She heard how awful she sounded. She sounded ill.

A moment later a man came on the phone. "Yes?"

"Mr. Feinstein, my name is Claire Hayden. I'm sorry to bother you, but I need to ask you some questions," Claire said, filled with pain. It was crossing her mind now that her relationship with Ian was over. And it had happened with the speed of light. But why?

Because he was going to destroy her father, one way or the other.

"How did you get this number?" he asked sharply.

Claire did not glance at Ian, who stood a few inches behind her, practically breathing down her neck. "From Ian Marshall. I'm here with him now."

There was a pause. "I see. May I speak to Ian?"

Claire handed Ian the phone.

"Hello, Leonard," Ian said after listening to the other man for an instant. "Yes, I'm fine. Look, do me a favor and answer Claire's questions. It's urgent. Thanks." He handed the phone back to Claire, giving her a hard look.

Claire hesitated. "How would you describe Ian, Mr. Feinstein?"

"Excuse me?"

She trembled. "I was told he might not be the most reliable of employees."

Feinstein actually laughed. "Who told you that? Ian is one of the most reliable individuals I know. He is also determined, thorough, and effective. The job he does for us is flawless, and that is no easy task in itself. You see, we are mostly an educational and research organization. His department is underfunded and understaffed. Yet somehow, over the years, he has brought dozens of war criminals to the attention of the appropriate authorities, both in this country and abroad. And some of them have been successfully convicted for their crimes. Ian is far more than reliable, he is resourceful. I would trust him with my life."

Claire didn't know what to say. She licked her lips. "Does the center think or know that Elgin is dead?"

There was a long pause on the other end of the line. Then, "We know no such thing. That is a very odd question. Elgin remains in the top five on our most-wanted list. He's still on Scotland Yard's most-wanted list as well."

"Thank you," Claire whispered, blindly handing Ian the phone.

She didn't move. She couldn't. Her body was shutting down just the way her mind was. The part of her brain that was still functioning heard Ian speak briefly with Feinstein and then hang up. Out of the corner of her eye, Claire saw him straighten and look at her. She couldn't face him now.

It was hard to get the words out. "I need to be alone."

She thought he said, "Claire? I hate that this is happening," but she could not be sure.

"Good night, Ian," she said, refusing to even look in his direction.

"I'm sorry, Claire."

She nodded, refusing to cry in front of him.

He backed out, shutting her door.

Claire left her bedroom the following morning before eight. She had cried herself to sleep but woken up periodically, the tears coming again and again. As a result, she felt more tired that morning than she had the day before, and she also looked like hell.

As she entered the living area, she could smell something delicious wafting out of the kitchen, which was one door down the hall, on the other side of the entry. She could also smell coffee. Claire hesitated. Ian hadn't left for his meeting with Frances Cookson. What should she do?

She could turn around and hide in the bedroom until he left. Or she could go into the kitchen to get a cup of coffee, which she desperately needed.

Claire crossed the foyer, apprehension rising in her. She reminded herself that they were both mature and intelligent adults. The kitchen had no door, and she paused on the threshold. Ian was at the stainless-steel stove, making French toast.

He had recently showered, and his dark hair was still wet. He was already dressed for his business meeting, in pale gray trousers, a white button-down shirt, and a flashy, colorful print tie. He was wearing his shoulder holster, and in it was his gun.

He was impossibly attractive.

Becoming involved with him had been the worst mistake of her life.

It hurt so much.

He turned to the opposite counter where oranges were cut up, awaiting their fate in the juicer, and he saw her. He went still.

"Good morning," Claire said quietly.

His gaze scanned her, lingering on her eyes searchingly. "Good morning. How did you sleep?" He did not smile. The tension was thick enough to stick in a bread slicer.

"Like shit."

He clenched his jaw. He moved past the oranges on the cutting board and poured her a cup of fresh coffee. He didn't ask her how she liked it; he already knew. Claire watched him add skim milk and half an Equal. He handed it to her.

Claire drank it, watching him add more French toast to the pan. He looked unbelievably good in the kitchen.

He lowered the flame and faced her, leaning his hip against the granite counter. "I'm sorry about the way we fought last night."

Claire nodded curtly. "Don't want to talk."

"Maybe we should," he said.

"Don't think so." She sipped more coffee, staring into the creamy brown liquid.

"Claire. You know you need to go home. You know it's best now."

She sensed another huge argument in the making. "I know nothing of the sort. I know only that you are a bossy pain in the butt. Ordering me around as if we're in the marines."

"I want you out of this."

"Well, maybe I won't go."

"Maybe I'm not giving you a choice," he said flatly. "Your tickets back to the Bay Area will be messengered over here before ten. Flight leaves at noon. Be on it."

She was so unhappy that her temper only prickled at his high-handed takeover of her life. How had it come to this? The child within her wanted to go to him, tell him she was sorry and that she still loved him, and lay her head on his chest while he held her. Had they become enemies?

"My father must be protecting his brother," Claire said flatly. She had thought it all out last night. Her father had lied about Ian and he had lied about Elgin, so there was no other option. "But he is not Elgin. He might even be the third brother. Remember? Lady Ellen had a child. We never asked her what happened to her son."

"I have to go—I'm late," Ian said, not looking at her now. He was turning the burner off. The French toast was done, but he hadn't eaten his breakfast and clearly did not intend to. Alarm filled her. "What?"

"I'm late," he said. "Here." He took a plate out of a cabinet for her. Still avoiding eye contact, he left the kitchen, leaving the oranges on the counter.

He was leaving, just like that.

Stunned and barely able to comprehend what was happening, Claire saw him emerging from the dining area, his jacket now on. He had his briefcase in hand. Her alarm increased. She wanted to call to him, beg him to wait, stop. She could not get a single word out.

He looked at her. His eyes seemed dark and determined, but they also seemed unhappy. "Have a good trip, Claire."

Claire couldn't seem to speak.

He waited another moment.

"Yeah," Claire said, oh-so-succinctly.

He turned and left. The front door closed with a terrible and harshly final sound.

Dazed, Claire took the French toast and put it on a plate; she juiced two oranges, careful not to think or feel; and, plate and glass in hand, she walked over to the breakfast nook and sat down. It overlooked a part of the terrace. It looked to be a beautiful spring day. There were even birds singing on the terrace. He had potted geraniums, and they were in bloom. Claire choked on a bite of the French toast.

She had never felt more miserable in her entire life.

The tickets came at a quarter to nine. Claire put them in the garbage.

How could she leave?

Her father could not be Elgin, and she had to protect him at all costs. If Elgin turned out to be Robert, Claire no longer cared—she would care only that Jean-Léon not pay any price for protecting his brother for so many years. If Elgin turned out to be William, which was extremely doubtful because of the way her father had lied, it would hurt, but she would survive. In any case, she could not go home and pretend this was not happening; she could not merrily go about her business as if nothing was wrong.

She had to get over to Frances Cookson's and find out what was happening—before it was too late.

But she did not have an address, and the meeting was about to begin. Claire didn't bother to try and call Ian on his cell—she knew he would not tell her where he was.

She ran into his office, and rushed over to the larger desk, which was covered with neat piles of paper, folders, and books. The first thing she saw by the telephone was a notepad. Scribbled on it was an address in the East Fifties and the time, nine A.M.

Sixty seconds later she was out the door.

Claire jammed the elevator button. It was ten to nine. It might take only ten minutes to get to the Sutton Place address. "C'mon," she growled at the bank of elevators.

William Duke couldn't possibly be their man, not when her father had told so many lies in order to protect his brother. And Ian did not have any photographs of Robert. Or did he?

Claire froze. *He did—if William Duke was really Robert Ducasse.*

If William was her uncle, it would explain his nearly lifelong friendship with her father and the fact that they had both emigrated from France. If William was Robert Ducasse, everything suddenly made sense. His love and kindness to Claire had been more than friendship—because he was really her uncle. God—how could she not have seen this before? How could she have been so blind?

The elevator door opened.

Claire leaped inside and pounded frantically on the lobby button.

But it also meant that William was a ruthless killer.

Frances Cookson's apartment was just off of York Avenue on a side street, overlooking the East River. It was an old, beautiful brownstone town house that had been converted to apartments. By the time Claire had pressed the buzzer in the lobby, it was a quarter past the hour. Ian had only a fifteen-minute head start on her.

Claire was filled with apprehension as she explained to Frances over the intercom that she was Ian's assistant and running late. Clearly Ian did not object, as she was promptly buzzed through the locked door leading into the building.

As there was no elevator, Claire walked up the narrow, carpeted stairs to the third floor. Now that Claire had made the connection between William and Robert Ducasse, she was stunned that she hadn't guessed earlier. She couldn't wait to tell Ian.

Frances had left her apartment door open, and Claire walked into a small, cozy parlor, filled with mismatched furniture and throws. The first person she saw wasn't her hostess, who greeted her at the door, but Ian, seated on a sofa in the living room. He was regarding her, but his expression was impossible to read. Instantly Claire was uncomfortable, but she knew he would not make a scene in front of Frances Cookson.

Frances appeared to be about seventy, and she was an attractive, naturally blond woman with Scandinavian features who seemed young and agile for her age. She led Claire over to the sofa where she had been seated with Ian, cups of coffee and a plate of cookies on the low table in front of them.

"Thank you for seeing us," Claire said, trying not to look at Ian. She failed. She sent him her society smile. "Sorry I'm late."

He stared at her. "No problem," he said.

The tension hadn't softened in the half hour or so that had passed since he left his condo, and Frances looked from the one to the other with obvious bewilderment.

"Let me get you a cup of coffee," Frances said, and before Claire could protest, she walked into the adjacent kitchen.

Claire realized she was unbearably tense, and she met Ian's gaze with trepidation.

"Did you get the tickets?" he asked quietly.

Claire sat down, not on the sofa beside him, but in a flanking chair. "Yes, I did."

"Good."

"They're rat food."

"What does that mean, Claire?" he asked somewhat darkly.

She smiled sweetly. "They're in the garbage. Where they belong."

"You belong on that plane," he shot back.

"The caveman act doesn't suit you, Ian. Besides, Jane has something to tell Tarzan."

"Has something else happened?" he asked flatly, but she saw the interest in his eyes.

"Not really," she said, smiling and looking all around the apartment as if taking cues on how to decorate for *Home Design* magazine.

"What does *that* mean?"

"William is my father's brother, Ian," she said. "William is Robert Ducasse."

He studied her. "I was wondering if that might not be the case myself."

"What? You *knew*?"

"Claire, I don't *know* anything for certain. I am *wondering* if William and your father are brothers. And if they are, then who is who."

Before Claire could comprehend that, Frances appeared and handed her a mug of steaming coffee. Claire set it down. Ian was still determined to believe that Jean-Léon was Elgin. "You are wrong," she snapped.

"I'm conducting an interview, Claire," Ian said warningly. "May I record our conversation, Mrs. Cookson?"

"Of course. But you do know that I already spoke to the police, not once but several times." She smiled, but sadly.

Ian said, "New York City, Frances Cookson, April thirtieth, 2001." He glanced at his watch. "Nine-twenty-five A.M." Then he smiled at Frances kindly. "Why don't you tell me what happened the day George saw Elgin? Beginning with what day it was."

"I will never forget the date—it was the day before he died." Her tone quavered. "April ninth. We had arrived in San Francisco on the seventh. He was so upset."

Claire went to the kitchen, which was separated from the living area by its counter, and pulled a tissue from a box of Kleenex. She handed it to her. Frances accepted the tissue with a small smile.

"Where did Suttill see the man he believed to be Elgin?" Ian asked, although they already knew this.

"We were in San Francisco on a holiday, you know. We prefer to eat a large lunch—usually we don't eat at night. It was at the Garden Court, and it was just after one."

"So Suttill had no doubt that the man he met there was Elgin."

Frances nodded. "I had never even heard of this Elgin until that day. We met about eight years ago, when he was on holiday here in New York, and we've been dating ever since. We are both very active people. We live in the present. We had never even discussed the war." She added, "I suppose I should be speaking in the past tense. It's so hard."

"What happened at the restaurant?" Ian said. "Would you mind very much recalling the conversation?"

"I'm not certain. I never saw anything or anyone—I was in the ladies' room at the time. When I returned to our table, George was paying the check, and he was extremely agitated. We hadn't even touched our food. I never saw this man—Elgin. George took my arm and we left the restaurant without a backward glance. It wasn't until we were in the car that he started rambling on about the war and a spy who had murdered a pilot and agents, and it hardly made any sense! I really could not comprehend a word he was saying, except he kept coming back to one name: Lionel Elgin. George did finally tell me that Elgin had been his superior during the war, and one day he just vanished, but they found all these incriminating things in his apartment, making it quite clear that he was a spy." She paused, staring down at her hands, which were ringless, the manicure nude and perfect, and she smiled sadly again. "And a day later he was dead."

"I am sorry," Ian said softly.

Claire reached out to touch Frances on the hand. "I am, too. If it's any consolation, we believe this man, Elgin, also murdered my husband."

Frances started. "Oh, dear, I am so sorry." Suddenly she flushed, looking from Ian to Claire. "I mistakenly assumed the two of you were a couple."

Claire felt her cheeks heating. "We're not," she said with a grimace. She had to glance at Ian.

He looked away, his expression tight and hard, to reach for his briefcase. Claire knew what was coming, and she tensed as he removed half a dozen photographs from his briefcase. "We really appreciate your help, Mrs. Cookson," Ian said quietly.

Frances covered her eyes with her hands. "Sometimes I wish I could forget that day, George, everything. I never thought to find love again, not at my age." She looked up. "My husband died in 1989. I wasn't looking for anyone, and then four years later I met George and it was the most natural thing in the world, being with him, falling in love all over again, like a foolish teenage girl." Tears slid down her round cheeks.

"Frances." Claire laid her hand on the woman's shoulder. "I'm so sorry." She felt terribly for the older woman. Her loss seemed so much greater than Claire's. Claire had her whole life ahead of her; this woman did not.

Elgin was not her father. Her father had not done this.

"George did not deserve to be murdered," Frances said on a long, shaky breath. "I miss him so. But time heals all wounds." She smiled bravely, and they all knew it was a facade.

Claire didn't know what to say.

"Mrs. Cookson, even though you say you never saw Elgin, I'd like to show you some photographs. Maybe one of these men will strike a bell. Maybe one will seem familiar. Maybe you did see Elgin without knowing it, from the corner of your eye."

Frances was surprised. "The police never showed me any photographs."

"I know," Ian said with a smile, laying the photos down on the table.

Claire went rigid. A part of her still dreaded that moment of ultimate revelation. She couldn't seem to move.

Ian spread out the six photos on the coffee table in front of the older woman. Claire glanced at them from where she sat—which meant that she was looking at them upside down. It hardly mattered. The first person she recognized was William Duke. The other five men were strangers.

Ian had not put her father's photo there.

Claire gasped, her eyes flying to his. She wanted to say thank you. Instead, tears of relief filled her eyes, and she turned her head away quickly so he would not see.

"I don't know," Frances whispered, studying the photos intently.

Claire found herself leaning forward. Frances's hand moved over the photos, and it seemed to hover above William's picture, as if she might lift it up. Then she picked up the sixth photo, studied it, and put it back down. She glanced up at Ian, shaking her head. "I don't know. I just don't know. I . . . I think I might recognize this man," Frances said, pointing at the sixth photo.

Claire closed her eyes. Amazingly, she was filled with relief. What if there was another explanation for Jean-Léon's lies?

Claire decided that she would continue to pray for both her father's and William's innocence.

"All right," Ian said finally. He was obviously disappointed as he stood up. "Maybe we can speak a bit more another time."

Claire's heart sank. She knew he hadn't shown the older woman Jean-Léon's photo because of some degree of sensitivity to her presence, but he would come back—alone—and do so.

"I am so sorry I can't be more helpful, Mr. Marshall," Frances said, walking them to the door.

"You have been very helpful," Ian assured her and said good-bye. Claire also smiled and said good-bye.

Outside, they were blasted with a gust of hot air. The day promised to be stifling. They paused on the curb. "Now what?" Claire asked.

Ian shoved his hands in his pockets. "She was probably a dead end. They're all dead ends." He shook his head. "This is the real problem, Claire, trying to identify someone after so much time has elapsed. The only person still alive who knew Elgin is Lady Ellen." He sighed and looked at her. "I'm going back to the office. You're going home. No ifs, ands, or buts about it. In fact, my sister Lisa, the fed, will escort you right to your flight, which you can still make. I'll call her now."

"Forget Lisa. I'm in this until the final buzzer sounds," Claire said, meaning it.

Ian looked at her. "Game's over, Claire. Don't you think you've had enough?"

"We're in overtime," Claire said grimly. "I can't bail out now. What kind of partner would that make me?"

"I saw your face," he said. "Why don't you try honesty for a change? You're scared, Claire. You think it's Jean-Léon, too."

"You're wrong," Claire cried furiously. "Bad call. You are wrong, wrong, wrong!"

"I think you protest overmuch," Ian said softly. "Why do you have to be so stubborn, Red? Has it ever occurred to you that I have your best interests at heart?"

Claire's heart turned over, hard.

"Claire." There was no mistaking the plea in his tone. Then he shifted toward her.

For one split second, Claire thought he intended to take her in his arms. In the next instant, he staggered hard toward her, as if struck brutally from behind, and there was no mistaking the shock on his face.

She caught him, but his weight knocked her down. Claire felt his blood and realized he'd been shot. She screamed.

PART
FOUR

AGAINST THE SUN

CHAPTER 14

August 1, 1940

Lionel had taken a flat in Knightsbridge in June 1939, on his seventeenth birthday. On that day, he had enlisted in the air force as well. He had lied about his age to both his landlord and the RAF recruitment officer. But because his father was both a baron and a leading member of the Conservative majority, he wasn't questioned about his age—or anything else. In fact, he was automatically given an officer's rank of lieutenant and sent to a special officer-training program created for enlisted personnel like himself in a time when war seemed imminent and unavoidable.

The timing was fortuitous—three months after signing his lease and one month out of the RAF officer-training program, war on National Socialist Germany was declared, an event that happened more through sheer default and ineptitude than moral rectitude or resolution on the part of Great Britain. Because Lionel was fluent in German, and because he had done rather poorly on the tests designed to distinguish potential pilots from the masses, he was assigned to an intelligence unit. His superiors then transferred him to the ministry of information the moment that it was created, shortly after Chamberlain's ouster and Churchill's advent.

Of course, he lived in the officers' quarters of his unit. But the flat was a necessity as far as he was concerned, and as he was a rich and titled nobleman, no one questioned it. Indeed, his fellow officers assumed that he kept a tart. Lionel did little to quell those rumors; instead, he fed them very deliberately. And although the flat was small, cold, and barely furnished, although the hot water rarely ran and the place was nothing like the lavish Elgin Hall, it suited him perfectly. In fact, he quite liked it.

Father hated it.

It had been a ho-hum and ordinary day, and Lionel was rather bored. But then, everyone was bored with the "phony" war. The battle for the English Channel continued. British radio reported the loss of eight RAF planes, with two pilots missing; it also claimed the downing of eighteen Luftwaffe bombers and four ME-109s. Lionel had been in his office with his aide, George Suttill, when he heard the report. Inwardly he had smirked. Suttill and another assistant had cheered. Lionel knew those reports were false and purposefully exaggerated for the sake of civilian morale. Everyone around him seemed to actually believe them when, for God's sake, they worked in the ministry of information, which in another country would be labeled the ministry of propaganda. It was their job to feed the public false cheer and to paint black pictures white, or at least an acceptable shade of gray.

He was surrounded by idiots and morons.

Lionel sighed and reached under his small bed to pull out his leather valise. He carried it across the flat's single room and set it down on the desk where he often worked late into the evening beneath the mandatorily dimmed glow of a small lamp. His windows were covered with black tape; the blackout had been in effect for more than a year. He opened the valise. Inside was a high-frequency radio transmitter and receiver. Very calmly, Lionel began punching out his coded message on the wireless.

Translated into English, the message read, "Urgent. RAF flight changes stop new patterns stop Four Finger formations." He signed off with his code name, Swan. The name was a nod to his cousin Rachel, whom he saw from time to time, inconclusively. She was a WAAF stationed at Fighter Command.

He knew she was stationed at Bentley Priory and that she was about to become engaged to some Jew. He made it his business to keep track of her. Deciding on the code name Swan had somehow pleased him. He knew she would hate it, but in a way, his choice had really been a compliment.

Lionel did not wait for an answering transmission. The fact that the RAF had changed their fighter tactics only spoke to the fact that the Luftwaffe had been outflying them all summer. The information was important but did not require an answer from his contacts at the Auslandsorganisation in Berlin. Besides, he was hardly the only agent in Britain, and perhaps another spy had already sent along the information.

It amused Lionel that the average person thought spying to be glamorous and exciting, when the fact was that there was little excitement about what he did. Espionage was mundane work at best. Lionel spent his spare time gathering technical data on the British military and then transmitting it to

Berlin. Only in novels did spies resort to force or seduction; theft and bribery were the most common techniques. It was amazing what a few pounds could do. And of course, Britain remained an open society in spite of some censorship caused by the war, which made his job ludicrously simple.

His knocker banged.

Lionel got to his feet, moving without haste. Three years ago, when he was fifteen, he had spent an entire summer outside of Berlin, ostensibly lured there by his German girlfriend, who was actually an Abwehr plant. There his induction into the German intelligence community had begun—he had spent two months at an estate called Park Zorgvliet, a spy school filled mostly with foreigners like himself, eager to serve the führer and the Fatherland for various personal and ideological reasons. At the A-Schule West, he had learned he was calm and rational by nature, that not much ever ruffled him, and that his fear, when it did rise, could be controlled. He had passed his courses with superior grades and, upon returning to Britain, had been careful to behave as the most patriotic of Englishmen, no matter how he wished to do otherwise.

Now Lionel closed the valise, and as he carried it to its hiding place beneath the bed, he called out, "Yes? Who is it?" But he already knew.

"It's your father," Lord Elgin responded from the other side of the door.

Lionel was pleased Usually his father made him feel all of thirteen years old, and he did not like being reduced to a nervous boy. But things had changed; no, things were about to change. For he had just received the most exciting instructions of his short career as a German agent.

He opened the door. "Hello, Father. This is a surprise."

Randolph Elgin did not smile in return. He had become portly in the past few years and now wore a steel-colored goatee. He entered, his expression indicating that he could hardly stand to do so in such an impoverished place.

Carefully, Lionel closed the door behind him. "Isn't it a bit late for you to still be in the city?" Elgin usually rushed home to Ellen, the horrid whore.

Elgin looked around with stiff disapproval, then walked over to the flat's single chair—other than the one at the desk—and sat down, removing hat and gloves and resting his cane against the arm of the chair. "I've been at Whitehall most of the day. It looks as if that bastard will finally invade, Lionel. Intelligence has learned of a new order, Eagle Day."

It usually went this way. The intelligence arms of both sides in a constant race, with neither side ever being much ahead—or behind—the other. "Really? And when will Eagle Day occur?" Lionel knew that this could not be true because he had not been notified, and if an invasion was imminent, his contacts would alert him.

"That's the problem. We don't know. Our sources can't pinpoint a precise date. Churchill has sent out a war alert to all of our forces and the Home Guard. I think it will sow panic. I wish he would rein in that brash nature of his. Jesus Christ."

"There was a time when you admired his audacity," Lionel commented, remaining neutral. "It doesn't behoove you, Father, to argue with him now."

"He can do more harm than good if he continues this way," Elgin said flatly. "Plus, I heard this amazing rumor. Apparently our intelligence people think we have a spy in our midst."

Lionel merely blinked. "Father, I hate to say this, but surely there are quite a few spies among us, it is a time of war."

"You are always so blasé," Elgin said with a flash of anger. "Do you not care if there is a traitor somewhere in our military?"

Lionel almost blinked. "Is that what they say? And why do they think such a thing?"

"There have been a series of advertisements placed in the *London Times*. Apparently those ads are coded instructions being read by the Abwehr in Berlin."

Lionel raised both brows. "Fascinating," he said. It was times like these that he found the most interesting. He felt oddly detached, almost as if he were not inside of his own body—so he could be a completely objective observer of the unfolding event. He thought with the utmost clarity. He had objected from the beginning that using the newspapers to send less urgent information was too risky, but his superiors had ignored him. Lionel decided that he would no longer use the *Times* to send Class 3 information, no matter what he was told to do. He had no intention of hanging as a traitor and a spy. The war had not even begun, not really, and it was much too soon for him to have to pack up his bags and flee.

An image of Rachel flashed through his mind. He dismissed it.

"Can you imagine the audacity? Using our own newspapers to communicate with the Nazis!"

"I think it is a rather foolish scheme," Lionel said calmly. "If indeed there ever was such a scheme."

"Mark my words. We will catch this man, sooner rather than later."

"I am sure that we will."

His father grunted and glanced around the flat. "I do not understand why you keep this flat." Elgin looked right at him. "I have heard the rumors. I have heard that you bring a woman here. A mistress. Is it true? They say she is lovely."

"She is very beautiful."

Elgin stared at him, his jaw flexing. He finally said, "I cannot imagine you in a relationship. I suppose I should be pleased."

"Yes, you should." Lionel smiled. It was so hard to contain himself.

Elgin made a cry of exasperation. "So how are things at the ministry? I saw the new poster: 'Keep mum, she's not so dumb.' Bloody good idea to warn our chaps about talking too freely, Lionel."

"It's catchy," Lionel agreed. He had tried to discourage the poster, as it was very effective, portraying two soldiers with whiskeys and cigarettes conversing carelessly in front of a gorgeous blond woman. The rest of the poster read CARELESS TALK COSTS LIVES.

"You haven't come home for dinner in weeks," Elgin said. Lionel had expected this tack. "We miss you. John keeps asking when you will visit. What should I tell your brother?"

My half brother, Lionel corrected him, but silently. "Tell him I will come home as soon as I have the chance."

Elgin stood up with the help of his cane. "Don't you care about him, even if you don't care about us?"

"Of course I care," Lionel said, not meaning it. His father had annoyed him—and angered him—his entire life. Fortunately, as he became older, he had learned how to see through and past his father, so that Elgin could no longer rile him. Lionel did not like becoming angry—it ruined his control.

Besides, very soon his father would never make him angry again. "You know, Father, you should really call before coming by."

Elgin flushed. "I am sorry. But surely you have nothing to hide, now do you?"

Elgin would *dare* to play cat and mouse with him? "I have nothing to hide, Father."

"Sometimes I wonder," Elgin said bluntly. "Sometimes I wonder about you."

"Really." Lionel turned away. He walked over to a real radio and turned it on. The strains of "We'll Meet Again" came on. Vera Lynn was singing.

"Why do you turn away? And shut that off."

Lionel faced his father slowly.

"Sometimes I think that I do not know you at all. My own son," Elgin said heatedly.

Lionel did not answer. In a secret pocket on the lining of his sleeve was a three-inch knife. The instructions he had so recently received would truly liberate him. His life would change forever—the way it had when he had gotten rid of Harry. From time to time he did dream of his brother, who remained seventeen, his eyes filled with hatred and accusations. But he had no regrets. Had Harry lived, Lionel would not be who and what he was today.

"Did you hear a word I said?" Elgin stomped past him with the cane and turned off the radio. The sudden silence after Vera's beautiful alto was startling.

"Of course I heard," Lionel said, maintaining a pleasant smile on his face. God, he hated this man. He always had and he always would.

"How can a father not know his own son? I look into your eyes, and I feel as if I have come up against a huge wall. A huge blank wall," Elgin said.

"Maybe you have," Lionel remarked. His tone was amazingly calm, and carefully, he slipped the knife into his right palm, keeping it concealed. "Just because you sired me, that does not give you a right to get into my mind."

"A right? But you are my son—and my heir! Why can't you be more like Harry? Why are you always hiding your feelings from me, from everyone?"

Lionel felt his face change. "Don't talk to me about Harry," he said very slowly, very succinctly, very dangerously.

"Why not? Surely you can cherish your brother's memory. Or have you already forgotten him?" Elgin challenged.

Lionel thought that his smile felt tight. "I will never forget Harry," he said. "Harry was—is—a god."

"How dare you speak so mockingly of your brother!" Elgin cried.

If only Father knew what was to come, Lionel thought.

"I don't think you ever loved him," Elgin said roughly. "That is the truth. I think you were jealous of him when he was alive, and I think you are still jealous of him. Dear God!" Elgin suddenly covered his face with his hands. His shoulders shook, as if he were crying.

Lionel watched him in surprise. What was this?

Elgin looked up. "Sometimes I wonder if that shot was really an accident," he said in a ragged whisper.

Lionel stared.

Elgin sighed, wiping the moisture from his eyes. "Are you going somewhere?" He had noticed the edge of the valise sticking out from under the bed.

Lionel's pulse remained absolutely steady. He smiled. "No."

Elgin faced him. "I don't know why I bothered to come. I must go. Has it begun to rain?" There was the softest sound of drizzle against the windowpanes.

"I think so."

"I don't have an umbrella. May I borrow yours? I have had this bloody bronchial infection for a month now, and the last thing I need is a summer chill." His father was looking at the empty umbrella stand beside the door.

"I lost mine," Lionel said. "I must have left it in a cab or some such place."

"Can I borrow a muffler, then? I parked a few blocks away."

Lionel smiled. "There is a scarf in the valise, I think," he said very quietly.

Elgin glanced at Lionel. "Is something wrong?"

"Not at all." Lionel continued to smile, and he nodded at the valise.

Elgin stared briefly, then bent and lifted the valise, which was considerably heavier than it looked. He grunted and put it on the bed, opening it. He stared.

He stared at the transmitter and receiver inside the case. He did not say a word. The light tapping of drizzle continued on the windows.

Lionel walked up behind him. "Have you nothing to say, Father?"

"Is this a bloody radio? This looks like a radio!" Elgin gasped.

"Yes, Father. I'm afraid it is a radio."

Elgin stared at him, turning white. Comprehension was in his eyes. "Oh my God," he whispered. "Lionel, no. Tell me no!"

"Yes, Father. *Yes*. I'm a fascist and a spy for the Germans and proud of it. You call yourself a Conservative? That's not what you are. What you are is a *fool*."

Elgin's eyes widened. "Dear God—"

"There is no God," Lionel said. He did not give him time to finish. He slid the small knife swiftly across his father's jugular vein. Too late, as the blood gushed, he realized the mess he'd made, and that he should have killed him another way.

Elgin remained upright and alive for several seconds, his eyes wide with shock and disbelief, then horror. The gurgling sound of his choking to death on his own blood blotted out the sound of the rain.

Lionel caught him as he collapsed, then laid him down on his back carefully, not wanting to spill any more blood. His own pulse began to accelerate. Christ. There was blood everywhere, on the floor, on his uniform, some had even splattered onto the bed.

He had done it.

He had gotten rid of the pompous bastard.

He was free.

Lionel smiled.

He walked to a corner of the room where he kept a single burner to brew tea, and there he wiped the blade on a rag. Wadding up the rag, he put it in a laundry bag. He cleaned the floor, stripped, changed his clothes, and wiped up. Everything that was soiled went into the bag, which he intended to burn. His father remained on the floor on his back, drenched in blood, his eyes wide and unseeing.

Lionel sat down at his desk, turning his chair to face his father. He must dispose of the body, he thought, in such a way that it would never be found. He pondered how he might do that, and the story he must concoct in order to appease the authorities when they eventually learned of Elgin's disappearance.

Lionel quickly decided what he must do. But as it was only seven in the evening, he must hide the body for the moment. He pushed his father under the bed. He would remove the body and all the evidence in the middle of the night, when his neighbors were asleep.

For the first time in years, Lionel feel asleep within moments.

CHAPTER 15

August 23, 1940

She'd been given a three-day leave, and today was the last day; tomorrow she would have to report back to her WAAF unit at Fighter Command. Rachel chose not to think about it. It was too pretty and pleasant a day—it was almost the kind of day where one could forget that the country was at war. The skies were blue and cloudless (she tried not to notice any vapor trails left over from air fights with the Luftwaffe), the day was warm and breezy, and it made her want to sing her thanks for being alive and whole. Just two days ago, the air station at Croyden, where Joshua was stationed, had been attacked. Only one soldier of the Royal Artillery had been injured this time; a few weeks ago, that had not been the case. Eleven airmen and one officer had been killed, not to mention hundreds of civilians, all in one monstrous air raid, which had been followed within days by another. According to Joshua, Croyden had looked more like the moon than the planet Earth.

After the first devastating raid, several squadrons had been transferred to the Midlands while the station was repaired. Rachel could not be more thankful that Joshua had survived the attacks unscathed, and she was grateful that thus far her father and sisters also remained unharmed and in good health.

Rachel had spent her leave at her home in the East End, and now she was on her bicycle, leaving London behind, on a pure whim. She would enjoy the day to its fullest, as if there were no war, because tomorrow and the next day and the day after that, she would spend twelve to fourteen hours daily wearing a pair of headphones, listening to and deciphering the conversations of the Luftwaffe as they battled the RAF overhead. There was no real end in sight.

Rachel was not complaining. She was proud to do her duty and proud to be a WAAF in Great Britain's time of need.

A butterfly drifted over the handlebars of her bike. A lorry passed her on the two-lane country road she rode on. She had ridden by Greenwich some time ago. The industrial blight of London's South End had been mostly replaced by pastures and grazing cows. True, some of the pastures were pockmarked with craters left by bombs. But even where the earth was scorched, Rachel could see tiny new blades of grass and yellow wildflowers emerging from the ashes and dirt.

She was alive, Joshua was alive, and in a way, the fact of war was a godsend. Because after it was over, if her father had his way, she and Joshua would marry.

Rachel tensed a little, slowing her bike as several couriers on motorcycles whizzed past her, followed by a rare civilian motorcar. Rachel felt like a traitor—how could she think, even for a moment, of the war as a godsend? The war was a terrible thing—the Germans had overrun Austria, Czechoslovakia, and Poland, not to mention Denmark, the Netherlands, Belgium, and France. And she did love Joshua. It was just that she wasn't ready to get married so soon.

Joshua wanted to marry immediately. She had known him for four years, ever since she was fourteen, and they had been given permission to date a year and a half ago, when Joshua had turned eighteen and promptly enlisted in the army. Even then, as much as Papa liked Joshua, he hadn't liked her dating when she was still only sixteen. Rachel had been eager to begin dating him—the thought of being courted with candy and going to the cinema with a boy who had admired her for years and who was now in uniform seemed so glamorous. The reality was a bit different. The cinema, the candy, holding hands, even the kissing, it was all nice enough. Somehow, though, Rachel had expected more.

She had never forgotten the way Harry Elgin had looked at Sarah and the way Sarah had looked at him. She had never forgotten the kiss they had shared, which she had witnessed on the day of his death. They had both been so young, but there had been so much passion. Rachel was too honest with herself not to know that she did not have that kind of passion. She loved Joshua, but her blood didn't run wild when she saw him or when they kissed. Rachel was afraid it was a matter of character. Sarah was the passionate, fiery one; she was outspoken, aggressive, brave.

Rachel remained kind and caring, the peacemaker, and until she had enlisted, both a surrogate mother to her sisters and a surrogate helpmeet for Papa.

So maybe the passion she did not feel had little to do with her love for Joshua and everything to do with her own calm nature.

Of course, he was perfect for her. He came from a good, hardworking, Orthodox family, Papa adored him, and so did she. One day they would marry. Rachel had no doubt. She'd have half a dozen children. Papa would move in with them. It would be a wonderful life.

She ignored a pang inside her breast and pedaled faster. *We'll win the war first*, she thought to herself. There was nothing wrong with putting duty ahead of self-interest. Even Papa would agree with that.

But yesterday they had fought for the first time over the telephone. Joshua had asked her again to set a date, and she had declined. He had clearly been hurt, but Rachel had cajoled him back into a cheerful disposition. Her stomach hurt a little, just recalling that unpleasant argument. Why did he have to be so impatient?

He did not know that she had recently been assigned to the top-secret Y unit. That had happened when her CO had discovered that she was fluent in French and Italian and could get by in German. She was immediately removed from her position as a radar operator and now spent all of her time listening to the enemy flying in the air above her.

Rachel's stomach growled, reminding her that she had packed a small picnic lunch and that she needed to find a pleasant spot to stop. She had also brought a book to read. She slowed her pedaling as several trucks passed her. Ahead was a fork in the road. Both roads appeared to lead to a smaller country lane. There were no road signs—they had been removed to fool the enemy should the Germans ever invade. A huge concrete box was also ahead of her, signaling the unpleasant presence of some sort of factory. Nowadays almost every factory, once used for civilian purposes, had been converted to wartime industry. Rachel did not want to think unkindly of the series of buildings with their sooty smokestacks, but they were a blight on the otherwise picturesque countryside and a reminder of the war that she wished to briefly forget.

She decided to take the left fork, which would take her north toward Eltham, a pleasant little town. And in the next instant she heard an all too familiar mechanical screaming high above.

Rachel slammed on her brakes and almost went over the handlebars, looking up.

A huge plane coming at an impossible speed seemed to be diving down toward her.

Abruptly it changed direction, moving back up toward the sun. But drifting down in its wake were black objects.

A second later, the bombs landed and the gray structure exploded. Rachel dove to the ground as another series of explosions sounded. The screaming of the German bomber faded as it left the scene.

Rachel spat out a mouthful of dirt and sat up and looked into the sky. She could see a tiny black speck, and then it was gone. She didn't bother to shake her fist at it. Still, this was the very first time she had been so near a bombing. She was shaken to the core.

Then she looked toward the factory.

It was in flames. She could hear sirens, and she thought she heard cries and screams. No longer thinking about herself, she grabbed her bicycle, leaped on it, and pedaled quickly toward the factory. By the time she arrived, she saw that several other civilians had gathered, along with an ARP warden, his motorcar, and several bicycles parked before the burning building. An entire half of the structure had collapsed on top of itself. Through an entrance on the erect side, people were staggering out.

Rachel left her bike and ran toward one of the workers, a woman who was coughing but unharmed. Rachel grabbed her. "Do you think there are people trapped in there?" she asked as a stream of factory workers continued to run out, a few wounded now appearing with the others. She was aware of another car coming to a stop in the lot before the building.

"Thank God it's mostly machinery in sections D and F," the woman said, wiping her grimy cheeks. "But there are at least the two supervisors and a team of engineers who work round-the-clock in those sections."

A makeshift ambulance was pulling into the parking lot. It had clearly been converted from a vehicle used by a company that made vacuums, as one of the company's slogans remained on the back door.

"Are you all right?" Rachel asked the woman, who nodded. Then she pulled free of Rachel, calling out to a friend. Rachel watched her run to a coworker who was holding her arm awkwardly to her chest.

"Rachel? Is that you?"

Rachel heard a vaguely familiar voice and she turned. Her eyes widened as she saw her cousin Lionel Elgin, whom she had not seen in about a year—and whom she preferred to avoid. "Lionel."

He walked over to her, looking quite smart in his dress uniform. Rachel had heard that he was in an intelligence unit and posted to the ministry of information. He paused beside her, his eyes meeting hers. Then he stared past her. "It looks as if they might have a few blokes trapped under the rubble. It might take the rescue squads some time to arrive."

"My thoughts exactly," Rachel agreed, as they started walking briskly toward the caved-in side of the building. It had become a way of life, she thought, to help those in need. Clearly, even her eccentric cousin had risen to the occasion of war. She heard a soft moan. "Do you hear that?"

"Yes, I do," Lionel said grimly. Simultaneously, they broke into a run.

Half a dozen women and older men joined them, and within moments, everyone was determinedly moving blocks of cement and girders of steel aside. For the next thirty minutes or so, Rachel and Lionel worked with the others soundlessly, managing to uncover and bring to safety three badly wounded workers. An ATF unit had arrived to help them and put out any fires. Finally the rescue squad arrived, and they were asked to move out of the way.

Rachel turned her back on the scene, now shaken and exhausted. She found a tree and slid down to sit at the base of its trunk, watching as the ambulances were loaded with the wounded. She counted two dead, and it saddened her immensely. She did not think she was ever going to get used to the war.

"You're crying," Lionel remarked.

Rachel looked up at him. "Yes, I suppose I am."

He scrutinized her, then smiled. "You haven't changed."

Rachel didn't know whether that was a compliment or not. "Actually, I have," she said, wiping her eyes.

He left her without a word. Rachel saw him go over to his motorcar. Even though he was in uniform, it was a civilian vehicle, and only the very rich could afford petrol for motoring. He returned with a thermos. "Tea." He smiled at her. "It's a bit weak." He unscrewed the cap and poured her a cup, handing it to her.

"Thank you, that's so kind." Rachel took a sip. It was indeed weak, and hardly sweet, but rationing had become stricter in the past month, and she did not blame him for reusing old teabags. She hadn't realized she was so thirsty, or that her hands were bleeding from scraping amid the rubble.

Lionel sat down at the base of the tree beside her. He dug a half-eaten chocolate bar out of his pocket and handed it to her.

"Are you sure?" Rachel asked hungrily.

"Absolutely," he said, smiling.

Rachel ate the stale but delicious candy.

"I heard you are stationed at Fighter Command," he said when she had finished.

"Yes, I am."

"What do you do?"

She lied. "I'm a radar operator." She was not allowed to tell anyone what she really did.

"How have you changed?" he asked.

Rachel started. "I'm eighteen now, Lionel. The first time we met, I was thirteen."

Lionel smiled softly—as if fond of the memory. "I remember."

Rachel got chills. Didn't he remember that his brother had died that weekend? Mistakenly shot by his own hand? She stood up, trying to brush off her skirt. The act was futile. "I think I had better go."

"Why? You're on leave, aren't you?"

She handed him the empty cup. "Yes, but my leave ends today. I'd like to spend some more time with Papa and Hannah before I have to go back to the base."

"How is your father? And your sisters?" Lionel asked, screwing the cup back on the thermos.

Rachel shivered again, though it was a hot August day. "Everyone is fine. Sarah drives an ambulance."

Lionel smiled. "That would be Sarah. In the thick of it. Is she still seducing boys?"

Rachel stiffened. "She seduces no one. Men try to seduce her. They cannot stay away."

He seemed amused. "Will you ever defend me that way?"

"Do you need defending?"

"Perhaps. I am family."

"Yes, you are. Lionel, I really have to go." She forced a smile. "It was nice to see you. Take care." She turned.

He caught her arm. "Did I hear something about an imminent engagement?"

"There is no engagement," she said more briskly than she intended.

"Are you in love?"

She stared at him. "Lionel—"

"You're not in love," he said. It seemed to Rachel that he was pleased.

She was not belligerent, like Sarah. When gauntlets were thrown, she turned the other cheek. She said, "Actually, I am in love. His name is Joshua Friedman, and he's a sergeant in the Royal Artillery, stationed at the Croyden aerodome. We're waiting for the war to end before we get married."

"Croyden got hit badly, didn't it?"

"Very badly," Rachel agreed. "Joshua said they lost the armory and the officers' mess completely. Of course, you know the reports to the public weren't accurate—it was so much worse than we were told. A hundred and eighteen civilians died, Lionel. Isn't that terrible? I'm so relieved he wasn't hurt."

Lionel looked through her. "The Gerries will get their due," he said finally.

He was so odd. "I do have to leave," she said.

"Don't you want to ask about my family?"

She looked at him. "I have merely assumed that Lady Ellen and your father are fine. And little John must seven or eight by now."

"Seven, I think," Lionel said. "You haven't heard."

"I haven't heard what?" Rachel asked, suddenly anxious.

"I'm surprised you haven't heard," he said slowly. "My father disappeared about three weeks ago."

"What?" Rachel cried in shock.

Lionel just nodded.

"How does one disappear?" she asked, disbelieving.

"I don't know. But the authorities have made some outrageous claims," he said very grimly.

"What kind of claims? And how is Lady Elgin?"

"She is hanging on. They claim to have found all of this secret correspondence hidden in his desk. They even found some sort of invisible ink. They say he is a Nazi supporter, perhaps even a spy, and they believe he has fled to Germany."

Rachel felt herself gaping. She closed her jaw abruptly. "What?" she managed finally. "They think he is a spy?" Their dinner at the manor in Wales came to mind. She clearly recalled Papa and Elgin arguing furiously. The rest of her recollections were somewhat vague, but hadn't Papa accused Elgin of being a fascist? Could it be true?

"I know. It's absurd. I am so angry every time I think of it."

Rachel looked at him as he sighed. He didn't seem angry, just resigned. But if there was one thing she knew about him, it was that he was not emotional by nature. "I am very sorry, Lionel," she said, meaning it.

"Thank you," he said. "I knew you would be. I know you are the one person in my family I can count on, Rachel."

She was taken aback. They were family, but hardly close. Blood was thicker than water—that was one of her father's favorite expressions. Still, Papa's feelings for the Elgins had not changed. Rachel felt quite certain he was excluding them from the equation whenever he expressed such a familial sentiment.

"Well, I have to get back to the ministry. I was on an assignment this morning. Do you need a lift?" he asked.

"No, that's quite all right," she began, when she heard a familiar whirring noise. "Oh, no," she cried.

And then she heard the screaming, growing louder. In unison, they both looked up.

The sun was in their eyes. For a moment, Rachel was blinded, and she lifted her hand to shield her gaze. In the next moment, a black T-shaped object emerged from behind the sun. As it did, machine guns began firing high above them, their noise unmistakable.

Rachel gripped Lionel's arm as another plane became visible, chasing the first.

Lionel ran to his car. Machine-gun fire continued to sound. He returned, peering upward through a pair of binoculars.

"What's going on?" Rachel cried anxiously, also gazing at the sky and trying to watch the dogfight.

"A Spitfire on the run from an ME-110," Lionel said flatly. He handed her the binoculars.

Rachel trained them up at the sky, just in time to see the Spitfire bank so tightly it was almost impossible, wheeling away from the Luftwaffe fighter plane. The Spitfire banked again, coming back toward the ME-110. "Yes," Rachel cried, her heart feeling as if it were wedged in her throat. She focused the glasses briefly on the Spitfire's markings. Her heart lurched as she realized the plane was K 5281, and that it belonged to the Seventy-second Squadron. She knew the plane. Just like she knew the pilot by voice and name. She must have listened to a dozen conversations in which "Hawk" was the RAF adversary in a dogfight with the Luftwaffe. He stood out from his peers; not only was he American, he had that distinctive and funny New York accent. He had scored three kills since July, and as he was the first American to down a Luftwaffe plane in the war, he was rather infamous. But perhaps his infamy came from the rumor that he had claimed to be a Canadian in order to enlist in the RAF. Rachel had heard that his actual name was Eddy Marshall.

Machine-gun fire burst out another time. But this time it was the Spitfire attacking the ME-110 from behind.

Before her very eyes, the German fighter exploded in midair.

"What happened?" Lionel asked calmly beside her.

Rachel was about to hand him the glasses when she realized something was wrong. The Spitfire was wobbling from side to side as it began its descent. "We got the bloody Emil," she said, "but something's wrong. Hawk Marshall is hurt." She realized his fighter must have been hit in the initial round of firing.

He was descending now rapidly, at a steep, unusual angle. Rachel could hear his engines, and she had been around planes enough by now to know that this one didn't sound right.

"He's going to crash-land," Lionel said matter-of-factly.

Her heart felt like it had stopped. Rachel watched the Spitfire trying to correct the angle of its descent by lifting its nose. It was flying over the burning factory now. But every time the fat nose bumped up, it came down heavily again. Suddenly the roaring engine began to whine.

The fighter somehow cleared the building by inches, not feet. It was flying so low now that Rachel was afraid it would crash into the roof of the farmhouse in the field behind the factory. As it angled down, cows scattered, bellowing. A dog in the barn began to bark wildly. The plane managed to clear the rooftop of the house.

The fighter was about to hit the ground. However, a patch of trees was directly in front of it. Rachel now saw that one of the wings was flapping at its tip, as if broken, like a chicken wing. The front two wheels touched down. The plane screamed and bumped up again.

The group of close-knit trees was just meters ahead. The Spitfire went down another time. This time it stayed down, brakes screaming now as it headed directly for the trees.

Rachel watched the plane start to collapse onto one side, swerving ever so slightly, enough to avoid a head-on collision with the trees. But instead, the trees sheared off the plane's other wing, metal screaming and shrieking.

The plane continued past the trees, wingless on one side, and finally came to a shuddering stop in the center of the field.

Rachel turned to look at Lionel, and together they ran to his car, jumping into it, Lionel gunning the engine. He jumped the curb of the parking lot and plowed through the fence enclosing the pasture. All the cows had fled to the perimeter. They bumped and bounced over the rutted ground. And as Lionel halted the car a few meters from the Spitfire, Rachel saw the pilot's helmeted head appear from the open cockpit. She jammed open her door and ran toward the plane.

He tipped up his goggles and tore off his helmet, tossing it away. He began climbing out. Rachel reached the broken wing just as he leaped to the ground. He staggered, and she caught him. His full weight landed on her, pushing them both against the side of the Spitfire. The metal skin was burning-hot to the touch.

Rachel gripped him more tightly, until they both regained their balance by leaning on the plane. "Are you all right?" she asked anxiously.

As she spoke, it struck her how big he was, at once tall and strong, and there was something odd about his being in her arms—it felt familiar, either that or it felt right.

He looked down at her.

Rachel froze. Any further words she had been about to utter escaped her now. Any air she'd had in her lungs was lost. Time stood still. The past disappeared, and the future and the present became one. Looking into a pair of smoky green eyes, she had the craziest thought: *I know this man.*

And then the thought was gone.

"I'm fine . . . now," Eddy Marshall said.

CHAPTER 16

Rachel couldn't seem to find her voice. His smile reached his eyes. He had amazing eyes. "I think I've crashed right at the feet of an angel," he said. "Are you an angel?"

There was laughter in his tone. It sparkled in his eyes. He had just crashed, perhaps even destroying his plane, and he was joking with her. Rachel was oddly immobilized. The soft sound of Lionel's steps brought her out of her strange paralysis. "Is the plane safe?" she managed.

"She won't blow. I got hit in the windshield and the wing. She's okay, we can save her," Eddy said. His gaze remained unwaveringly upon her. He still wore a slight smile, and now Rachel noticed two deep dimples, which intensified the sense one had that he was extremely good-natured.

Suddenly he glanced past her at Lionel.

Rachel stepped back, out of their mutual embrace. She realized he had several cuts on his face, which were bleeding. They looked superficial. "Are you hurt?" she asked.

"Sprained my wrist," he said. "Banged up my knee. But I think that's it."

Lionel paused before them. "Nice flying," he said. "I'm Lieutenant Lionel Elgin."

Eddy turned. "Sorry, bud, can't shake. Squadron Leader Eddy Marshall. Number Seventy-two, out of Biggin Hill."

"You're an American," Lionel commented.

"Damn right, I'm a Yank through and through." But Eddy was looking at Rachel again.

She became aware of the disconcerting intensity of his gaze. She knew she was blushing. "We had better get you to a hospital. You need to have your wrist looked at," Rachel said softly.

"Only if you are a nurse in disguise," he returned.

"I'm afraid I'm not a nurse," Rachel replied, wishing she were.

He met her gaze, his smile fading. "It's just a sprain. My knee's okay. We need to call this in. I need to get back to base."

He was a heroic man, Rachel couldn't help thinking. Heroic and handsome, thinking of his plane and his duty first. Rachel felt overwhelmed by the pilot standing before her—and she was acutely aware of being overcome. "Please, have a doctor look at your wrist. And at your knee and those cuts. You really should."

"All right," he said softly, as if they were alone. "Has a guy ever refused those eyes of yours?" But he wasn't smiling anymore and he flushed.

Rachel felt her cheeks heat up like boiling water again. Quickly she turned aside, ducking her head. *He is only flirting with you,* she thought. But deep in her heart, she didn't believe that at all.

"The medics are busy at the factory. There's a hospital a few kilometers from Eltham. I'll take you there," Lionel said, a rude voice cutting between them.

"That would be great." Eddy glanced briefly at Lionel before looking at Rachel again. "You haven't introduced yourself," he said.

"Rachel Greene. I'm Lionel's cousin, actually, although we met by chance today."

"I see." He smiled at her. Rachel looked away. The trio began walking back to Lionel's Bentley. Rachel's arm bumped into Eddy's. She moved aside, putting more distance between them. He kept glancing at her, but she pretended not to see. She felt very small beside his much larger frame—she guessed he stood an inch or so over six feet, and he was a broad-shouldered man. Of course, his flight suit was padded with thick fleece. She had heard it was horridly cold up there in the skies above London.

He could be a poster boy, she thought, *for the RAF. He should be a poster boy for their recruiters.*

It struck Rachel like a bolt out of the blue that she was being unfaithful to Joshua by being so fascinated with Eddy Marshall. She stumbled.

"Hey!" He caught her, sliding his arm around her waist. "We don't want you to sprain something, too, now do we?" He smiled into her eyes.

She was in his arms again. It was doing crazy things to her body. Rachel pulled away. "I'm fine, thank you."

His expression faded. He gave her an odd look. They continued back to the Bentley in silence, Eddy studying the ground.

She hadn't meant to reject him. He was only flirting, only being friendly. But of course she had to reject him—she had a serious boyfriend whom she intended to marry one day.

Rachel told herself that it was absolutely normal for her to react as she had to this handsome American fighter pilot. All the RAF pilots were notorious and dashing to begin with—when they weren't fighting Stukkas and Junkers, they were drinking and gambling and chasing women. This particular pilot had undoubtedly left a string of broken hearts all over southern England, she decided with determination. Rachel knew she was not the first woman to become all fluttery in his presence. It did not mean she did not love Joshua.

Lionel opened his door as Eddy went around to the car's other side. "We'll pick up your bicycle and throw it in the trunk, if you'd like to ride with us."

Eddy, about to use his left hand to open the passenger door, froze.

Rachel looked at Lionel. She had no reason to go to the hospital with them. Then, aware of Eddy's stare, she slowly looked at him.

Suddenly his hand went to his head and he staggered a little, as if he'd lost his balance. "Wow," he said. "This huge pain just went though my head." He leaned against the side of the car, as if faint.

Rachel was already running around the trunk to him. She thought he was engaging in theatrics to keep her attention, but she couldn't be sure. He had just crashed in a Spitfire. He could have a concussion. She put her arm around him, and he leaned against her. It was a hard male body—she had never had this kind of awareness before. "Are you dizzy?"

He blinked at her. "Suddenly I'm seeing double. There's two of you, angel, two beautiful blondes."

She met his very lucid gaze; he looked away with a smile he failed to hide. He was pretending to be dizzy. Still, Rachel did not move away. She couldn't help being flattered. "Maybe you'd better sit down."

"Yeah," he said roughly. "Maybe you'd better help me." It wasn't a question.

Their eyes locked.

Her heart began catapulting around inside her chest. "I'm afraid to let you go. God forbid you should faint and hit your head again."

His smile widened. "God forbid. God forbid I should drop dead, go to heaven, and find an angel there like you."

"You are a terrible charmer," Rachel said with a smile, still supporting him.

"Honey, I'm a man," Eddy said.

Ridiculously, she blushed again, but this time they both laughed a little. Feeling happier than she ever had, Rachel opened the door and helped him into the front seat. "Don't abandon me now," Eddy said. "You're my good-luck charm."

"I'll come to the hospital, but just for a while, since I have to get home," Rachel conceded, trying to be prim.

Eddy did not try to hide his delight.

A few minutes later, the bicycle was sticking somewhat precariously out of the trunk, and they were on their way.

"That was some dogfight," Lionel commented once they were back on the motorway. "Not many pilots could land a plane in that condition in a cow pasture and simply walk away."

"Thanks," Eddy said. "I've been flying since I was a kid."

"Really?" Rachel asked, impressed.

He twisted to look at her in the backseat. "I started flying when I was ten."

Her eyes widened. "Is that possible?"

"I love planes. My dad would take me out to a small private airfield on Long Island, and one of the pilots there took a liking to me. Now, I didn't solo until I was thirteen," he added with an infectious grin.

"Only thirteen?" Rachel quipped.

"Only," he said.

"You're from New York?" Lionel asked, interrupting them.

"Sheepshead Bay, Brooklyn," he said cheerfully.

"What brought you to Britain?"

Eddy finally faced Lionel. "That damned megalomaniac, Hitler," he said, no longer smiling and deadly serious. "He has to be stopped. Obviously. I got tired of waiting for America to join the war. I think we will. But later, rather than sooner." He turned to wink at Rachel. "I'm an impatient guy. I can't sit around twiddling my thumbs when I can be doing something—like shooting down German bombers."

Rachel smiled at him.

Lionel glanced at her in his rearview mirror. "Well, I am afraid that this time they shot *you* down."

"It was the first time, but I doubt it will be the last," Eddy said.

"Don't say that!" Rachel cried, aghast. "You might jinx yourself!"

He gazed at her. "So you care," he said.

She stiffened. "Of course I care."

He turned away, smiling and satisfied.

Lionel met her gaze in his rearview mirror again. Rachel looked away instantly. Whatever had made her declare herself like that? And what would Joshua do or say if he knew about this day?

"And you, Rachel? Do you work in that factory we were just at?" Eddy asked.

She shook her head. "I'm a WAAF at Fighter Command."

"Really?" he exclaimed, twisted around again so he could converse with her. "How come I haven't seen you at any of the clubs or pubs in town?"

Lionel remained quiet, as if concentrating on driving, but Rachel knew he was listening intently. Rachel hesitated. "I don't really go out like that. I work double shifts and long hours. When I have enough free time at night, I go home to see my father and my sisters."

"Where do you live? When you're not in the ladies' barracks at Bentley Priory?"

"My home is on Fournier Street. I'm sure you've never heard of it. It's the East End," she added, without any shame.

Eddy shrugged. "I don't know where that is. I've been to a few pubs, but I don't know my way around London. At least not yet. Maybe you could show me the city sometime?" His eyes met hers.

He was asking her out. Wasn't he? She shot a glance at Lionel. Of course, she should tell him she was practically engaged. That she wasn't available. Rachel could not get the words out.

Fortunately, Lionel had just entered the hospital car park.

"Oh, we're here," Rachel cried instead of answering Eddy. She avoided looking at him now. She knew he was startled by her failure to say yes.

Doors slammed as they all got out and entered through emergency. Lionel and Rachel waited while Eddy went to the nurse at reception. Rachel watched him speaking with the redhead. She wasn't particularly attractive, but she was very busty, and she had a porcelain and perfect complexion. She began to giggle. Rachel couldn't hear a word that they were saying, but she knew Eddy was flirting with her. In a way, she was relieved.

On the other hand, amazingly, she was jealous.

The redhead came out from behind the desk.

"I can wait," Eddy was saying. "Take those factory workers before me." Gurneys carrying victims of the recent bombing waited in the hall.

"You come with me, Lieutenant," the nurse said firmly. "We don't make pilots wait. Especially not handsome ones like you." She smiled archly.

"Hon, I will wait my turn, as I am hardly bleeding to death." He patted her arm. "I'll be sitting right over there." He pointed at a row of empty chairs. "Okay?"

She finally acquiesced, going back to her duties behind the desk.

Eddy came back to Lionel and Rachel. "Keep me company?" he said to Rachel.

"I really have to go." It was absurd, her eavesdropping on him and the nurse and being insanely jealous. "I'm really late."

"You're not going to bicycle all the way back to London, are you?" he exclaimed.

"Yes, I am."

His face fell. Rachel realized that he understood she was rejecting him. "Well, I hope we'll meet again. Sometime soon." His gaze was searching.

She bit her lip. It was now or never. Give him what he wanted—or never see him again. "I'm sure we will. I'm . . ." She paused.

"You're what?" he asked quickly.

"I'm glad you're all right," Rachel said in a rush. She turned abruptly, almost blindly, crashing into Lionel.

"I'll help you get your bike out of the car," Lionel said. "And I'm happy to wait, Marshall. I can give you a lift back to Biggin Hill if you want."

For a moment Eddy was silent. Rachel felt his eyes on her back. She wanted to cry. What was wrong with her! "The boys will be picking me and Betty up at any moment," he said.

Rachel turned. "Betty?" she asked, instantly thinking of the redhead.

"My plane," he said, staring at her.

He had a girl. Her disappointment was vast. "Oh."

"My mom's name is Betty," he said.

Rachel started. "Really?"

He nodded. "I'm renaming her, though, today."

Rachel didn't move.

"I'm naming her Angel," he said seriously. "Because for the first time in my life, I have met one."

Rachel was speechless.

Rachel's family lived just a few blocks from the Whitechapel High Street synagogue, on a small narrow cobbled street lined with two-story brick homes and a few scanty trees. Most of the homes were divided among two or three families. Here and there the lower floor was devoted to a cobbler's shop, a butcher store, a grocery, or a milliner. Gardens and yards were out back. Clotheslines hung from house to house, stretched across the street, drying clothing fluttering over the heads of passersby, wheelbarrows, bicycles, and carts like so many multicolored flags. Before the war, the elderly used to sit out on their front stoops in good weather, simply to watch life in the neighborhood pass by and to gossip whenever they could.

By the time Rachel had arrived in front of their two-story white plaster house, her thighs and calves were burning with fatigue from the long bicycle ride. She carried her bicycle up the three steps to the front stoop and left it there. Her neighborhood was small and close-knit. There was no theft.

The sun had begin its descent. Rachel knew that dusk would soon follow as she pushed open the screen door and entered the small, narrow parlor, thinking about a long, hot bath.

Hopefully Sarah wasn't home. If she were, their single bathroom undoubtedly would not be available.

Delicious odors drifted to her from the kitchen, and Rachel realized, with no small amount of guilt, how late it was. She should be helping Papa in the kitchen. He still worked long hours, tending both his shoe store and his factory. A widow from down the block came most days to help him and Hannah with the evening meal, out of the goodness of her heart and the hope that Papa might marry her. Knowing that Rachel was home for a few days, Mrs. Winkle had stayed home.

The BBC radio was on. As Rachel hurried into the kitchen, she recognized the radio commentator's voice. He was mocking the latest German propaganda efforts to sway the British to Hitler's side. Periodically London was barraged with leaflets and flyers dropped by the Luftwaffe in lieu of bombs.

She was ravenously hungry. She hadn't eaten all day, she was very tired, and she just might fall asleep in her bath when she had the chance to take one, but that wasn't all she was thinking about.

He would name his plane Angel after her.

"Rachel!" Hannah appeared from the narrow, carpeted stairwell, shrieking. "Where have you been? Joshua wants you to call him so he can see you tonight. And someone named Eddy Marshall called *three* times."

Rachel stared at her eleven-year-old sister, whose dark hair was pulled into pigtails with pink ribbons, her glasses slipping down her small nose, her ankle socks bagging about her scuffed and worn Mary Janes. They could easily have new shoes from Papa's factory. But of course, they would not think of breaking the law by violating the government's rationing orders.

"Did you *hear* me?" Hannah cried.

Rachel's heart was skipping uncontrollably. "Yes, of course I did. How could I not? Being as you are always shouting," Rachel said evenly. She was trying to marshal her thoughts and emotions. Eddy Marshall had called three times? What could he want? And how had he gotten her phone number?

She had left immediately, while Lionel had stayed. That was it. Lionel had given Eddy her number, even while knowing that she would one day be engaged to Joshua. Rachel had to close her eyes. She had the distinct impression that Lionel had done so on purpose, solely to cause trouble.

The way he had fed Ellen's fish to the swans.

Rachel did not know what to do.

"Who is Eddy Marshall? He's an American! How did you meet him? Is he a diplomat?" Hannah asked, tugging on her hand.

"Hello, Rachel-lay," Papa said, coming out of their small kitchen and wiping his hand on one of Mama's old aprons. "Is everything all right?"

"Everything's fine," Rachel lied, filled with desperation.

He wasn't Jewish. What had she been thinking—even if with the back of her mind? He wasn't Jewish. Papa would never allow anything to happen between them.

And Eddy would be shocked if he realized she was a Jew. Rachel felt sure of it. Gentiles were always stunned to learn that someone was a Jew. It was as if they expected horns on your head or a scarlet letter hanging on your chest, and if there wasn't, then you couldn't possibly be Jewish.

"Joshua wants Rachel to go out tonight, he must have gotten the night off," Hannah cried. Rachel gave her a warning look. Hannah ignored it. "And an American keeps calling her."

"What's wrong?" Papa asked quietly. "And who is this Marshall person?"

"He is an RAF pilot who crash-landed not far from Greenwich today," Rachel said briskly, as if reciting mathematics to a teacher. "It has been a horrid afternoon." She walked past them both and into the kitchen. There was a pot of stew on the stove. It was mostly potatoes and onion, but there were carrots and peas from their garden, and Papa had put a few pieces of chicken in as well. Automatically Rachel began to stir it.

Her sister and father came to stand behind her.

"First bombs fell on a factory. I ran into Lionel. We dug out three workers before the rescue squads came. Then there was a dogfight. He downed a Luftwaffe fighter first, but he was hit, and he crash-landed in a field right next to the factory." Rachel felt breathless and despairing. "Somehow he survived the landing and was barely hurt. Lionel drove him to the hospital. I went with them."

"He left a number for you. Are you going to go out with him? And if you do, what will Joshua say?" Hannah asked, knowing full well that she was causing trouble.

Rachel turned, finally looking at Hannah and Papa. "What makes you think he wants to ask me out, Miss Trouble?"

Papa turned and walked out of the kitchen without a word.

Rachel stared in surprise and then concern. "Papa?"

"Why does he keep calling if he isn't trying to go out with you?" Hannah said.

"Mind your own affairs, Busybody," Rachel cried in a whisper, yanking hard on one of her sister's pigtails.

"Ow," Hannah screeched, tears coming to her eyes.

Rachel let her go, shocked by her own temper. "I'm sorry!"

Hannah shot her a baleful glance, her eyes filled with tears, then turned and fled up the stairs. "I hate you!"

Rachel could not believe that she had hurt her sister. What was happening to her? She looked up to find Papa standing in the doorway, studying her.

Rachel flushed, thinking, *He knows. He knows I like this American pilot, he knows.*

"Did you eat anything today?" he asked.

"I had two cups of tea this morning before I left the house," she said, wanting to smile and failing. "With sugar and lemon."

He seemed to accept that answer. "Sarah is not coming home tonight. Take a bath and we will eat."

Rachel nodded. Sarah was lucky enough to be able to come home every night to sleep when she was not on a night shift. However, sometimes she chose to sleep over with other ATF drivers who shared a flat in Cheapside. Rachel knew that on those nights she was out dancing, smoking, and drinking in the city's various nightclubs with her girlfriends and soldiers. Sarah seemed very happy in spite of the war. No one knew how to enjoy life more.

Papa knew. He knew about her girlfriends, none of whom were Jewish. He knew about the cigarettes, the drinking, the soldiers. He had never said a word, but Rachel saw the sadness and resignation in his eyes, and she knew he felt that he had lost Sarah, and that he had given up on her.

Rachel secretly admired her sister for having the courage to live as she pleased, but she wished she could be just a bit more circumspect. In the end, when Sarah married a Jew, Rachel knew it would all work out.

Rachel walked over to the phone and dialed up Croyden. It had been a civilian aerodome until a few days before the war began. Although many of the squadrons were housed in buildings outside of the station, Joshua's unit was in barracks that had been built the previous year, inside the grounds. There was no telephone in the barracks. Five minutes passed while Joshua was located. When he came on the line, he said, "Rachel! It's the last night of your leave and we haven't seen each other. I miss you terribly. How about dinner and dancing?"

"I have had a terrible day," Rachel said, gripping the phone too tightly. She felt ill and she didn't know why. Tears filled her eyes. "Oh, Joshua. I rode my bike to Eltham and a factory was bombed right before my very eyes. I helped rescue some workers, and then a pilot from Biggin Hill was shot down in the field next to the factory. I ran into my cousin and we drove him to the hospital—"

"Rachel! Stop and take a big breath. I'm sorry you had such a day. You must be exhausted."

"I am," Rachel said, trying to do as he had asked. She continued to shake. She felt like an adulteress. Had she committed adultery in her deepest thoughts? But she wasn't even married!

"Which pilot? Maybe I know him."

"The American, Hawk Marshall, out of Biggin Hill."

"I've heard of him. He's a brash fellow, they say," Joshua remarked.

Rachel froze. "What?" But of course he was brash; she had seen that firsthand.

"They say he's brash as can be when he flies. A daredevil pilot, will try anything. Likes to take 'pleasure spins,' looking for Gerries to fight. Was he an interesting fellow? The way he sounds?"

Relief washed over her. She had assumed Joshua meant brash as in bold with the ladies. "He was interesting." Oh, God. He was far more than interesting, and he had called. *Three times.*

"I think you need a fine meal and some dancing. Haven't you been begging to go dancing for months and months now? We could go to the Savoy. I know it's not our kind of place, but it is grand. We—"

"I'm too tired," she whispered, but the truth was, she was too frightened. What would happen if she called Eddy back?

They would go out. Papa would shout and scream.

And what if they fell in love?

Rachel shuddered at the notion. She could not call him back. It was as simple as that.

Joshua was silent for a moment. "I understand," he finally said.

And Rachel knew that he did. Because he was so very understanding—except on the issue of their marrying. Now she was consumed with guilt. "I have to be at Bentley Priory at six A.M. I must have ridden fifty kilometers today. I—"

"Rachel, I understand. We have our whole lives to go to the Savoy and dance the night away. God willing," he added. "You get a good night's sleep. Call me tomorrow after your shift."

"I'm working a double," she managed. "I'll call you the following morning."

"That's fine," he said. "Sleep tight. And Rachel? I love you."

A huge lump in her throat was choking her, preventing her from making a reply. Fortunately he hung up, sensing that the conversation was over.

Rachel stared at the receiver in her hand before slowly hanging up. And then tears filled her eyes, spilling over onto her cheeks, as a very vivid image of Eddy Marshall filled her mind.

"You should meet him tonight," Papa said.

Rachel whirled, wiping her eyes. Papa stood in the doorway.

"Do you want to tell me what this is really about?" he asked too quietly.

Rachel couldn't meet his gaze. "It isn't about anything," she said, a terrible lie, and to her own father.

The telephone rang.

Rachel whirled to stare at the black receiver hanging on the wall. She knew who it was. She just knew.

Papa moved past her and lifted it. Rachel tensed with dread and expectation.

"It's for you," Papa said, handing her the phone. "It's Mr. Marshall."

Rachel did not take the phone. She shook her head, soundlessly forming the words *No, not now. I'm not home.* She shook her head again, backing away.

Papa spoke. "I am afraid my daughter cannot come to the phone right now, Mr. Marshall. Might you state your business?"

A long silence seemed to ensue as Eddy spoke to her father, Rachel desperately wishing that she knew what he was saying. And all she could think was *Please, Eddy, don't tell him the truth.*

Papa nodded and said, "Good night." He hung up the phone and turned. "This man seems to be interested in you. He asked you to please call him."

"He's just a friend," Rachel said too quickly.

Papa just looked at her.

When they had finished their meal, she shooed her father out of the kitchen, guiding him to his favorite chair in the parlor. Benjamin sat in his rocker with a pipe, listening to the radio. Back in the kitchen, Rachel handed Hannah a towel. "I'll wash, you dry."

Hannah gave her a dirty look. She had decided not to forgive Rachel for the mean-spirited yank on her pigtail.

"I'm sorry I lost my temper and hurt you," Rachel said, filling the sink with sudsy warm water, to which she added their dirty dishes and spanking-new pots and pans.

Hannah did not reply.

Rachel sighed. They had given all of their old, heavy cookware to the ministry of supply, for use in the manufacture of airplanes. As a result, they had bought new pots and pans, which were delightfully lightweight. But now she was thinking about airplanes. About Spitfires. About *Angel* . . . about Eddy Marshall. "I wonder where Sarah is tonight," she said, attempting to break her own train of thoughts.

"In a nightclub," Hannah said meanly.

Rachel scrubbed a plate, dunked it in a bowl of clean water, and handed it to her little sister. "I'm sure she's still working, Hannah. And don't speak so loudly."

"Papa can't hear. He doesn't hear well anymore."

"I told you I'm sorry," Rachel said, washing another plate.

Hannah put the dry plate in the cupboard. "Why did you do that? You've never been mean before."

"Maybe it's a lesson. Maybe sometimes you shouldn't be a snoop." Rachel kept her voice kind.

"But he keeps calling!" Hannah exclaimed.

"I don't even know him," Rachel said firmly, her heart skipping a series of beats.

They washed and dried in silence until Hannah said, low, "Last night she came home at four in the morning."

Rachel, dunking the plate, purposefully splashed her sister with dirty water. "That's her affair."

"Hey! You did that on purpose."

"Yes, I did. And how would you know what time Sarah came in?" she whispered. But she was thinking that Sarah must have had a reason to come home and not go to the shared flat in Cheapside.

Hannah shrugged. "I heard her. Them. She wasn't alone." She sent Rachel a sidelong look.

Rachel stood still. "She did not come home alone?" She was scandalized.

"They stood on the front stoop kissing for hours and hours."

What was wrong with Sarah! "That's enough. Sarah is an adult. Her life is her own affair. When will you stop minding everyone's business?" Rachel said tersely. She finished the plates and began washing the silverware. She could not manage this new burden now.

"I think he's a new boyfriend. I heard her call him John. Her last boyfriend was that captain in the navy, Ted. Or maybe she has two boyfriends?"

Rachel was distressed, and she hit Hannah with the soapy dishrag. "Enough. Quit spying on Sarah. You should pray that one day you are as beautiful and brave as she is."

"I'm the ugly one," Hannah said. "I will never look like Sarah or you."

Rachel froze. "You're not ugly," she began, horrified that Hannah would think such a thing, when there was a knock on the front door.

"You and Sarah are both blond and fair, and I'm as dark as a Spaniard," Hannah said. She shrugged. "And I wear glasses."

Rachel looked at her, but before she could respond, she heard Eddy Marshall's voice in the parlor. The pot she was then scrubbing slipped from her hands, landing on the floor with a loud bang.

"It's the American," Hannah cried gleefully, setting the last dry plate in the cupboard. She grinned at Rachel and ran from the kitchen.

Rachel just stood there, unmoving. All she could think was *Oh God*.

He was talking to Papa, explaining how he had met Rachel earlier that day. "I hope you don't mind that I came by unannounced, but I just had to thank her for helping me out of my plane and staying with me at the hospital," he was saying.

Papa was silent. Rachel cringed. Finally he said, "Rachel is a dutiful daughter. And a dutiful soldier. I am very proud of her. She is always helping everyone, even the neighbors."

Rachel came to life. She retrieved the pot, took off her rubber gloves, and patted the waves of her hair, which she had set three days ago. There was now a silence in the parlor. Dear God, what should she do?

And did she have rouge on? Lipstick? Oh, God! She hadn't put on a stitch of makeup after her bath!

"It's very late for callers," Papa suddenly said.

"I'm really sorry," Eddy said. His tone sounded subdued, as if he had figured out that Papa was not friendly. "But I caught a ride with a bunch of soldiers on a delivery truck. It's pretty far from Biggin Hill to London."

There was another silence. Rachel crept to the door, straining to hear.

"Did you walk?"

"A bit," Eddy said. Then, "I'd really like to thank your daughter properly." He was not going to give up.

Papa sighed. "I'll tell her you are here."

It was too late to change her plain old blouse for her favorite pink cashmere twin set, and there was no time to put on even a speck of rouge. Inhaling hard and shaking like a leaf, Rachel stepped out into the parlor.

He was standing in the center of the room when she walked in. He had put on his dark blue dress uniform and beret, and his left arm was in a sling. There was also a tape high up on his right cheekbone where he'd been cut in the crash. He had several officer's bars and one medal pinned upon his chest. Upon seeing Rachel, he smiled.

It was reflexive; Rachel smiled back.

Hannah was devouring a bag of jellybeans. "Look at what he brought me," she cried.

Rachel couldn't look away from Eddy. They grinned at each other.

"You didn't return my calls," he said simply, as if no one else were present.

"I was going to," she managed. And then she stopped.

Papa stood there staring at them both.

Rachel felt all of the color draining from her face. "Papa?"

"It's late, Rachel," he said heavily. "Hannah, it is time for bed, say good night to the guest."

He had called her Rachel. He never called her Rachel.

Hannah protested, then bid Eddy and Rachel good night. She left, and ignoring them now, Papa walked into the kitchen and outside into the garden, where Rachel knew he would sit and smoke in solitude. The screen door creaked closed behind him.

Eddy had been watching him leave, too. He looked at Rachel now, no longer smiling. "I shouldn't have come uninvited," he said.

"No!" Rachel plucked his sleeve and then dropped it. "It's all right. I mean, Papa didn't mean to be rude."

Eddy studied her. "Is it all right, Rachel? I'm sorry to have upset your father, but if it's truly all right with you, then I can live with that."

The truth came out of her mouth, seemingly of its own accord. "It's more than all right, Eddy."

He smiled, a smile she had so quickly come to love. "Can we take a walk?" he asked, gesturing toward the front door.

Rachel hesitated for only an instant. "Yes."

"Good." He took her hand. "Let's go."

Rachel was anxious and excited, and she felt the conflict not just in her heart but all the way to her bones. "Papa? We're going to take a walk."

There was no answer.

CHAPTER 17

They slipped out into the night, hand in hand. Eddy smiled at her, but he didn't speak as they began strolling down the block. The silence wasn't awkward: instead, nothing felt as right as holding his hand and bumping against his hip as they walked. It was wonderful; Rachel felt as if they were a couple.

Of course they were not. There was Joshua and, even more importantly, Papa.

A few of her neighbors were still cooking their suppers, and spicy-sweet aromas wafted from the open windows of their houses. The sun had set, and because of the blackout, they had only the moon and the stars and the white strips painted on lampposts and sidewalks to guide them. Rachel still found it awkward to walk anywhere at night in such a manner; clearly Eddy did not.

But then, he was a fighter pilot. The night would not deter him from anything, not when he had the courage to fly against the Luftwaffe.

It crossed Rachel's dazed mind that he didn't even have to fight this war. He was an American. He could be safely at home with his family, his friends.

She glanced up at him, suddenly shy. He glanced down at her, and they both smiled.

"This is nice," he said.

"Yes, it is."

They smiled again and lapsed into another easy silence.

His hand was warm and strong. His stride was long yet unrushed. She had to hurry a bit to keep up with him, even though she knew he was walking slowly so she wouldn't have to exert herself. Why couldn't Papa see that he was a wonderful man? Kind, strong, heroic?

Because he wasn't Jewish and he would never be Jewish . . . Rachel didn't complete her dismal thought.

But it was as if he read her mind. "Your father doesn't like me."

"No, that's not true!" Rachel cried automatically.

They paused, facing each other. "I've met reluctant fathers before. But I've never cared about a girl before. Not this way."

Rachel felt stunned. *He cared.* "But we only just met."

"Believe me, I know." He rolled his eyeballs a little.

Rachel laughed. He joined her. "Does your arm hurt?" she asked.

"No. But it's badly sprained." He grimaced. "They won't let me fly for a few days, maybe even a week."

"That's why you're free tonight," she realized.

"Yeah. Why doesn't he like me?"

Rachel stiffened. She didn't know what to say. Her neighborhood was obviously Jewish, at least to her—on the corner of the street was a small shop selling prayer books and seder plates, menorahs and mezuzahs, and other Judaica. But on the other hand, most gentiles had never met a Jew, and he might not realize the truth.

"Is it because I'm a Yank, a Protestant, or a New Yorker?"

He was trying to make light of the situation, but she couldn't smile. He knew.

"Rach? It's because I'm a Christian, isn't it? If I were Jewish, he wouldn't give a damn."

She wet her lips. Her pulse raced forcefully. "You know."

"I know what?"

"That we're Jews."

He seemed a bit puzzled. "Hon, half the people in this neighborhood are speaking Yiddish. There are Jews in Brooklyn. Quite a few, actually. One of my mom's good friends is Jewish—although she married a Catholic, a fireman."

Rachel was breathless. "She married a Catholic fireman?" How had she ever managed that?

"Yeah. Her name's Ruth Watts, and she's happy as a clam. You'll see when you meet her." He took her hand, tucked it firmly in his, and they started walking again, turning back around.

Rachel was stunned anew. He seemed to assume that one day she would be in Brooklyn, meeting his mother's best friend. Her heart skipped in joy. But then she thought of Papa and was filled with despair.

"I'll win him over," Eddy suddenly said with determination.

Rachel looked at him. "He's a very stubborn man." She didn't want to tell him about Mama. And then there was Joshua.

He gave her a grin. "Hon, I don't quit. When I set my sights on something, I *always* win."

Her heart ballooned with admiration. "That's why you are such a wonderful pilot."

He agreed. "That's why."

"And modest." She laughed.

"Terribly modest." He halted in front of her house.

Rachel's heart slammed to a stop. He was going to kiss her good night. She knew it.

He studied her. "I think I've broken enough Greene rules for one night, and you had better go back in."

She couldn't laugh this time. She couldn't even speak.

"He will come around. Would it help if I ask him permission to see you?"

"No!" Alarm filled her.

"That's what I thought." He sighed. "Life can be short these days, Rachel. There was a scramble just before I left to come visit you. One of the guys got it. A frigging Emil tore up his fuselage. He crashed over the Dover Cliffs." He looked at her, his green eyes impossibly sad.

"I'm so sorry."

For a minute, Eddy couldn't speak. He cleared his throat. "His name was John. We called him Joe. Don't ask me why. Jonathan Edward Litton." He paused. "Joe was nineteen years old, and last Sunday he got married."

Now Rachel couldn't speak. Tears filled her eyes.

"Hey! I didn't mean to upset you, hon. But damn it, this is a war, and it's real bullets we're shooting up there."

"I know. I'm a WAAF, remember?"

He gazed into her eyes. "No. I don't remember. When I look at you, I see an angel. We only met today. Can you believe it? I can't. I feel so happy, Rachel."

"Me, too," she whispered.

He had the use of only one arm, so he took her elbow and pulled her toward him. He was facing her house; she had her back to it. Rachel tensed, knowing he meant to kiss her.

"Rach?"

She had to look over her shoulder. As she did, she thought she saw someone standing in one of the blacked-out windows. They had put up blackened cardboard with black tape, so it was hard to tell, but she thought she saw a movement where there should have been none.

"The windows are blacked out," Eddy said softly. "He's not there."

She met his gaze, not telling him that Papa would have to rip off only a small piece of cardboard in order to spy on them. And she thought, *This will kill him.*

Eddy smiled a little and leaned over her, and the next thing Rachel knew, he brushed his mouth briefly over hers.

Her heart tightened, and her breath got lost, and excitement slammed all over her.

He straightened. "When can I see you again?"

She could hardly breathe, much less speak. And the kiss had been chaste. "I . . . I go back to Bentley . . . Priory . . . in the morning."

"I know. How about a few hours after your shift? I'll wine and dine you." He smiled at her.

"It's a double." She hesitated. She couldn't tell him about the Y unit. Even when she was off duty, it was very hard for her to get off the base without a leave. But of course they could always stay on base.

"Then the night after tomorrow. I can meet you at Command HQ around eight. You do want to see me again, don't you?" The slightest light of anxiety flickered in his eyes.

"Of course I do!" Rachel cried.

Eddy grinned. "Okay, then."

They had a date. Just like that.

"Good night, Angel," he said.

Papa was waiting for her.

Rachel slipped into the house, quietly closing the door behind her. Foolishly, she was hoping that Papa had gone up to bed, but he hadn't. He sat on the sofa in the parlor in the shadows of the room's single lamp, waiting for her. His hands were folded in his lap.

She couldn't face him now. Not when her heart was singing with joy and hope. Not when she was falling in love.

Rachel almost reeled. *She was falling in love.* With an American pilot named Eddy "Hawk" Marshall. With a gorgeous, green-eyed, daredevil, do-good American pilot.

Papa stood. "I do not want you seeing him again."

The floor beneath her feet tilted wildly, impossibly. It took Rachel a moment to recover her balance, and she actually looked down. The wood floor wasn't moving. She was surprised to find it so still.

"Did you hear me, Rachel?"

She looked up. "He is not what you think."

"Oh, so he is Jewish?"

She wet her lips, her mind racing frantically, uselessly. "He volunteered to fight our war, Papa. He's an American, from Brooklyn. Only a few hours ago, one of his squadron was killed. He crash-landed, Papa. Can't you see? He's a good man, a strong man, a heroic man and—"

"Is he Jewish?"

"His mother's best friend is a Jew."

"What does that have to do with anything?"

"She married a Catholic," Rachel whispered.

"He's Catholic?" Papa asked, his eyes widening.

For him, the only thing worse was Muslim—or fascist. "No. Protestant."

"I thought so." Papa turned to walk away.

Rachel stared at his retreating back, horrified. She ran after him, in front of him, halting him in his tracks. "Don't do this! Please, Papa, don't do this, and don't make me choose!"

His eyes widened. "Choose? I do not give you a choice, Rachel. And I know you will not behave as your sister does."

"But this is different. I am falling in—"

"No. This is not different." He cut her off. "He is a wild pilot, and you are a good girl. These pilots—these gentiles—they are all the same. Different from you and me. They will never be like us. Does he follow the Shabbat? Is he kosher? Is he circumcised?" He did not wait for her to answer. "I forbid you to see him again."

Rachel cried out.

Papa walked upstairs.

*   *   *

Another agent had given Lionel a special lens for his Leica camera in the first days of the war. The lens enabled him to reduce film to microdots, which provided him with an extremely safe way to transmit information back to Berlin. Each microdot was so small that it was size of a dot made with the tip of a marker pen or a child's crayon. It was easy to affix the microdots to the inside of an envelope, where only someone looking for them would discern their presence. Of course, microdots could be hidden in just about anything—the sole of a shoe, for example. Mailing them back to his colleagues was also a simple matter. Either neutral countries were used, or the mail was sent to actual prisoners of war in German camps, whose mail was intercepted by fellow agents.

His flat was also set up so he could develop film—including microdots—himself. Before his death, his father had thought him to be an amateur ornithologist. Lionel had told his peers in the ministry that he was an avid birdwatcher and that ornithology was his hobby. Upon occasion, Lionel made sure to take snapshots of birds and ducks, and actually, it was a great cover as far as photographing various aspects of Britain's defenses went.

Recently he had changed his routine. That was very important, and he had learned that while at Park Zorgvliet. Now he came back to his flat for lunch so he could work, instead of doing so in the early evening hours. In a few months, he would change his routine again.

He had received a letter from a colleague via Lisbon and was now developing microdots, having turned his small room into a darkroom. The first microdot appeared to contain a list of newly coded names for his contacts and for various military terms. In his business, everyone was extremely cautious.

There was a knock at his door.

Lionel straightened over the pan of developing fluid, surprised. He had a meeting tomorrow with the agent he reported to; had he misunderstood? He stared at the door, wondering if it could possibly be Ellen, his grieving stepmother. (To his amazement, she actually was grieving.)

There was another knock and then he heard, "Elgin? Are you in there? Elgin!"

Christ! It was the American pilot he had chauffeured to and from the hospital yesterday. Lionel grabbed the pan and walked briskly to the closet, placing it inside. Using tongs, he removed the mostly developed document of new code names and clipped it to a wire hanging beside his uniforms and shirts. Marshall knocked again.

Lionel hurried; he didn't want the pilot to go away. He closed and locked the closet door, turned on the lights in the room, glanced around, saw the envelope from Lisbon. It was in the wastebasket. The other three microdots were in the desk drawer in a small tray of paper clips. "Right there!" he called out.

He opened the door to find Eddy Marshall standing there, smiling. "Hey! I stopped by the ministry of information, and your aide said you went out for lunch." He glanced past Lionel. "I hope you don't mind my dropping by like this. Back home we're pretty informal."

"Of course not," Lionel lied. How did Eddy know where to find him? His radar went up.

On the one hand, it was no secret that he had this flat. On the other hand, yesterday he'd had a private and extensive tour of the Biggin Hill aerodome, and Eddy had even shown him into three hangars. Lionel had left Biggin Hill elated and had spent two hours sitting in his motorcar on the side of the road, drawing up a map of the air station and listing all that he had seen, right down to the number of damaged planes in the shop. In spite of being in the RAF himself, it would be too suspicious for him to find ways to tour these air stations when his job was strictly limited to the ministry of information.

Still, there was no reason to be suspicious. Suttill must have told Eddy the flat's whereabouts. "It's a pleasure to see you again," Lionel said, smiling. He led Eddy in, thinking now about the looks he'd witnessed passing between Eddy and Rachel yesterday. He had been bothered by their mutual attraction ever since.

Eddy glanced around as Lionel closed the door, sniffing. "It smells like a darkroom in here," he said with a smile. "Have you been developing film?"

Lionel remained smiling as well, hardly perturbed. "I am an amateur ornithologist," he said.

"What the hell is that?" Eddy asked, finally returning his gaze to Lionel.

Lionel wondered if Eddy had just scrutinized his flat. It was hard to tell. But for all his charm, Eddy Marshall did not seem overly bright. Most of the RAF pilots, while brave, were stupidly so. Mostly they were immature boys who liked to fly and fight. "My hobby is birds," Lionel said.

Eddy blinked. "Birds?"

"Yes. I watch birds and I photograph them." Lionel watched him.

He saw Eddy bite back a real laugh. "You'll have to show me some-time."

He might actually be a moron, Lionel thought. "I'm a rather clumsy photographer, so I do not show my work."

Eddy shrugged. Lionel thought the subject was over. But Eddy said, "My best buddy back home is into photography. Where's your equip-ment?" he asked, looking curiously at Lionel.

Lionel felt his smile stiffening in place. Maybe it was too soon to judge Eddy "Hawk" Marshall. He might seem glib, boyish, and easygoing, but just how easygoing could he really be? He was a top fighter pilot, no easy achievement. But could he really be any kind of a threat?

Lionel had been taught never to underestimate the enemy. So he reminded himself that in spite of a quick smile and good looks, Eddy wasn't that stupid, and right now, even though he seemed guileless, he was asking questions. "I keep everything down in the cellar," Lionel lied. And he almost smiled. For he certainly did.

Eddy nodded. "What do you shoot?" he asked.

"Ducks and geese. Robins and jays. Swans." Lionel smiled again. "So what brings you here?"

"I thought I'd take you to lunch," Eddy said. He held up his arm in the sling. "Can't fly. Got some free time. How about it? You don't seem to have dinner on." He grinned. "I owe you one."

Lionel felt his smile vanish. He had told Suttill he was leaving to take a bite at home, Eddy knew that, and had apparently noticed that there was no sign of a midday meal in progress. Yet he had not once looked at the hot plate where, on occasion, Lionel heated a pot of water or boiled an egg. "How's the café downstairs?" Eddy asked.

"Not too expensive," Lionel said calmly.

"It's my treat. It's the least I can do," Eddy said, shifting as if restless, which most of these pilots were. But Lionel became intrigued. Because

Eddy was now facing his desk, even though his single glance at it was nothing but indifferent. "This flat's a good idea," Eddy said. "So who is she?"

Lionel smiled. Was Eddy stalling or sincere? There was nothing but pads and pens on top of the desk, and although Lionel had been writing down several of the new code names on one scratch pad, he'd burned that piece of paper. Still, the top pad bore the imprints of what he'd written, but Eddy could have hardly noticed by glancing once and so blandly at it.

Lionel did not take his eyes off Eddy. He wanted to catch him regarding his desk. "Gentlemen never kiss and tell."

Eddy laughed. "Very true. Sorry I asked."

Rachel popped into his mind, and Lionel felt his body tighten unmistakably. She'd had stars shining in her eyes when she had been with Eddy. It was amusing; it was sickening. "Shall we?"

Eddy nodded with a grin. He turned, causing his line of vision to sweep over the desk.

Lionel continued to smile calmly. Had Eddy seen the envelope in the wastebasket? Lionel glanced directly at it: the envelope was faceup, and the Lisbon return address glared up at Lionel in black handwriting. Still, if Eddy had seen it, it was impossible for him to have read the address, and even if he had, Lionel already had a plausible story about whom he knew in that foreign city.

"Boy, I could eat a horse," Eddy was saying easily.

As they crossed the room, Lionel began to tingle with a slight excitement. If Eddy was astute and not what he seemed, then Lionel's life might become very interesting indeed.

They walked downstairs and entered the small restaurant, where they were promptly seated. Both Eddy and Lionel were accorded the utmost respect by the proprietor, with Lionel in full uniform and Eddy in a casual, well-worn RAF flight jacket and cap. The waitress fawned over them both. They ordered shepherd's pies and ale.

"I saw Rachel last night," Eddy said, using his cigarette lighter to light a cigarette. He smoked Lucky Strikes—many Americans did. He offered one to Lionel, who declined. Eddy took a drag, leaning against the banquette, seeming happy. "In fact, we have a date tomorrow night as well."

Lionel was not surprised. So this was why Eddy had come calling. Not because he "owed" Lionel anything, but because he wanted to fuck Rachel.

The entire sordid affair reminded him of Harry. It reminded him of the way Ellen had wanted him, the way so many other beautiful girls had, the way Rachel's sister had. *But Rachel hadn't looked at Harry with stars shining in her eyes.* She had liked him, admired him, trusted him. But she hadn't wanted him that way.

He had never seen such a look in Rachel's eyes before.

Lionel sipped his ale, feeling a faint stirring of anger. He shoved it away, and having to do so made him even angrier. Thinking about Rachel—and Eddy—had been tormenting him ever since yesterday. Yet he knew he had nothing to worry about. In fact, he should be happy. Because if she was falling in love with the American, it would eventually kill her. Lionel knew she would never defy her father over a man.

Eddy was speaking, his eyes bright, and Lionel tuned in. "Your cousin is amazing, isn't she? What a heart of gold."

Lionel smiled at him. "Rachel would cry if you decided to set traps for a mouse."

"She wouldn't hurt a fly," Eddy agreed.

Lionel decided to tell him about the swan. "My stepmother had three beautiful swans. When we were children, one of the swans died. Rachel is the one who found it. She wept over that useless bird."

"She would," Eddy said. "She's a very caring girl. I like that."

"So I can see," Lionel said, debating how much to tell Eddy. He doubted the difference of religion would affect the American. But Lionel would take bets on his being possessive and jealous. He would also bet a stack of pounds on the fact that Eddy did not yet know about Joshua Friedman.

"And she's a knockout. A drop-dead gorgeous woman. And smart!" Eddy exclaimed. "All the beautiful girls at home are bimbos." He shook his head as if he could not get over it.

"Rachel likes to read. Ask her what she's reading now," Lionel prompted. "She'll tell you Dostoyevsky or Tolstoy or some such thing."

"Who?" Eddy asked blankly.

Lionel wanted to laugh. He wasn't surprised that Eddy wasn't well read. "Where did you go to school?" he asked.

"You mean college?"

"Yes, I mean university," Lionel said. Now he suspected the other man of not even attending a university.

"I went to a community college," Eddy said.

Lionel felt satisfied—the man had no education to speak of.

"But just for my freshman year. Then I got a scholarship to Fordham U." Eddy smiled at him. "I was going to graduate this year, but the war put that on hold for a bit."

"Your major?"

"Phys ed," Eddy said promptly. "I plan to teach physical education after the war." He added, "I like kids."

Gymnasium, Lionel thought, pleased. The man wasn't that bright—he was going to become a gymnasium teacher to a bunch of brats if he survived the war. If Rachel was falling in love, it wouldn't last, even without the obstacle of her father and their religious differences. Rachel was an intellectual through and through. Eddy would soon bore her.

Then Lionel thought about the fact that he was very handsome and in uniform and a pilot. It might be a while before Rachel figured out that they were not compatible at all.

"How well do you know Rachel?" Eddy asked.

"Our families aren't close. Still, I am very fond of my cousin, even though we have not spent much time together."

"Are you Jewish, too?"

The question shocked Lionel. "Of course not."

"I didn't think so. So what's her story?" Eddy asked. "What's a doll like that doing unattached? And what about her old man? Is he the reason she's fancy-free?"

Lionel sat back, folding his arms, pleased with the turn of the conversation. "Rachel is hardly 'fancy-free,' as you put it, Marshall."

Eddy sat up. "What?" His smile was gone. His eyes were no longer lazy. They were piercing.

"Rachel is very much spoken for."

Eddy slowly stubbed his cigarette out in the ashtray, taking a long time to do so. He looked up. "What do you mean?"

Eddy didn't look like a man who would one day teach snotty children how to throw a ball. There was nothing lazy about the light in his eyes now. In fact, he looked every bit a fighter pilot—rather intimidating and even dangerous.

"Everyone knows that it is just a matter of time before she marries Joshua Friedman."

"Joshua Friedman," Eddy said slowly. Lionel smiled, but only inwardly; outwardly, he kept his expression bland. He could not take his eyes off the American.

"Who the hell is Joshua Friedman?" Eddy said very calmly.

"She didn't tell you?" Lionel asked.

"No, she did not."

It was almost nine; Eddy was late.

For two days and two nights, Rachel had not known what to do. It had been impossible to sleep, just as it had been impossible to concentrate while on duty. It seemed that all she could think about was Eddy, while yearning to be with him, but Papa's stubborn refusal to allow her to see him again haunted her. Rachel was torn. Should she follow her heart—or break Papa's?

She felt certain that was what it would come down to: if she dared to defy Papa, she would hurt him terribly. He had never recovered from Mama's death, Sarah was a huge disappointment, but she was his Rachel-lay, the apple of his eye. If she saw Eddy, if she fell in love with him, he would wither up and die, an old and bitterly defeated man.

Rachel stood nervously outside the security gates, where two benches were placed. Three soldiers and another WAAF waiting for friends, family, and rides were seated on the benches, the pair of airmen flirting with the WAAF. Rachel didn't know anyone except in passing, and she kept her back to everyone, as she did not want to be friendly now. Partly because she was so anxious about seeing Eddy again. He didn't know she could not go out with him now. She had tried to call him four times earlier in the day, but he had not been at the base. What would he do when he found out?

But the real question haunting her was would he hate her for her choice?

Rachel stopped pacing. She glanced at her small gold wristwatch. It was almost nine-thirty now. Surely he wouldn't hate her for doing what was, ultimately, right.

Rachel peered up and down the road. Because of the blackout, and the fact that high beams were illegal, one could not discern an approaching vehicle until the very last minute. The night was spectacular in its darkness. Other than the glow of one of the soldier's cigarette tips, and a few stars overhead, the road, the security gate and booth, and the airbase were cast in shadows and darkness.

Rachel couldn't believe that he had changed his mind about their date. Her stomach sickened at the very notion. Her heart knew better than to believe that. Had something happened?

She could not help being frightened, which made her more nervous than she already was. What if he was in the air? He could be scrambling even now, while she was waiting for him. What if he had refused to stay grounded; what if he had flown and been hurt? He could hardly fly his plane and man the machine gun with one hand!

She would die if something happened to him.

Rachel wanted to cry. The extent of her feelings told her that she truly loved this man. How had this happened? Why couldn't Papa see that he was wonderful? But Papa wasn't going to change, Rachel thought miserably.

If only she could be more like Sarah. Sarah would never let Papa keep her apart from the man of her dreams.

A pair of dimmed low beams suddenly became visible, and a moment later a motorcar's engine could be heard. Rachel stiffened, even though she doubted it was Eddy—where would he get an automobile? Unless, of course, he had gotten a lift. The motorcar paused before the security gates, and a man called out. One of the soldiers returned the greeting, and Rachel's heart sank. As she had thought, it wasn't Eddy.

Two soldiers left. A few minutes later the WAAF was boarding a small bus headed for Islington, and Rachel was alone.

She shivered even though she wasn't cold, her thoughts returning to her family. Tomorrow was Shabbat. Because of her religion, she was exempt from duty on the Sabbath, and she would go home before sundown, returning after sundown the next day. In the past, Rachel had always enjoyed Shabbat, when the family sat down to a fine meal together. Even Sarah never failed to be present for their Friday night celebration. Now, for the first time in her life, Rachel dreaded going home.

Rachel suddenly stiffened. A man was walking toward her. He formed a dark, indistinct shadow, emerging from the even darker night—clearly he had come from the underground, which was a few blocks away. Her heart jumped in relief and excitement and even more fear as she recognized the way he moved, the tilt of his head and the width of his shoulders.

"Hello, Rachel," Eddy said quietly, pausing before her.

It was hard to make out his features in the dark, but she didn't have to see his face clearly to know that something was terribly wrong. She heard it in his tone. Her apprehension, the feeling of nausea, increased. Did he somehow know what she was going to say? "Hi, Eddy."

"You didn't change."

She remained in her uniform. "Eddy . . ." she began, wringing her hands.

He just looked at her. A beam of moonlight illuminated one side of his face.

"I . . . I . . . I hate doing this—"

"You should have told me right away," he said abruptly. "But I still don't believe it." He was harsh.

Rachel was confused. "What are you talking about?"

"Joshua Friedman."

She gasped in surprise.

He peered more closely at her. "Isn't that what you were going to say? That you can't see me because of your fiancé?"

"We're not engaged," she managed. "I meant to tell you, but . . ." She stopped.

"But what?"

She said truthfully, "It just didn't seem to matter."

"I don't understand. Lionel said the two of you have an understanding, and that you will get married after the war."

Lionel! Rachel found herself taking his arm. "Lionel likes to make trouble, I think. I . . . it's not Joshua."

"What? What do you mean?"

She wished she could see him better. "It's Papa," she cried. "He's forbidden me to see you ever again!"

Eddy stared, and then, before she knew it, she was in his arms. He was not wearing his sling, she realized. "Do you love Joshua Friedman?" he asked.

"No," she returned, hardly able to breathe.

"Are you supposed to marry him?"

"Papa wants it," she said honestly, becoming acutely aware of how impossibly good it felt to be held this way, in his strong embrace.

"I think I see. You didn't tell me about him." His gaze was searching hers.

"When we were together, I forgot about him," she whispered.

Slowly, he began to smile. "Do you love me, Rachel?"

She bit her lip and slowly nodded. "God help me, I do."

His smile broadened, and he swept her up against his chest—which was astonishing in its hardness—and covered her mouth with his.

Rachel was electrified; and then his lips were asking hers to open, and they did, and his tongue was inside her mouth, and she was amazed, and she felt as if they were spiraling way up into space, far above the clouds and the earth.

Eddy broke the kiss. He stroked her hair. "No more Joshua," he said. "You're my girl now."

For one instant, elation swept her even farther above the atmosphere—perhaps to heaven itself—and then she came back to earth with a thud. "Eddy. No. There's Papa," she said.

"God," he said.

"I have never disobeyed him in my life," Rachel whispered, still in the circle of Eddy's arms. "I have never broken his trust."

He studied her. "Do you want to stay on base?"

Rachel nodded, since she didn't have permission to leave.

He slid his arm around her and they walked back through the gates, Eddy showing his ID as they did so. "We have to talk about this, Rachel," he said. "You can't be Daddy's little girl forever."

"It's not so simple," Rachel returned, at once ecstatic and miserable. "Even now, I am betraying Papa by being with you."

He halted and cupped her face in his hands. "Look. Where there is a will, there is a way."

Rachel tried to smile. "I want to believe you."

"Then believe, Rachel."

She searched his eyes and she believed. Rachel nodded and smiled.

Relief filled his gaze. "How about a coffee in the canteen?"

Rachel knew what he meant by "canteen," and she nodded. "The NAAFI is to our right," she said.

They headed that way, walking past several large barracks and several groups of airmen and WAAFs. "I happen to be a catch," Eddy said with a smile. "I come from a good family, I have a good job, a solid future. Maybe in time your father will come to see me in a different light."

Rachel didn't think so. "What did you do before the war?" She realized she didn't even know how old he was. "How old are you, Eddy?"

He laughed. "I'm twenty-two, Angel." He hesitated. "This is off the record, hon. Okay?"

She blinked at him. "You mean what you are telling me is a secret?" His slang was endearing.

"Well, we don't need to advertise, because it might affect my relationships in the squadron. I'm squad leader, Rach. The guys look up to me. There can't be any doubt. When you're flying against the sun, you have to trust your wingmates completely—one hundred and ten percent."

"I understand," she said, wondering where this would lead.

"I graduated from NYU a year ago—a year early, in fact. I skipped a year in high school," he added. "I have a B.A. in political science."

"NYU," Rachel said. "Is that a university in New York?"

"Yeah. It's a pretty good school." He shrugged. "My family doesn't have money. We're like your family, hardworking, decent. I got a partial scholarship and I worked a part-time job to get through. And I had some help from Uncle Sam."

"The government?"

"As a sophomore, I was recruited by the FBI," he said. "They helped pay the bills."

Rachel stared at him.

"Of course, I quit the bureau when I decided to fight Hitler." He smiled at her. "But my old job's waiting for me when I get home."

Rachel didn't know very much about the FBI, but she knew it was some kind of investigative government agency. She didn't know whether to be proud of him or afraid for him. "Is it a dangerous job?" she asked carefully.

He was pulling a pack of cigarettes from his pocket. He offered her one. Rachel declined—she didn't smoke. "Do you mind?" he asked.

"No."

He lit up. "Hon, after this war, my answer's got to be no."

Rachel studied him. She wasn't reassured. "You like danger," she suddenly said. "You like living on the edge."

He slid his arm around her as they continued to walk. "Would it bother you terribly if I said yes?"

She hesitated, thinking about it. "No. It's who you are. It's part of what makes you so exciting."

"I like that," he said, and he tossed his cigarette aside, but only so he could sweep her into his arms for a very long and even more thorough kiss. Rachel was shaking and boneless by the time he was done.

"Wow," Eddy said.

Rachel smiled. "Can I second that?"

He laughed. Suddenly he gave her a look. "Hey, what are you reading?"

"What?"

He repeated the question.

"I'm reading Somerset Maugham," she said with puzzlement.

"No Tolstoy?"

What was this about? Rachel wondered. "I've read *Anna Karenina* three times."

Now he smiled. Then his expression changed. "Rachel, about your cousin Lionel," he began. "He seems a bit strange and—" He was cut off.

Somewhere not far away, a series of huge explosions sounded.

Eddy pushed Rachel to the side of the building, covering her body with his. In unison, they turned to locate the origin of the sound. Beyond the base, somewhere to the southeast, the night was on fire—the sky red and aglow—illuminating the skyline of London and St. Paul's tall spire. More explosions sounded, one after another, and as it struck Rachel just what was happening, they saw the sky brighten again and again, the circle of fire expanding. Air-raid sirens began screaming.

"They're bombing London," Eddy said, stunned. "The frigging Gerries are bombing the city!"

Rachel stood immobilized with disbelief as the sirens continued to scream belatedly, and as more explosions thundered, ripping apart the night.

CHAPTER 18

London had been attacked. What was worse, the news traveled like wildfire, and by the time Rachel was dismissed, she knew that the areas where the bombs had hit included her own neighborhood. Rumor had it that the old church at Cripplegate had been destroyed. Other neighborhoods had been attacked as well—Islington, Finchley, Stepney, Tottenham, and Bethnal Green.

Rachel hitched a ride in a supply truck that was passing through London. She was no longer in shock, but she was afraid. She kept reminding herself that the odds of her own home having been struck were low. But all she could think of was Hannah and Papa, who would have been in their beds last night when the bombs fell. And what if Sarah had decided to go home last night?

She squeezed her eyes closed. Many children had been evacuated to the safer area of the countryside early in the war. Some had returned, not liking it, others had stayed in their foster families. She, Papa, and Sarah had decided that Hannah could stay in the city. Now she was determined to see her little sister placed in a safe home.

She was so afraid.

Rachel stared out of her window. The effects of the bombing were everywhere. She saw the rubble of crumbled buildings and stores as the supply truck passed through Islington. Pubs and cafés had been hit and destroyed. Fires still burned in places, although sporadically; the fire squads and AFS had put out all of the larger infernos. Rescue squads were working the rubble, and ambulances were parked haphazardly by the bombed-out sectors, awaiting the arrival of the wounded and the dead. In certain areas soldiers patrolled and checked ID, in others, the Home Guard. And at every site of devastation, civilians were apparent, men too old to be in the Guard, women too old to be in the ATF or so young they had babies in their arms, and boys and girls too old to have been evacuated outside of the city. Some loitered; others were digging through the rubble to help the overtaxed rescue squads.

"I can swing by your house, Rachel, if you like," Sergeant Thomas said.

"That would be great," Rachel whispered.

"Damn Nazis," he said.

Ten minutes later the truck was cruising past the synagogue on Whitechapel High Street. Amazingly, the tiny, beautiful temple where Hannah went to school, and where she and her family worshiped, was still erect. The buildings on either side of it were demolished.

"I'll get out here," Rachel said.

She wasn't even aware of the truck stopping, saying good-bye, or getting out of the cab. Rescue workers were going through the rubble with a "sniffer." A dozen civilians watched, gentile and Jew alike. An old grocery truck converted into an ambulance was parked at the curb, awaiting victims; a warden was directing the traffic around it. A housewife with the WVS was handing tired workers cups of tea from a makeshift stand.

"Rachel?"

At the sound of Sarah's voice, she jerked and saw her sister sitting in the ambulance. She was the driver, and another woman Rachel knew, Felicia, sat beside her in the passenger seat. They were both in their navy blue ATF uniforms. Rachel ran over to the cab and gripped the door, as Sarah had her window rolled down.

Sarah stepped out, and they embraced briefly but hard. "Are you all right?" Sarah asked. She appeared exhausted. There were circles beneath her eyes, and her cheeks were very pale.

Rachel nodded. She wondered if she was as red-eyed as her sister. "Papa and Hannah? Have you seen them? Are they all right?"

"They're fine. Our block is fine. The Goldbergs were hit, Rachel. The roof collapsed, the house was entirely destroyed. Rescue squads are there now, trying to dig the Goldbergs out." Sarah's voice broke on the last note.

Rachel managed to digest the news about their neighbors, who lived two blocks away. They were an elderly couple, with married children who had moved away. "They're both missing?" she whispered.

Sarah nodded, then said viciously, "Hitler swore he'd never bomb the city! Damn those bloody Nazis!"

Rachel had to close her eyes, and the sisters clung together again.

"How was it last night at Command HQ?" Sarah asked hoarsely. Tears had filled her eyes.

Rachel hesitated, then gave her a look that she knew Sarah understood. She had confided in Sarah when she was transferred into the Y unit. Very low, she said, "There's a new code word. We are working around the clock to figure out what it signifies."

Sarah nodded. "You will figure it out. We are the best of the best." She smiled bravely at Rachel, then her smile crumbled. "It's been nonstop since midnight. It seems like there's no end to the wounded, although right now we're pulling out more corpses than anything else."

Rachel took her hand and squeezed it.

The ARP warden suddenly came up to them. "That's it, Sarah. Everyone's accounted for. No bodies here." He was grim, and like Sarah, he appeared dirty and exhausted. Rachel saw that the crews were breaking up.

Sarah jumped back into the cab of the ambulance. "I have to go." The radio within the cab was crackling, and Felicia picked it up.

Rachel froze. "Sarah? Today is Shabbat."

Sarah turned on the ignition. "God will forgive me," she said.

Rachel realized what was happening and gasped, "But Papa won't!"

Sarah shot her a grim and tired smile, backing away from the curb. Rachel had no choice but to step aside as the ambulance roared past her. She was aghast.

No one was at home. It was almost six o'clock—they still had two good hours before sundown. On a normal day, their dinner would be simmering on the stove, as no cooking was allowed once the sun set. But there was nothing on the stove now.

Rachel could guess where Hannah and Papa were. Still a bit shocked that Sarah had chosen to completely break with tradition, she hurried outside and around the block. The scene of devastation at the Goldbergs' was every bit as terrible as she had imagined. Their house had been reduced to dust, rubble, and pieces of charred and scorched wood. As Rachel approached, she saw Mrs. Goldberg being carried into an ambulance on a stretcher. She was alive; her eyes were open and she was trying to speak.

Papa was with her, accompanying the gurney on its way to the waiting ambulance. He was trying to soothe her.

Rachel scanned the scene and located Hannah behind a small card table that contained a Soyer boiler and several thermoses. She was working with a WVS volunteer, offering tea and lemonade to the various workers. Rachel smiled a little at the sight of her urchin sister, and she ran over to hug her.

Rachel stroked her unruly hair. "I am so relieved that you and Papa are all right," Rachel said. "I could hardly think of anything else all night and all day!"

"Don't cry, Rachel," Hannah said, tugging on her hand. "It was just one of those nasty bombs. From now on, Papa said we'll sleep in the shelter." A year and a half ago they had put an Anderson shelter in their backyard, but they had never used it, as it was so cramped and uncomfortable.

Rachel sniffed and nodded, holding back her tears with an effort as Papa came over. She took one look at him and knew something was wrong. "Papa?"

"Let's go home," he said with a sigh. His overalls were covered with dirt and dust. There was even a bloodstain on one thigh. "It's over, Rachel-lay, and we have Friday-night dinner to make."

"Can I stay and help Millie clean up?" Hannah asked.

Rachel guessed that Millie was the woman with the WVS. Papa nodded, and Hannah ran back to the woman, who was packing up her things on the tea stand.

Papa took Rachel's hand. Her heart began to beat with unease as she looked at his grim profile. He said, not looking at her, "Saul is dead."

Rachel was stunned. She could hardly think. She had always known the Goldbergs, and now Saul Goldberg was dead . . . killed by a German bomb.

They had been at war for almost a year, but until the summer, it had been a "phony" war, and until now all of the fighting had been in the air or out at sea. In fact, the ones who had been dying were the pilots, and as horrible as that was, the only pilot she knew was Eddy. There had been very few civilian casualties thus far.

For the first time since Britain had gone to war, Rachel knew someone who had died. The war had finally come home.

They walked home in silence.

In the kitchen they methodically began to put together a meal. Papa took lard and soup bones out of the icebox, while Rachel went into the garden for carrots and string beans. When she returned to the kitchen, Papa said, setting a kettle to boil, "Sarah is late. It's almost seven."

Rachel did not look at him, but every muscle in her body tensed as she went into the pantry for an onion, potatoes, and flour. She said, "Sarah is working tonight."

Papa faced her as she came out. "If Sarah does not come home tonight, she will never be welcome in this house again."

"Papa!" Rachel dropped the potatoes on the kitchen table, or perhaps she threw them down. "It's a war, Papa. God will forgive her," she cried, using Sarah's own words. "Why can't you?"

Papa's face was set. "Because my daughter is a whore." He looked ready to cry.

Rachel froze. Had she just heard what she thought she had?

Papa turned back to the stove. His shoulders were shaking.

Rachel ran to him. "How could you say such a thing? Sarah is beautiful and brave, Papa. More women should be like her!"

He did not look at her. "Do you take me for a fool, Rachel?" he asked wearily.

Rachel did not know what to do. In fact, she wasn't even certain that Sarah was a virgin, so she did not dare get into that. She said, "Please allow Sarah to save the lives of Hitler's innocent victims tonight. Please."

Papa did not answer. He was peeling carrots, the skins flying wildly across the kitchen counter.

"Please, Papa. For me."

He stiffened and his hands stilled. And he nodded.

Rachel sagged against the counter, flooded with relief. She said a prayer of thanks to God, for surely, this once, he had been listening.

The telephone rang.

It was automatic—both Rachel and Papa looked at the clock on the wall, as the phone could not be answered once the sun went down. It was seven-fifteen. Rachel raced to the phone to answer it, already knowing who it was.

"Eddy," she cried, realizing too late that Papa was present.

"Rachel. Are you okay?" he asked quickly.

"Of course, I'm fine!"

"Is your family okay?"

"Yes, we're fine. And you?"

"Thank God," he said, relief evident in his tone. "I called the base the moment I had a chance, and they said you'd gone home, and I was afraid something had happened to your family."

Love filled her chest, making it almost impossible to breathe. But in the next breath, she had an inkling, one she did not like, not at all. "Tell me you're not flying?"

"Honey, I had to go up. A fractured wrist isn't going to stop me. My squadron wasn't going up without me, Rach. I'm the squad leader."

"So now your wrist is fractured?" she said, aghast.

"Well, it's hairline, which means it's no big deal. Take heart. By the time we got up, the Gerries were halfway across the channel. We couldn't catch them, and you know we're a lot faster than they are."

Rachel wanted to beg him to stay on the ground until his wrist had healed. Papa said, "Rachel. Today is Shabbat." There was tremendous censure in his tone.

"Eddy, this is a bad time for us to talk. It's a holy day."

"I understand," he said, and he hesitated.

There was something about his silence that filled her with dread. "What is it?" she asked quickly.

"Damn. Rachel . . . my squadron's being transferred to the south. We leave tomorrow."

"What?" Rachel reeled as if struck. "Transferred—where? Why?"

"The war is heating up. Hitler attacked London, Rach. Innocent people were killed last night. Customers leaving the cinema. Men and women leaving the pubs. This was an attack upon innocent civilians, not factories or airfields or munitions or supplies. We're being moved closer to the action."

"Where are they transferring you?" Rachel whispered, unable to fight the anguish. They had only just met. They had only begun to fall in love. They needed more time. Just a little more time . . .

"Tangmere."

"Tangmere?" Rachel echoed. Tangmere was in the south. It wasn't far from Portsmouth. It was so far away from her. . . .

"Rachel, we have dinner to make," Papa said sternly.

Rachel didn't even look at him. She was frantic now. She turned her back on her father. "But when will I see you again?" she asked. "You're leaving *tomorrow?*"

"Rachel, I will find a way. It might be a few weeks, but as soon as I have the chance, I'll take a leave and come up to London. I promise."

Terror overcame her. He would forget about her. Find someone else. Or worse, he would be hurt, killed, and she would never see him again.

He was flying with a fractured wrist.

"Eddy, you don't have to do this. Your wrist—"

His tone changed. "We're short of pilots, and you know it."

She did know it. "I'm sorry."

"I don't want you to worry," he said, his tone easing. "Not about me and not about us." Then he added, a smile in his voice, "I'm in charge of all the worrying around here."

Rachel had to smile a little, but she couldn't speak.

"I have to go, and I know I'm holding you up. I'll write as soon as I get settled in. And I'll call."

He would write. He would call. Rachel felt tears sliding down her cheeks. She knew she should not be so selfish, this was war. But she remained terrified that she had lost him when she had discovered him only a few days ago.

"Rachel, are you there?"

"Yes," she managed.

"I love you," he said. There was no hesitation.

She didn't hesitate, either. "I love you, too." And she knew Eddy was smiling as he hung up.

Rachel gripped the phone to her breast. It was as if he had already gone. But he hadn't left. He wasn't leaving until the morning.

There was always tonight.

But it was Shabbat. Rachel hung up the phone, and there was no internal debate. There was no choice. Slowly, she turned.

"So I've lost you, too," Papa said, his eyes finding and holding hers.

"No, Papa. You haven't lost me, and you never will." Rachel went to him and kissed his cheek. "Let's finish making dinner," she said.

Rachel walked the distance from the underground station to the entrance to Biggin Hill. It was late, and there were no vehicles on the road for her to get a lift. It had taken her nearly two hours to get to her destination—it was almost midnight. She hadn't realized that this air station was so far from London. On the map it seemed much closer.

The base was, of course, blacked out. It loomed ahead of her, indistinct and shadowy. The gates were closed. Security guards stood in front of them, two vague human shadows. Another guard would be seated in the security booth behind the closed gates, but Rachel could distinguish only the booth and not the soldier inside. As Rachel approached, she heard planes overhead. She looked up. A squadron was taking off. Against a panoply of stars, the dark silhouettes gleamed silver, streaking up into the night.

Eddy could be in one of those planes. On the other hand, his squadron was being transferred in the morning—he wouldn't fly now unless it was an emergency and most of 11 Group was scrambling.

The two guards eyed her and shone a flashlight on her briefly as she paused before them. She wasn't in her uniform, so they did not mistake her for one of their own WAAFs. "Can we help you, miss?"

This was the hard part, Rachel knew. She swallowed down her apprehension—she had come this far, defying both Papa and God to do so—she could not back down now. "Would you please tell Eddy Marshall that I'm here."

The guards looked at each other. "Do you have a pass?"

Rachel shook her head.

They looked at each other, slyly now. "So you want to see Hawk, eh?"

"Please," she said imploringly. "He's being transferred tomorrow. If he hasn't scrambled, he'll see me, I know he will."

The guard looked doubtful. His buddy jabbed him. "She seems upset, Frank. Might as well give him a ring."

"Thank you," Rachel said.

Ten minutes later, as she stood outside the closed gates, Eddy appeared, hurrying toward her from the other side, clad in trousers and a bomber jacket. He was carrying a small penlight, shining it downward. "Rachel!" He broke into a run. "Open the damn gates," he shouted.

The guards hurried to obey, pushing open the big wire gates. Eddy caught her in both arms, crushing her to his chest, in spite of the sling he was once again wearing. Rachel held on to him as if her life depended on it.

He set her back an inch or so, so he could look down at her face. "I don't know what possessed you, but I love you for it," he said. "I really missed you." And he kissed her for a long time.

The guards cheered and whistled.

Being in his arms again felt like the best thing that had ever happened to her.

"Damn," Eddy said, appearing flushed as he broke off the kiss.

Rachel was flustered, out of breath. "I had to come. I missed you, too."

"But it's Shabbat," he said, peering at her closely in the dark. "I did some reading . . . it's a big deal. You've broken the law or something."

"It's a covenant with God. I think he'll understand," Rachel murmured, as they remained thigh to thigh and chest to chest.

Eddy just stared at her. Then he took her hand and kissed it. "I am glad you did this, Rachel."

"Me, too." And she was. Because she was so afraid of what the war might bring. This time there not only hadn't been any choice, there hadn't been any conflict, either. But she would not lie to Papa.

It was as if he read her mind. They started walking along the road, away from the entrance to Biggin Hill. "What will you tell your father?"

"The truth." She hesitated. He was already heartbroken over Sarah, and now he would be over her as well. "Let's not talk about Papa now. Please. We have this one night."

"I am in complete agreement," he said. "But there'll be more nights, Rachel. More nights and more days."

Rachel prayed that he was right. She had never been a pessimist before. Her worry frightened her now. "You're wearing your sling."

"It hurts a bit," he admitted.

"How many sorties did you fly today?" she asked, trying not to be critical.

He hesitated, as if debating whether or not he should tell her the truth. "Six."

"Eddy," she whispered, dismayed. But the squadrons were all flying round the clock.

"Honey, what can I do? My men need me. They're exhausted, demoralized. We've lost so many pilots," he said, lowering his voice to a whisper. Suddenly he stopped and faced her. "The Luftwaffe just seem to keep on coming, their numbers just don't seem to be diminishing. My boys need a break. But they're not going to get one. I can't stay down."

It was the first time she had ever heard fatigue, frustration, even anguish, in his tone. "Are you scared up there?" she whispered.

He smiled a little. "You know what they say—only fools feel no fear."

"I'm so proud of you," she said, more than meaning it.

"I'm proud of you, too."

They smiled at each other and leaned on the split-rail fence of the property they were standing on. A farmhouse seemed to be in the distance. Rachel could hear the bell of a cow. Eddy slid off his jacket, tossing it over the railing.

"Can I smoke?" he asked.

"You never have to ask," Rachel said, not quite sure she meant it.

He laughed. "Angel, I will always ask." He lit up and inhaled deeply. "You know, it was a mistake."

"What was a mistake?" She was so happy that they were together. She also leaned on the rail, not caring if she tore her pale pink cardigan.

"The bombing of London. Two of the Luftwaffe pilots lost their way, can you believe it?" He leaned more heavily on the fence. "And they were running out of fuel, of course." Everyone knew that the German bombers only had about ten minutes at most of flying time once they reached the British coast.

"They had no choice but to drop their bombs, lighten up, and race for home. What crap," Eddy said with heat. Then he looked at her. "I curse too much, don't I?"

"It's all right," Rachel said softly.

Eddy lapsed into silence. Rachel didn't mind. She could hear crickets singing now, and one of the cows sighing. The breeze was soft, warm, almost balmy. It was a beautiful night.

If only this moment would last forever, she thought.

"How well do you know your cousin?" Eddie suddenly asked, stubbing his cigarette out on the railing.

Rachel started. "Lionel? Not well. I've spoken to him only a dozen times in my entire life."

"Why? Because his family is a bunch of snobs and your family is Jewish?" Eddie asked.

Rachel blinked. "Yes, that's exactly why."

"Have you ever seen his photography?" he asked.

"His what?" She was surprised by the question.

"He likes birds," Eddy said. "I stopped over at his flat one day, and he was developing film. Claims he's an amateur photographer and that he takes pictures of birds."

Rachel stared at him, but all she could recall was Lionel feeding Ellen's fish to her swan. "He claims . . . what is this about?" She was filled with unease.

"I don't know. Something feels so damn odd about him. I think I might have walked in on him doing something he did not want me to see or know about. Or maybe he's protective about his birds." Eddy smiled at that but looked carefully at Rachel. "Surely you knew your cousin likes birds?"

"Actually, I didn't know, but I'm not surprised."

"Why?"

Rachel hesitated. Eddy was so intent. "It has to do with an incident when we were all children. He seemed very interested in his stepmother's swans."

Eddy was listening. "He told me about the dead swan."

"He did?" Rachel was surprised.

"So you can see him being a bird-watcher—an ornithologist?"

"An orni—what?"

"Ornithology is the study of birds. I had to look it up," he said with chagrin.

"Eddy, why are you asking me these questions?"

He shrugged. "I did a bit of checking. The authorities think his father might have turned fascist, been a spy, and fled to Germany."

"I heard that."

"From who?"

"Lionel told me the day you crashed near Eltham."

They both smiled a little at the memory.

"Like father like son?" Eddy asked.

"What?" Rachel gasped.

"I'm only fishing, hon. Relax. It's just that he's weird. And cold. He smiles all the time, but have you ever noticed how amused his smiles are? And they don't reach his eyes."

Rachel was becoming chilled. "Yes, I have, and the truth is, I have never liked him. He can't be a fascist, Eddy. He's in the RAF, just like you."

Eddy smiled at her. "Did you know his father?"

"Yes, but we only met a few times." She knew what he wanted to know. "I believe Lord Elgin could have been a fascist. But the person you might want to ask about that is Papa."

Eddy nodded. "I will." He paused, gazing into the night.

"What is it? What are you really thinking?"

He smiled and slid his arm around her. "Do you already know me so well? It was too easy at Elgin Hall. They found all kinds of German-made paraphernalia. Invisible ink. A paper opener made in Düsseldorf. A list of code names in German. No self-respecting spy would leave such incriminating evidence around."

Her heart was beating very loudly—surely Eddy could hear. "He might, if he was planning to disappear and didn't care what the authorities found."

"Good point," Eddy conceded.

"How would you know about this? You're not family."

Eddy hesitated. "It's not top secret. I asked around. The story's a big deal—it's floating all over the place."

Rachel believed him until he looked away. She suddenly wondered if he wasn't telling her the entire truth. Still, Rachel trusted Eddy completely. If there was something he wasn't telling her, there was a good reason for it.

"I think the best thing might be if you steer clear of your cousin for a while," Eddy said.

Rachel nodded. "I have no problem with that. His company isn't exactly enjoyable."

"Good." Eddy stared at her.

Rachel let him. It was funny, how a long look from him could make her start thinking about being held and touched and kissed. One long look, and she was melting all over and wanting what was impossible—and what no self-respecting girl should even think about.

Tomorrow he was leaving.

"Eddy?"

"Yeah?" he asked roughly, reaching for her hand and holding it hard.

"You're going to see a lot of action now, aren't you? Tangmere is so close to France."

"There'll be a lot of action," he said.

"I am so scared," Rachel said in a whisper.

His eyes widened. "For me?"

She nodded.

He pulled her into his embrace. "I don't want you worrying about me, hon. I'm one of the best, Rachel. Trust me. I'll come home in one piece."

"I hate those words!" she cried, clinging to him.

"Don't be afraid," he said urgently, cupping her face in his hands.

He was forgetting his sling again. "Your wrist."

"I don't care about my wrist," he said with a smile, and he kissed her again.

This time they were all alone. The crickets sang and the moon beamed and Rachel swayed in his arms as his mouth plied hers hungrily; their bodies seeming to fuse. It was pleasant out, but Rachel became warm as the kiss continued taking on a volatile life of its own. Eddy's strong hands slid down her back, then up again, and finally settled low on her hips. Rachel wanted to moan into his mouth, but she did not dare.

Eddy's mouth tore free of hers and suddenly he was kissing the underside of her neck. One of his hands slid up over her rib cage, pausing beside her breast.

Rachel wanted to die. If he did not touch her breast, she might. His mouth moved to her ear. Rachel could no longer control herself, and while she meant to sigh, she moaned.

He crushed her hard, finding her mouth with his again. This time, Rachel felt his hardness against her thigh. She knew what it meant, even though she wasn't supposed to. Excitement made her tremble from limb to limb. It made her giddy and reckless. Somehow, Rachel Greene had disappeared and a wild woman had taken her place.

Planes sounded overhead.

The roar was rude and loud, as if the flight was just a few meters above them, not hundreds or thousands of feet. Rachel stiffened as Eddy ceased kissing her, holding her so hard that she could feel his wildly pounding heart against her bosom. She felt certain that her heart was the faster of the two.

"Oh, God, Rachel," Eddy whispered against her hair.

Rachel couldn't speak. She had never been consumed with desire before, but now she understood what passion was. She could not move.

Eddy remained standing that way, holding her and breathing hard. "I want you so much," he said in a rough whisper. "We had better stop—this is too tough."

"I want you, too," Rachel heard herself say. "So much."

Eddy tensed even more. He seemed to stop breathing as well.

Rachel could hardly believe herself. First violating the Shabbat and defying Papa, and now she was turning into a tart. "You're leaving tomorrow," she said.

He finally pulled an inch away and looked down at her face. "Yes, I am. But I'll be back."

The fear almost choked her. She could not voice it either, but it was there, consuming her—what if he did not come back? Saul Goldberg was dead, and he had been an old man, a civilian. This man flew a dozen sorties every day—every day he faced and taunted and tempted death.

"Rachel? I will be back. There's no need to rush, as much as I want to." He tried to smile and failed.

"I love you, Eddy. I want to stay here tonight with you," Rachel said, not quite sure what she meant.

His eyes widened. "What are you saying?"

"I don't know!" she cried. "But we have tonight, for certain, and it's a magical night, isn't it?" Now she was the one to take his beloved face between her hands. "Kiss me again."

He stared. "But it's too hard. It's harder for a man to control himself."

"I know." She hesitated. Her mind raced, spun. She couldn't think it through. Didn't want to. "So don't."

His eyes widened almost comically. He gripped her arms. "Are you asking me to make love to you?"

Her heart beat hard. It was like a drum, and then there was not enough air, and that was almost suffocating her. She felt light-headed, faint. "Yes," she whispered.

For one moment he did not move, and then he crushed her to his chest again. Rachel felt his heart beating madly beneath her cheek. "Hon. I can't. I respect you too much, Rachel. When we make love for the first time, it will be in a bed with satin sheets—on our wedding night."

Rachel jerked to look up at him. "What?"

"You heard me." He smiled a little and made a funny face. "I can't believe I just said that, but I did. And I meant it. We'll make love for the first time on our wedding night," he said, this time very firmly.

He wanted to marry her. The planes were gone, but the acrid smell from their engines remained in the air. Eddy was a fighter pilot and the war was real. *He might never come back.*

"Eddy?" Rachel whispered, filled with trepidation now. But her determination was even greater.

"What?" There was the slightest hint of wariness in his tone.

She hesitated, then slipped his hand over her breast—then beneath her cardigan and into her blouse and over her lace brassiere.

Eddy was still.

So was Rachel.

Their eyes held while her heart beat insistently, and then he slid his hand beneath the cup of her bra and her breast filled his palm. Her nipple hardened immediately.

Rachel heard a small moan escape her as her eyes drifted closed.

"You've never been with a man," Eddy said, and it wasn't a question.

"It doesn't matter."

"It matters to me."

She opened her eyes and looked at him in time to realize that he was not going to reject her—his arms were going around her and he was lifting her up. "I am going to marry you when I come back," he said.

"I know," she whispered, as he carried her over to the gate. Without letting her down, he unlatched it and butted it open with his hip. He did not bother to close it. His strides increased, and then Rachel found herself on the ground, on her back, beneath a spreading oak tree. Eddy slipped the cardigan off her shoulders, tossed it aside, and as he knelt over her, he smiled.

She smiled back, happy and excited all at once.

He moved on top of her, their mouths melding, and for one instant it was gentle. And then no more.

His hands were on her breasts, teasing her nipples again and again, through silk and cotton; his lips were demanding, his tongue inside her mouth; he reached down and tossed her skirts up, sliding his hands up her thighs, over her gartered nylons. Rachel cried out. Eddy's fingers brushed over her cotton panties.

This time Eddy cried out, and suddenly he was helping her remove her blouse and skirt while shrugging off his own shirt. Rachel took one look at his muscular, broad, bare chest and she wanted to cry—he was the most beautiful man, the most beautiful person, the most beautiful thing she had ever laid her eyes upon. He stood up, to hop out of his pants. "What is it?" he asked.

"You're beautiful."

He sank back down, in only his boxers and socks. "I'm a guy," he said roughly. "You're the one who's beautiful, Rachel." He pulled her back into his arms.

It was the most natural thing in the world to let him settle himself between her thighs and to hook her ankles over his calves. But Rachel hadn't expected the shock of excitement from having his hard loins against her own. Eddy was kissing her, but he must have been jolted too, because he buried his face against her neck, and they lay like that for a long moment, the heat building between them.

"I want you so badly. Can you feel that?"

She had to smile. "How could I not?"

He began gently rocking his erection against her. "I want this to be good for you."

Rachel actually couldn't speak. An odd sound escaped her, like a whimper.

"I want you to come when I'm inside you," he whispered, still moving his hard length back and forth over her womanhood.

Rachel had no idea what he was talking about. It didn't matter. Her body had taken over. *Please,* she thought, aching and dying. *Please!*

"Rachel?" he half murmured and half gasped. He was reaching down between them. His fingers stroked over her panties, between his manhood and herself.

Rachel couldn't breathe. She couldn't think. She could only feel.

He said something incoherent, pulling off her panties. Rachel gripped his shoulders more tightly, and she heard herself whisper, "Please, dear God, please." And it somehow crossed her frantic mind that she should not be using the Lord's name just then. But she could not dwell on it.

Eddy suddenly gasped, but Rachel didn't really hear, because the huge tip of him was pushing against her where she was soaking wet and waiting.

"Eddy!" she moaned.

"Oh, damn," he cried, surging into her.

Briefly, there was a tearing pain. Rachel stiffened, and then it was gone. What remained was the most amazing fullness inside her. Rachel began to cry.

This was Eddy. They were one.

"Did I hurt you? Are you okay?" Eddy was asking, a frantic note in his hoarse voice.

"No, no," Rachel gasped, rocking him now, using her hips and her pelvis and body parts she hadn't ever paid attention to before.

Eddy began moving.

Rachel felt herself spiraling out of all earthly existence; the universe shattered, and so did she.

Birds were singing. It was their cheerful chirping that woke Rachel up. Stealthy fingers of light were slipping over the field as Rachel opened her eyes. She lay stark naked in Eddy's arms, their legs entwined, her buttocks spooned into his groin. Her skirt and his shirt were covering the lower halves of their bodies as a makeshift blanket.

Rachel did not want to move. Her body felt tired and sore from all the times they had made love—and dear God, now she began to blush, thinking about the things they had done that she just knew weren't proper—but the reason she did not want to move was that maybe being held like this was even better than making love. It was a difficult if not impossible question that Rachel decided to debate at a later date.

She felt elated, but now she sobered, because it was almost dawn, and it struck her, cruelly, that Eddy was leaving for Tangmere in an hour or so, while she would have to go home to face Papa and the wrath of God—the very same thing.

"Good morning," Eddy whispered, kissing her forehead.

He was awake. Rachel smiled up at him, refusing to think about her father now. "Good morning," she said.

"I love you." His green eyes smiled at her and moved slowly over her face.

Her heart joined in the chorus coming from the treetops. "I love you, too."

The smile in his eyes faded. "It's five. We leave at six. I have to go."

"I know." She felt tears begin to gather in her own eyes. She turned away. He had many battles to fight, and she would not send him to war with tears and sorrow.

He hadn't seen, though he was loath to release her. He handed her brassiere and underwear to her. Even though he knew every inch of her now, Rachel blushed and held her skirt over her nakedness.

"You don't have to hide from me," he said softly, stepping into his boxers.

Rachel blushed just looking at *him* in near daylight. "I know. I need some time to get used to this."

"I know." He smiled briefly at her as they both began dressing. He didn't look directly at her again and Rachel loved him even more, if that was possible, for his kindness. "Hon, I'm worried."

She was alarmed and stopped buttoning her blouse. "Why?"

"Your father. What will he do to you when you get home—after you've spent the night with me?" He finally looked at her, tucking his shirt into his slacks.

"I don't know," Rachel said truthfully, a bitter and fearful pang finally going through her. "I just don't know."

Eddy seemed upset. "I can't regret what we did, but Rachel, if he somehow hurts you—"

"Papa would never hurt me." But now, thinking about her father, she was feeling sick. She had never lied to him, but if he asked her about last night, did she dare tell him the truth? The extent of her dilemma was beginning to sink in.

"You could always tell him that we're getting married," Eddy said.

Rachel began to realize the vast sum of her actions. She had violated the Shabbat, she had disobeyed Papa, *and* she had slept with a man. *Papa would never forgive her.*

"You've turned white," Eddy said anxiously. "Damn it!"

She looked at him and somehow smiled. "Eddy. Don't worry. Papa will be very angry, but I am his favorite. He will forgive me in time." She hated lying to him. She had never lied like this before. But she could not let Eddy go into battle with his mind full of worries about her and her father. He had the Germans to worry about. Dear God, surely that was enough. "We will argue. Shout. Even cry." She held back the tears. "But truly, that is all. In another week or so, Papa won't even remember that I stole out of the house to see you."

Eddy did not look convinced.

Rachel kissed his cheek, smiling. "Papa loves me, Eddy."

"I know that," he said, still grim and drawn. He sighed. "If only I were a Jew. C'mon. I've got to report to duty or I'll find myself in the brig."

She had no idea what the brig was, and just then she couldn't care. All thoughts of facing Papa fled. She took his hand, overcome with an anguish of their impending separation. In just a few minutes, she would be taking the tube back to London and he would be flying *Angel* to the aerodome at Tangmere.

"It will be a few weeks, Rachel. Just a few weeks," he said.

She nodded, and felt the tears filling her eyes. She did not believe him.

What was worse, she was finally aware of a small voice in her head. Perhaps it was intuition or even a premonition. But now she understood why this night meant so much to her—why she had sacrificed her family and her religion in order to come to this man, in order to be with him.

Somehow, she knew that they were never going to have a wedding day.

She prayed that she was wrong.

CHAPTER 19

It was past eight by the time Rachel reached London. Her heart felt as if it were broken, she missed Eddy that much. Yet she was also ecstatic; she was truly in love, head over heels in love, for the first time in her life. Never had life seemed so bittersweet. Never had the future felt so fragile.

As her train traveled through the city, Rachel's thoughts veered from Eddy to her father. The sweetness of her joy and the hard edges of her anguish softened as she began to contemplate facing him. Rachel decided to get off the tube at Piccadilly Circus; walking a few extra blocks might help clear her head and prepare her for what surely would be the worst argument of her life. It was too much to hope that Papa would still be asleep and that he might not have noticed that she had disappeared in the middle of the night.

He was going to be furious. Would he strike her?

He had never hit her. Papa did not believe in smacks or slaps. Yet once, when she was a child, she had seen him strike Sarah—her older sister had said something rude to Mama, and Papa's reaction had been instantaneous. Rachel had recalled being stunned; Sarah had fled to their bedroom, locking herself in, while Mama had cried. Papa had gone about his business, but he had seemed more upset than anyone.

Rachel almost felt that she would deserve it if he did strike her. But she was an adult, and she could not imagine him doing so. There was only one other possibility. He would disown her the way Elgin had disowned Mama.

She reached the outskirts of her neighborhood, wishing Sarah was home, as if her older sister, who was so brave, might transmit some courage to her. At least she had reassured Eddy; at least today, as he scrambled time and again against the Germans, he would not have her to worry about.

It was still shocking—the gaping spaces between upright buildings, when once the block had been whole. Rachel passed the synagogue, finally succumbing to guilt. In a few minutes the morning services would begin.

Her feet dragged. Ahead was her house. There was no sign of activity from this vantage point, of course, but Rachel knew what she would find when she stepped through the front door. Papa waiting for her, Papa enraged, Papa telling her that she was no longer his daughter, Papa telling her to leave the house.

She was sick inside, in her heart, her stomach, her very bones.

Rachel pushed open the front door and was stunned to find the parlor empty. The house was deathly silent. Her unease escalated wildly.

Hannah stepped into the room, from the kitchen. She stared wordlessly at Rachel, her eyes wide, her face white. She did not say a word.

More fear—real fear—overcame Rachel.

"Hannah?" she tried.

Hannah stared at her as if she were a ghost. Then she turned and fled upstairs.

Rachel hugged herself. This was wrong, very wrong . . . She stepped into the kitchen. Her heart stopped.

Papa sat at the kitchen table, reading the Torah. He was dressed for temple, in his suit and *kipa* and talit. He did not seem to hear or notice her.

"Papa?" she said hoarsely.

He did not look up.

Rachel was trembling now. She cleared her throat, nervously toying with the hem of her cardigan. "Papa? Good morning."

He continued to read. It was as if he did not hear her.

For one instant, Rachel was alarmed—was he ill? Had he lost his hearing? "Papa?"

He turned the page as if she weren't standing there in the doorway, attempting to speak to him.

It struck her then that he was ignoring her. Was this how he intended to punish her? Or was he so hurt he could not look at her, speak with her? "Papa? I am so sorry! Please try to understand."

He continued to read. It was as if he was stone deaf, or as if she did not exist.

"I love him. I know he's not Jewish, but he's a wonderful man. Please, please try to understand—tomorrow he might be dead! He's being transferred far to the south—I had to go see him last night. Papa? Think of how it was when you met Mama—"

Papa stood, closing the Torah, and Rachel stopped in midsentence, hope soaring in her breast. But he looked past her, through her, and called, "Hannah, we must go."

Amazement stiffened her.

Papa walked around her, not once looking at her.

"Papa!" she cried, turning as he went past. "I did what I did for love, Papa, and I am so sorry to hurt you! To have disobeyed you! Please try to understand."

"Hannah?" Papa said, giving no sign that he had heard her.

Hannah trotted downstairs. She wore the same frozen, terrified expression as before. Her eyes met Rachel's. She did not speak.

"Please, wait," Rachel said with sudden desperation. "I should change. I am coming with you, of course."

Papa took Hannah's hand. He tucked a stray hair behind her ear. "Ready?" he asked her.

Hannah nodded, darting a fearful glance at Rachel.

"Then we shall go." Papa tried to smile but failed miserably. He led his youngest daughter through the parlor and to the front door.

Rachel felt her world beginning to crumble all around her, the way the walls of the Goldbergs' house had crumbled, into heaps of rubble and piles of dust. "Papa!"

They walked through the front door.

He wasn't going to speak to her; he wasn't going to acknowledge her. This, then, was her punishment, the price she would pay for her defiance and her love. For one moment, Rachel could not move. The front door creaked closed.

For how long could he do this? Surely he must speak with her again eventually! Surely they would shout and argue in time. Perhaps he would even disown her. But to pretend that she did not exist?

Rachel covered her face with her hands. She was shaking wildly. This silent treatment could not go on for very long, she told herself. But she was not convinced. This, certainly, was far worse than anything she had imagined.

She fought back tears. She must not miss the morning service, but she could not go in these grass-stained clothes—the clothes she had made love in. Rachel turned to run upstairs and change. As she entered the bedroom she shared with her sisters, she caught a glimpse of her reflection in the mirror on the wall. It was terrified. Rachel opened the closet, choosing a dark, somber dress. She began to choke on the tears she was fighting.

Papa was the most stubborn man she knew. Rachel had a terrible feeling—that he would never speak to her again.

Shabbat. Rachel now dreaded returning home for the holiest day of the week, but she could not stay away and hide behind her job at Fighter Command, as much as she would like to do so. That would only make everything worse. As Rachel entered the house four weeks later, she was assailed with the smells of roasting chicken, potatoes, and onions. She had no appetite—she hadn't had an appetite in weeks, and she was very slender now.

Sarah came out of the kitchen in an apron, smiling and beautiful. She hurried over to Rachel and kissed her cheek, but her eyes were anxious. "Hi, sweetie. We're having roasted chicken tonight."

Rachel nodded, although she could not care less. She bit her lower lip and inhaled, trembling. "Is Papa in the kitchen?" she asked with dread.

"He's in the backyard."

Rachel hugged herself. "Surely he'll talk to me tonight. It's been over a month, Sarah. He has pretended that I don't exist for an entire month." Rachel's gaze locked with her sister's. She did not know how much more of this she could take—she had broken Papa's heart, but now he was breaking hers.

"I know." Sarah hugged her again. "I know and I'm sorry. You're not the one who deserves this. I'm the one who should be treated this way."

Rachel only shook her head. To make matters even worse, she had received one short letter from Eddy a week after his transfer, and she had not heard from him since. She was becoming doubtful; she was beginning to wonder if their love really existed. Or what if the reason she hadn't heard from him was that he was hurt—or worse? Three weeks ago, when he had not replied to her letter, she had learned from an airman at Fighter Command that he was fine. The battle for Britain had become very intense, and the RAF was flying constantly in response to the Luftwaffe invasions. Last week, the silence growing ominous, Rachel had tried to speak with her source again. All the airman would tell her was "I can't say much, but he's not wounded or missing, Rachel." And what did that mean? Was Eddy now a part of some classified action? She was torturing herself with worry.

"Do you want me to come with you?" Sarah asked, breaking into her thoughts.

Rachel shook her head, overwhelmed. The war was taking a terrible toll on everyone now—the bombs fell not just on the RAF airfields, on factories and munitions dumps, but on the city, both day and night. Hitler had vowed to bring Britain to its knees, and his efforts were concentrated on London. It was so bad that they no longer went to temple on Friday night; they ate their Shabbat meal in the Anderson shelter by candlelight, while Hurricanes and Spitfires roared overhead, taking on the Junkers and Stukkas sent to inflict what damage they could upon the civilian population. As they prayed, bombs exploded in the distance. More often than not, the distance wasn't great—the East End and Cheapside were being the hardest hit thus far by the Germans. Many of her neighbors were outraged by the unfairness of it all.

It was all too much to bear: not hearing from Eddy, the air raids, the bombs, the war.

But facing Papa was perhaps the most difficult task of all.

Rachel crossed the kitchen and opened the back door. Papa sat in his rocker, rocking in silence. But the silence was narrowly contained—somewhere up above them Rachel could hear fighter planes, and somewhere to the south, she could hear bombs exploding. "Hello, Papa," she said.

He didn't flinch, stiffen, or turn. It was as if he truly did not hear her; as if, for him, she did not exist.

Rachel turned and walked back inside. How did joy become despair so quickly and thoroughly? Was it only four weeks ago that the future had seemed so bright in spite of the uncertainty of the war? Only four weeks ago she had been in Eddy's arms.

Pilots were notorious for loving and leaving their women.

"You're skinny," Sarah said, handing her a soiled envelope.

"What's this?" Rachel asked, not caring.

Sarah smiled. "I didn't think Papa should see it. It's from Church Fenton." Her smile increased.

"Church Fenton?" That was an air station. Her pulse began to skitter wildly as she looked at the envelope. "It's from Eddy!" she cried.

Sarah laughed with happiness.

Clutching the letter to her breast, Rachel ran upstairs and into their bedroom. Flopping on the bed, she tore the letter open as Sarah came in, closing the door behind them. Something wrapped in yellow paper fell onto the bedspread. Rachel began to read the letter. Sarah reached for the carefully folded paper square.

"Sarah!" Rachel cried as she read and began to understand why she hadn't heard from Eddy. "A squadron of Americans has been formed, and Eddy was transferred to it! They're calling it Eagle Squadron . . . they're at Church Fenton, Eddy is wing commander . . . there's a USAAF liaison! He misses me!" She hugged the letter to her breast.

"Rachel." Sarah held up a tiny, glittering object.

Rachel froze. *It was a ring.*

It was a gold band set with one very small solitaire diamond—it looked exactly like an engagement ring.

"This fell out of the envelope, Rachel," Sarah said huskily, with barely repressed excitement, her eyes huge.

"Oh, God," Rachel prayed, taking the ring from her. It was the most beautiful ring she had ever beheld, and tears filled her eyes.

"What does the rest of the letter say?" Sarah demanded.

Rachel blinked back the tears. She skimmed over three long paragraphs devoted to the training of the raw American recruits and Eddy's impatience and frustration at not being in battle. Then he wrote: "I've enclosed an engagement ring. I know it's not much, but it was hard to find, Rachel. I hope you like it—I really wanted to give you something so much better. I promise that one day I will. So, here goes. Will you marry me? As soon as I can get away I am coming to see you, and I promise, no matter what, I will make it to London for the holidays. I think we should make plans to tie the knot then—if you'll have me. So what do you say? You know I will not take 'no' for an answer." He signed the letter simply, "Love, Eddy."

And there was a postscript, which Rachel did not share with Sarah. "I am so glad that your father did not cause you too much grief over the night you spent with me. I cannot even begin to describe how relieved I am." Rachel had thoroughly glossed over her situation at home in the letters she had sent to him at Tangmere.

Now, slowly, stunned, Rachel looked up.

Sarah whooped and dove onto her, knocking her back on the bed. "You're getting married! To a hero!" She whooped again.

Rachel was breathless as they both sat up. "I'm getting married. Oh my God. Eddy and I are getting married—we're engaged!" It was truly beginning to sink in.

"Put the ring on," Sarah urged.

Rachel burst into a smile and slipped it onto her fourth finger. She held out her hand.

"That is so beautiful," Sarah gasped.

Rachel just stared at the ring. "I'm engaged," she whispered, the joy beginning to take root within her.

"Yes, you are." Sarah stood. "I had better go check on our supper."

Rachel suddenly stood. "I can't wear this." If Papa saw, or guessed, or knew, it would truly be over between them—if it wasn't already. Rachel's joy abruptly dimmed the way one might turn off a lamp.

"No, you can't," Sarah said realistically.

Rachel had two necklaces. The string of pearls had been Mama's, and she wore it all the time. The other necklace was a gold chain with a Star of David pendant. It had been a birthday gift from Papa, given the year after Mama died. Rachel walked over to the room's single bureau, which the three sisters shared. She had her own jewelry box—it, too, had belonged to Mama.

She removed the chain and took off the Star of David, refusing to think about Papa now. She slipped on the ring and put the chain around her neck, tucking it under her blouse and out of sight. Her happiness was now tainted with guilt.

"Let's go downstairs," Sarah said, taking her hand and squeezing it. "You had better start thinking about the wedding ceremony now. He's Protestant, you're Jewish. Who will perform it? And where will it be?"

Rachel took a breath. Sarah was right. It would take some effort on her part to make the arrangements, and of course, there would not be a wedding, just a small, secret ceremony. Impulsively, Rachel gripped Sarah's hands. "You'll be there, won't you? No matter what? Please, Sarah." She wished that Hannah could be present, too, but it would not be fair to burden a child with such a secret.

"Of course I'll be there," Sarah said, and as they went downstairs, Rachel knew she was thinking just as Rachel was, about what it would be like not to have a real wedding, with all the food and guests, the dancing and a big white wedding cake. Rachel thought about standing in front of an air force chaplain without Papa there. Her happiness seemed to vanish.

In three days it would be Christmas—in another hour she would be with Eddy.

Rachel stood in front of the open but guarded gates at Bentley Priory, unable to contain herself. She clutched a bouquet of roses to her chest, her heart beating wildly. The artillery guard standing behind her were grinning at her, and Sarah, wearing a rather prim navy blue dress and coat and a pair of new black patent-leather pumps, was also smiling foolishly.

The day was grim and cold, the threat of rain imminent. Rachel was not wearing a coat, but she was not shivering. She was warm. Hot. Faint. Disbelieving.

A military jeep approached.

As it came closer, Rachel began to shake and tremble—she saw Eddy in his dress uniform sitting in the front seat beside a BEF officer. Two other officers, both BEF, were in the back. The jeep came to a lurching halt beside Rachel, and Eddy leaped out, eyes wide, staring at her.

Rachel could not move. It had been almost four months since she had last seen him and she had never been this happy in her entire life.

"You are so beautiful," Eddy gasped.

Rachel said, "I know it's bad luck to see the bride, but—"

"Like hell it's bad luck," Eddy cried, and he lifted her high and whirled her around and around, her white satin wedding gown flying about them, until they were both laughing, until everyone was laughing, and then he slid her down his body slowly, and his expression changed, as did hers.

In his arms, her feet still off the ground, Rachel looked into his eyes and felt her heart expanding to impossible dimensions. In that moment, she felt as if she were weightless; that they were floating up in the clouds. He set her down and they kissed, clinging.

"Enough," Sarah cried eventually. "The chaplain's waiting, we have a wedding to perform!"

Eddy and Rachel moved slightly, reluctantly, apart so they could smile into each other's eyes. "You are the most beautiful woman I have ever seen," he said huskily. "Is the dress your mother's?"

Rachel nodded, tears coming to her eyes. "Yes." How she wished Mama were still alive. If she were, Rachel knew how happy she would be for her and Eddy, and if she were, she also knew that Papa would be speaking with her. Papa did not know that they were getting married that day, and obviously, he had no idea she had gone into the attic and borrowed her mother's lovely wedding gown.

"You must be freezing," Eddy said then, sliding his arm around her. "What are you doing, waiting for me out here in that dress without a coat?"

"It's been so long, Eddy," she whispered as they walked back to base, Sarah falling into step beside them.

"I'm sorry, hon, I am. But the boys were so damn raw when I got them, not to mention us being stuck with a bunch of old Brewster Buffaloes. We're getting our Spitfires in another six weeks." His eyes brightened even more. The squadron also had several Hurricanes, one of which was Eddy's. Rachel had kept abreast of the Eagles' situation from the moment she had learned of Eddy's transfer in October. He currently had fifteen kills to his credit, an amazing record. No American had more. "Man, do I miss my old girl."

Rachel knew he meant his old Spitfire from Biggin Hill. "I'm not even nineteen, dear," she said primly.

He laughed and turned to Sarah. "Hi. I'm so glad we finally get to meet."

"So am I," Sarah said with a smile. "Rachel did not exaggerate when she spoke of you."

Eddy gave Rachel an affectionate glance and bounded ahead of them to open the door. The chapel was housed in a small brick building with a whitewashed porch.

Sarah said to Rachel, under her breath, "Boy oh boy. Handsome, dashing, and a real gentleman."

"I know," Rachel whispered back, clutching her roses tightly. "I am the luckiest girl alive."

*   *   *

They got out of a cab on a quiet street in Knightsbridge. It was lined with white-plaster two- and three-story homes. Tall trees shaded the street. Every house had a small grass lawn in front, and one neighbor had a stone walkway with hedges lining the property. In the summertime, the azalea bushes would be in bloom.

"Where are we?" Rachel asked, still dazed. *They were married. Eddy was her husband. She was wearing a small, antique gold wedding band to prove it. And they had papers.*

She was now Mrs. Edward Marshall.

Eddy grinned and swept her up into his arms and carried her up the stone walk, Rachel clinging to him. An idea was occurring to her—but it was impossible—wasn't it?

The front door and window boxes of the house were a freshly painted shade of evergreen. Eddy used his hip to open the front door, which was unlocked, and he carried her inside.

Rachel felt her eyes widen. They had stepped into a small parlor with shining wood floors, what looked like a brand-new couch, a pretty antique coffee table, and freshly painted, canary-yellow walls. A fire was burning in the stone hearth. Still clinging to Eddy's broad shoulders, she took in the yellow and white curtains. Narrow stairs led to the next floor; ahead, Rachel could glimpse a kitchen that had recently been painted white. She glimpsed blue and white gingham curtains inside, which looked brand-new, as did the white enamel stove and refrigerator.

"Do you like it?" Eddy's voice in her ear, his breath feathering her neck, jolted her out of her amazement.

She blinked at him, her body stirring, tightening. "Like it? I love it! Whose house is this?"

"Ours," he said, sliding her to the floor.

Rachel would have stumbled in shock and disbelief if he hadn't been holding her. "What?" she gasped.

"I've leased it for us. You can stay here now, and I'll come as often as I can. Maybe you might want Sarah to move in." He was smiling. "I think she'd be happy to."

"What have you done!" she cried, throwing her arms around him.

"You're my wife," he said simply, embracing her hard.

Tears filled her eyes. *This was their new home.* Of course she would ask Sarah to move in! "But how can you afford this?"

He smiled a little. "I'm not a poor man. I wired home for some of my savings. And two of my brothers sent us some dough as a wedding gift."

Rachel could not speak.

"Do you really like it, Rachel?" he asked in a husky tone.

"It's the most beautiful house in the world," she managed.

His gaze seemed to turn to smoke before her very eyes. "I am glad." Then, "You have made me the happiest man on this planet, Rachel."

Rachel thought she saw tears sparkling on his eyelashes.

Eddy released her and turned away. Rachel let him compose himself. He walked over to the hearth to prod and poke the fire. Then he turned and he was himself again. "Sarah did the decorating. I hope that's all right."

Rachel nodded, starting to cry.

"Rachel!" He rushed over to her.

"I'm so happy it hurts," she whispered.

"Good." He was fierce. He cupped her face and kissed her, hard.

They hadn't seen each other, or touched each other, or kissed in four months—not until that morning. Rachel sank into his arms, opening hungrily for him. She had not been exaggerating. The beauty of her love was painful. It crossed her mind as they sank onto the rug that she wished he weren't a pilot.

He settled on top of her, amid the ballooning skirts of her wedding dress. An instant later he was propped up on his elbows above her, and they were both laughing. "That dress is beautiful *but*," he said.

"It's a big *but*," Rachel agreed.

The dress was removed, as were her slip, garters, nylons, brassiere, and panties. Eddy's clothes followed, tossed into the same pile, much, much more quickly.

He loomed over her. Rachel touched his face. "I love it when you look like this," she said. "So intense, so determined."

His jaw was flexing. So were the muscles in his arms and chest. "I am determined. I can't wait."

"Then don't," she said, and as he slid into her, she closed her eyes and held him, and the love inside her breast expanded impossibly until she thought that her heart would burst.

*   *   *

They paused outside their home in the gray dawn of the following morning. Rachel had to be back at Fighter Command by six-thirty, and she had just learned that a second Eagle Squadron was being formed. Eddy had to report to Bentley Priory at nine for several staff meetings before he would rejoin his men. They had about an hour left before Rachel reported to duty. It was still as dark as night outside, and here and there, a few fat raindrops were falling.

Eddy locked the door. "We're just a few blocks from your cousin's."

Rachel was hardly awake. They had made love all night. Now she no longer feared a pregnancy; in fact, they both wanted a child, and soon. She yawned. "What?"

But Eddy was fully awake. "Elgin. His flat is a five-minute walk from here. Would you mind if I put you on the underground by yourself instead of taking you back to base?"

Instantly Rachel was fully awake. She was too alarmed to be disappointed. "Why? What are you going to do?"

He looked at her. "Drop by." He smiled, but it did not reach his eyes. "After all, I'm in the neighborhood."

Rachel had never seen such a hard light in his eyes, and she shivered. What was going on? "Eddy, it's a quarter to six."

"I know. I'll hang out at the café for an hour, then see if he wants to have a 'spot o' tea.' " He mimed her accent for the last three words.

Rachel could not be amused. "But you don't like Lionel."

"Hon, just trust me on this one," he said lightly. He took her arm and started walking.

Oddly, panic surged within her breast. "I'm coming with you," Rachel said determinedly.

"No. Definitely not."

"Eddy, I'm coming with you."

He glanced at her as they crossed the deserted street. "You'll be late."

"Yes, I will. But he's my cousin. And—" She stopped and faced him, barring his path. "What is this about, Edward?"

His eyes widened at her language and her tone. Then he smiled and said, sheepishly, "You're acting like a wife."

"I *am* your wife. Why would you visit my cousin now, at this hour? I don't like this."

He sobered. "It's official," he finally said.

That was the very last answer she expected. She stared. A raindrop plopped down on the tip of her nose.

"Look. My superiors have asked me to check into strange . . . circumstances. That's all I'm doing. We both think Elgin's strange. I need to see a few of his bird pictures. That's all," he repeated.

Rachel found it difficult to breathe. She wasn't an idiot. She worked at Fighter Command, in an intelligence unit. His "superiors" were in the air ministry. Weren't they?

But this was war. Panic and propaganda were everywhere. Average citizens were warned to be on the lookout for German agents and members of the Fifth Column. In fact, German agents were constantly found in the most unusual places within Britain—strangers would suddenly appear in a small coastal village, carrying German-made flashlights or speaking with an unmistakable foreign accent. They were arrested immediately, usually by the Home Guard.

"It's not a big deal, Rachel," Eddy said.

Rachel hugged herself. "Good. Then I can come with you."

He sighed and rolled his eyes. "Are you always going to be difficult like this?" But his voice was tender.

"Yes," she said, and her tone wasn't light, it was filled with tension.

"Okay. We're wasting time." He took her hand and they hurried briskly down the block.

Rachel hurried to keep up. "I still think you are wrong about Elgin. Lionel has always been odd. He's still odd. He was an eccentric boy, and now he is an eccentric man."

"I call it 'better safe than sorry,' " he said firmly.

They continued in silence for several blocks. Finally they were about to turn a corner when Eddy yanked her back around it and pulled her against the wall. "Well, well," he said, a low murmur of satisfaction.

Rachel's heart skipped a series of beats. "What is it?"

He didn't answer, peering cautiously around the side of the building, clearly not wanting to be seen. He popped back behind the corner. "This is our lucky day." He smiled at her. It was a smile she had never seen before.

It was chilling.

Rachel stared at his set face. He had a ruthless resolution now that she had never suspected existed. But this had to be why he was such a successful fighter pilot. This was why he was still alive. "What is it?"

Eddy continued to peer around the side of the building. "He's leaving. Getting off to an early start. I didn't realize these ministries started their business at the crack of dawn."

They did not. Not usually.

Eddy pulled her out from behind the corner. "He's gone. He just drove off in that Bentley of his. Funny, he's still using that car, with all the petrol rationing."

They crossed the street, watching carefully for traffic in the near-dark dawn, as a few motorists and cyclists had appeared. An old limestone building faced them. The café was on the ground floor, but its windows were all gone, as was the front door. Someone had boarded up the entrance. The building next to it had been partly demolished by a bomb. The blast had damaged the café as well. An OUT OF BUSINESS sign was tacked onto a board.

The building was a walk-up, Rachel saw, and it housed two apartments to every floor. The front door, massive and wooden with a small window, was locked. Rachel looked expectantly at Eddy as he tested the knob. They would have to abandon their plans, Rachel thought, not at all disappointed.

Eddy took an object out of his pocket. It was long and thin. Rachel saw him insert it in the lock. "That's a pick!" she cried.

"Ssh. I told you what I did before the war," he said in a low voice.

Rachel stared as he pushed open the door, having effortlessly picked the lock in seconds. She did not like what was happening, what she was seeing—it was almost as if she were with a stranger.

But that was impossible. This was Eddy, her husband.

They hurried upstairs, Rachel following a step behind and filled with trepidation. As they paused in front of apartment 2, Rachel asked, keeping her voice down, "Are we breaking in here, too?"

"Yes." Eddy tried the knob; the door was, unsurprisingly, locked.

"This is against the law."

"So are a lot of things." He picked this lock with more difficulty—he had to take a shorter and thinner pick from inside his jacket to do so. It took him about three minutes.

Rachel was bewildered. "I'm not sure we should be doing this," she tried nervously, glancing across the hall at the opposite door. "What if the neighbor steps out?"

"If you keep talking, he undoubtedly will," Eddy said, opening the door and shooing her in. He closed and locked it behind them.

Rachel was relieved that they had not been caught. She glanced around the small flat nervously. "So what is it that you did for the FBI?" she asked.

He did not answer her.

Instead, he walked over to the wastebasket and dumped it upside down. Rachel could only stare. He sorted through a few tissues and papers, as if looking for something. Curiosity overcame her worry. "What are you looking for?"

He said, "Remember when I told you Elgin received mail from Lisbon? I'm looking for unusual mail."

Rachel came over. "Why, Eddy?"

He said only, "Nothing useful here." He stood and looked at the neat top of the desk where a pad and a few pens lay. He opened the drawer— inside were various items, including a lead pencil. He picked up the pencil and darkened the entire top page of the pad. Rachel peered curiously over his shoulder, forgetting her fears.

Words had emerged through the lead. "Tantallon Dec. 24 0700," she murmured. "That sounds like a time, date and place."

"Where's Tantallon?" he asked, tearing off the top page and putting it in his pocket.

"Up north on the coast in Scotland," she said, and she began to have an inkling. She shivered. "What are you thinking?"

Going through the two drawers, he did not answer. Rachel saw more pens, stationery, and a small tray with paper clips. There was also a pot of ink that looked new and unopened, as well as a small jar. Eddy picked up the jar and opened it. He sniffed, stuck a finger in. "What is this?" He showed it to her while tasting his fingertip with his tongue.

"I don't know. It looks like a powder."

Eddy grimaced at the flavor. He tore another page from the pad, poured some powder on top, folded the page securely around the powder, then put that in his pocket, too. He replaced the jar of powder in the drawer.

Rachel hugged herself. "You're intelligence," she said hoarsely, filled with fear. Fear for him, for them.

Eddy slowly turned to face her. He was so grim.

"Tell me the truth," she whispered.

"It's better if I don't." He crossed the room. "I'm a pilot, Rachel. I'm a goddamned pilot who can smell the enemy a mile away." He had his back to her now, trying the closet door. It was locked. "I can feel those Gerries before I see them. I can't explain it. No one can. Maybe I just have a stronger intuition than the rest of my men. It's why I have so many kills. I'm never taken by surprise." He took a third pick from his pocket.

"I'm your wife!" Rachel cried.

Eddy quickly unlocked the simple closet door and turned to her. "I know. And you're the best thing that's ever happened to me, Rach. I swear."

"We can't have secrets—and lies—between us!" And she thought about her own secret, her own lie. "I'm in the Y unit. And I never told you the truth about Papa. He hasn't spoken to me since that first night we spent together. He has shut me out of his life, he has buried me alive!"

Eddy stared, turning white. He did not move.

"I lied to spare you," she said in a more subdued but anguished tone. "The way you are doing now, to me."

He swallowed. After a long moment, during which they gazed at each other, he said, "They didn't let me out."

"What? I don't understand."

"When I left the States to fight Hitler, they asked me to help. Last June they put me in a new, elite unit. The SIS."

"They?" Rachel asked, clenched with fear. "Who are they?"

"Uncle Sam," he said abruptly. "The FBI."

Rachel could only stare. *He was with American intelligence.* Her mind raced.

"Don't doubt me," he said, coming to her with hard strides. He gripped her arms. "I'm an RAF pilot first. You know that. I put my life on the line every single day, a dozen times, maybe more, when I go up. There's no conflict of interest. You know that. My fighting the Germans up there for your country, or down here for mine—in the end, it all comes out the same."

Rachel wasn't sure. She felt like she was reeling. She felt faint. She heard herself say, "And if Lionel is a German spy, then who will you tell? Your CO here, or someone in the States?"

He couldn't respond.

She had thought so.

"Rachel?"

"It doesn't matter," she said, shaking her head fiercely, coming to her senses. "You're an American, and you're right, the final goal is the same. We all want this war over, with Hitler's defeat. But . . . this is worse. Before I only had to worry about your being shot out of the sky. Now I have to worry about your being stabbed in the back by some damned German spy!"

He smiled a little and said, "Hon, no one's going to stab me in the back. I promise you that."

Rachel wished she believed him. She was so afraid.

He released her and turned back to the closet. An instant later he said, "Well, he lied."

Rachel hurried across the room.

"He said his equipment was in the cellar. Here's a Leica, two lenses, and everything he'd need to develop his film. The Germans use Leica cameras, Rachel."

Lionel wasn't German. The room felt so still around her, around them. She looked from the camera and lenses to Eddy.

"But he's good, I'll hand him that," Eddy said, showing her half a dozen oversize photographs of birds. The first one was of a beautiful white swan, floating in a rippling pond. Rachel shivered.

Eddy went through the closet with incredible efficiency. Rachel said, "You were right. He's an agent. Oh, my God." As Eddy was going through the pockets of Lionel's suits and uniforms, she said, "We had better leave, Eddy." She glanced nervously at the front door of the flat.

"A German-made camera, imprecise notes, and what might be powder used to develop invisible ink is not enough to hang him." Eddy closed and locked the closet after putting everything back where he had found it. He turned to look at her. "I want something big. A code list. Important contacts. And where the hell is his radio? He's got to have a transmitter."

Rachel watched him fearfully as he walked past her and dropped to his knees, peering under the bed. He stood. "Nothing's there. There was a suitcase under the bed the last time I was here. It's not in the closet. He must have it with him. He must be going out of town."

Rachel said, "December twenty-fourth. That's tomorrow. Maybe he left for Scotland today."

Eddy smiled at her as if he was enjoying himself.

Rachel froze. "What are you planning!"

"Hon, relax. I know what I'm doing."

"Do you?"

He came to her and guided her to the door. "It's only six-twenty. You can be at the base in twenty minutes if you rush."

"What are you going to do?" she asked again as he opened the door.

"I have a few more things to check out."

"Here?" she whispered, aghast.

They stepped into the hall, and Eddy closed the door. From the outside, he could not lock it.

"He'll know that we were here," Rachel exclaimed in a whisper.

"He'll wonder if someone was here; he'll wonder if he forgot this once to lock the door behind him," Eddy said calmly.

"I'm scared," Rachel cried as they hurried down the hall.

"Don't be. Elgin doesn't scare me, Rachel. If he's a traitor, I will bring him down, just the way I would a Luftwaffe pilot." He finally smiled at her. "Don't look so worried."

"How can I not be worried!" she erupted furiously. "Every single day you take that Spitfire up in the air, and it's either you or some German boy who dies! And now the danger is even worse. God! I think I heard some gossip a few years back, that he had a German girlfriend. I think he spent some time with her in Germany before the war."

"Perfect," Eddy murmured as they reached the ground floor.

"You're enjoying yourself," she accused. There was no doubt in her mind now. He thrived on challenge, on danger.

They heard a noise behind them.

Someone was coming downstairs.

Rachel's heart dropped and she whirled. Eddy whipped her into a different stairwell. The door closed behind them, and they were in the pitch dark. They could hear footsteps going past them. Eddy turned on his small penlight. Rachel realized this stairwell led down into the cellar below the closed café.

"I want to take a quick look at the cellar," Eddy said. "With the café closed, it would be a perfect place for him to hide more equipment."

At least he was no longer insisting that she leave without him. "Okay."

Eddy led the way down, and a moment later he pushed open a heavy, scarred wooden door. A dark, cavernous room faced them. Rachel could not see much other than beams and shadows, but she was assailed by the odor of decay. It was so strong that it made her stomach roil.

Eddy froze. "What the hell," he said, low. He glanced around in the dark, then hit a wall switch. Nothing happened. "Stay there," he said, shining his penlight around the dark space. It seemed to be filled with boxes and old, broken-down or unused restaurant equipment.

Rachel nodded, even though he couldn't see her response. Unease assailed her. What was that horrid smell, and what was Eddy doing?

Suddenly a single overhead bulb came on—Eddy had found the string. The large cellar came into view. In its center was a plain wooden table with several boxes on top of it. A few boxes were placed along the walls, and so were an old, large icebox and a very old four-burner stove. Another table was on the far side of the cellar, with a toolbox, some saws, tins of nails, and a hammer on its surface.

Eddy looked around grimly.

"What is that smell?" Rachel whispered, feeling as if she might retch.

He strode over to the icebox and yanked the door open. And cried out.

Rachel ran to see what had stunned him so.

"Rachel, no!" He moved to bar her way, but it was too late.

Lord Elgin's body was stuffed inside the icebox. He had been cut in half so he would fit.

CHAPTER 20

It was instinct that made him look back while he was at the first inter-section and less than a block away from his flat. Lionel glanced in his rearview mirror and then turned his gaze ahead; instantly, he did a dou-ble take. Someone honked behind him. Lionel twisted to turn around now. Even in the dark of dawn, he was certain that he had just glimpsed Eddy Marshall and Rachel.

They were in a hurry.

They were heading toward his building.

The calm overcame him like a huge, peaceful wave. Lionel stepped on the gas pedal, made the next turn, and found a place to park. He got out of the car and locked it carefully, then began to smile. His life had just become very interesting indeed.

What were Marshall and his cousin doing at his flat? Was it a social call?

It was only six in the morning. Somehow he doubted it.

At the corner he paused and peered around at the front entrance to his walk-up; there was no sign of either Marshall or Rachel. Lionel had grabbed his binoculars before leaving his car, and now he trained them on the single window of his flat. At first he saw nothing and no one. But in a few moments, he was rewarded as a man's form passed by the win-dow, and even though there was no way Lionel could get a good look at him, he knew who it was. A moment later he glimpsed Rachel.

They were in his flat.

This time Lionel really smiled.

Eddy Marshall was on to him. His cousin Rachel and Eddy Marshall.

Lionel turned and went back to his car. He had business to attend to, and none of it had anything to do with the day's agenda for the ministry of information. And he had a trip to make.

Which was why he was dressed as a civilian.

Someone had done his or her best to make the dormitory for the WAAFs as comfortable as possible, but it remained a spartan affair. Most of the girls preferred returning whenever possible to their families, if their families lived in the London area, or chose to share a flat with other WAAFs just off base. Rachel preferred to sleep in the dorm, since her unit was pressed into double and even triple shifts so often. Even now that she had her own house, traveling back and forth from Knightsbridge was too time-consuming, unless Eddy was there.

She had just finished two back-to-back eight-hour shifts. It was almost midnight. Sleeping, however, was the last thing on her mind.

She sat on her small bed in a room that slept four, her hands in her lap, her mind racing. In a way, coming to the base after finding her uncle in the icebox had been a relief. She had spent the past sixteen hours with a pair of headphones clamped to her ears, listening to too many conversations in the skies above her to even count. There had been no chance to think of anything other than the pilots in combat above, speaking in both German and English and sometimes in Polish or French.

She twisted her hands in her lap. Who could have done such a brutal thing to Lord Elgin? Who?

She felt like throwing up. Her stomach had miraculously held on to whatever she had consumed that morning; Eddy had told her to go directly to the base, and that he would report the murder to the authorities. Which authorities had he gone to? she wondered. Scotland Yard, the London police, or military intelligence? The FBI?

Who had murdered Lord Elgin, and why?

Surely Lionel had not murdered his own father.

Rachel's head hurt her terribly now, but she usually suffered from migraines after long, stressful shifts. She told herself that just because Lionel's father had been found dead in an old icebox in the cellar of Lionel's building didn't mean that Lionel had murdered him. But why did she have to recall now, of all times, Harry's accidental death in 1935? Lionel had mistakenly killed his own brother. And now his father was cut in half and stuffed into an old icebox.

Why hadn't Eddy called her? She had tried to call him three times that day, twice on short breaks and just a few minutes ago after being dismissed. Unfortunately, every time she called, he hadn't been available, and Rachel knew what that meant. It meant he was in the air, fighting to protect her country and its citizens.

Or was he on his way to Tantallon?

Tomorrow was December 24. Was something going to happen up there on the Scottish coast at 0700 hours?

"Rachel?" The door to the small bed-crammed chamber opened and a WAAF popped her head in with a smile. "You have a telephone call."

Eddy. No small amount of relief washed over her. Rachel was on her feet and dashing past the other woman before she could even say thank you. If he was intending to be at Tantallon tomorrow morning at seven A.M., she did not want him going alone.

There was one phone in the common room that they used for smoking and chitchat. Rachel reached for the dangling phone and cried, "Eddy?"

"Rachel, it's Lionel."

She froze. Her mind seemed to go blank. At the same time, her heart lurched with sickening force, with dread. *Her cousin wasn't just eccentric; he was a fascist, a spy.*

"Rachel? Are you there?"

She told herself to be calm, rational, to think. She told herself to act positively normal, or he might suspect something. "Lionel!" She forced some cheer into her breathless voice. "This is a surprise!"

"God, Rachel, I am so shaken, I can hardly talk!"

Rachel was already tense. Lionel did not sound like himself. Cautiously, she asked, "Is everything all right?"

"No!" He sounded almost hysterical. "God, someone found my father—he was murdered, Rachel, murdered—someone found him in my cellar—in the bloody cellar of my building!"

Rachel did not speak. She couldn't seem to think. "What?" she finally managed.

"I've been down at Scotland Yard. I didn't know what to say. I'm as surprised as anyone!"

They had released him. Where was Eddy? Rachel needed to talk to him desperately now. "Do they have any suspects? Do they have any idea what happened?"

"No. It might be a prank. When they got to my building, the body was gone. So it's the word of one witness who had sworn the body was there in my cellar against the fact that right now, there is no body anywhere."

The body had been removed. Rachel realized her hand was cramping from how tightly she was gripping the phone. "Who saw the body?" she whispered.

"I don't know. They won't say. But whoever it is, he has some kind of credibility with the authorities, because they seem to be certain he is telling the truth. God! Someone murdered my father, Rachel, and whoever it is, he's removed the body . . ." Lionel trailed off. He sounded almost on the verge of tears. "You're family, Rachel. You're the only one I could think of to turn to."

He did not sound like a guilty man or a spy. Maybe the powder was something innocent. Maybe he preferred the German camera to an American-made one because it was superior. There had been pictures of birds, for God's sake.

And at least he did not know that it was Eddy who was the witness—Eddy and her. "I'm so sorry, Lionel."

"Rachel, I have a favor to ask of you. No, to beg of you," Lionel said.

Rachel was assailed with a fresh wave of unease. "Of course," she said automatically.

"They've interviewed my stepmother. She is hysterical, as you can imagine, thinking about my father having been murdered. I'm not at Elgin Hall—I'm on duty, and I won't be home until Christmas Eve. You're the only one I could think of to call. Could you come out? She needs to be with another woman right now, Rachel. I beg you. She's alone and distraught. I'm afraid she might do something to hurt herself in her grief. If you could just stay with her until I can get back. I beg you, Rachel."

Rachel stared at the greenish wall behind the phone. "I hardly know Ellen. I haven't seen her since that weekend in Wales when I was a child."

"The two of you hit it off when you met. I remember it very clearly. Please, Rachel. She has no one else."

Rachel imagined what it must be like for Ellen just then. God, she hoped no one had told her what had really happened to Elgin. "Where are you?" Rachel asked cautiously. Was he on his way to Tantallon?

"I'm in the south," he said. "At Dover. It's ministry business."

He could be telling the truth. Elgin had just been found, gruesomely murdered. Lady Ellen might very well be distressed. Rachel's mind spun so fast and hard that she became light-headed.

Poor Lady Ellen.

Rachel had liked Ellen that single time they had met. She had also felt sorry for her, being married to such a cold older man. Her only remaining family was Lionel; her parents had been dead for years, and she was an only child. And of course there was her young son.

"I'll come," she said, the decision made. But she was no fool. She would bring Sarah, and she would leave Eddy a message, explaining where she was—and why. Besides, Lionel wouldn't even be there. He was in the south—or in the north. "But I can't stay, Lionel. I can come tonight, but I must be back on duty tomorrow morning."

"Nonsense," he said. "Your uncle has been murdered, I will make arrangements for a few days' leave. You can spend Christmas with us. Thank you, Rachel. I'll tell Ellen to expect you tonight." He hung up.

Rachel wondered if he had forgotten that she was Jewish. She hardly cared about spending Christmas at Elgin Hall. Rachel managed to reach Sarah, explaining what had happened. Sarah was shocked but agreed to meet Rachel at the hall as soon as her shift was over, which was in a few hours. But she might not be able to stay long, either.

"I am on at noon tomorrow," she said. "But I'll see if one of the other drivers can cover for me."

"Thanks," Rachel whispered, suddenly bone-tired.

"Rachel? How do you like your new home?" Sarah asked slyly.

She had forgotten all about her new home and Sarah's role in furnishing it. "I love it, Sarah. Thank you so much! And we had the most wonderful wedding night. It could not have been more magical," she said, clenching the phone. Her wedding night felt as if it had happened in another life, not a mere twenty-four hours ago.

"You're welcome," Sarah said cheerfully. "See you at Elgin Hall."

Rachel could not reach Eddy—he had not, as it turned out, arrived back at the air station yet. He had been due back hours ago.

Rachel was afraid. She left another message.

* * *

The first thing Eddy had done that afternoon was take a train north to Berwick-upon-Tweed, hoping bombing would not delay him, as the Luftwaffe often targeted the railways. It did not. He arrived in the city late in the afternoon, and promptly stole a motorcycle. It was raining, the skies gray and heavy—soon it would be dark. The ride up the rugged Scottish coast took another hour and a half, and the rain became frigid. By the time he arrived in the village closest to Tantallon Castle, he was thoroughly soaked and frozen to the bone, and darkness had cloaked the land. He did not worry about catching pneumonia. He was newlywed—he had no intention of dying anytime soon.

He had an entire night to kill, but he didn't dare take a room in the village's single inn or even linger in the town's pub. He was an American and would stand out like a sore thumb. And then there was his quarry. Eddy had no intention of turning a corner and coming face-to-face with his adversary.

Instead, he rode through the town at a sedate pace, the only motorized vehicle on the blackened road. It was very hard to see where he was going—this far north, the Scots hadn't bothered to paint any white strips on the road or any lampposts. Road signs were also missing, but he had expected that and had memorized his way very carefully. He continued up the winding road slowly. On his right was the sea. Rock cliffs fell hundreds of feet to meet the surf below. The wet moors rolled away on his left. He saw the small signal light that was just off the coast, the "Haven of Thomptalloun," blinking in the night. It should have been blacked out. He knew then that Tantallon Castle lay ahead.

Eddy was not coming in blind; he had done a bit of research. Lionel had clearly activated the signal light, for no U-boat could get close to shore because of the rocks. Eddy was expecting some kind of rendezvous, and any sub doing so would have to launch a dinghy.

There were other alternatives, of course. One was that the scrawled message—"Tantallon Dec 24 0700"—was in code and did not mean what it implied. The other was that Lionel Elgin had decided to call it quits, and that a U-boat was coming to pick him up and whisk him away to the safety of European shores.

Eddy did not think so. Elgin was in too deep; there was no reason for him to run for it now.

Amazing, how his father's body had so suddenly and conveniently disappeared.

Eddy slowed his motorcycle fractionally as the soaring stone towers and walls of the old Scottish castle came into view; looming and forbidding black shadows. He did not pause. He saw no cars parked anywhere; no sign, in fact, of any other visitor. But then, it was dark out and hard to see, and he might be wrong. He continued on.

His motorcycle was very loud. Except for the crashing of the surf on the rocky beach below, it was the only sound for miles in the silence of the night.

A few miles up the road, he drove off on a cow path and hid his bike behind some trees, removing his pack. In it were binoculars, a loaded gun, a camera, a multipurpose penknife, a penlight, a flashlight, another knife—this one lethal—a nylon rope, some rations, and a pair of dry socks.

Eddy walked slowly along the road, on the alert for company. By the time he crossed over and began his approach to the castle, he felt quite certain he was alone. He was approaching from the northwest. Ahead, the castle sat on an outcropping of cliff. Below, there was a small strip of pale beach. He could also see the winking signal light in the sea, within swimming distance. Eddy paused to scan the beach below, the tower ahead, and the central section of ruins with his binoculars. He could make out nothing more than a juxtaposition of dark shapes. He continued on.

The moat, now dry, caused him to veer to the east and wander parallel to it. He did so with great caution—there was only one bridge, and he and Elgin would both have to use it. At the bridge, made of wood and constructed by local officials for prewar tourists, he squatted and lifted his binoculars again. Somewhere to the east was an incomplete sea gate. He wondered if the U-boat would attempt to launch a dinghy in that direction instead of the western beach that he had previously passed.

He saw nothing. Not even the briefest flash of movement. Eddy thought that Elgin would arrive sometime before dawn, so as not to spend any more time than necessary in the inclement weather. Eddy slipped the binoculars back into his rain jacket and hurried across the bridge. He ran across the open space of what had once been an outer ward, and by the next bridge, he crouched again, waiting to see if he had alerted anyone to his presence.

The minutes ticked by. The air was very wet—or had it begun to drizzle? Eddy scanned the outer walls and the towers of the castle, which were only yards away now. He saw nothing.

There was just one way to get inside the ancient fortress. The entry was an arched entrance that formed a short tunnel. It was the perfect trap.

He had no choice.

Eddy slipped his revolver into his hand. He leaped up and ran across the few feet of the bridge, then darted across another short open space and into the vaulted entrance. His footsteps echoed loudly. A stone, displaced by his feet, skittered across the stone and earth floor, finally crashing down an incline somewhere.

Once inside, he veered left, disappearing between crumbling walls and nooks and crannies. He took a moment to catch his breath and listen for Elgin, his back to the wall. He took out his penlight but did not turn it on, waiting for his eyes to adjust to the darkness.

The surf roared. Its sound was intensified by the stone walls.

There was no question about it—he was alone. Eddy turned on his penlight but kept it trained upon the rough stones at his feet. He crept through one hall and then another, until he came to what he felt certain was the unfinished sea gate. Here the rock floor fell abruptly into the sea; hundreds of years ago, it would have been an ideal place for a ship to berth and unload its cargo and passengers. Eddy studied every detail of the tower, then turned and retraced his steps, finally ending up back in the central section of the ruins. He had to proceed with caution, as the center did not exist—it plummeted down hundreds of feet where once there had been floors. He finally entered the tower where a guidebook had said the Douglas family had lived. At its northern edge, he looked out of a portal and saw the beach just below, to the north. The signal light was blinking directly to his west.

It would be the beach, Eddy decided with satisfaction. No U-boat captain would have the nerve to try to come alongside the incomplete sea gate. The rocks were too jagged, and discharging a passenger—or picking one up—too dangerous.

Eddy shone his light up the walls of the tower where he stood. He finally saw the perfect spot: a small room on the floor above. He looked around and realized that the spiral stairs had been destroyed. He would have to climb, which was even better. Because if his enemy ever discovered him, he would have to climb up as well.

Eddy secured his pack. He put his rope around his waist and tied it to a solid stone arch. He put his penlight between his teeth and began to climb.

Half an hour later, drenched with sweat, he swung up into the room above, where he lay on the broken stones of the floor, panting and out of breath. Then he sat up and quickly inspected his pack. He would assemble his equipment after he ate; he settled down for the night.

"I'm so glad you came, Rachel," Ellen said, reaching for her impulsively with both hands.

Rachel smiled at her. "I'm so sorry about your husband," she said.

Ellen blinked at her. She was pale, although not teary-eyed or red-nosed; it did not look as if she had been weeping. "I am simply stunned," she admitted, leading Rachel through the foyer and into a large, opulent salon. "Who would do such a thing?"

The question did not require an answer, and for an instant, Rachel forgot about the murdered lord. She was in a huge room with two crystal chandeliers and marble floors; the furnishings were fabulous, the furniture gilded. There were works of art on the walls; there were huge mirrors, beautiful tables, and candelabra. She had seen rooms like this only in museums and rendered in art. She could not believe that, particularly in a time of war, anyone lived in such luxury.

"Are you hungry?" Ellen asked. One of the room's many tables contained beautiful tea sandwiches and a pot of tea. "Or would you like a glass of wine?" She seemed a bit hopeful that Rachel would agree to her last suggestion.

But Rachel was exhausted. She glanced around, afraid that Lionel would walk through that door at any moment.

Perhaps he was on his way to Tantallon right now.

"I could use a sandwich," she said. "I suppose Sarah has not yet arrived?"

"Sarah is coming as well?" Ellen seemed relieved. "This is wonderful. It's horrible being here alone. Especially on such a night."

Rachel wondered if Ellen had volunteered for the war effort. She did not dare ask. She sat down, accepting a small plate of assorted sandwiches and a cup of tea. The rain began again, tapping on the windowpanes. Ellen poured herself a glass of white wine from the dry bar, a cart on gilded wheels, stationed not far from where they sat.

Ellen took a seat on the red velvet settee beside the chair where Rachel perched. "So you must tell me what it is like to be a WAAF," she said, smiling. "It must be very exciting indeed." And then she saw the ring.

The sun was on the horizon, a bare intrusion of shimmering light in a rainy gray day. Below, Lionel Elgin stood on the strip of beach, his hands in the pockets of his wool peacoat, his head ducked slightly against the rain.

Eddy studied him through the binoculars, filled with excitement. Elgin wore the clothes of a civilian, including a wool cap.

He trained his binoculars on the sea, and his pulse increased. A submarine was breaking through the surface of the water. It was a German U-boat. It didn't have to fly a flag—which it was not—for him to recognize it. *He had been right.*

Eddy picked up his camera.

A dinghy was launched. Four sailors began rowing it to the shore where Lionel waited. There was a fifth man sitting in their midst. Eddy focused, and as he began taking photographs, another man bundled up in a black wool coat and cap appeared on the beach, beside Elgin.

They arrived within half an hour of each other. It was late afternoon of Christmas Eve.

Sarah had left to rejoin her ATF unit earlier in the day, and Rachel sat with Lady Ellen in the salon, John upstairs napping. As it turned out, they had exhausted idle conversation; Ellen was knitting and Rachel trying to read without much success. The only sound was the wind rattling the windows and the ticking of a huge bronze grandfather clock.

She had attempted to reach Eddy five times that day—he still had failed to report to his command. If he did not do so soon, he would be AWOL. Rachel knew where he was; he was in Scotland, chasing Lionel Elgin.

The front door in the huge marble foyer opened and closed. Lady Ellen jumped to her feet, clutching her knitting and needles. Rachel looked from her tense, pale face to the threshold of the salon, and the thought struck her quickly and hard: *She is afraid of Lionel.*

Her cousin appeared in the doorway, clad in his uniform, smiling at them both.

"Hello, Lionel," Ellen said stiffly.

Lionel was looking at Rachel now, and slowly, she got to her feet. Every single hair on her body seemed to be standing on end, and she wanted to scream at him, *Where is Eddy?* She did not say a word.

Instead, she watched Lionel cross the room and pause to kiss Ellen's cheek. Ellen actually backed away from him, and his lips brushed only the air. "How are you?" he asked.

"Fine." Ellen's smile was brittle.

Lionel clearly knew her feelings, and as clearly didn't care. He turned to Rachel. She realized she had been holding her breath. "Hello, Rachel. You look lovely. Miserable day, isn't it?" He shivered as if for effect.

She realized she despised him. "Yes, it is. And now that you are here, I must return to Fighter Command."

He kissed her cheek before she could imitate Ellen and move away. "But you have a leave. They aren't expecting you back until tomorrow. It's Christmas Eve." He smiled. His gray eyes remained amused.

Rachel felt as if she were a trapped mouse being toyed with, while he was the hungry but lazy cat. "I don't celebrate Christmas," she said too harshly. "Or have you forgotten?"

"Of course I haven't forgotten. But your husband has," he said.

Rachel started. "How—"

"I rang up Ellen earlier and she told me the wonderful news. Congratulations to you both. I left a message for Eddy, inviting him to join us for a Christmas Eve supper tonight." The words were hardly out when the doorbell rang.

Rachel's gaze shot past Lionel into the foyer. The Elgins had kept two servants, a housemaid and the cook. Now the maid opened the door.

Relief made her sag. Eddy stepped into the foyer, wearing his bomber jacket. Instantly their gazes met and held.

He was all right.

"Speak of the devil," Lionel murmured. He smiled widely at Eddy. "Did you get my message?"

"Yes." Eddy wasn't smiling. He walked right up to Rachel, who met him halfway, walking into his arms.

She did not speak her thoughts—*Are you all right?* But his eyes under-stood and gave her the answer she wanted—*Yes.* He smiled and gave her a tiny, nearly imperceptible thumbs-up.

Whatever had happened, it had been successful, and Eddy was pleased. Rachel wanted to weep with relief, instead, she leaned forward on tiptoe, and he kissed her.

"Newlyweds," Lionel murmured from somewhere behind them. While his tone was not disparaging, Rachel sensed the mockery.

"I think it is wonderful to be so in love," Ellen said tersely. Then, from upstairs, the baby began to cry. "Excuse me," Ellen said, hurrying from the room.

Rachel pulled away from Eddy and looked at him with all the worry she felt. She wanted to tell him that something was terribly wrong with Ellen as far as Lionel went. They needed to be alone. She had to find out where he had been during the past twenty-four hours.

"So," Lionel said casually, as Eddy and Rachel returned to the salon and he poured them all drinks, "have you heard? They found my poor father. Murdered and cut in two. Imagine that?"

Eddy did not bat an eye as Lionel handed him a Scotch. "No, I didn't hear. I am sorry," he said.

Rachel looked from one to the other, chilled. Lionel was smiling, Eddy was not.

The moment they were alone in the guest room, she turned to Eddy, who instantly gripped her arms. "How could you come up here by yourself?" he cried. "Rachel, I could strangle you!"

They had just finished an endless Christmas Eve supper, and everyone had retired for the night. "Well, where have you been?" she shot back. "I think I know!"

"I went up to Tantallon Castle," Eddy said grimly, not releasing her. "He's our man, Rachel, and I have the evidence that will convict him for high treason." He released her, sighing. "I'm tired," he said abruptly.

She melted; she touched his stubbled cheek. "What kind of evidence?"

"Photographs. Rachel, this is not a good idea. Jesus! I almost had a heart attack when I got your message that you'd gone to Elgin Hall. Didn't it ever occur to you that this is a trap?"

She stared. "Yes, I guess it did. But I felt sorry for Lady Ellen."

"You felt sorry for her?" He was incredulous. "I smell a rat," he said. "He's used you to lure me here, by damn."

Rachel stared in growing horror.

He softened. "He won't trap me. Don't worry—I can take care of myself."

She folded her arms. "Like the time you ditched out over the channel?"

His eyes widened. "How in hell did you hear about that?"

"You never told me!" she accused. That had been months ago, and he was very lucky to be alive—a dinghy with rescue workers had fished him out of the freezing water almost instantly, before he got hypothermia and died.

"I didn't want to worry you," he said.

"You can't keep secrets from me anymore," she begged. "I'm your wife. Whatever you are involved in, we are in it together."

He was silent for one moment. "Rachel, as your husband, it's my duty to protect you."

Rachel saw an argument in the making, and that was the last thing she wanted. She put her arms around him and laid her cheek on his strong chest. "Let's not fight. Let's get out of here."

He stroked her hair and kissed the top of her head. But he did not answer her.

Fear stabbed through her. "Eddy?" She looked up at him and saw the determined look in his eyes. "We can't stay now! Not if this is a trap!"

"We'll leave in the morning. I don't want to spook Elgin. He has no idea I've got the goods on him, Rach. We'll go to bed and first thing tomorrow, I'll drop you at Bentley Priory and take care of business. If we bail out now, he might go underground, or he might even flee the country."

Her heart was booming now. "I don't like this," she said.

He hesitated. "Neither do I. But it's too goddamn late to back out now."

CHAPTER 21

Their bodies had become one.

They moved in perfect unison. It was so new, so wondrous, so exhilarating, yet it was as if they had done this many, many times before. Rachel held his shoulders as Eddy moved over her, inside her, his strokes long, slow, exquisite, the tension escalating between them, the pressure building within her. And just when she could not stand it anymore, just when the power of love and desire became unbearable, his rhythm changed, becoming faster, harder, more urgent. Rachel felt the cries being ripped from the very core of her being. She wanted to be silent—the master suite was at the end of the hall, and God knew where Lionel slept—but her will failed her. Eddy's name filled the room; it filled the night as he filled her.

Afterward, he rolled onto his side and pulled her into his arms. Rachel burrowed there against his chest, spooned into his large, muscular body. Her breathing began to slow. Her mind clicked into its customary coherence, and images from the evening began tumbling swiftly there.

It had been an evening filled with tension and undercurrents.

Eddy suddenly pulled her onto her back, moving over her. "You're not asleep," he said.

Rachel's heart lurched. "No. Eddy, Lionel knows."

He did not have to ask what she meant. "Yeah. Somehow, he figured out I'm no ordinary pilot. He's smart."

She wanted to beg him not to finish what he had begun. But how could she? His courage and determination made him the man that he was, the man she so desperately loved.

He crushed her in his arms, not even kissing her. "I have to go."

"No!"

He sat up, tossing the sheets aside.

Too late, the words tumbled forth. "Eddy, please don't. So far nothing has happened. In the morning I will go back to Bentley Priory, and you to North Weald. *Please.*" She hadn't realized until that exact moment just how desperate she was. "You don't have to do this!"

He stood, sliding on boxers and pants. "Nothing's happened? Not only did he murder his father, Rachel, he's a frigging Nazi spy."

"I mean, nothing has happened between you and him," she pleaded, almost in tears.

He was pulling on his shirt, his expression grim. He finally looked at her. "I can't quit now. I just can't. It's not who I am."

Rachel clutched the covers to her chest. "What are you going to do?"

He glanced at his wristwatch, which had an illuminated dial. "It's two. He should be sound asleep by now. I am going to take a peek around the house." His tone was easy, his gaze was hard. "You don't have to worry."

"But why? You already have those photographs! And maybe he isn't asleep," she tried. "Maybe there isn't anything in the house. He must have gone back and removed the body after we found it! He is very clever!"

Eddy was dressed. He walked over to a chair and lifted his bomber jacket, then dropped it back down. Rachel gasped when she saw the small gun in his hand. "What is that?" she cried.

He tucked it into the waistband of his pants, then slid on the worn leather jacket. "Look, hon. I'd like to find a list of contacts. He isn't the only agent operating here in Britain."

"You could search the house another time—after he's arrested."

He came over to her swiftly and kissed her forehead. "You worry too much. I'm a tough guy, and Elgin's a pansy." It was clear now that he was no longer thinking about her, that he had other matters on his mind. "Try to get some sleep," he said, and he was gone.

The huge horrible realization of what was happening—and what might happen—hit her now. Eddy was hunting Lionel. Lionel—who was a killer.

Rachel leaped up from the bed, uncaring that she was naked. She ran after him, pausing in the doorway. "Please," she whispered, clinging to the door. She was so afraid now that her fear blinded her.

He did not hear her, for he was disappearing down the stairs.

He was gone.

Rachel froze, clutching the door. She faced her very worst nightmare—the certainty, in every fiber of her being, that she had seen him for the very last time.

He did not make it to the library. In fact, he did not make it downstairs.

A door was wide open at the far end of the hall, and two small lights were on inside. Eddy took one glance into the room and realized it had to be the parlor of a suite. A large sofa faced the fireplace, brilliant works of art covered the upholstered crimson walls, and a desk that was clearly in use was against an adjoining wall. Eddy did not hesitate. He knocked on the open door. "Lionel?" he called quietly.

There was no response.

He tried again, with the same effect.

Eddy stepped into the parlor, glanced around, reassuring himself that no one was present. Then he crossed it to the next open doorway, where he was greeted with the largest bedroom he had ever seen, with a huge canopied bed in its center. These walls were done in a softer shade of red that was more salmon-hued. Here was another sitting area and another fireplace with a marble mantel. One small nightlight was on; no one was in the bedroom.

"Lionel? It's Eddy. You still up?"

There was no answer.

Eddy quickly returned to the sitting room, going straight for the desk. He explored every inch of the surface but found nothing incriminating. There were three drawers, but again he found nothing. Lionel was being very careful now. Eddy felt certain that if he ever searched his Knightsbridge flat again, there would be nothing there except pictures of birds.

Eddy glanced at his watch. He'd been in the master suite for less than three minutes. He'd give himself three more. He looked around the parlor and finally saw a small valise under a settee. It was the size of an overnight bag, so he had no reason to be suspicious of it; on the other hand, it should be in the bedroom, not the parlor. He quickly crossed the room, squatted, and opened it. He was expecting to find a radio. Inside was nothing but items of clothing.

Footsteps sounded in the hall. *The valise was a decoy—a trap.*

Eddy had processed the film he had taken at Tantallon, and four microdots were inside a slit in the sole of his shoe. He was going to hand-deliver the microdots to his contact at the American embassy tomorrow.

He did not have to make a conscious decision—his every instinct told him to secure the microdots before he came face-to-face with Elgin now.

Eddy left the valise open and in full view at the foot of the settee. He leaped up as he grabbed two of the four microdots, missing the others. The footsteps were just outside the door. He had about fifteen seconds to act.

Eddy crossed over to the fireplace. Just above the mantel was a beautiful painting of two nude women and a parakeet. As he pressed the two dots between the gilded frame and the canvas, the words "Venus and Psychée" caught his eye. He turned away, shoving his hands in his pockets.

Lionel entered the parlor. He stopped short, eyes widening.

Eddy was sweating. He didn't really know what reflex had caused him to hide the microdots that would definitely incriminate and probably convict Lionel as a traitor, but his reflexes had saved his life too many times to count, and he did not question his own motivations now.

He hardly had the time.

"Eddy?" Lionel wore trousers and a smoking jacket that was an exquisite shade of lapis. He was also wearing black velvet slippers with his initials embroidered on the toes in gold. He glanced from Eddy standing before the masterpiece to the open valise on the floor by the settee.

"I couldn't sleep. I was going downstairs to find a book when I saw the lights on and the door open." Eddy smiled. His gun felt hard against his waist. He was acutely aware of it as he slowly removed his hands from his pockets and let them hang loosely at his sides. Lionel would not get the jump on him, oh no. "I was hoping for some company."

If Lionel realized what Eddy had been doing, he gave no sign. Nor did he question the fact that Eddy was wearing his jacket, and he did not glance again at the obviously ransacked valise. He returned Eddy's brief smile with one of his own. "How about a nightcap downstairs?"

"That's a great idea." Eddy was on alert now. Lionel was too clever to be so dumb; he should be very suspicious of Eddy's being in the master suite at this hour. Eddy had no doubt that this was a trap and he had no intention of being caught in it.

Lionel stepped aside, but Eddy smiled and said, "After you." He would not give this man his back.

Lionel suddenly looked at the doorway. "Rachel?" he asked.

Eddy started, turning to look, thinking, *Damn it, I told her to go to sleep.* He was expecting to find her standing in the doorway of Lionel's suite, but he was wrong. The threshold was vacant. *It was the oldest trick in the book.* And as he was faced with a glimpse of the empty hall beyond, he felt the knife slicing across his throat and jugular.

As he gripped Lionel's wrists, he heard the gushing of his own blood, and in the mere seconds of life that were left to him, he thought, *I'm dead. He's won. The fucking bastard has won.*

A split second of life was left to him as Lionel released him and he fell, hard, to the floor. Blackness shrouded him.

His last thought was *Rachel.*

The blackness fell.

Beyond it, there was so much light.

Eddy did not return.

The sun was shining brightly, as if it had not rained through half the night. It was a quarter past seven on Christmas Day, and Rachel was fully dressed. Where was he? Why hadn't he come back?

Rachel thought she might die of grief. Surely he would walk through her door at any moment.

She had not gone back to sleep. About an hour after Eddy had left her, she hadn't been able to stand the suspense any longer, and she had crept down the hall with a small candle. She had found the door to a man's suite wide open, and two small lights burning within. The sitting room and the bedroom had both been empty, although a valise was at the foot of the settee, left carelessly open.

She had seen dark, wet stains on the rug. Rachel had been afraid that they were bloodstains. An inspection had told her she was looking at soap and water.

She had continued down the hall and through the house, telling herself that anything might have spilled on the rug, requiring Lionel to clean it up. The house had been huge and frightening, all darkness and shadows, and she had not been able to find either Lionel or Eddy.

Now she heard footsteps in the corridor outside her bedroom door.

Rachel dashed to the door and flung it open. She gripped the knob in shock, for Lionel was just coming in, clearly having taken an early morning horseback ride. He was in his riding boots and a hacking coat, and mud covered the leather uppers. "Lionel!" she exclaimed.

"Oh, good morning, Rachel." He smiled pleasantly at her, removing leather gloves. "It's such a beautiful morning, I've been out riding. Did you sleep well?"

Had he been out riding all night as well? "I haven't slept at all," she cried, her heart hammering uncomfortably. "Where is Eddy?"

He stared. "What do you mean, where is Eddy? Isn't he with you?" He blinked so innocently at her.

She glared furiously at him. She was shaking now and only just aware of it. "He couldn't sleep last night. He went downstairs, maybe for a drink, I don't know. I haven't seen him since!"

"Really?" Lionel was so calm. He seemed mildly surprised. "Maybe he went out for a walk, the way I went out for a ride. I'm sure he'll be back at any moment; after all, he has to report back to his command." He came closer and took both of her hands in his. "Your hands are so cold!" he exclaimed.

Rachel stared at his smooth, boyish, handsome face. She wanted to retch, for she was filled with revulsion, but she couldn't seem to move and didn't try to pull free of his grasp. "Where is he?" she whispered. "Please tell me what you've done with him!" Even as she spoke, Eddy's words returned to haunt her.

I smell a rat . . . he's used you to lure me here.

"Rachel, are you ill? You seem hysterical. What are you saying? I haven't seen Eddy since we all retired last night."

Rachel shivered violently. *Eddy had to be all right.* Just because he hadn't come back to their room did not mean that something horrible had befallen him. *It didn't mean that he was dead.*

"Rachel? Maybe you should sit down."

Rachel blinked and found herself staring into Lionel's gray eyes. His tone had been concerned, but his eyes reflected nothing but emptiness.

The comprehension seared her. *He is a madman.*

Eddy's voice filled her mind, so loud and clear it was as if he were standing right there beside her, speaking to her in that very moment. *I think the best thing is for you to steer clear of him.*

Rachel whirled because she felt him there beside her, and she really did expect to see him standing behind her, smiling at her. No one was there; she faced a smiling portrait of an Elgin ancestor instead.

Stay away from him, Rachel.

The words were so crystal-clear. Perhaps she was the mad one.

"Rachel." Lionel took her hands again. "Do you want to lie down? Should I call Ellen? Perhaps you need a bit of tea."

She looked wildly at him. She couldn't seem to think clearly now, no, she couldn't seem to think at all. All she could seem to focus on was staying away from Lionel—she must stay away from him—it was what Eddy wanted. "I have to go, I'm late," she cried, tearing herself free of his grasp and hurrying down the hall.

Lionel followed her downstairs. "Rachel! Where are you going? Are you all right?"

Rachel ran faster, tripping in her haste. She had to get away from him, she had to!

"Rachel! Your coat!"

Rachel flew across the foyer, hearing him, but only vaguely. His words did not sink in. She knew only that she had to get away from him and it was crucial, it was urgent. Her brain had formed a series of words, and it was a chant she could not shake.

Eddy was dead.

Rachel knew it because a few hours ago, a part of her had died as well.

Rachel wandered into her father's house. Papa and Hannah were in the kitchen, sipping tea and nibbling on toast. Papa was also reading the newspaper.

He did not look up. Hannah did, and she cried out, leaping to her feet, when she saw Rachel's expression.

Rachel staggered into the doorway and hung on to it for her life.

"Rachel," Hannah whispered, all the color draining from her face. "Rachel, what is it? Oh God, has someone died?"

Rachel nodded, the tears coming now in endless, silent streams. The pain inside her would kill her as well, and soon, she realized. She did not care.

"Not . . . Sarah?" Hannah gasped, unmoving.

Papa looked up, eyes wide.

So he had heard; so he was human after all. "Eddy," Rachel whispered, and then the pain went through her like a lance, and for the first time in her life, she fainted.

*   *   *

She awoke on the sofa. Sarah had laid a wet compress on her head, and Hannah held her hand. Papa stood in the center of the parlor, his eyes upon her. Rachel looked at Sarah.

"What happened?" Sarah asked, ashen.

"Eddy has disappeared," Rachel said, struggling to sit up.

"He's disappeared?" Sarah cried.

Rachel nodded, and the tears began all over again. It was impossible to speak.

"You mean he was shot down?" Sarah asked grimly.

Rachel looked from one sister to the other. Then she looked at Papa. "My husband is dead," she whispered. The grief was too strong, she could not speak. But Papa met her gaze for the first time in four months, just before she collapsed, sobbing, in her sister's arms.

Also weeping, Hannah fled upstairs.

Papa came over and laid his hand on her shoulder. "I am sorry," he said. It was too late.

That afternoon Rachel told the authorities all that she knew. But Eddy Marshall had disappeared, and it was two weeks before his body was found in a lake just north of Elgin Hall. It was the same day that Rachel learned she was pregnant with his child.

PART
FIVE

A STRANGER IN OUR MIDST

CHAPTER 22

Claire paced the waiting area of the emergency room at New York–Presbyterian, choking with fear. She had one coherent thought. *She could not lose Ian now.*

A police car had actually been driving by as the shooting occurred, and while the shooter had gotten away, an ambulance had arrived only moments later. Claire had given her statement to the police, while Ian was being sped toward the nearest hospital. She had then called Leonard Feinstein, Ian's boss. Both of his numbers were stored in Ian's cell phone. She had snatched it from him while he was on a stretcher awaiting surgery in the chaos of a corridor in emergency, all the while trying to tell her that he was okay and that being shot in the back was no big deal.

It had been a rotten time to play hero, Claire thought now, tears coming to her eyes.

And the last thing he had said to her, or tried to say to her, as he was being wheeled away was "Lisa, Claire. Call Lisa."

His FBI-agent sister. Claire didn't even know her last name, but if she was single, it was Marshall. And it might still be Marshall even if she was married.

"Claire?"

Claire looked up at the sound of a stranger's voice. A middle-aged man with dark hair and graying temples was approaching. He wore an impeccable suit and was rather good-looking; he also exuded an aura of wealth and authority. "Is he still in surgery?" he asked.

"Are you Leonard Feinstein?"

"Yes. Are you okay?"

Tears filled her eyes. "No. Damn it, I'm in love with him," she heard herself cry.

Leonard was grim. "Let me find out what's going on," he said.

Claire nodded and watched him walk over to the reception desk. She had no doubt that he would get the answers she had not been able to get herself. Claire looked at Ian's phone. Then she sank into a chair and opened up the digital phone book. Sure enough, Lisa Marshall had three listings. Claire chose the number of her cell phone and dialed. There was no answer, so she left a voice mail.

Leonard returned. "He's being taken to his room. She was reluctant, but I told her that you're his fiancée." He smiled a little. "He's okay, Claire. They dug a slug out of his shoulder; Ian's lucky the shooter missed."

Claire shuddered. "Thank God."

"What happened?" Leonard sat down next to her. "Did you see the shooter?"

"No. And I already told the police everything about Ian and Elgin. I hope I did the right thing."

He patted her hand. "You did. We're the good guys, remember? We follow the rules, we don't break them." His expression changed. "Shall we go see how our buddy's doing?"

Claire nodded, grateful to no longer be alone. Apparently Leonard had asked directions—either that or he knew his way around this particular hospital—and a few minutes later, Claire found herself peering into a private room where Ian lay in bed, pale but alert. He seemed to be arguing with a nurse.

"Thank God you guys are here," Ian said with irritation.

The nurse said tersely, "He should sleep." Before she turned and walked out, she gave him an annoyed look.

"Claire, did you call Lisa?" Ian asked immediately.

Claire couldn't believe it; he had been shot, and he was thinking about protecting her. She walked over to the bed, and without thinking about it, she took his hand and clasped it. Then she closed her eyes, trying to hold back the tears of relief. She lifted his hand and kissed it. The tears fell anyway, silently.

He met her gaze. "I'm okay, Claire. I'll be released first thing tomorrow. It was only a graze."

She shook her head, incapable of speech.

"It wasn't a graze," Leonard said, from the foot of the bed. "They pulled a slug out, Ian. Did you see the shooter?"

"No. He fired from behind. And if I don't miss my guess, I think he was up above, maybe in the window of an upper-floor apartment across the street."

Claire remembered that Bill Marshall had been struck from behind as well. Had Eddy been taken by surprise, too?

Dear God, she just could not imagine William Duke being such a ruthless killer. But he must be Elgin.

"So he was a sniper," Leonard remarked.

Ian said, "He was waiting for me to leave Frances Cookson's apartment." Suddenly he paled.

"What is it?" Claire asked quickly.

Ian struggled to sit up. His color had worsened.

"Slow down, bud," Leonard said.

"Cookson. I'm worried that she needs police protection, Leonard. She couldn't ID Elgin, but I'm afraid we led him right to her. And he doesn't know that she can't make him."

"Got you." Leonard walked out of the room, already on his cell phone.

"Damn it," Ian said. "They'll never put a man on her." He winced as he tried to sit up.

"Ian, stay still. You'll hurt yourself. Is it time for another painkiller?" Claire asked.

"I'm not taking painkillers, Claire. I can't think clearly if I do." Then he smiled at her, but it was lopsided. "Hey, this is new. The little-mama side of you."

Claire stared, unable to think of any smart reply.

"Honey, it's all right."

"How can you say that?" Claire whispered. She gripped his hand more tightly. "You were right, Ian. Elgin is after you. Not me. We were yards apart. Do you think it was Elgin himself? Could he be such a marksman? At his age?"

Ian hesitated. "I don't know. But if it was Elgin, he'll have left us a small memento of the day's work."

Claire looked up at the ceiling in real despair, then walked away from him. She could feel Ian watching her. What would happen next?

"Claire?"

She turned.

"Call Jim, my assistant. I need to speak with him. Also, try to reach

Frances. Ask her if she can go visit her relatives again for a while. I hate the idea of her being here in New York and so easy to find."

She walked back to his side. "Ian, you are in no shape to pursue Elgin now."

"I'll be as good as new tomorrow. Maybe a little stiff and sore, that's all."

"Please rest here for a few days," she begged.

His eyes darkened. He reached for her with his left hand. "Claire, try to understand. I've waited years and years for this moment. Elgin killed my uncle and my father, and now he's gunning for me. I'm not going to sit here and twiddle my thumbs while he either vanishes again, this time for good, or devises another plan to knock me off. I cannot."

She stared at him and loved him for his courage. "All right," she finally said. "I'll call Jim and Frances, but you are not doing anything without my help."

"Claire," he began, clearly in protest.

"Tough luck, macho man," she said. "You couldn't get rid of me now if you tried."

Claire couldn't bring herself to leave Ian's side. It was amazing how almost losing the one you loved could put your entire life—and your feel-ings—in total perspective.

He had a stream of visitors: the police, his sister Lisa, three other sisters, someone's husband, several teenagers who turned out to be nieces and nephews, and his assistant, Jim, who wound up making a list of notes. Murphy appeared. He briefly cleared the room to ask questions privately. In that interim, Claire managed to reach Frances and persuade her to go visit her daughter in Atlanta for a few days. Around noon the hospital room was suddenly empty, and Ian fell instantly asleep.

She watched him dozing for a long moment, once again thanking the universe and the fates that he was okay. Then she got up and left the room.

Claire took his cell phone out of her back pocket. Images tumbled impossibly through her mind, mostly of William and her father. The urge to call Jean-Léon was overwhelming now.

Claire had reached several conclusions. After fifty years of marriage, Elizabeth had to know the truth about William. She could not be the highly ethical woman Claire had believed her to be. Still, Claire hoped she did not know that William was a murderer. It was possible that she was aware of his having been a spy years ago but had no idea how ruthless he actually was.

There was also the possibility that the Dukes had lied about returning to the States. At this point, William would be crazy to come back. By now, he should be in Timbuktu.

On impulse, Claire dialed their New York town house. A maid answered, and Claire learned that the Dukes were out but were expected back around six.

So they had returned stateside after all.

Would a guilty man come back? Claire supposed he might, if he was sure of his ability to cover his tracks. So far, Elgin seemed to have a surplus of self-confidence.

Claire paced. Her mind veered from the Dukes to her father, and almost automatically, her breathing became constricted. Her father was protecting William, but surely he knew nothing of the extent of William's criminal behavior. Surely he did not know that Ian had just been shot.

Claire gave up. Leaning against the wall outside Ian's room, after reassuring herself that he was still soundly asleep, Claire reached Jean-Léon's housekeeper and was told that he had left town. Claire was surprised. For a moment, she felt as if a band were being tightened about her chest. She reached him on his cell phone. "Dad, where are you?"

"I'm in Chicago," he said briskly, as if in a rush, "on business. Where are you, Claire?"

"I'm in New York." She ignored an intern wheeling an empty gurney down the hall. She inhaled deeply. "Someone tried to kill Ian Marshall a few hours ago."

There was a measured silence on the other end of the line. It frightened Claire. The silence somehow did not sound or feel surprised. "Dad? Are you still there?" she asked cautiously.

"Yes, I am. How is Marshall?"

"Do you care?" Her own words—and her terse tone—surprised her.

"What kind of question is that?"

"I'm sorry. I'm upset." *That's an understatement*, she thought. "He's okay. The shooter missed, fortunately." Claire hesitated. "Dad, you lied to me. You lied to me about Ian's reputation and about Elgin, who is very much alive. He's on Scotland Yard's most-wanted list, damn it."

"Why won't you stay out of this, Claire?" was Jean-Léon's overly calm response.

"The man I love was almost murdered! Someone tried to shoot him in the back!" She was shouting. Two nurses walking past turned to look at her. Claire flushed and lowered her voice. "Elgin tried to murder him."

"So now you are in love with him?" Jean-Léon asked. He sounded resigned.

"Yes, I am," Claire said firmly.

"Has it ever occurred to you that I am trying to protect you?" he returned. "And I did a bit of checking. There was a rumor that Elgin died, and maybe it's true. And I certainly did not lie about Bill Marshall. The police believe the murder to have been a pointless mugging."

"It wasn't a pointless mugging," Claire whispered.

"Why can't you let things alone?"

"I can't because I love him and he could be dead right now. Elgin has to be caught, Dad."

"Has it ever occurred to you that he is using you, Claire? Ruthlessly, for his own ends?"

She took short, hard breaths. "No, Dad. It has not occurred to me that he might be using me," she said, but his words struck a painful and frightening chord. Ian had used her initially to try and get close to David. But Claire would not consider that he might still be using her. Now she summoned up all of her courage. "What's occurred to me is that you are trying to protect Elgin," she said.

Absolute silence fell.

"Dad?"

"I am trying my best to protect you, but you aren't being very cooperative, Claire," her father rebutted.

"I know that Elgin is your brother."

He was silent again. He did not deny her words.

Claire tried to tell if the silence was one of surprise and shock, or resignation and acceptance. She could not tell. "Dad? He's a killer. *A ruthless, cold-blooded killer.* He has to be brought in. You can help. *Please help.*"

"I need to think about this," Jean-Léon said. "I'm going to come to New York tonight. We should meet. We'll talk about everything then."

"All right," Claire said, sagging against the wall. *He hadn't denied it.* She had been hoping, foolishly, that he would. The child who lived within her harbored a foolish notion that Elgin was not William Duke and that William wasn't Jean-Léon's brother, and that there was some reasonable and sane explanation for everything. Claire felt overwhelmed. Could she really handle this?

"Claire? We have to meet tonight, as soon as I get to town," Jean-Léon said firmly.

Claire gripped the tiny phone. "Okay. I can meet you tonight. When and where?" she asked harshly—before the phone was ripped right out of her hands.

Claire cried out. But it was Ian who had ripped the phone from her hand, snapping the lid closed.

Claire stared at him in absolute disbelief.

He stared back, his eyes wide, incredulous, angry. "What the hell do you think you are doing, Claire?"

"I . . ." Claire gasped, still shocked that he would tear the phone right from her hand. She had never seen him so angry, and she flinched. "I was trying to help. I asked *him* to help *us*."

He was so angry that he couldn't speak. Claire's own anger disappeared as he turned and walked back to his bed. He was wearing a hospital gown that was gaping in the back, and in other circumstances, it might have been funny or awkward, but it was not. He climbed into the bed, where he seemed to collapse. Perspiration beaded his brow.

"I was trying to help," Claire insisted.

He turned his head to look at her. "Do you want to be the death of me, Claire?"

She stiffened as if stabbed with a red-hot poker. "That's not fair."

"No, that's not fair, and neither is life. Eddy's death, my father's, David's, none of that is fair. I do not trust your father, Claire." He stared at her. "And neither should you."

She was frightened all over again. "But it's William," she whispered.

He hesitated. "That's your theory, not mine."

"No, Ian." Claire shook her head. "Please don't do this."

He had closed his eyes. For one moment, Claire blinked, thinking he had fallen asleep. But his lids lifted, and his regard was direct. "There's a reason I wanted you to go home. Now you know what that reason is."

Claire didn't want to hear any more.

"I am going to do whatever I have to in order to end this hunt once and for all. I will bring Elgin in, Claire—no matter who he really is."

Claire didn't know what to say. She couldn't think. She could only feel sick with fear.

There was a knock on the door. Claire was relieved by the interruption. Lisa Marshall, Ian's sister, was standing in the doorway with an armful of flowers. They had met briefly earlier; Lisa was small and blond and very pretty, too pretty, Claire thought, to be in the FBI. She was chic in a pleated, navy blue skirt that did not cover her knees, and a short matching jacket. She smiled at Claire, her eyes shining with excitement, and deposited the flowers on the windowsill with half a dozen other arrangements.

"You're back," Ian murmured.

"Not only am I back, have I got news," Lisa said, settling down on the foot of his bed. "Guess what we found in the apartment across the street?"

"Spent casings?"

"No kidding. Guess again. There's more." She smiled at Claire.

"I'm too tired to play twenty questions," Ian said.

"He's done it again, Ian. He left this behind." Lisa tossed a tiny object in a plastic bag onto the bed.

Claire stood up in order to see and realized she was looking at an extremely small knife, the size of nail clippers. It looked unused. Claire came closer. "Oh my God," she said. "Is that what I think it is?"

"Yes," Ian said harshly. "It is. It's a goddamn thumb knife."

"He's playing with you, Ian," Lisa said, no longer smiling. "This looks to be new and clean as a whistle. Still, he dropped it off as his calling card. I don't think he even meant to kill you. I think he meant to miss."

"That's pure speculation," Ian said.

Lisa stood. "It's my gut." She picked up the bag. "This is going to my favorite lab rat, and how much do you want to bet this is the exact type of weapon that did in Hayden and Suttill?"

Ian did not answer.

Claire stared at the knife, thinking how strange it was that such a tiny object could inflict so much death.

"After this one, bro, you owe me big-time."

"Anything," he said, waving somewhat tiredly at her.

Lisa grinned. "Set me up with that hunk Feinstein, will you?"

Claire realized that Ian was exhausted. She moved to his side. "You need some sleep, Ian."

"She's been mothering me for hours," Ian said to Lisa.

"Smart woman. The way to his heart is Gap jeans and chicken soup, but make sure there's toe cleavage."

Claire looked at her. She was too numb to reply.

Lisa turned to Ian. "Duke's in custody right now. He has an alibi for the time of the shooting."

"No surprise there."

"No. And we still can't make the hit man from Wales." Lisa hesitated and glanced at Claire. "We're going to get a search warrant for William's residence, Ian. See if we can't find a trail tying him to either hit, or Hayden, or even Elgin."

"About time," Ian said.

Lisa shrugged. "Hey, we're the best."

Claire looked from one to the other, her fear far more intense now.

Lisa glanced at her again.

"What is it?" Claire whispered, unable to move. "What is it that you're not telling me?"

"I need to speak with Ian alone," Lisa said.

It was about Jean-Léon. Claire just knew it.

"Give us a moment, Claire," Ian said kindly.

Claire looked at him, and her eyes felt pried open with crowbars. She turned and left the room, but she did not shut the door. It was almost impossible to get enough air now. Her breathing was harsh, making it impossible to eavesdrop, which was what she had to do.

But as she stood outside the hospital room, Lisa came to the door. She smiled at Claire, then closed the door in her face.

Claire fell against the wall, overcome with panic. What were they discussing?

"Hi, Claire. What are you doing?"

Claire blinked and saw Leonard Feinstein standing before her, holding a paper bag. Succulent aromas were coming from it. Claire had to guess Chinese.

Claire tried to find her voice. "Hanging." Her smile felt sickly.

"Are you all right?" He looked closely at her.

To her horror, she shook her head no and felt tears welling.

"Can I help?" he asked.

She swallowed. "Only if you produce Elgin—and he isn't someone I love."

Feinstein stared. Before he could respond, the door to Ian's room opened.

"Oh," Lisa said in real surprise. "Didn't expect to see you again."

Feinstein seemed to be flushing. He held up the bag. "Can't let our big guy starve."

"Feinstein to the rescue," Lisa agreed, sniffing. "Chinese?"

"French Thai."

Claire hardly heard their exchange. She walked slowly past them and found herself staring at Ian. He stared back.

Claire didn't know how long she stood in the center of his room, locking gazes with him. But there was no mistaking the look in his eyes—he felt sorry for her.

Lisa breezed in. "The Feinstein Food Squad is here, and I gotta go. Sleep tight, bro," she said, leaning over Ian and kissing his cheek. "No naughty dreams." She smiled at Claire. "Are you going to stay for a while?"

Claire nodded.

"If you wait a minute, I can give you a ride," Leonard said somewhat stiffly to Lisa. "I have a driver downstairs."

"Too cool," Lisa said, with nonchalance that belied her previous statement of interest in the man. "But I wouldn't want to put you out."

"You won't," he returned. He walked over to Ian. "Is there anything else you need?" he asked, placing the bag of takeout on the bureau.

"Let's touch base first thing tomorrow," Ian said.

"Okay."

Claire didn't like their conversation. She felt an unspoken communication between them. Or was she now thoroughly paranoid?

Leonard picked up his briefcase. "You be careful," he told Ian. "And you have one helluva woman to count on, so listen to her if she has something to say." He smiled at Claire. "I'm sure we'll see each other again soon."

Claire nodded, trying to smile. It was hopeless.

Lisa suddenly came up to Claire and hugged her. "Take care of him," she said with a smile, but she mouthed, *Be careful*, and then she and

Leonard waved and walked out. Lisa's voice drifted back from the hall: "Hey, what about a quick martini?"

Claire faced Ian again. "What is it?"

"Your father has disappeared, Claire."

Claire stared, his words echoing in her mind. "That's crap. He hasn't disappeared. I just spoke to him. He's in Chicago."

"Claire. The police want to bring him in for questioning, and he has disappeared—no one knows where he's gone."

Claire inhaled hard. Tears burned her lids. A memory she had forgotten for too many years to count suddenly assailed her. She had owned a horse as a child, and when she was about thirteen, it had run away with her. She had fallen off while on the trail.

Claire remembered returning home, bruised and still frightened, knowing how hard it would be to take her horse out on the trail again. Jean-Léon had been on the phone when she walked into the house, and even though he saw her, he nodded at her to wait. William had been sipping a drink on the patio. He had taken one look at her, seen that something was wrong, and sat her down and gently encouraged her to tell him what had happened, and finally, to reveal her worst fears. By the time Jean-Léon joined them, Claire wasn't afraid of the idea of taking the horse out again, and she had been smiling and laughing at William's jokes.

William Duke had always been one of the kindest men she knew.

Her father had been the one who was remote and difficult to reach.

"We had better talk."

Claire wanted to weep. "Not tonight."

"Then when, Claire? You tell me when."

She bit her lip. Her pulse felt explosive now. "All right. Because I can't take it anymore. *You think Elgin is my father.*"

"Yes, I do."

"You don't know anything!" she shouted. "So why did you arrest William if you are really after Jean-Léon?"

"William hasn't been arrested—no one has. And I am not the one who arrests anyone. And"—he hesitated—"damn it, Claire, I hope I am wrong."

"I have to go. I need to crash. It's been a long day." She whirled away.

"Wait! He'll contact you again!" Ian cried.

That stopped her in her tracks. Slowly, Claire turned. "What?"

"I heard a part of your phone conversation. You agreed to meet with him."

Claire was stunned. "That was before."

"No," Ian said.

"Don't do this, Ian. Not if you care about me."

He was the one to make a harsh and ragged sound now. "This is bigger than you and me, Claire. Why can't you see that?"

She shook her head. "It's my life. My life, my father—the only family I have."

"Elgin has done despicable things. But it's more than Eddy's murder, it's more than the others. He was a part of the Nazi war machine, Claire. Just one tiny cog, but he was a part of it. And that is inherently unforgivable, and there must be retribution."

"I'm going home," Claire said, then realized that the only place she had to go was Ian's condo. Of course, she would not stay there now. She would never stay there again.

"Please. Wait."

His tone was anguished, but Claire was having trouble with her limbs, anyway. Her body did not seem capable of obeying her brain.

"I would never hurt you," he said, his gaze earnest and pleading all at once. "Not intentionally. That has never been my intention."

Claire was reeling. "I think it's too late." And it was. It was just too damn late for sorrow and regret, and it was certainly too late for them.

"Claire, I love you."

She almost laughed, but it would have been a tearful sound. "I have to go." She knew she would have given anything to hear those words in another time and place. Now they didn't matter.

He's using you ruthlessly. Out of nowhere, her father's horrible statement pierced her mind. Of course, Jean-Léon was wrong. Ian was not using her. Claire knew that for a fact.

I love you . . . He's using you.

Ian's words, her father's words. Suspicion rose within her.

"Claire? We need you now," Ian said.

CHAPTER 23

Claire prayed she had not heard him correctly. But he said again, "We need you now."

She shook her head. "No."

Ian's gaze was intense. "Claire, I wish it didn't have to be this way."

"It doesn't."

"You're upset and angry—understandably so."

"Don't you dare pretend to understand how I feel or what I'm going through," she warned.

"Okay." He raised both hands. "I won't. And you're right. I can't possibly comprehend how you're feeling now." Ian pushed the covers aside and swung his legs over the bed.

Claire watched. She made no move to help him.

After a pause, he stood. "I sort of liked it when you were a mama hen."

Claire's face felt impossibly rigid. She did not respond.

He walked over to her. Claire flinched as he reached for her hands. "If your father is innocent, Claire, he'll be able to prove it. If not, he has to pay for his crimes."

Claire jerked away from him. She was shaking. "He's innocent."

"Do I have to remind you how many innocent people have died because of Elgin? I could be dead now, Claire. You could be dead!"

She refused to meet his gaze. "You have made your point. A killer is on the loose. *A monster*. But it is *not* Jean-Léon."

"If he's innocent, the truth will come out," Ian said firmly.

"What do you want from me?" she cried, finally meeting his gaze. "What?"

"Call your father," he said. "Arrange a meeting. I'll take care of the rest."

"You mean you and a hundred cops will swarm all over him. You mean I should be the *bait* in your *trap*."

Ian was so very calm. "If he's innocent, it won't hurt anyone."

"You want me to trap my own father!" she screamed. "You know what, Ian? *Go to hell.*"

Claire did not wait for his reaction. She rushed from the room and out the door.

The street was residential. Old town houses, mostly brick and all converted to apartments, lined the block, as did reed-thin and apparently unhealthy elm trees. Here and there, a tree was fenced off from the neighborhood's dogs, and daffodils smiled happily at the world. Not a single parking space was available; cars lined both sides of the street, a few of them junkers. And there was a plainclothes police car parked across the street. It stood out like a sore thumb.

Did they really expect that car and the single detective in it to stop anyone?

It was ridiculously easy to walk up the block toward the apartment building where Frances Cookson lived. Blending with the pedestrians was almost as simple as getting through the locked lobby door by claiming to be an early guest of a tardy resident. In fact, it was amazing how old age opened up so many doors so easily—no one ever suspected an elderly person of being anything other than needy and feeble and sweet.

A quick inspection of Frances Cookson's door told the intruder that it was double-locked and chained. A knock would have to do.

"Yes? Who is it?" an elderly woman's voice said from the other side of the door.

There was no doubt that Frances Cookson was peering through the peephole now. There was also no reason to assume a new alias. The identity established over half a century ago would do.

Frances Cookson opened the door, her eyes somewhat wide with surprise. "Can I help you?" she asked in confusion. "Do you have the right apartment?"

"Yes, I do." The knife followed the smile. The movement was so quick that it wasn't until the small blade had arced across the jugular vein of the blond woman that she realized what was happening. In that moment, their gazes met, the woman's wide and astonished.

"I'm sorry." The words were sincere.

But no link could be left to the past.

Claire paused blindly on York Avenue outside the hospital. Her father's ugly words echoed in her mind, and clearly, he was right.

I love you.

Once, Claire would have believed such a declaration from Ian. Now she must not even consider it, she must not remember it, she must not. She hurried across the street, moving with several other pedestrians, and it was only when she was halfway across that she realized the light was red and traffic was coming uptown and she had better move out of the way, fast.

She ran to the safety of the other sidewalk, panting and out of breath. Ian wanted her to set a trap for her father; she would never do it.

Her cell phone rang.

Claire stumbled and reached for Ian's phone, stashed in her pocket. But it was silent.

Her own phone was in her purse. The ringing ceased.

Claire moved into the shadows of a deli's awning, looking at her caller ID. She was afraid it had been Jean-Léon, who even now might be back in the city. But it was not. Elizabeth Duke had been the caller.

Claire hesitated, then called her back unthinkingly, her grip clammy on the phone.

"Claire! Did you hear what happened?" Elizabeth cried, sounding distraught.

"What happened?" Claire managed numbly.

"They had William in custody all day, Claire, all day, questioning him for the crimes of that spy, Elgin. But he's home now, thank God; in fact, he is so upset he is drinking a Scotch in bed. Claire!" She started to weep.

Claire found it impossible to find compassion for the other woman. She was too frightened for herself—and Jean-Léon. "I'm sorry."

"He's innocent," Elizabeth said, choking on tears. "Thank God they realized that."

"Yes. Thank God."

"Claire? Are you nearby? He's asked for you."

Claire stiffened as a million warning bells went off at once in her mind. "What?"

"He's asking for you."

Claire tried to cope with this startling bit of information. What if William were Elgin; what if the police—and Ian—were wrong?

Why else would he ask for her now?

Was this a trap?

"Claire? It would be lovely if you could drop by. We both need you," Elizabeth said.

Claire swallowed hard. And if William was innocent? Then he was an old man in failing health who had gone through a terrible ordeal. And his request would make sense—she was the daughter he had never had.

"I'll try," Claire said, and it was a lie. There was no one and nothing that could make her go over to their house now.

"Please come soon. In the state he is in, I expect him to be asleep within the hour."

"All right," Claire managed, and it was another terrible lie.

You think it's Jean-Léon.

Yes, I do.

Claire hurried up the block. Someone was innocent, and it was either William or Jean-Léon, but it could not be both.

Oh God, what was she going to do?

Go home. Except going home would not change anything, and it would not make this nightmare go away.

Claire shut her eyes as if, in doing so, she could shut out the truth. How could her father be Lionel Elgin? How?

The answer was simple: he had never been there for her. He was so remote. She had never had that hug she had craved her entire life. His only love, his true love, was art.

It was, in fact, very possible. She had been speaking with Jean-Léon from the moment she had met Ian. Elgin seemed to know their every move—and so did her father.

Her father's words, Ian's words, echoed relentlessly in her mind. Claire wanted to clap her hands over her ears and scream in frustration and despair.

The telephone rang again.

Claire paused on the corner of Sixty-seventh and First Avenue, looking at it. It continued to ring. Insistently, incessantly.

Claire knew who it was. This time it was not Elizabeth. She hesitated, but there was no caller ID. He was calling from a blocked line.

"Dad?" she asked warily.

"I've finally caught up with you," Jean-Léon said abruptly. "I'm in the city, Claire. Where are you?"

Claire hesitated. She was afraid to tell her father where she was.

"Claire?"

"I'm—downtown."

He seemed to accept that, but then why would he suspect his own daughter of lying? "We have to meet, without Marshall. I'll explain everything then."

What explanation could he possibly make?

"Claire? Are you there?"

"Yes, I'm still here," she said, and she felt the kind of anguish she had felt when her mother died. The sense of loss was acute. The loss—and loneliness.

"Is Marshall still in the hospital?"

"Yes," she said dully. This was, she thought, the blackest day of her life. Worse than the day her mother had died.

"When is he being released?"

"I don't know." She had somehow turned into an incorrigible liar, lying to everyone she loved most.

"Meet me tomorrow morning at six, in the park. Enter at Eightieth Street by the Met. Walk straight west and through the first tunnel. When you come out, continue on until you reach the Great Lawn. Start across it. Keep walking until I meet you."

Claire hesitated, and she could not seem to speak. The conflict engulfed her. Making a decision now seemed an impossible feat.

If he's innocent, the truth will come out.

He's using you ruthlessly.

I love you.

"Claire? Are you there? Damn it, I have to go!"

"I'm here," Claire whispered, feeling faint. "All right. Central Park, six tomorrow morning. I'll be there."

* * *

The sun was rising at six the following morning. It was cool out as Claire approached Fifth Avenue, the huge Metropolitan Museum of Art ahead of her, taking up almost four blocks. She paused for the light, as there was some traffic even at this early hour. She wore a sweater, but it could not chase away the chill within her, which cut through every fiber of her being. Claire was sick inside.

The light changed. She was the only person to cross the street.

As she walked into the park, she left the huge building of the Met behind. A woman was walking a German shepherd, and a homeless man was sleeping in rags on a park bench, but otherwise she did not see anyone.

Claire had never felt so alone in her entire life.

The path began to fork; ahead was the tunnel her father had spoken about. She veered to her left, moving away from the back of the museum. The tunnel was dark and cold. Claire began to tremble with dread.

Could she really do this? Did she even want to?

But she had to have answers. She just had to.

She was walking between two fields. Two men playing with their dogs were on her left. Ahead, Claire saw the Great Lawn.

A man appeared in the midst of lawn, far away, a distant silhouette. Claire's heart turned over.

Last night, Ian had told her that Frances Cookson had been murdered.

Claire reached the lawn. She continued in the same direction, now walking across the soft wet grass. Jean-Léon was walking toward her. As he came closer, Claire faltered, filled with fear.

How could she do this?

She wanted to turn and run.

He waved for her to come toward him when he was still twenty yards away.

Claire continued on. Never in her life had she felt so miserable.

Her father halted in front of her and smiled. "I am so glad to see you," he said with emotion.

Claire bit her lip to keep it from trembling uncontrollably. "Dad. Frances Cookson is dead."

"Who?" His opaque gray gaze was searching. "Claire, you don't think—"

She hugged herself. "Did you . . . ?"

He stared. "Jesus! I don't even know who the hell Frances whatever-her-name is!" He seemed angry.

"Did you kill her?" she asked harshly.

He stared, at her. "Is that what you think?"

"Just answer me!" she cried.

"No, Claire, I did not."

Claire stared back at the man standing before her. He was seventy-eight—or so he claimed—and looked amazing for his age. He was as handsome as Paul Newman, as youthful, as virile. He might as well have been Paul Newman, or John Doe, or anyone. Did she love this man? She didn't even know this man. He was a stranger—he had always been a stranger. She had certainly craved his love. Now, she did not know how she felt.

"Is William your brother?" she whispered. "Is he Robert Ducasse?"

"No, Claire. My brother is dead."

"Robert Ducasse died in a POW camp during the war," Claire whispered. "His brother, Jean-Léon, died fighting in France."

He blinked. "Jesus! They were cousins—my grandfather was one of four brothers—the family is huge!"

"You said you were going to explain," Claire tried.

"Did I say that? I said we had to meet. I don't like what's happening, Claire. You're afraid of me, I can see it on your face and in your eyes, and I'm your father. It's Ian Marshall. He's brainwashing you. And I can't stand it."

"Dad—did you murder David?"

He seemed startled and then furious. "Is that what you think?" he exclaimed. "Claire, how could you think such a thing!"

"I don't know," she cried back. "Are you really Lionel Elgin? Did you murder Eddy Marshall? Did you kill his wife, Rachel? Were you the one who murdered Bill Marshall? Please, Dad, I have to know!"

"You know who I'm going to kill?" he said coldly. "I'm going to kill that fucking Ian Marshall for putting all these ideas in your head—and for putting you in the middle of a dangerous investigation that you have no right being a part of." He glanced at his watch. "C'mon. Let's walk. I have a breakfast meeting at seven."

Claire didn't move. "Why did you disappear?"

"Disappear? What are you talking about! I haven't disappeared, I'm right here."

"The police want to question you. They said you disappeared."

"Christ!" Jean-Léon cried. "They're idiots, Claire, and so is my secretary—she knew where I was. And I'll be happy to speak with the police and give them a piece of my mind."

Claire was shaking her head. She couldn't speak now. But there was one question she had to ask, since it had been haunting her forever. Still, it was almost impossible to get the words out, maybe because the prospect of his answer terrified her.

"Claire?"

"I'm a Jew, Dad. You married a Jew. Didn't that bother you?" she asked in a whisper.

"What?" He seemed disbelieving. "No, Claire, it did not bother me and it does not bother me, for God's sake, you are my daughter!" He hesitated. "Claire, I—"

His words were cut off by the deafening sound of a helicopter. Startled, they both looked up.

The helicopter appeared overhead, hovering. The wind from its rotor blades gusted hard at them, causing them to career into each other. "You are surrounded, Elgin," a voice boomed over a megaphone. "Raise your hands and surrender now."

Claire met her father's eyes. His were wide with the comprehension of what she had done, and Claire felt herself begin to flush in guilt.

"Hands up, Elgin," the voice boomed. "You are under arrest. Give yourself up."

Claire looked past her father and saw the SWAT teams and police officers at the edge of the clearing, using the far line of trees for cover. Huge gusts of wind from the helicopter's rotors were blowing grass, dirt, and debris around them. Claire continued to stagger from the strength of the gusts.

"How could you?" Jean-Léon asked tremulously.

"I'm sorry," Claire whispered, but she did not know if she meant it or not.

Jean-Léon took a gun out of his suit-jacket pocket. Claire blinked at it but did not move away from him. "What are you going to do?"

"I don't know," he said.

"Drop the gun!" the voice cried. "Drop the gun! Claire, move away from him!"

Claire felt as if she were in the midst of a dream. But she obeyed the impersonal voice over the megaphone, and she began backing away from Jean-Léon, leaving him standing there alone, a gun in his hand.

Their eyes met.

"There is no way out," the officer continued over the megaphone. Claire realized he was standing on the edge of the field behind them, where more SWAT team members and more policemen crouched. Jean-Léon had seen them, too.

As Claire walked away from her father, she glimpsed Ian among the police and SWAT teams standing a hundred feet away in the line of trees, but the sight of him gave her no comfort, and he was too far away for her to make out his expression.

Suddenly all hell seemed to break loose. All of the police and detectives and SWAT teams began rushing toward her.

Claire froze, but the dozens of men ran past her, and she turned.

Jean-Léon had thrown down his gun and stood with his hands up in surrender.

"Dad," Claire cried, and in the next instant a dozen uniforms were on top of him, handcuffing him.

"Claire!" Ian was at her side.

She couldn't look at him now. She shoved past him, hurrying to the paved walk ahead, wanting to leave this nightmare behind.

The roar of the helicopter began to diminish as it lifted up and left. The barked commands of the police sounded behind her. Marked and unmarked cars were pulling up in the field. Siren lights were flashing.

"Are you okay?" Ian demanded, catching up to her.

She was so angry it was hard to speak. "What the hell do you think?"

Ian stopped in his tracks, and she left him behind.

A man in a tweed jacket and felt fedora came up to her. His name was MacIntyre, and he was from Scotland Yard; Claire had met him last night. "Thank you," he said with a smile.

Claire lifted her sweater and T-shirt, revealing an expanse of flesh and the microphone taped and wired to her body. A man from the FBI came over and removed it. She remained mute. She had nothing to say to any of them. In that moment, she was filled with hatred, no small amount of it directed at herself.

On impulse, she turned. Her father was being pushed into the backseat of a squad car. Ian stood beside the car with Lisa. Claire watched until he sensed her stare and turned to look at her. She abruptly turned away.

She hoped he was happy. God knew she was not.

And then she saw William Duke standing farther back, behind several policemen, behind one unmarked car. Surprise stiffened her, but only briefly. There were tears in his eyes.

Claire began to walk away from it all, the black and whites, the congregation of uniformed and plainclothes officers, the feds, MacIntyre, Ian. Her pace increased. She ran.

William held out his arms and she rushed into them.

It was the safest haven she had ever known.

"I'm so sorry, Claire, so sorry," William said, his voice hoarse with emotion.

She couldn't speak. She could only nod. He held her another moment, until she managed to get a grip. Finally she straightened. "Yeah." She sniffed. "So am I. I'm sorry I doubted you. I don't know how I could have ever had such doubts."

"It doesn't matter. All that matters now is you." He smiled sadly at her. His gaze was searching.

"I'll get over it." She didn't think she ever would. "What are you doing here?"

"I was on my way to your hotel to leave a message for you—I saw you and followed you here."

He hesitated. "Claire, there's no gentle way to say this."

Claire waited, bewildered.

"I'm your real father," William Duke said.

CHAPTER 24

William and Claire walked through the tunnel, back the way Claire had come. Claire wasn't reeling, because she was numb. "I don't understand." She paused on the other side of the underpass, a stone's throw from the Met.

"Your mother and I agreed to never tell you the truth." He touched her, moving hair away from her face. "But given all that has happened, I realized today I had to come forward, Claire. Let's sit down," he suggested.

Claire nodded, still stunned, as they walked over to the nearest park bench. The park was filling up now, mostly with dogs and their owners. "But you and Elizabeth have a wonderful relationship," Claire said.

"Yes, we do. Claire, we've been married fifty-six years. That's a long row to hoe, and we had our ups and downs. We separated just after our twentieth anniversary," William said gently, his gaze upon her unwavering. Claire looked into his eyes. She saw so much affection there. "And you had an affair with my mother?" Claire whispered.

William nodded, his eyes on her face. "Cynthia was very unhappy, Claire. I'm sure you can imagine why."

Claire could. Her mother's marriage must have been one of loneliness and even despair. Had there also been doubts, suspicions, shadows? Claire shivered. "Maybe it was a blessing that she passed away when she did." She never would have thought to see the day when she would think such a thing.

"Our affair happened accidentally, I guess. She was lonely, and like most men, I wasn't about to be alone, even for a day. But I never stopped loving Elizabeth, and we had to break it off. Elizabeth and I, of course, realized that our differences meant nothing in the light of our love and friendship, and we've never thought about breaking up since."

This man was her real father. She was not Jean-Léon's daughter. Elgin was not her father. "This is a miracle," she managed hoarsely. But confusion settled in on the heels of shock. And there was no denying it. While it was easy to admit that she was very fond of William, a part of her would always cling to Jean-Léon. A part of her still needed him and his love. Claire didn't want it to be this way, but it was.

"Not really. Had I been a more sensitive and less virile man, I would have spent my separation thinking things out, instead of sleeping with your mother."

Claire met his watery gaze. "I don't know what to say, or what to think."

"That's understandable, Claire. I know that you will always have strong feelings for Jean-Léon, one way or the other."

"Does he know?" Claire suddenly asked with trepidation. And she had an image she wished she would never again recall—Jean-Léon standing there beneath the howling helicopter, his hands up in the air.

He hadn't admitted anything, she realized with a pang.

"No. He has no idea. We were very careful."

Claire heard William, but she had begun to analyze the conversation she had just had with Jean-Léon. She was uncomfortable and disturbed, as she should be—she had been the bait in Ian's trap, a role she had sworn she would never perform. Claire had to shake off her thoughts. She stood. "I wonder if he will ever forgive me for what I have done."

William also stood, using his cane, and put his arm around her. "I believe he loves you, dear. In his own way. Love is about forgiveness."

Claire ducked her head against the brightening day. The past was flashing through her mind, images tumbling and juxtaposed. Jean-Léon hardly ever present, William always somehow there, in the midst of her life. Suddenly Claire thought about his wife, whom she loved also. "Does Elizabeth know?"

"Yes. She's known from the beginning, there are no secrets between us. She encouraged me to tell you the truth, Claire."

Claire took a deep breath. She looked up at the sky. It had become a robin's-egg blue. In fact, the sun was bright and shining. It was over, she realized. The nightmare was finally over.

But Jean-Léon had denied everything.

But then, Elgin would hardly break down now, after all these years, and confess.

Claire forced a smile. "I had better go. I'm exhausted, and I'm taking an afternoon flight home. I stayed at the Helmsley last night; my stuff is at Ian's."

William looked at her closely. "Is something wrong?"

"Of course not," Claire whispered, but dear God, she had a thought she wished she hadn't—what if they had captured the wrong man?

"Shall I give you a lift? My driver is waiting in front of the Stanhope."

"I'll walk. It's only a few blocks." She hesitated. "William? You're not his brother, are you? You're not really an Elgin?"

William looked amused but did not laugh—it was hardly a laughing matter. "No, dear, I am who I say I am, and I really went to school with Harry Elgin, whom I adored."

Claire nodded and they began to walk out of the park.

"Are you certain I cannot give you a ride? In fact, if you like, you can come back to the house for breakfast. Elizabeth should be up in a half hour or so." He smiled at her.

"Thanks, but I'll walk. I need to pack and I need to think. This has been a very confusing morning." It was perhaps the hardest act of her life, but she turned on her best, most perfect, high-society smile.

William smiled back.

Claire had keys, of course, and the moment she had let herself into Ian's apartment, she went still. Something wasn't right.

The apartment's atmosphere felt laden and combustible. The silence seemed fraught with tension, and thick enough to cut with a knife.

Claire told herself she was overwrought and justly so. "Ian?"

There was no answer.

Claire remained standing in the foyer, and now the hairs on her neck were prickling sharply, warningly, at her. "Ian?" she tried again.

There was no response.

But she hadn't expected him to respond, because she had last seen him speaking with Lisa, MacIntyre, and half a dozen other detectives in the park.

So what was wrong?

Claire realized she was filled with dread. She realized that she expected another blow to come her way at any moment. She realized that the apartment did not feel empty—which was absurd, the result of her well-earned paranoia.

What if they had captured the wrong man?

Claire didn't want to go there now. She turned and double-locked the door. As she crossed the hall to the kitchen, her sandals made a loud clicking sound on the wood floors. In the kitchen, she dutifully put fresh grounds in the coffeemaker, added water, and turned it on, trying not to think. Then she turned, leaning against the counter, listening to the silence of the apartment. But what was she listening for?

Behind her, something scratched. Claire jumped, whirling, and saw a cat outside on Ian's terrace, scratching at the windowpane. She inhaled shakily. Clearly the cat belonged to Ian's neighbor, whose terrace adjoined Ian's.

Claire took a sip of water and crossed the apartment again. She might as well pack her few things while waiting for the coffee to brew, but why did her footsteps sound so loud? Why was her breathing so harsh?

William claimed to be her father. She should not doubt him; plus, a DNA test could settle that question sooner or later.

Claire opened the door to her bedroom—and cried out.

Elizabeth was standing directly in front of her on the other side of the bed, in front of the room's large window. She was backlit by the early morning sun, and it was hard to make out her expression in the glare. "I didn't mean to frighten you, Claire."

Her heart was beating hard and fast, hurtfully. Claire laid a palm on her breast. "Good God. Didn't you hear me? Why—" She stopped in shock.

Elizabeth pointed a small black gun at her. "You are all fools," she said softly.

Claire stared, transfixed by the small gun, trying to understand what this meant and failing. "What . . . what are you doing?" she managed, somehow looking up and into the other woman's eyes.

Elizabeth sighed. "My dear, the Swan is dead. He died in late 1944. In fact, he died on Christmas Eve of 1944, and I thought that touch rather amusing myself."

This could not be happening. "I don't understand." But she did—for an inkling of an idea was beginning, one so fantastic and incredible that it was mind-boggling.

"I killed him, Claire. We had lost the war, and he knew too much, and it was time to get rid of him." Elizabeth smiled at her. "You see, he reported to me. I was his superior, my dear. In a way, we were a team."

Claire sagged against the wall. "Oh my God."

"God will not help you now," Elizabeth said flatly.

Claire stiffened instantly. This woman was a killer—maybe she had killed everyone—Jean-Léon was innocent—and she, Claire, was in grave danger. Instantly, Claire decided to play for time.

"I don't understand," she said breathlessly. "How could this be? You're a woman. I mean, I just don't understand. I've known you my entire life—you became a mother to me when my mother died."

"There's very little to understand, my dear," Elizabeth said easily, "except that you and Marshall have both gotten far too close for comfort—which is what David and Suttill did as well—and like them, you must be removed."

Claire blinked. She was sweating now, and perspiration trickled down her brow and into her eyes. It gathered between her breasts. It made her hands wet. Had this woman killed David and George Suttill? *How could this woman, whom she had loved and trusted her entire life, be a ruthless killer?* "You killed David?" Claire gasped.

"I most certainly did. It was the bloody worst luck, to be having lunch with him and to have George Suttill recognize me as Lionel's old wartime girlfriend. I was Elizabeth Longford then, but no matter, Suttill knew. He recognized me. You see, when Lionel disappeared, the authorities tried to find me in order to question me. The world believed Lionel and me to be lovers. It was so convenient to be his girlfriend, as I could go to and from his little flat as I pleased. When Lionel 'vanished,' I, of course, had to disappear, too. I colored my hair and changed my name and the way I dressed, the tart becoming a princess, and the idiots never found me, when all along I was right under their noses."

Claire could only stare. "So you began dating William. And four years later, he took you to France."

"William was the perfect cover for me, which was why I married him so quickly. Of course, I lied about my age, to throw everyone off. I was eighteen in 1940—not fifteen." She paused. "I have survived all of these years, Claire, by never allowing any link with the past to remain."

"So since George Suttill recognized you as Lionel's old flame, you killed him? And you killed David just because he was there at the restaurant and heard the exchange?" Claire could hardly believe what she was hearing, but then she was faced with a ruthless sociopath, not the woman she had known her entire life. That woman had never existed; that woman had been an illusion.

"Yes and yes. But David also happened upon me while I was removing Suttill. Which made him a witness to murder, Claire. And as you know, I have no intention of spending even one day behind bars."

Their gazes locked. Claire realized her time was running out. An image of Ian flashed in her mind—if only he would return to the apartment to try to speak with her. But after the way she had turned her back on him, Claire felt quite certain he was not about to come to the rescue now. She was on her own.

"You know, I am genuinely fond of you," Elizabeth said, moving away from the window, toward the foot of the bed.

Claire went rigid. *Shit.* What should she do? "Was David stupid enough to be blackmailing you, too?" she asked, sidling to her left. She wanted to keep a distance between them—not that it mattered, as Elizabeth had the gun.

Elizabeth smiled and shook her head. "No, he was not. I deposited the cash in his account to lead the authorities astray. In fact, I used the thumb knife to pin the murders on Elgin—a dead man. I knew Marshall would think David had uncovered Elgin and was blackmailing him. Brilliant, don't you think?"

Claire hardly knew what to think. She nodded, unable to tear her gaze away from the other woman.

"Also your Father had that Courbet, linking him to Elgin. I stole it at the end of the war because I needed the money; it was pure coincidence that he bought it from a fence in Paris a few year later." She smiled. "I must admit, when we became friends, the first time I saw the Courbet I almost fainted."

Claire remained speechless.

"Surely you have more questions, Claire. Surely you want to know about your lover's uncle, his father?" She smiled serenely, as if enjoying herself.

"Why do you want to tell me?" Claire asked, sick with fear. There was a lamp on the bureau behind her. It was large. If she let Elizabeth get close enough, could she slam her with it and somehow not get shot? Or worse, killed?

It was a catch-22. To really hit Elizabeth with the lamp, she would have to let her come closer. But in doing so, the odds were greater that Elizabeth, who would clearly shoot to kill, would not miss.

"You won't live to tell anyone about it. And neither will your lover," Elizabeth said in a matter-of-fact tone.

"Did you murder Eddy Marshall? And Rachel? And what about Harry Elgin and Lionel's father?" Claire's mouth seemed numb. It was hard to form the words. Was the lamp within reach? It was plugged in. She knew that from the other night. If she flung it at Elizabeth, would the cord prevent her from doing so effectively? *Damn.*

"My first victim was Lionel. I don't enjoy killing, Claire. Lionel enjoyed the power of dispensing life or death. I feel only regret that after all of these years, I am now reduced to the status of a common killer. I am not a killer, Claire. Ideology motivated me during the war. I am a highly ideological person."

"You're a fascist."

"Please, Claire. Don't start with the Jews now. I am not really an anti-Semite. And in fact, you know my beliefs. I have been on the far right for years."

Claire inched back another step. Unfortunately, groping behind her would be too obvious. Just how close to the lamp was she?

"Lionel murdered his brother when he was a boy, out of jealousy, I believe. But it was the right move, as he became the Elgin heir with all of the rights and power that entailed. Lord Elgin needed to be removed, as he was in our way—I gave Lionel permission to act on it. As for Eddy? He was in American intelligence, Claire. He uncovered Lionel. I could have been next. He had to be removed."

The anger overcame Claire then, and its force was stunning. "And did you have to get rid of his wife, too? How ideological is that?"

Elizabeth shook her head. "Why are you angry, Claire? You didn't know Eddy, and you didn't know Rachel. Lionel thought she knew too much. I agreed. She was a liability. She claimed Eddy had taken photographs—we had to silence her."

Claire wet her lips. She had to make her move now. "Did he take photographs?"

"I have no idea," Elizabeth said.

Claire stared. Elizabeth stared back.

"Move away from the bureau," Elizabeth said.

"Okay," Claire whispered, and the word came out as a high-pitched squeak. She did move—whirling and grabbing the lamp at the same time. As she flung it, the gun went off. Claire felt an unbelievable burning sensation in her chest, and the bullet's impact hurled her backward against the bureau, and to the floor.

But Claire didn't pause. Elizabeth cried out as the lamp hit her in the face and chest, causing her to stagger backward several steps. Claire managed to get up onto all fours. Elizabeth was lifting the gun. Claire leaped up and out through the door as another shot rang out.

Jesus. Claire felt another burning in her back as she slammed the door closed behind her, about to race for the front door—which she had double-locked.

But Elizabeth would be able to mow her down in the hall outside or in the stairwell, if she tried to flee down that.

Claire looked around and grabbed the first item she saw that might be helpful as a weapon: one of the framed photographs from the bookcase in the living area. The frame was sterling silver. Claire shrank against the wall, by the corner, waiting for Elizabeth to come out of the bedroom. She held the photo high.

She promised herself that she would not miss—she would break the other woman's skull in two.

But the bedroom door did not open.

Seconds passed.

Claire heard her own heavy breathing. She gulped down air. Sweat blurred her vision. Why wasn't Elizabeth coming out? Had she been hurt by the blow from the lamp?

Claire inhaled, trembling. Her arm began to hurt her from holding the picture so high for so long.

An instinct made her turn.

Claire saw Elizabeth on the terrace outside, aiming the gun at her, the glass door between them. As the shot sounded, Claire dove around the corner of the wall to the other side.

She scrambled up against the wall, panting and shaking. This time, Elizabeth had missed. She heard the glass door sliding open. Now what?

She was so wet. Claire glanced down, and her eyes widened in shock. Half of her white T-shirt was crimson with her own blood. *Was she dying?*

Right now it didn't matter. What mattered was Elizabeth, in the adjacent living area, creeping closer—or to a better vantage point from which to gun Claire down.

Claire glanced behind her, at the damn double-locked door. Elizabeth would have a perfect shot if Claire dared to run to it.

She could go back in the bedroom.

Claire didn't hesitate. She jumped up and grabbed the knob and tried to push open the door. It wouldn't budge. *Elizabeth had locked it before she had used the window to climb outside onto the terrace.*

Claire looked down the hall to the master bedroom at its end.

She ran.

Inside, she closed and locked the door, but the lock was pitiful—undoubtedly anyone could open it with a hairpin. Claire didn't hesitate. She ran to the bedstand and opened the drawer. She rummaged through papers and receipts. No gun.

She ran to the other bedstead, with the same result.

She froze as she heard the lock on the bedroom door clicking open. Then she dashed into the master bathroom, closing and locking that door. She needed a weapon and she needed it now.

An electric razor lay on the marble vanity with a can of shaving foam. So did a bar of soap, an electric toothbrush, and other toiletries. Then Claire saw the scissors.

They were small, but she grabbed them and ran back to the door, positioning herself flat against the wall, so that the door would hide her when it opened.

The lock clicked open.

Claire couldn't breathe. Cotton filled her mouth. Sweat poured down her body in rivulets—or was it blood? Claire glanced down and saw the bright red drops on the marble floor.

The door began to open, inch by inch.

Claire lifted the tiny scissors.

"There is no way out, Claire," Elizabeth said softly.

Claire turned her head, otherwise not moving. Through the crack in the door by its hinges, she saw the other woman's form.

"I know you're standing behind the door, Claire," the other woman said.

Claire launched herself around the door with a scream of rage, slicing the scissors down. The gun went off again, but not before Claire felt the small blades tearing through flesh and muscle, not before she heard Elizabeth's cry, and this time, Elizabeth missed.

Claire smiled at her father. Except Jean-Léon wasn't really her father. He smiled back.

Claire lay in bed in a hospital room. She had been taken to Lenox Hill.

Her father sat by her hip. He held her hand. "Thank God this is over," he said, not for the first time.

The painkillers were beginning to fade. Her chest, above her left breast but below her collarbone, was beginning to really hurt. But at least she could think more clearly now. "It's finally over," she agreed. Elizabeth had been taken into custody.

"I am angry at you for ever becoming involved," Jean-Léon said hoarsely.

Claire met his opaque gray eyes. It was so obvious now that he cared for her. She felt horrible for ever believing him to be Elgin, even for an instant. She should have held fast to her convictions.

She would never tell him the truth about her paternity. If he suspected, she had no clue. She would go along with the arrangement they had had their entire lives. "Dad? Can you ever forgive me for not trusting you? For trapping you?" Tears came to her eyes.

"Don't worry about anything now, Claire. And of course I forgive you. I blame Marshall for everything."

Her heart rate seemed to increase at the sound of his name.

"He brainwashed you, he went off half-cocked. I wasn't lying when I said he's reckless, a cowboy. It would have been neat and convenient for him if I was Elgin." Jean-Léon was clearly angry.

Claire wondered just how neat and convenient it would have been. She didn't want to recall Ian's declaration now, but she did. *I love you.* Three such simple words—with so much damn power.

"Dad? How did you know so much about the investigation?" This had been bothering Claire.

He seemed surprised. "When Marshall first appeared in your life—royally upsetting it, I might add, I did what any father world do—I checked the guy out. And you know what? Men like Marshall, who lead complicated lives, never provide neat answers. There were so many questions from our preliminary investigation that I told my guys to go all the way. Which is how I found out about his hunt for Elgin and his father's murder."

Claire realized that she should have known.

"What is it?" Jean-Léon asked.

Claire sighed. "If you met the Dukes in the late fifties, why did they lie about it?"

Jean-Léon shrugged. "People like Elizabeth are liars, Claire."

She winced. "How is William?"

"I don't know. I imagine he is astonished. It will be some time before he will be able to comprehend all of this."

"We need to be there for him," Claire whispered.

His gaze met hers. "Yes, you do," he said evenly.

Claire started. In that moment, she realized that he knew the truth—he knew that William was her biological father.

Awkwardly, Jean-Léon patted her hand. "I'll call him if you like."

"Please," Claire managed, still stunned. "I'd like to see him."

Jean-Léon nodded. Someone coughed from behind them.

Claire turned and became rigid. The mere act of stiffening caused more pain to course through her chest. The back wound had been only a graze.

Ian stood on the threshold of her room.

Their gazes locked.

"Get out," Jean-Léon cried, on his feet. "Haven't you done enough damage? Get out before I have security throw you out."

For another heartbeat, Ian stared at Claire. She felt anguish and sorrow, anger and despair.

"I need to speak with Claire alone, Ducasse," Ian said. "I'm sorry. I'm sorry for making a terrible mistake."

"An apology will not do," Jean-Léon said stiffly.

"Dad!" Claire cried, surprising herself with her protest.

"It will not do," Jean-Léon reiterated.

Claire swallowed. A part of her mind told her to let Jean-Léon chase Ian away. Another part cried out for her to forgive and forget and do anything not to lose this man. "I need to speak with Ian," Claire whispered. "Alone."

Jean-Léon was incredulous. After a curt nod, he left.

Ian approached. "Thank God you are okay."

Claire did not reply.

"Claire?"

She swallowed a sob. "How is William holding up?"

"Not well. He's at home, sedated. He loved Elizabeth very much." Ian's gaze was somber.

"He didn't know, did he? He did not have a clue."

"No, he did not. He's in shock, Claire. I imagine he will be for a while." His gaze was searching.

"William Duke is my biological father," she said. "He told me this morning in the park."

His eyes widened. "What! What—when—how did this happen?"

"He had an affair with my mother. Apparently she was very unhappy in her marriage."

"I don't know what to say. Are you okay with this?"

"I've always loved him. He's always been the one to put the Band-Aid on my knee and the smile on my face. Now I know why he was always around."

"And Jean-Léon?"

"He's pretending not to know. I'll go along with that." She felt a tear slip free. "It could be worse. I've got two fathers now." Her gaze felt belligerent. "And they're both innocent."

"I made a mistake, Claire. I'm only human. But I can defend myself until kingdom come, can't I, and you will never forgive me."

"You made me trap my father."

"No. I asked you to help. You agreed. You did what you thought to be right at the time."

Claire knew that. She didn't respond. What point was there? He had wanted her to bait the trap, and yes, she had, and it was over now. It was done. In fact, everything was over.

"Don't look at me that way," he whispered.

"Why not?"

"Because I can't take it. Not from you." He tried a smile and failed. "C'mon, Red. Where's that famous smile of yours?"

Claire was silent. A question was burning within her. Had he ever loved her? Or had he only used her?

"We need to talk, Claire," Ian said roughly. "But not this way. We're both adults. We need to sit down and communicate."

"We are talking. We're communicating."

"No, we're not. I'm talking, begging, actually, and you're staring at me sullenly with accusation in your eyes and your mind made up. Why are you pushing me away? Don't do this, Claire."

Briefly, Claire closed her eyes. "I have been through hell," she said. "And I am really tired."

His eyes widened. "So now you want me to leave?"

"I think that would be best."

"You're a fool," he said angrily. Then he turned and raked his hair before facing her again. "When are they releasing you?"

"Tomorrow or the next day."

"And when are you going home?"

"We're going to stay at the St. Regis until I am a bit stronger. I'd like to be off the painkillers before I travel—and I want to be around William," she said.

He absorbed that. "I'll come by later, before visiting hours are over."

She shook her head.

"Claire!"

"What's the point? I still love you, and even if I forgave you, it wouldn't solve anything."

"Why the hell not?" he ground out, ashen.

"Because I can't trust you," Claire said.

He stared.

"And I never will."

A long, tense moment passed. Claire said, "I'm tired." What she meant was, *Please go.*

His jaw flexed. His eyes were dark now with anger. He turned and strode for the door. But once there, he paused to look at her. "I told you I loved you and I meant it. But I guess in your book, that doesn't mean very much—it must have all been a lie on your part."

The door slammed behind him.

It was just past nine in the evening, California time, when she got out of a taxi in front of her rental home in Mill Valley. Two weeks had gone by. She looked around at the shaded street, the other houses, the woods, feeling bewildered. This wasn't home. She hadn't spent even a single night in her rental house. Maybe she should have gone to Tiburon with Jean-Léon.

Jilly, her poodle, started to bark wildly, frantically. Various personnel from the Humane Society had been taking care of her while Claire was away, but the dog had been dropped off a few hours ago in anticipation of Claire's return. Her furniture had also been moved in while she was away. Claire dashed up the stone walk to her front door, forgetting her bags on the street.

She thrust open the door and the dog jumped on her, tail wagging, panting hysterically, happily. Claire got down on her knees, hugging her hard. But all she could think about was New York.

Ian hadn't tried to see her again.

She had not lifted the phone, not even once, to open up a new dialogue with him.

She had known the moment that the big Boeing 747 had lifted off that running away was not the right thing.

Claire closed her eyes and tried to think while holding Jilly. Images of New York City danced in her mind. The Bay Area had lost its allure. A lifetime ago, it had been the perfect place for her and David. Now she felt lost, homeless.

Ian probably hated her now. Claire felt like she hated herself. "Oh God, Jill, what have I done?" Never had she felt so desolate, regretful, and confused.

Jilly wagged her short tail at her.

Claire stood almost blindly. She had to go back to New York. She had to see Ian, begin the conversation he had wanted to have two weeks ago. But she was scared. What if he had washed his hands of her? What if too much stood between them now? What if she couldn't trust him, no matter how hard she tried?

What if she could?

The answer was so breathtakingly clear.

"You left these out on the street. Not to mention your front door wide open," he said.

Claire blinked, whirling around.

And Ian was standing uncertainly in the doorway, holding her two bags. He was *not* a figment of her wishful thinking.

"What are you doing here?" she gasped.

"I knew that you were leaving New York. William has been kind enough to keep me up to speed these past two weeks." He shrugged. "I just couldn't let you leave. I meant to let you go, Claire. I really did. And then, damn it, an hour before your flight left, I found myself racing to the airport, intending to stop you. I got a bit nervous about the scene I might make and picked up a seat on standby instead." His gaze never left hers.

Claire ran to him, amazed—exultant.

Eyes wide, he dropped her bag so he could catch her and wrap her in his arms. Claire held on to his neck and shoulders. Her plan was to never let go. "I take it this means you've had a chance to come to your senses?" he asked.

Claire nodded speechlessly against his neck.

He slowly let her slide down his body to the floor. He gazed down at her; she gazed up at him. "You scared me, Claire."

"I scared myself," she whispered. "I'm still scared."

"So am I. So now we're in this together, right?"

She gazed into his eyes and nodded. "Yeah." And she meant it, oh yes, she did.

He dipped his head and Claire leaned up. Their mouths melded, melted, fused.

When they came up for air, she said, "Make love to me, Ian. Right now."

"Now? Here?" He was incredulous.

She nodded, already unbuttoning his shirt. She had never wanted him more.

His slight smile vanished. Transfixed, he watched her opening his shirt, his belt, his fly. Claire took him in her hands.

"What are you doing?" he managed.

"You know." She bent over him, smiling.

A few moments later she was on her back, completely naked, and he was sliding deeply into her. Claire held him, closing her eyes, as he carried her into another universe. Afterward, they held each other as he stroked her hair.

Claire smiled.

"What's so funny?" he asked, propping on one elbow.

"I'm just wondering how I could have been so stupid to walk away from you. You make me happy, Ian."

"You make me happy, too, Red."

Claire rolled onto her side so they were facing each other. "If I paint my toes taupe, are you going to call me Taupe?"

"No, I'll call you Greige."

"Smart guy," Claire whispered. "Smart and sexy and resolute. I'm a lucky lady."

"Claire. How can I make everything up to you?"

"Marry me," she said with a smile, and then she realized what she'd said and her cheeks turned blazing hot.

He grinned at her.

She was aghast, appalled, horrified. "I don't know how that popped out!"

He laughed. "You opened your mouth, Red. And spoke your heart's desire."

"That is not my heart's desire," she cried, still mortified and lying through her teeth.

"No? So what is?"

"A hot fudge sundae, with those silly red cherries on top," she scrambled.

"Bullshit."

"It's not funny. Stop laughing at me! I didn't mean it. I don't know where those words came from," she cried, stumbling over her sentences.

"But it can be arranged. Set a date," he said.

"What?" She sat up.

"You heard."

She became watchful. "September. September, oh, fifteenth."

He nodded. "Smart girl. Four and a half months. You might be able to pull it off. Big wedding or small?"

"Small. Romantic. Old-fashioned." She could hardly breathe.

He nodded again. "Here or there? And please, no Beijing."

"I hate Beijing. There. I'm becoming very fond of the Big Apple."

He smiled. So did she.

"So it's settled?"

"Yep." Claire could hardly believe it. Were they really getting married? In four and a half months? "Shake." She held out her hand.

He sobered. "What—don't trust me?"

She met his eyes. "I am going to try very hard. Just give me some time."

He nodded and slipped his hand over hers. "Time is something I have, sweetheart."

Sweetheart. That was almost as good as Red. "I'm starved." She stood up and slipped on his shirt. "Let's order two large pizzas. One for you, and one for me."

He sat up, superbly naked and as immodest. "Two large pizzas?"

"Yeah, two. I am ravenous," Claire said happily, buttoning his shirt. But instead of reaching for the phone, she turned from where she was standing in the foyer and looked at the hall closet.

Ian was smiling a cat's I-Just-Ate-the-Cream grin, apparently enjoying watching her. "What?"

She gave him a look. Claire went to the closet and pulled out the large Courbet painting. "We need to sell this," she said. "You know that I'm moving to New York, don't you?"

"I assumed we'd live together once we're married," he said wryly.

Claire propped the nineteenth-century oil up on the wall and stared at it.

Ian slowly stood.

She looked at him—then did a double take. "Boxers, anyone?"

His expression was strange. "Yeah, sure," he said, as if he'd forgotten he was naked. He stepped into his shorts and came to stand beside her.

"You don't like this painting, do you?" Claire said, studying him, not the painting.

"It's beautiful," he said. "And I happen to like Courbet."

"I don't want to keep it."

"I understand." He seemed mesmerized. "This painting bothers me," he said abruptly. "It bothered me the first time I saw it at your house in the city, and it bothers me now."

"What do you mean?" Claire asked very quietly.

"I'm not sure. I don't know. It draws me like a magnet." He hesitated. Claire waited.

"Don't laugh." He glanced at her.

"I won't."

"I can almost feel Eddy standing behind my shoulder. I felt it at David's birthday, too. It's like he's here, beside me, telling me something. I can *hear* him, Claire. I just can't hear what he's saying."

"Wow, you're a romantic. Romantics believe in ghosts," Claire said, more than fascinated. She was tingling all over.

"I don't believe in ghosts," Ian said flatly. "Never have and never will. It's my imagination, obviously. Maybe it has something to do with repressed feelings about his death and my father's."

"Okay," Claire said. She liked the ghost theory better. "You never heard his voice anyway," she pointed out.

"But the feeling is so damn strong," Ian said, walking over to the painting. He began running his hands over the surface.

"Ian, don't. It's old. You'll damage it."

He didn't seem to hear her, stroking the gilded wood frame.

"Ian?"

He squatted to run his hands over the bottom of the frame. And then he froze.

"What is it?"

"Bubbles." His tone was tense. He went to his trousers and pulled a small penlight out of a pocket "You don't happen to have a magnifying glass, do you?"

"Only God knows where. Nothing's unpacked," she said, turning on the rest of the lights in the hall. "What is it? What have you found?"

"Holy God," Ian cried. "Claire, there are two tiny dots here—and if I don't miss my guess, they are microdots." He turned to look at her with wide, excited eyes.

Claire stared, stunned. Her mind raced. "Ian? Maybe you've found the photos Eddy claimed he took!"

He stood. "That is exactly what I am thinking. I've got to call Lisa to get the experts to take care of this." He tripped over his words in his excitement. He was already at the phone.

Claire watched him, with excitement. Would life ever be the same? she wondered happily. "Hey, Ian?"

"What," he said, dialing.

"Want a partner?"

At first he didn't get it, then he dropped the phone and stared. "You're kidding, right?"

Claire grinned.

One year and several months later

The doorbell rang. But Jilly was already barking.

It was Friday, and Claire had left work at noon. She had taken office space to continue all of her charitable work, just a few blocks from their new apartment—after their wedding eight months ago, they had realized they would need a three-bedroom, at least. On Fridays she liked to get home early and prepare a festive family dinner, one far more elaborate than usual. In a way, it was her tribute to Eddy and Rachel.

The microdots they had found stuck between the canvas and the frame on the Courbet had been the photographs taken by Eddy just before he died. In them, he had captured the young Lionel Elgin meeting a German U-boat officer, and at Lionel's side had been a young woman in men's clothes: Elizabeth.

Her trial was pending in another month. She was having the book thrown at her, and there was little doubt that she would be convicted for every single one of her crimes.

Jean-Léon remained in Tiburon, completely immersed in the world of art. They spoke over the phone every week or so, and once in a while Claire saw him when he came to New York on business.

William had sold every single one of the homes he had shared with his wife. He had bought a penthouse apartment in New York, where he spent most of his time, although he had also purchased a villa in St. Lucia. Claire saw him several times a week, and they had become very close. He had not spoken to or seen Elizabeth since her incarceration. As far as he was concerned, she had died.

If he was grieving for what he had thought he had, Claire did not know. He seemed to be going on with his life in a forceful and determined manner. He would be joining them for dinner that night—he never missed a Friday-night dinner unless he was out of town.

Now Claire wiped her hands on a kitchen towel, wondering why the dog-walker hadn't let herself in, as it was about that time.

But the doorbell rang again. Obviously it wasn't the dog-walker, who had keys.

"Should I get it?" Ian called from one of the bedrooms. He tried to take half days on Fridays, as well.

"No, I'll get it." Claire crossed the hall and opened the door, Jilly on her heels.

And she almost fainted.

The young man half smiled and fidgeted nervously, finally removing a pair of sunglasses. Green eyes met hers.

"Eddy?" Claire whispered, stunned. He was a dead ringer for Eddy Marshall. The curling black hair, the fair skin, the height, the build. He was even about the same age; Claire pegged him at twenty or so.

"Ma'am?" He hesitated. "I'm sorry to just drop by." He spoke with a British accent. "I'm looking for Mr. and Mrs. Ian Marshall."

"Ian!" Claire called, trembling now. "Come in, come in," she said to the young man.

"My great-aunt seemed to think I could call on you and that it wouldn't be terribly improper," he continued, fiddling with his sunglasses.

"Your great-aunt?" Claire whispered in shock.

"Hannah Blenheim, but she used to be Hannah Greene."

He was Rachel and Eddy's grandson!

Ian came out of the office, holding Rachel Anne in his arms. She was only two months old, and she was watching her father with wide, unwavering blue eyes. Ian saw the young man in the baggy jeans and backpack standing in their foyer, and he turned white, halting in his tracks.

"And you are?" Claire whispered.

The young man flushed. "I forgot to introduce myself. I'm Neal Marshall." He smiled uncertainly.

Ian handed Claire the baby and said, staring as if Neal were one of the ghosts he did not believe in, "You're Eddy Marshall's grandson."

Neal nodded. "I guess I should have called. I don't know. But I finally got the courage to meet you."

"You didn't have to call—we're so pleased to meet you," Claire cried.

He glanced at her uncertainly. "My father died a few months ago of a heart attack. My mother's in a nursing home. Ever since, I've been obsessed with finding my family. There's only Hannah left on the Greene side, and one cousin from my mother's side. But my father always said there were Marshalls in New York."

"I'm your cousin," Ian said softly. "Eddy was my uncle."

Neal smiled a little, still uncertain.

Ian clasped his back.

Claire blinked back hot tears. They looked so much like father and son.

"How old are you?" Ian asked. "How long are you here? Can you stay with us? The rest of my family will want to meet you."

Claire bit back her smile. Neal had no idea what he was getting into—their small, intimate wedding had numbered 105 guests. Claire had invited only a dozen of her closest friends, William, and Jean-Léon. Every other guest had been a Marshall: an aunt or uncle, brother or sister, cousin or in-law. No to mention their kids.

"Actually, I'm going to NYU this year. I'm a junior," Neal said. "I'm going to finish up my B.A. over here. I've always wanted to live in America." He shrugged as if that made no sense.

"That's great!" Ian exclaimed. "Can you stay for supper?"

"Well, yeah," Neal said, looking from Ian to Claire.

"We would love to have you," Claire said softly.

Suddenly Ian grabbed him. "Hey, do you like to fly?"

Neal brightened. "I love to fly! I've been flying ever since I was thirteen years old."

"That's great! I keep a twin-engine out at Teeterboro. Want to take her for a little spin tomorrow?"

Neal's eyes were wide. "I'd like nothing more," he said.

Rachel Anne had fallen asleep in bed between them. Claire was reluctant to move her to her crib just yet. She stroked her downy hair, filled with a mother's infinite love.

Ian leaned over the baby toward Claire. "I can't get over it."

"I know." She met his shining eyes. "It's almost a miracle, Ian. Rachel gave birth before she was killed. Her sister Sarah raised the boy. And today their love lives on in Eddy's grandson, Neal."

Ian smiled at her. "You are so romantic."

"I am so happy." They smiled at each other. "Ian, this feels so right. I mean, the moment I saw him, before he even said who he was, I was overcome. He feels like family."

"He is family, Claire," Ian said firmly. "He's our family."

Claire sighed and stroked the soft crown of Rachel Anne's head again. "If I ask you something, will you promise not to laugh at me?"

"I promise," Ian said, kissing the baby's tiny little hand.

"Do you think that maybe, just maybe, we could buy a bigger apartment—just in case Neal needs his own room to come to now and then?"

Ian smiled, but he did not laugh. "How come we think alike?" He leaned over to her until their lips were brushing.

"Great minds," Claire whispered.

"Yeah, Red," Ian said—a long time later.